Charlie Higson
Roald Dahl **Anne Fine**
Gordon Brown
N**a Bawden** Raymond Briggs
Roddy Doyle
y Strong Terry Jones
chael Morpurgo

... even Tom from McFly!

o time to read? Read this!

WOW!
366

Speedy stories in just 366 words

◣SCHOLASTIC

First published in 2008 by Scholastic Children's Books
An imprint of Scholastic Ltd
Euston House, 24 Eversholt Street
London, NW1 1DB, UK
Registered office: Westfield Road, Southam, Warwickshire, CV47 0RA
SCHOLASTIC and associated logos are trademarks and/or registered
trademarks of Scholastic Inc.

This edition published by Scholastic UK Ltd, 2009
The moral right of the contributors to this collection to be identified
as the author of their work has been asserted by them.
The pages at the end of this book constitute an extension of this copyright page.

ISBN 978 1407 11602 0

Printed by CPI Bookmarque Ltd, Croydon, Surrey
Papers used by Scholastic Children's Books are
made from wood grown in sustainable forests.

1 3 5 7 9 10 8 6 4 2

www.scholastic.co.uk/zone

Welcome to *WOW! 366*

As parents, we know how hard it can be to make time for reading. That's why we know this book will be so helpful to you. These stories take minutes to read, are great for dipping into, and introduce young readers to a huge range of brilliant authors.

It's vital that kids read – not only for their educational development, not only because reading is a crucial life skill, but because it introduces them to different worlds and experiences. Last year we were delighted to extend the Richard and Judy Book Club to include kids' books for the first time. When deciding which books to feature, we deliberately chose entertaining books to make getting to grips with reading fun. Enjoyment has to be where it all starts…

But we also know that it can be hard to find the time to read stories, with everything that has to be done in a day. *WOW! 366* is the answer. Just ten minutes a day can make all the difference, even if it's a simple bedtime story. You're spoiled for choice when you do grab those ten minutes: there are ghosts, monsters, fairies, dragons, aliens and much, much more! And with contributions from so many of today's biggest authors, including wonderful writers like Anne Fine, Michael Morpurgo, Roddy Doyle, and Charlie Higson, there really is something in here for everyone.

This collection is unique. It's designed to encourage children to go on and discover books for themselves. After each story, there are suggestions for other books by the author, or books he or she feels children will love. As well as being quick and easy to read, the collection will also lead children to go on to more work by the authors they find and enjoy here.

Reading should be fun, and getting to grips with reading should be fun too. The mini stories in this collection are great fun, but more importantly, they open doors, and fire imaginations.

We hope you enjoy the collection as much as we did.

Happy reading!

Richard and Judy

366 words about reading...

Everything starts with reading. It has always been important, of course, but now, in the digital age, it isn't just important – it's vital. If you read, life can be a global adventure bursting with opportunity (if you want all that excitement, that is – it is always important to read, whatever you decide you want out of life!). If you don't read, it can be hard to stay in touch with friends, let alone with the rest of the world. Reading is essential for daily life, and it offers us a great joy as well. It frees us, fuels ambition, opens doors, changes our world views and underpins our confidence.

Isn't it brilliant that a vital skill is also such good fun, though? Reading isn't just about getting the right grades at school. If you love music, fashion, film or gaming, want to take over the world (or save it?), go for gold at the 2012 Olympics or bake the perfect cake, you can read about it – in newspapers, magazines, websites, blogs, books, downloads, graphic novels and comics. Read those, and you will then have the skills to share your frustrations, ambitions and inside knowledge with fellow enthusiasts anywhere in the world.

Reading is at the heart of the things we love, and we should love what we read. So you are right to choose what you know you will, or think you might, enjoy – and that includes song lyrics and football journalism, poetry and comics. Don't forget to share your enthusiasm with others, too. (Reading might change your life, but it ought to be fun along the way.)

Let's shout a loud "thank you" to the writers in this fabulous book – a sweetie jar of funny, clever and unforgettable ideas, stories small enough to hold in your hand and share in just minutes. Brilliant. It is really tricky to produce a perfect little story of exactly 366 words. Try it for yourself and see just how frustrating and fiddly it can be. Without great writers, none of the best bits of reading would exist. So, three cheers for writers everywhere, and also three cheers for readers, who bring their words to life when they read them.

(…and yes, that was 366 words long!)

Honor Wilson-Fletcher

Project Director, National Year of Reading
www.yearofreading.org.uk

WHEN I WAS TEN | GORDON BROWN

When I was ten my parents gave me an encyclopaedia, a book like a dictionary but more interesting. I didn't read it all at once – it was huge. But I read it, going back to it again and again. And every time I went back to it I found out something new and interesting.

All of the stories were true, but not at all boring. There were pictures, mainly in black and white. And I can still remember those stories and pictures.

Mainly, I remember that reading that book was a time of discovery. I was only ten, and like most boys of that age, I hadn't travelled much and didn't know much either.

But every time I went back to read another bit of my encyclopaedia, it was as though I had been on a journey and come back from it knowing a little bit more about the world.

From my bedroom, or lying on the hearthrug in front of the fire, I went off on my travels again and again, and always came back for more.

I learned that fifty years before – five of my lifetimes ago – someone called Captain Scott had set out for the South Pole, a place far, far away and very cold. But when his team reached the South Pole, they discovered someone else had got there first. And on the way back to their ship it got worse. They ran out of food and died in the cold.

It was a sad story, but the name of his ship, *Discovery*, seemed right, and the rest of the book was full of discoveries too. I learned about dinosaurs and galaxies and looked for them – galaxies, not dinosaurs – in the sky at night from our back garden. But what interested me most were the people and their adventures – brave people like Scott and Shackleton, sporting heroes like Stanley Matthews, and even some politicians – though at ten it was hard to know what they actually did.

I know I'll never be an explorer or a great footballer, but I am quite happy as a politician. And, in a way, my life is still a voyage of discovery that began with reading books.

Gordon recommends:
Thomas the Tank Engine by the Rev. W. Awdry and
The Complete Brothers Grimm Fairy Tales by the Brothers Grimm

"A good short story," announced Rabbit, "must have a proper beginning, middle and end."

"Beginning, middle and end," nodded Lambkins, writing it down in his notebook.

Pig put up his trotter.

"Yes, what is it?" asked Rabbit.

"Any particular order?" asked Pig.

"What do you mean 'any particular order'?" asked Rabbit.

"As long as the story has a beginning, middle and end, does it matter the order they go in?"

Rabbit sighed. "The beginning should go at the beginning, the middle in the middle and the end at the end," he said.

Lambkins wrote that down.

"Oh," said Pig. "OK."

"What about a twist?" asked Ratty, who'd been sitting very quietly at the back. "Shouldn't a short story have a twist at the end? Something unexpected?"

"Like 'it was all a dream'?" Pig suggested.

"No, NOT like 'it was all a dream'!" snapped Rabbit. "Twists are fine. A twist where it was all a dream is *not*."

TWISTS ARE FINE, Lambkins wrote. "IT WAS ALL A DREAM" IS NOT.

"I think it's time for a break," said Rabbit. He produced a carrot from his briefcase and began crunching it noisily.

Ratty chewed quietly on a piece of electrical cable. Lambkins

3

enjoyed a grass sandwich (on wholemeal) and Pig ate a truffle. None of them spoke.

Soon it was time to get back to the lesson.

"I'd like you all to do an exercise," said Rabbit. "I want you to write a story where there is no conflict. There are no arguments, misunderstandings, grievances or annoyances. Everyone gets on well with everyone else."

"OK," said Pig.

"No conflict," nodded Lambkins.

"Splendid," said Ratty. "This is going to be such fun."

"I agree," said Lambkins.

"I don't," said Rabbit. "The point of the exercise is to show that all good drama – all good storytelling – is based on conflict. It's very difficult to write a short story without it."

"Liar!" snarled Lambkins, leaping to his hooves. He waved a broken chair leg above his head.

"Which brings me to characterization," said Rabbit. "A character should never act out of character simply to advance the plot."

Lambkins returned to his seat. He wrote that down too. And underlined it.

Twice.

If you enjoyed this story, why not try some of Philip's books: The *Eddie Dickens Trilogy* and the *Unlikely Exploits* series

MOODLEPOPS AND MAIDLEYBUG
ELIZABETH LAIRD

Melanie Spencer's Auntie Flo looked at her calendar and shrieked.

"The twenty-first already! Oh no! It's Melanie's birthday tomorrow and I haven't posted her birthday card!"

First she couldn't find her glasses, then she couldn't find her pen, and then she'd lost her postage stamps, but at last she was ready to write the card. Just as she was licking up the envelope, she looked out of the window and saw that the mail van was already driving up to the postbox. Quick as a wink, she scribbled Melanie's name and address on the envelope, raced out of her house and ran down the street. She got to the letter box just in time.

The next morning, the postman in Melanie's street stood looking at the envelope. He scratched his head and turned it upside down to see if it would be easier to read.

The name looks like Moodlepops Spinach, he thought. *Must be the café on the corner.*

But the lady in the café gave the card straight back to him.

"Not for me," she said. "Anyway, I think it says Maidleybug Spider. Try number 7. They are very keen on insects."

The lady at number 7 was so busy feeding her pet cricket that she hardly glanced at the envelope.

"No one ever writes to me," she said. "I prefer insects to people, anyway. Try Motorbike Speedo at number 10."

Motorbike was revving up his Harley Davidson but he peered at the envelope through his black visor. Then he waved a gloved hand towards the end of the street and spoke.

It sounded like "Maclemumble Spogliwook."

"Pardon?" said the postman.

Motorbike tried again.

"Do you mean Maclehose Sporran?" asked the postman. "Hm. Must be those Scottish people at number…"

But before he had finished speaking, Motorbike had taken off with a screech of his tyres and was whizzing down the street. He stirred up such a tornado that the card flew up out of the postman's hand and went twirling through the air till it floated down and landed with a final flutter on Melanie Spencer's doormat.

And that's where she found it when she opened her front door and set off for school.

If you enjoyed this story, why not try some of Elizabeth's books: *Secret Friends* and *Oranges in No Man's Land*

FOOTBALL JOURNEY | DAN FREEDMAN

This is a true story.

I actually enjoyed going to school. Well, on Wednesdays, anyway.

On Wednesdays it was Jack's turn to give Adam and me a lift in to school.

Jack was my neighbour Adam's dad, and he had the best job in the world. He was a writer. He'd written lots of things that had been on TV and he'd even written films too.

That meant that he was brilliant at telling stories. With only his deep, rasping voice, he could make his stories as exciting as watching a film at the cinema.

"Tell us a story, Jack!" we'd say as we got into his car.

Sometimes he wasn't in the mood, but we always knew how to wear him down.

"Go on!" we'd beg. "Tell us a football story."

Jack smiled. He loved football as much as we did.

I'll always remember one of Jack's stories about a striker called Derek Dooley. Jack said Derek Dooley was the best striker he'd ever seen.

He was big, strong and quick – unstoppable. He scored 62 goals in his 61 games and the whole country knew about him. He was going to be a star.

Derek Dooley was just about to play for England when he got injured. He'd gone in for a tackle with a goalkeeper and broken his leg. His leg became infected with something called gangrene. In the end, he had to have his leg cut off.

"What?!" Adam and I said. "He had his whole leg cut off? What happened to him?"

But it was too late. We'd already got to school. The journey had gone in a flash.

"I'll tell you another story next week," Jack promised. "Only seven days to wait."

I went into school and spent the rest of the day thinking about Derek Dooley and what he might have achieved if he hadn't broken his leg.

That was twenty years ago and I'm grown up now, but I can still remember those stories and those journeys to school.

I like to think that Jack would have been happy at what I did when I grew up.

I became a writer. I tell stories to children. Often about football…

If you enjoyed this story, why not try some of Dan's books:
The Kick Off and *Shoot to Win*

I HATE JENNIFER JONES | JEAN URE

"Where's Jenny?" said Mum, as I got into the car after school one day. "Wasn't she coming back for a sleepover?"

I said, "I'm not talking to her any more. I *hate* Jennifer Jones."

"Jenny? But she's one of your best friends!"

"She was," I said. "But now I *hate* her."

Mum shook her head. "What's brought all this on?"

"She's gone and ruined my new top!" The words came wailing out of me. "*Look.*" I pulled it from my bag and held it up for Mum to see. "I wish I'd never lent it to her!"

I'd only let her have it 'cause I felt sorry for her, 'cause she was going to this party at her cousin's and I knew she didn't have anything to wear.

"I'm sure she didn't ruin it on purpose," said Mum.

"*She* said someone jogged her elbow and made her spill stuff."

"Well, there you are! It was an accident. The poor girl probably feels terrible about it."

Poor girl? How could Mum say *poor girl?* I tossed my head.

"I hate her for it! I'm never going to speak to her again."

"Oh, Maisie, come on! I'm sure she apologized."

"Only to begin with." To begin with she was all like, *I'm sorry, I'm sorry*, pretending to be upset. "Then she got mean!"

"And what did you do?" said Mum. "When she said she was sorry?"

"I yelled at her!" Anyone would have yelled at her. Ruining my new top! "That's when she got mean. Said I was *spoilt*. Said I had

9

more clothes than I knew what to do with."

"Poor Jenny has hardly any at all. It must be hard for her," said Mum. "Don't you think?"

I was quiet for a bit; and then reluctantly I said, "Maybe."

"You could go into town any time you like and buy yourself another top. Couldn't you?"

"I s'pose."

"How often does Jenny have anything new?"

Practically never. Most of Jenny's stuff came from charity shops. I would really hate that!

"I wonder whether we should go back and get her?" said Mum. "Will she still be there?"

"Might be," I said.

She was! I was so glad.

If you enjoyed this story, why not try some of Jean's books:
Star Crazy Me and *Pink Knickers Aren't Cool*

MAX | KAREN WALLACE

Max was a mouse who wanted to be a magician.

"A mouse is too small," said his mother.

"A mouse is too quiet," said his father.

"Who ever heard of a mouse magician?" said his big sister Mary.

Then she rolled her eyes and laughed.

Max stood on a pair of stilts to make himself tall.

"I WANT TO BE A MAGICIAN!" he yelled.

And he woke up Wise Owl, who was dozing in a tree.

"Anyone can be a magician," said Wise Owl.

"You need a wand and a cloak and a big top hat."

Wise Owl yawned.

"And you need to learn some magic tricks."

So Max's mother gave him a wand and a cloak.

His father gave him a big top hat.

Wise Owl gave him a book called *Teach Yourself Magic Tricks*.

Max's big sister Mary didn't give him anything.

"A mouse can't be a magician," she said. "NO MATTER WHAT!"

All day Max taught himself magic tricks.

He made doves fly out of his cloak.

He made flowers pop out of his wand.

But when he turned his top hat upside down

and shouted "ABRACADABRA!"

no rabbit came out.

Max ran to Wise Owl's tree.

"WHERE CAN I FIND A RABBIT?" he shouted.

But Wise Owl wasn't there.

He'd flown away to find a quieter place to sleep.

"Can I help you?" squeaked a rabbit from behind the tree.

"I've just moved in!"

The rabbit was big and white and fluffy.

He was absolutely PERFECT!

"You certainly can!" cried Max.

"I'm a magician and I need a rabbit."

"FAR OUT!" squealed the rabbit.

"I've always wanted to be a magician's rabbit!"

So that night, Max put on his first proper show.

He pulled flowers out of handkerchiefs.

He pulled ribbons out of thin air.

He made his rabbit appear out of his top hat and FLY across the room!

Everyone clapped and cheered.

Even Wise Owl fluffed up his wings proudly.

Max's big sister Mary rolled her eyes.

"Huh," she said. "Call that real magic?"

Then Max smiled a mysterious smile.

He waved his wand and shouted,

"ABRACADABRA!"

And a huge custard pie landed SPLOT in his big sister Mary's face!

If you enjoyed this story, why not try some of Karen's books:
Thunderbelle's Spooky Night and *Alice Goes to Hollywood*

MOON CAKE | GERALDINE McCAUGHREAN

Have you noticed how, whenever the moon appears, one star hangs below it, as if by a chain? It's the anchor, of course. And the gondolier who punts the moon's frail crescent along the canals of night is Giacometti. It used to be flat-bottomed, like any gondola. They say its keel sagged because Giacometti liked his panettone too much. Slanderous lies!

Giacometti plies the tiny islets of the Milky Way, taxiing ice cream to interplanetary kiosks during the cool of the night, collecting dirty laundry from the better-class hotels, and delivering fresh. And of course, being a gondolier, he carries young ladies to their lovers and young men to their pizzas.

One night a couple boarded, bound for Biddaboom, that heart-shaped planet hidden behind Orion's breastbone. The lady, Hallie, was delightful, but Yob was sarky, sour and short of cash.

"You expect me to pay that?" Yob complained, seeing the tariff pinned up in the boat.

"The fare is fixed, *signor*," said Giacometti.

"For that price I wanna blanket."

"Of course, *signor*."

"And wine. And cake. Hallie likes cake, don'tcha."

"Help yourselves, do."

"And you: *SING*."

Ah!

"Regretfully, *signor*, Giacometti does not sing."

Yob jeered. "All gondoliers sing!"

"The moon is glass, *signor*, and my voice is high."

Yob stood up. Hallie tugged at him. The moon rocked dangerously. "I said *SING!*"

Giacometti apologized. Hallie wept. Yob triumphed: "Then I'm not paying!"

So – despite warnings nailed to every striped mooring-pole from Libra to Leo – Giacometti sang. His song spiralled, high and higher, like a finger rubbing the rim of a wine glass. His boat too hummed – shivered – sang – high and higher, to within one note of shattering!

…Giacometti broke off and began to whistle instead.

Dark darkened. The swell swelled. The black depths heaved. For Giacometti had whistled up the wind!

Over went the fragile craft, and sadly – so sadly – no, *really*! – Giacometti was able to save only ONE of his passengers.

Shaking Hallie by the ankles, to empty out the dark, he dropped anchor, then shared with her his moon-white cake.

Hallie loves panettone – can eat it all night, and does. Or the gondola moon might still be as flat-bottomed as any cruising night's canals.

If you enjoyed this story, why not try some of Geraldine's books: *Smile!* and *Six Storey House*

THE BIONIC BABY | LIZ PICHON

Mr and Mrs Boggle had always longed for a child.

They had been married for ten years before Mrs Boggle realized that at last, they were expecting their first baby.

Mrs Boggle began to crave strange combinations of food.

She ate bananas covered with motor oil. She scrunched on spaghetti with wire.

Mr Boggle thought it was odd, but Mrs Boggle and the baby seemed healthy, so he fed her computer chips and peas whenever she wanted.

When the baby was born, Mr and Mrs Boggle were delighted to have such a beautiful bouncing baby boy. They called him Billy and couldn't wait to bring him home.

But very soon Mr and Mrs Boggle realized that Billy wasn't like other babies.

Billy didn't drink milk. He had nice shiny metal teeth and ate anything he wanted…

Billy was exceptionally strong. He could walk and push his own pram. He could even run and jump incredibly high.

All the people in the town could see that Billy was different.

They didn't like him much and called Billy a freak.

But Mr and Mrs Boggle were just happy to have such a wonderful son.

Until one day the whole town got together and decided that

Billy wasn't normal and everyone was scared of him. "But he's only a baby!" Mr and Mrs Boggle told them.

"Exactly," the mayor said. "Who knows what he'll do when he's grown up!"

So the Boggle family were forced to move out.

But that night, there was a terrible storm. The river overflowed and water tumbled ferociously into the town, where everyone became stranded. They scrambled on to the rooftops to try and save themselves. Mr and Mrs Boggle could hear people screaming and didn't know what to do … but Billy did.

He was strong enough to pull a huge boat through the water, and they all jumped into it and were saved. The mayor declared Billy a hero and invited the Boggles back and made sure that Billy was never teased again for being different.

And months later, when Mrs Boggle began craving toast with metal, it wasn't long before Billy got a baby sister … and she was even stronger than him!

If you enjoyed this story, why not try some of Liz's books: *My Big Brother, Boris* and *My Little Sister, Doris*

THE STICKLER | LESLEY HOWARTH

"Stickler" is spelt S-T-I-C-K-L-E-R. It means "someone who insists on a certain type of behaviour". My embarrassing mum never goes anywhere without a felt-tip pen. Wherever it crops up, correcting careless spelling is her mission. Over Christmas she corrected "miseltoe" (m-i-s-t-l-e-t-o-e) and "sesonal" on signs around the village.

Now it's the new year, and for once, I wish she'd stop. We live in the country, where people put out home-grown flowers and vegetables for sale. Yesterday we pulled in at a stall beside the road. I groaned when I saw the list of items for sale. She got out her felt pen. "Please, Mum," I said, "just this once, don't—"

"Hold this cabbage."

She was just correcting "Cabage" and "Lily's" (l-i-l-i-e-s, no apostrophe) when a small girl came out and said, "What are you doing?"

Even my mum looked embarrassed. "Your sign – 'lilies' has no apostrophe."

"I'm Lily," said the girl. "And it does."

"You grew the flowers?"

Lily took Mum's pen. She drew out the long red felt strip that was inside and posted it down a drain. She put the pen together again. "Now it can't hurt people's feelings."

My mother looked at Lily. "Your turnips look nice. Can I have some?"

"You can, if you've got the right money."

The red metal cash box gave no change.

"Will this do?"

Lily shrugged. "Can't you count?" she said.

My mum looked at Lily and Lily looked back. Then my mum laughed. "You're right – who do I think I am, correcting other people's signs? Thanks for the lovely veg." And she put in double the money, and we waved, and went home.

And I swear, from then on, my mum's different. Last night she stood next to a sign reading MUSIC AT THE KINGS ARMS TONIGHT WHETHER PERMITTING without flinching, even though it was the wrong sort of weather.

We'll wave at Lily's stall every time we pass, and I swear my mum's less tense already, since she hung up her felt-tip. To make doubly sure that she has, this morning I tested her with a sign that read "NO STIKLERS HERE" and so far she hasn't tried to put the "C" in – not once.

If you enjoyed this story, why not try some of Lesley's books:
Calling the Shots and *MapHead*

COLOUR ME HAPPY | **PIPPA GOODHART**

Donald lived on his own in a small grey home. The house was grey. Everything in it was grey. Even Donald was grey.

But one day in school Miss Rainbow said to Donald's class, "I want you all to make a picture of your home." Miss Rainbow put out paints and pens and crayons and coloured cloth to be cut and stuck. But Donald just picked up a pencil and drew his small grey home with no colour at all.

"Oh, dear, Donald," said Miss Rainbow. "Your home looks sad. Take some paint home with you and colour it in."

So Donald took pots of paint from the cupboard and carried them home. He painted a blue sky, a blueberry pie, blue swings, blue butterfly wings and lots and lots of other things. Then he got a pot of red paint. He painted red cherries, red berries, a bright red door, a red rug on the floor and lots and lots more. Next he got a pot of yellow paint, and he painted a big yellow sun in the sky. He bent down low to paint the yellow dot in the middles of daisies. He painted buns from the oven, bananas on a plate and a big bright yellow front gate. Donald looked around.

"Now I need green."

So he mixed blue and yellow to make green. He painted gooseberry pies and green cat eyes and leaves on trees, grass stains on knees and ribbons in a little sister's hair. Then he mixed red and blue to make purple for purple pansies, purple plums and jams, jellies and juice. He mixed yellow and red to make orange for round orange oranges, marigolds in pots, and lots and lots of dots on the curtains.

But still something was missing.

"I know!" said Donald. "I need brown!" So he mixed every colour all together to make brown for painting soil and skin and walls and feathers and warm wriggling fur and more until … it all looked finished and fine!

"There!" said Donald, and he shouted, "Come and play at my house!" And everybody did.

"I think you've painted yourself very happy, Donald," said Miss Rainbow.

And he had.

If you enjoyed this story, why not try some of Pippa's books: *You Choose!* and *Three Little Ghosties*

LANGUAGE PROBLEMS | PAUL STEWART

Xorg Xorgos of the planet Kren was on an important mission.

He, with thousands of others, had been dispatched in hyper-warp-drive spaceships by the Krenian High Council to scour the universe for signs of intelligent life. Their task was to teach other planet-dwellers how to live in peace and harmony, so that they might avoid the centuries of war, famine and disease that had afflicted Krenians before the Great Enlightenment.

Xorg arrived on a small blue and green planet at 23.32 on December 31, 1999, local time. He landed his spaceship at the edge of a flat concrete area in the middle of a jungle of succulent green leaves and broad yellow flowers. He climbed outside and tested the air.

"Seventy-eight per cent nitrogen. Twenty per cent oxygen. Trace elements – argon, neon, krypton… The usual." He paused. "But too much carbon dioxide. I shall also have to teach the creatures here how to prevent global warming."

Out on the street, he passed a bony creature asking for money; then a coughing, smoking creature, the seeds of cancer already rooted in its lungs. A bank of screens in a shop window all showed the same bombing raid on a city.

"The High Council was wise indeed to send me on such a mission."

He headed for a bright building called Joe's, where the laughter and song led him to believe he would find a friendly welcome.

Harry Enderby, a food health and safety inspector, sat at the bar, glass in hand, about to toast the new millennium. Just then, he saw a huge orange insect standing up on the counter, bold as you like, buzzing and trembling and waving its antennae about.

"The secret to eternal harmony and everlasting peace," Xorg was explaining, flapping his wings for emphasis, "is…"

As the clock struck midnight, Harry flicked the disgusting creature off the bar and ground it into the floor with his heel – thereby ensuring that the third millennium would be as full of war, famine and disease as its predecessors. And far, far hotter.

What was more, two days later, he had Joe's closed down for flouting city regulations on hygiene.

"Cockroach infestation," he wrote in his report.

If you enjoyed this story, why not try some of Paul's books:
Fergus Crane and *Beyond the Deepwoods*

APOLLO AND THE SUNFLOWER
ALAN TEMPERLEY

All day long Apollo, the sun god, drove his chariot across the sky. In the cool of a summer evening, crowned with a wreath of laurels, he stepped down from heaven and walked on the bank of a beautiful river.

There he met Clytie, an innocent nymph with golden tresses that fell about her shoulders. Apollo, who was exceedingly handsome, stopped to talk to her, and Clytie, like many a poor girl, fell in love with him.

Each day, when his journey was done, Apollo descended with his lyre to enchant Clytie with his music and pour his loving words into her ear. All night, when he had gone, she dreamed of him; all day she longed for his return.

But Apollo was fickle and loved many pretty girls. By and by he met her sister, the white nymph Leucothoe, and turned his light upon her. Clytie was forgotten.

She was very unhappy.

Soon Apollo tired of Leucothoe also, and left the groves by the river, never to return.

He broke poor Clytie's heart. Sitting on the riverbank she wept and the gods wept with her so that their tears filled the river to overflowing. Every day Clytie watched her lover's journey across the sky in his chariot of golden fire, drawn by a team of horses almost as glorious as Apollo himself.

Her sorrow did not pass and after many days, to bring her

peace, the gods turned her into a flower. Her feet became rooted in the earth. Her yellow hair became a crown of petals. The nymph Clytie became the very first sunflower.

The floods retreated. Beneath the burning gaze of Apollo the midsummer earth became brown and parched.

But the beauty of Clytie remained, and still remains, as fresh and fair as in life. All day long she turns her head to follow her lover Apollo as he drives across the sky. At dawn, as he appears above the eastern horizon, she opens her petals to greet him. At noon she gazes full into his glorious face. And at dewy dusk, as his prancing steeds return to their stables, she closes her petals once more and dreams away the hours of darkness.

If you enjoyed this story, why not try some of Alan's books:
Harry and the Wrinklies and *The Magician of Samarkand*

THE NIMPSTER | MARTINE OBORNE

There are five people living in our house.

There's me, Mum and Dad, baby Lucas … and the Nimpster.

We all make quite a lot of mess.

But nothing like the mess the Nimpster makes.

Every day, when Mum gets home from work, she says, "Who made all this mess?"

"It wasn't me," says my dad.

"It wasn't me," I say.

"Not me," says Lucas.

It was the Nimpster.

When Dad comes into the kitchen, he says, "Who made all this mess?"

"It wasn't me," says my mum.

"It wasn't me," I say.

"Not me," says Lucas.

It was the Nimpster.

When I go into my bedroom, I say, "Who made all this mess?"

"It wasn't me," says my dad.

"It wasn't me," says my mum.

"Not me," says Lucas.

It was the Nimpster.

(When Lucas crawls into a room, he doesn't say anything – even if it is really messy. Because Lucas likes mess.)

One day I decide to CATCH the Nimpster.

It's a Saturday and so I hide under my bed all morning waiting for him to come. I wait a long long time and nothing happens. I can hear Mum and Dad chatting downstairs. I can smell lunch cooking. I can hear Lucas playing with my remote control car (something he is absolutely NOT allowed to do).

I am tempted to give up. But I don't. I stay there.

And then SUDDENLY he's there.

The NIMPSTER!

He pulls books off the bookshelves.

He gets all the toys out of their boxes.

He opens the drawers and tries on my clothes – even though he's MUCH too fat for them.

There's now so much stuff on the floor that the Nimpster stumbles and falls and squashes my doll's pram.

Right. *That's it*, I think. I crawl out from under the bed.

But the Nimpster has gone.

Mum's head peers round the door.

"Who made all this mess?" she asks.

I open my mouth to reply but Mum goes on. "Don't tell me," she says. "It was that Nimpster again."

"Yes it was," I say. "Really."

"I believe you," says Mum. But I don't think she does.

Then she opens my wardrobe door and…

AAAAAARGH!

It's the Nimpster!

If you enjoyed this story, why not try Martine's book:
Hamilton's Hats

HUNT! | JOAN LENNON

We were running flat out in the moonlight, my friend and I, and the Hunter was right behind us. I knew my friend would head for the woods. Once in among the trees, we just might have a chance…

Round the back to the bins, knock the last two over, hope the Hunter wouldn't notice – CRASH! CLATTER! SPLAT! We'd tricked him! But it only bought us a moment. The Hunter was back on his feet, bits of rubbish hanging from his hat, and if he'd been mad before, now he was *furious*!

Off again! There had to be a dozen gardens between us and the woods. We leapt over one fence, dragged ourselves under the next, wriggled through hedges and dashed across vegetable patches and flower beds. Harsh, hard lights came on in the houses as we passed. Angry owners stuck their heads out of bedroom windows and yelled, "*What's going on out there?!*"

But the Hunter didn't answer. He just ran grimly on, focused entirely on us, and he was getting closer every minute. I risked a glance back and saw the enraged look on his face. It made my heart jump into my throat. I looked across at my friend and I could tell that he was almost at the end of his strength.

But the last fence was in sight. One final mighty leap … and we tumbled into the woods and flung ourselves behind a tree.

The Hunter was just too late!

"You rotten foxes!" he wheezed, and when I peeped out from behind the tree, I could see him standing by the fence, shaking his fist in our general direction. "You ... you ... vermin! I HATE foxes!"

I looked at my friend and my friend looked at me.

"That was close," I said solemnly.

"It certainly was," he agreed.

"I thought he was really going to catch us this time," I said.

"Yeah, me too!"

For a moment, we lay on our furry tummies, panting, waiting for our heartbeats to come back to normal. Then my friend said casually, "So, shall we do it again tomorrow night?"

I didn't answer him right away. Then, with a big foxy grin, I said, "You're on!!"

If you enjoyed this story, why not try some of Joan's books:
The Wickit Chronicles and *Questors*

SCAREDY-CAT | GILLIAN SHIELDS

I was scared of Julie Clegg. She was in my class and could do somersaults and swim twenty lengths. But I couldn't, so she laughed at me and pushed me around. Not enough to get into trouble, but enough.

There was a big climbing frame in our playground. Julie swarmed up easily, right to the top.

"Look at me!" she shouted.

But I didn't dare climb more than a few rungs.

"Cowardy-custard!" Julie jumped down and pushed me with her jabbing little hands. "You're a scaredy-cat!" Suddenly, a crowd of girls was laughing and jeering. "You daren't do anything!"

"I dare walk through the old graveyard after dark!"

There was a horrible silence. The old graveyard was really creepy. Nobody ever went there. People said it was haunted.

"All right," grinned Julie. "Show us after school."

"All right," I said defiantly. But inside, I was petrified.

By four o'clock it was dark, a thick November dusk. I set off, surrounded by Julie and her gang. We reached the gate of the gloomy graveyard.

"Go on then," Julie taunted. "You have to touch the broken grave. And bring something back," she added.

Slanting trees met overhead, shutting off the sky. Birds cried eerily. I could just make out the broken grave in the shadows. It was an old stone tomb, like a chest, and one side of it had cracked open with age. People said that was where the ghost came out.

I set off, my heart hammering. And then, I heard it.

A thin, wailing voice.

The girls by the gate screamed. But I carried on. I had to prove that I wasn't afraid, even though I felt sick. I walked right up to the grave. Something white was coming out of the gaping hole!

I ran, helter-skelter, back to the gate.

"Scaredy-cat!" sneered Julie.

"I'm not!" I panted triumphantly. "I touched the grave and brought something back."

I opened my jacket. Shivering next to me was a tiny lost kitten, as white as a ghost…

Later, Mum said I could keep him, so I called him Spook. After that, I wasn't scared of the old graveyard again. And I certainly wasn't scared of Julie Clegg.

If you enjoyed this story, why not try some of Gillian's books:
The *Mermaid SOS* series and *The Perfect Bear*

A PIG'S TALE | MATTHEW SKELTON

I swear I'm not making this up. My parents don't believe me (they say I'm telling tales), so I'm writing to you instead. To warn you of my sister. She's an evil genius, a criminal mastermind.

This afternoon I was innocently minding my own business (NOT sticking my nose in her diary, as she claims), when my Evil Older Sister grabbed me by the arm and pinned me to the ground.

"Pig!" she shouted (for no reason at all). "Pig!"

At first I thought she was going to tickle me to death, but then it got worse.

Much worse.

She ripped off my T-shirt.

(Not that it's any of your business, but I should probably point out here that my belly button does just that. Points out. Don't laugh! I'm really sensitive about it.)

"Ha! Looks just like a pig's snout!" she teased while I grunted and squealed, trying to get away. But she was too heavy to throw off. Before I knew what was happening, she'd grabbed a felt-tip pen and was using it to draw something on my tummy. In permanent ink, too!

I screamed and struggled, but the more I tried to defend myself, the more I got red ink all over my hands. First she drew a balloon-like head, then two triangular ears, then a roly-poly body and four pink trotters. Then, with a gleeful giggle, she added a long squiggly tail.

"Oink, oink," she said and finally let me go.

I cried all the way home. Well, all the way to my mum.

"What have you been doing?" she shrieked when she saw the pig's face around my navel.

"It was her," I blubbed, pointing at my sister, who beamed angelically round the room.

"I tried to stop him, Mum," she lied, "but he insisted on making a pig of himself. Just look at his hands."

Dad held them up for his inspection.

"Looks like you've been caught red-handed, young man," he said, and sent me straight to bed without supper.

So here I am, in my room, while my big fat sister has roast beef and I have none.

I hate her.

(Her lousy diary wasn't even that interesting, anyway.)

If you enjoyed this story, why not try Matthew's book:
Endymion Spring

FAMOUS DAD | TONY DE SAULLES

My name is Harry Cook and my dad is a celebrity chef on the telly.

How cool is that?

Not very.

I hardly ever see him these days – he is too busy being a celebrity. I don't see much of Mum either. Not since she became Dad's personal assistant. She organizes his diary and travels everywhere with him. Mum and Dad say they're both thrilled with how everything's going.

Mr Cook Cooks! (my dad's TV show) is on every afternoon at four-thirty. He cooks meals for famous people and chats to them about their lives. *Mr Cook Cooks for Alan Shearer!*, *Mr Cook Cooks for Jacqueline Wilson!* – that sort of thing. I used to watch it on my own after school but not so much recently. I've got a new friend, Eddy, and I would rather be playing football at his house than watching *Mr Cook Cooks!* I wish I had a dad like Eddy's dad. They go to the cinema and do paintballing and stuff.

They even invited us to play in a Dads and Lads football match next week but, of course, my dad is too busy for stuff like that.

It's an extra-special programme today – *Mr Cook Cooks for the Prime Minister!* I couldn't miss that. I've been sat here for twenty minutes waiting for the exciting bit.

Exciting bit?

Er, yes, well ... Mum and Dad were in a hurry this morning before they left for the TV studio, so I helped to pack the cooking ingredients. That's when I had my brilliant idea.

Ooh, here we go. The Prime Minister's munching a mouthful of Dad's red-pepper salad. Hope he didn't mind me swapping the peppers for red-hot chillies. Wow, the PM's eyes are bulging! He's clutching his throat! Now he's glugging red wine to wash the chillies down. Wonder if he can taste the vinegar I added. Hmm, I think so. The PM is gagging and spluttering! The audience is gasping! Dad's face is frozen in a terrified stare. Somebody wearing headphones is loosening the PM's tie.

He'll be OK.

Excellent.

I think I'll phone Eddy and tell him Dad will probably be around for the football match next week after all.

If you enjoyed this story, why not try some of Tony's books:
Dino Doggy and *Horrible Science: Disgusting Digestion*

THE GREAT ZAMBINI | SAM OSMAN

Charlie led a blissful life. His father was Carlo Zambini – the one and only Great Zambini of Zambini's Travelling Circus. Every night Charlie watched proudly as Carlo coiled Emily the performing python around his neck and soared through the air on the flying trapeze.

Charlie's Uncle Lionel led a dreary life. He was a thin, weaselly man who did conjuring tricks in the circus car park. Every night he too watched the Great Zambini, his greasy moustache quivering with envy.

One dreadful day Charlie's parents disappeared.

"I am the Great Zambini now," said Lionel. He coiled Emily around his scrawny neck and took up the trapeze.

"You cost too much," he told Charlie. He fed him on scraps and beat him when he cried.

One morning Charlie was feeding Emily when the clowns walked by.

"If Lionel disappeared," said Bobo, "Charlie would be the boss."

"Wouldn't that be wonderful," sighed Jojo.

The next day Emily stopped eating.

"She's fine," said the vet. "Snakes can go for ages without food."

But weeks passed and still Emily would not eat.

"She misses Carlo," said Bobo.

"Rubbish!" roared Lionel. "She adores me. She even stretches out next to me while I'm taking my afternoon nap. She never did that with him."

"She's fine," said the vet in the next town. "Snakes eat when they want to."

But spring came and still Emily would not eat.

"It's strange," mused Lionel. "She's been stretching herself so much she's nearly as long as me." He glared at Charlie. "But it's your fault she won't eat. If she starves to death then so will you." And he went for his afternoon nap.

Charlie ran to find another vet.

"I am an expert on snakes," said the vet. He listened to Charlie's story and grew deathly pale. "Six months of starving and stretching herself? Quickly, before it's too late. Run and tell your uncle she's preparing to eat him!"

Charlie ran as fast as he could, but by the time he got back, nap time was over. He found Emily lying on Lionel's bed looking rather plump. She raised her head and, whispering in his ear, she said:

"You are the Great Zambini now."

Sam recommends:
Moonfleet by John Meade Falkner and *The Secret Garden* by Frances Hodgson Burnett

PRIDE COMES BEFORE A FALL | ANNA WILSON

Tilak was a very proud turtle. He was proud of his shiny shell. He was proud of his neat flippers. He was proud of his elegant swimming strokes.

And he did not like being laughed at.

So when Chintana the chimpanzee cackled, "You are the funniest animal I have ever seen!", Tilak bristled.

"Actually, I am a most *talented* turtle."

Chintana laughed so hard, she fell off her branch.

Tilak snorted. "You know what they say? Pride comes before a fall. You wouldn't catch *me* falling from a tree like that."

Chintana sneered. "Oh yes? And how would you get *up* there to start with?"

"I'd fly," said Tilak rashly.

Chintana guffawed. "Oh stop!" she said. "You are priceless!"

"I'll prove it," Tilak retorted.

He shouted to a parrot overhead. "Hey, Parul!"

Parul landed gracefully. "Yes?"

"Help me out," Tilak demanded.

Parul looked at Chintana, and the chimp winked.

"All right," said the parrot. "What's the big idea?"

"See this stick?" Tilak said. "You take one end, and I'll take the other, and let's prepare for take-off."

"Are you sure?" asked Parul.

"Just get on with it," Tilak said.

So Parul grabbed the stick and Tilak took the other end in

his mouth.

"Now what?" said Parul.

"Mmmfugle!"

"What?"

Tilak let the stick drop. "Fly, idiot!" he shouted.

"Yes, sir," Parul muttered, and beat her wings, "but you'd better keep your mouth shut!"

Tilak bit the stick again, and Chintana gasped as the turtle and parrot rose up into the brilliant blue sky.

The turtle felt prouder than ever. *I can fly!* he thought.

He looked down at the chimp who just minutes before had laughed at him, and who was now speechless with wonder.

"Ha!" Tilak yelled. "Not so funny now, am I?"

But in opening his mouth to jeer, Tilak had let go of the stick. He had not kept his mouth shut as Parul had warned.

He was falling, falling. . .

SPLASH! He was back in the river, speechless with shame and fury.

The chimp clutched her sides and laughed until she cried, while Tilak hid his head in his shell.

"You were right all along!" squeaked Chintana. "Pride *does* come before a fall!"

If you enjoyed this story, why not try some of Anna's books:
Nina Fairy Ballerina and *Puppy Love*

ROBIN HOOD TAKES A BATH | DAVEY HEITLER

Robin Hood, Master of Disguise, needed a bath. It had been a particularly hot summer, and spending it with a group of sweaty outlaws in Sherwood Forest did not help.

"Get the soap!" Maid Marion complained, increasingly loudly.

However, Robin didn't want to bathe in the cold stream that was the Merry Men's usual bath. You see, although Robin was very noble, stealing from the rich and giving to the poor, he was also a little spoilt. Bathing in a stream without even any bath bubbles didn't sit well with him, especially when it was so *very* cold. Robin, however, had a plan...

Later that day, an old washerwoman hobbled into the Sheriff of Nottingham's castle. The guards weren't particularly nice to her, calling her names like "hag" and "bag lady". The washerwoman didn't pay any attention, though – she was probably used to people being rude like that. She headed towards the bathhouse, muttering to herself in the way that old people sometimes do.

"I'm here for the towels," she cackled at the two guards outside the bathhouse.

"Through here," one of the guards grunted, whilst the other pulled faces behind her back.

Presently they heard some strange sounds coming from the bathhouse.

"What is that awful noise?" they asked each other.

Deciding to investigate, they cautiously approached, swords drawn.

"On my word, we charge," whispered the captain. "NOW!"

The door burst open, and the guards rushed in. The old washerwoman was nowhere to be seen. Instead, there was Robin, who stopped singing mid-note and gave a sheepish grin. He was trapped.

Quickly, though, before they could stop him, Robin jumped from the bath and dived out of the window, landing with a splosh in the moat below. I don't know if you know anything about castle moats, but I can tell you they are not the cleanest of places. Although he was able to swim to the opposite bank and scamper away (stark naked, I might add), Robin was even smellier than before. Maid Marion was most unimpressed.

"Get the soap!" she commanded.

So Robin did as he was told. It was the coldest bath of his life, but at least he smelled good afterwards.

Davey recommends:
The Hobbit by J.R.R. Tolkien and
The Wee Free Men by Terry Pratchett

GREAT GRANNY | ANN BRYANT

Sometimes Tom's granny picks him up from school. Ben Brown always says rude things about her, like, "Why is she so old?"

Tom gets cross. "Because she's a *great*-granny!"

Ben just laughs.

Granddad died when Tom was teeny. Tom's seen some photos, though. There's one of Granddad with Tom on his lap. Tom is wearing a necklace. It's a bit embarrassing.

When Tom has tea at Granny's, they turn the den into a pretend aeroplane so Tom can play pilots, while Granny goes on her computer and writes and writes.

Mrs Fuggle has been talking about the Second World War at school. She invites Granny to talk to the class. Tom is cross. Ben Brown will only say nasty things.

Granny tells the class a story about a plane that drops out of the sky because the enemy shot at it. The plane lands in the sea, but the pilot is trapped inside the cockpit and some of the plane is on fire.

Tom wonders what's going to happen to the poor pilot. Will he die because of the fire? Or drown because of being trapped?

Granny explains that there is a Royal Navy ship nearby and the rescue team go to the plane. But the pilot looks dead, so most of the team go to help other trapped people. One lady from the team stays behind, though. She stays for ages in the freezing cold sea and eventually she manages to free the pilot.

Then Granny holds up the photo of Tom sitting on Granddad's

lap, wearing the necklace. How embarrassing. "This is Tom's great-granddad," says Granny. "When he was a young man, he was a pilot. In fact, he was the pilot in my story." Granny's voice goes quiet. "And the lady was me."

Ben Brown gasps, and everyone in the class says how brave Granny was.

"This medal that Tom is wearing in the photo is the special medal I got from the prime minister at the end of the war," explains Granny. "And now I'm writing a book on my computer, all about the story of me and Granddad."

"Your granny *is* great, actually," whispers Ben Brown.

"Told you," says Tom.

Yessss!

If you enjoyed this story, why not try some of Ann's books:
Billie and the Parent Plan and *First Term at Silver Spires*

THE GARDEN ON THE HUNDREDTH FLOOR
MARY HOOPER

Apparently, so they said, the lift had a sign by the button saying "Out of Order".

Well, if it *was* there, I didn't see it, because I was thinking of a hundred other things, wondering whether to get my hair cut really short and what my new school was going to be like, you know, stuff like that. I breezed into the lift, pressed the button for the twenty-seventh floor and waited.

As soon as the doors closed, I turned to look at myself in the mirror and shuddered. Yeah, I definitely needed a good haircut. I was just turning to get a look at the back when – *whoosh* – there was a crazy white-noise strobing, like the sound when a bluebottle hits the killing screen in the butcher's, and a incredibly brilliant white light.

Wow, I thought. *Whassat?*

A voice, an in-lift voice, announced, "This is Floor One Hundred", and I remember thinking that this was a bit mad, seeing as I knew I'd pushed the twenty-seventh button. I went to push it again, to go down, but as I put my hand out, the doors suddenly opened and I stood there, gaping. It was just *amazing*: I could see for miles and there was sunshine, flowers, trees with blossom, birds singing and a fountain making rainbows – all that dazzling sort of stuff.

I couldn't believe my eyes. I took a step forward to go out but the doors closed – *wham!* – in front of me. I gave a yell of fury and then, suddenly, I was lying on the floor of the foyer and there was a load of people standing around me.

"Sssh. You're all right," a man with the word AMBULANCE CREW written on him said. "I'm afraid you had a little accident."

"What? What sort of...?"

"An electric shock from the faulty lift. It was rather a violent one and you passed out."

"I didn't," I said rather indignantly, "I went to the hundredth floor."

"But, sweetheart, you've been clinically dead," said the man gently.

"No! I went to the hundredth floor."

"You didn't go anywhere," said the man. The people around me exchanged glances. "Besides, this building is only thirty-three storeys high."

If you enjoyed this story, why not try some of Mary's books:
The Remarkable Life and Times of Eliza Rose and *Newes From the Dead*

MY MAGAZINE ABOUT ME | ANNE FINE

I thought that the idea was brilliant: a magazine about me.

Yes, me. Pip Harlow. Red-haired. Learning to play the recorder. And fairly good at sports.

I didn't have to think too long about the title. I called it *Pip*. And underneath I wrote a banner headline: *The Magazine All About Me*.

First, I wrote an article about my average day. You know the sort of thing: "On school days, poor Pip is woken by the alarm clock..."

I had a column down the side: *Pip's Favourites*. In it, I listed all the books and films and bands and foods I like the best.

I wrote an article about my pet. (That's Digger. He is a terrier, and my dad says that if he digs one more hole in the lawn, he's going to die.)

You have to have pictures, so I spent hours trying to insert a photo of myself. Then Dan came in (Dan is my brother) and he set up the magazine properly, and Photoshopped me into a wicked pair of sunglasses, and took off the damp field behind me in the photograph to shove a Californian beach behind me instead.

How was it my fault that, when Togs rooted through my school bag looking for a pen, the magazine fell out?

"What's this?"

"Nothing."

Togs looked up. "This is a magazine called *Pip*!"

I thought Togs was getting at my name. So I said, "*Loads* of people are called Pip."

"Rubbish," said Togs. He looked more closely at the magazine. "Look! It *is* you! I'd recognize you even in those sunglasses." He read a bit. "Hey, Pip! This really *is* about you, isn't it? I *know* your dog's a terrier. And you love chutney! So it *is* you!"

So that's how I became so famous in my school for being so famous that there's a magazine about me. Everyone thinks they can't find a copy in Smith's because I'm mostly famous back in California, where the photo was taken.

I keep on trying to explain. But they just think I'm trying to preserve my privacy, and being modest.

So it was really an all-round success, this Magazine About Me.

Try it yourself.

If you enjoyed this story, why not try some of Anne's books:
Ivan the Terrible and *The More the Merrier*

THE BREAD PUDDEN WARS | BRIAN JACQUES

ONE

1946. Post-War Britain: a land for heroes, and all those kids who attended the Saturday matinee. My local cinema was fondly dubbed "The Bug House". It cost tuppence (1p in today's money) admission, to sit on wooden plank seats. But nothing bothered us kids, we were cowboys, just like in the movies. Much better than the reality of war-damaged Liverpool. Our parents were poor working class, and shortages were rife. Everything was on ration. Luxuries like sweets, chocolate, fresh fruit and eggs were in short supply, even to those with money. So, you made the best of what you could get in the pre-technology era. We were cowboys with a difference.

Apart from wellingtons, our Western gear was the wooden stock of a 303 infantry rifle, and a wide brimmed ex-army tropical helmet. These were obtained by bartering worn-out clothing, scrap metal, or jam jars, with the rag-and-bone men, who pushed carts around the streets. Seven-year-old kids wearing helmets, ten sizes too big, carrying huge wooden rifles, we were real cowboys. Off we went to the matinee, armed with newspaper parcels of Bread Pudden.

TWO

In those days of scant rations, mothers used what they had. Bread Pudden was merely stale bread crusts, a pinch of spice, and a handful of raisins (when available). These were soaked, baked and left overnight. The result was a congealed, rubbery mass which could have been used to repair Liverpool's bombed docklands.

Packed into the matinee, we sat waiting. Once the lights dimmed and the film began, the Great Bread Pudden War erupted with a ferocity that equalled any war ever fought.

Helmeted urchins bombarded indiscriminately, flinging grenade-sized chunks of Bread Pudden everywhere! Up on the screen, Custer might be fighting the Indians, Wyatt Earp might be shooting up the O.K. Corral, or cattle might be stampeding o'er the plains. But in the real world, cinema ushers were pleading for ceasefire, diving for cover amid a soggy hail of Bread Pudden. Battered but unbowed, we battled on, fielding stray cobs with our rifles, taking on all comers amid lethal barrages. After the matinee, we limped victoriously out of the Bug House. Out into peace-time Britain, a land fit for cowboy heroes.

If you enjoyed this story, why not try some of Brian's books:
The *Redwall* series and *Castaways of the Flying Dutchman*

HAPPY HALLOWEEN | PETE JOHNSON

It's Halloween: I'm doing a dare, as I'm the new boy. And I've got to prove myself.

"You knock on the door," this boy says. "A really scary-looking guy will answer. You shout out: 'Mr Mason, I know your secret. You're a mad magician who puts spells on people. You're also very ugly. Happy Halloween!' You can run for your life then."

The boys watch me slowly walk up to Mr Mason's house.

I ring on the doorbell.

"Good luck," whispers a voice. "You'll need it."

The door rattles and opens. Mr Mason glares down at me. I shout out everything I've been told to say. "Happy Halloween!" I end.

Suddenly Mr Mason's hand springs forward and pulls me inside. I hear the boys gasp.

I start to shake with laughter. I know Mr Mason – or my mum does. He is her great-uncle. But they had lost touch for years.

Last night I told him about the dare. He just put back his head and laughed. "Of course I'll play along," he said. He even suggested pulling me into the house.

"I can see your friends hiding outside," he says, laughing. He's so cheerful. How can he have got such a bad reputation?

"When this is over," I say, "I will tell my friends what you are really like."

"Shall we play another little joke on your friends?" he asks. He brings out a vampire mask. "I found this in the loft, why don't you try it on?"

It fits perfectly.

"This will give your friends a shock," he says.

I stagger outside. I shout, "He's turned me into a vampire!"

The boys' faces bob up. But they are so horrified they can't speak. They all run away.

A shiver runs through me. It is starting to get cold. A bird shrieks, making me jump. I've had enough of jokes at Halloween. I try and pull off the mask. I can't move it.

I see Mr Mason glide towards me. "Will you help me?" I begin.

He shakes his head. "I'm afraid your friends are right – I do put spells on people. And that mask doesn't come off … ever." He starts to laugh again. "Happy Halloween."

If you enjoyed this story, why not try some of Pete's books:
The Ghost Dog and *Help! I'm a Classroom Gambler*

STOP ME | ALI SPARKES

I like to tube-surf. I stand in the middle of the carriage, even when there are seats free, bending my knees slightly, balancing while the train ducks and dives, singing along the dark track.

I look down through the windows of the connecting doors, to see how the carriages ahead are moving; to warn myself of a lurch to the left or a dive to the right. I don't often look through the windows at the side of the carriage. But on this day I did.

We'd slowed down between Leicester Square and Charing Cross, and for some reason I glanced left, through the glass to the blackness and the sooty snakes of power lines.

And I saw a girl. Her face was a picture of terror. And so it should have been. She was pressed against an underground tunnel, desperately trying not to get flattened while a tube train skimmed past her, centimetres from her nose. Her hair was whipping across her cheeks and her eyes were round with fear. And she mouthed something at me, in that single second that I saw her.

"STOP ME."

I nearly fell into the gap, getting off at Embankment. I'd seen a girl in the tube tunnel. I must have been eating too many E-numbers. It couldn't have been real.

Except that I saw her again. The next day, in the same spot. For one second. Eyes round with fear, hair across her cheeks. "STOP ME."

The third day it happened I actually asked if anyone else had seen her. Nobody spoke. They just read their papers harder.

On the fourth day she got on to the train. The same girl. At Tottenham Court Road. Grabbing the handrail next to me, she looked haunted and grim. Determined. When we got to Leicester Square, she got off. And so did I.

When the train had gone, she walked to the far end of the platform by the yawning dark mouth of the tunnel and swung one foot over the edge.

"I have to stop you," I said, and pulled her back. She stared, stunned, and then walked away. I never saw her in the tunnel again. I always look.

If you enjoyed this story, why not try some of Ali's books:
Monster Makers: Electrotaur and Slashermite and
Monster Makers: Stinkermite

THE STORYTELLER | SUSAN COOPER

Once upon a time there was a boy born in the Northlands. He had no brothers and sisters, so he was much alone. He didn't mind. He told himself stories; he played games of make-believe in which he was the cowboys and the Indians and the horses as well. He specially liked being the horses.

He learned how to paddle a canoe on the lake, and he went fishing often on his own, in the misty mornings. He loved to watch the birds, and his favourite was the osprey that coasted high overhead, the underside of its great white wings turned blue by the light echoing up from the lake. The boy longed to fly like the osprey, way up there, but he didn't know how.

He read books, and found that the world was full of stories, even better than those he made up for himself. He learned many of them by heart, and when he grew up, he took his stories to crowds all over the world, and became a master of his calling. He had a canoe of his own now, and he still went fishing, looking up at the osprey coasting overhead. Looking, yearning, but not flying. He flew only in his dreams.

On went our storyteller, acting out the world's stories for the children of the world, until he was past ninety years of age, and his time was nearly used up. Lying in his bed, he saw through the open window an osprey, coasting on its broad wings across the sky.

"Come on out," said the osprey.

The old man said, "I can't fly."

"You can now," the osprey said.

And the old man found himself flying, flying out through the window, over the land and the sea, in a wonder and delight that he had never known. He lay on the wind; he looked down at his world and all its stories.

"I must go back now, I suppose," he said.

"Oh no," said the osprey. "Now you have reached your own story. You don't have to go back."

So they flew and they flew, and there they are flying still, once upon a time and for ever more.

If you enjoyed this story, why not try some of Susan's books:
The Dark is Rising Sequence and *The Boggart*

THE MOUSE | CARLO GEBLER

"Watch now," his granny said. She baited the trap with chocolate and slid it under the sideboard in the front room where she had just seen a mouse.

The next day, sitting on the green sofa and laughing at Roger the Dodger in his *Beano Annual*, he heard the trap go off.

He lay down on his belly, pulled out the trap and ran with it to the kitchen, where his granny was peeling apples.

"We got the mouse!" he shouted.

"Great! Now get rid of it, there's a good boy."

He went out to the back garden, lifted the lever of the trap and dropped the mouse on to the ground. Up above he heard screeching from the hawk that lived in the old elm down by the road.

He picked the mouse up by its tail and noticed blood around its mouth. He touched its body. It was still warm, he noticed, and now he felt a bit sad. The hawk's cries sounded again, closer this time.

He went over to the hedge and flung the mouse away. He expected it to fall into the field behind but instead the hawk suddenly swooped down. In mid-air it snatched the mouse with its claws and then shot into the sky.

He ran back into the kitchen shouting, "Our hawk!"

"What, darling?"

"It took the mouse!"

"Well," said Granny, laughing, "he'll enjoy his dinner today. Now be an angel . . . go and set the trap again like I showed you.

Remember, mice like chocolate. There's some in the pantry. . ."

The next morning, hoping for something to lure the hawk back, he went to check the trap. No mouse. He kept checking it throughout the day.

The morning after, following breakfast, he was again down on the floor and peering into the dark, dusty space under the sideboard.

He saw that the chocolate was gone but there was no mouse.

"Granny!" he shouted.

She looked in the door. "Any luck?"

"He's taken the chocolate!" He showed her the trap.

"Goodness me!" she said. "He didn't want to be thrown to the hawk, obviously."

"Granny," he said gravely, "he's a clever one, make no mousetake."

"Yes," she agreed, "mousificent."

If you enjoyed this story, why not try some of Carlo's books:
Bull Raid and *Caught on a Train*

High in the hills of Wales there was a tumbledown farm. It had barns and sheds and a long, low farmhouse. In there lived the farmer. Over the years, work and weather had worn him away till he looked like a bone wearing a hat. Now he was old and sick, lying in bed with his three sons sitting beside him.

"Boys," he said, "this farm will be too small for you to share when you're grown men. So when I'm gone, one of you must have it all. Here are three coins, one for each of you. I want you to buy something that can fill this room. Whoever does that best will get the farm."

So the boys took the coins and headed into town. The eldest son knew exactly what he wanted to buy with his coin. Hay! He bought a full cart-load.

The second son went to a place that made pillows. He bought thirty sacks of soft, downy feathers.

The youngest son went to a hardware shop and bought two small things.

That night, the boys gathered at the bedside again.

"Well now," said the old farmer. "Are you ready to show me what you bought?"

"I am," said the eldest son, and he went outside and fetched the straw. But when the last bale was brought in and spread over the floor, the hay barely reached the top of the bedpost.

"I can do better than that, Father!" cried the second son. He brought in his feathers and threw them around the room until it looked like snow had come early. But when the feathers settled, they took up even less space than the hay.

The old man turned to his youngest son. "Well, Cal," he said. "Can you do better?"

"I think so," said the youngest son with a shy smile. And he reached into his pocket, brought out the two small things he had bought and together they filled the room, right up to the roof.

"Well done, Cal," said the old man. "The farm shall be yours, and may you live a long and happy life here, as I have done."

Can you guess what Cal bought?

If you enjoyed this story, why not try some of Cat's books: *Barkbelly* and *Snowbone*

Answer: He bought a candle and a box of matches and filled the room with light.

THE BING BANG BONG MONSTER | SUE HEAP

One dark sleeptime there was a BING BANG BONG noise.

"What a commotion!" said Mrs Woffle as she woke with a start. "Who on earth is that at the door?"

Mr Tumble woke up too. He lived in the flat next to Mrs Woffle.

The noise happened again.

"What a racket!" he shouted.

"Who's out there?"

"For goodness' sake, BE QUIET!" He sighed.

Mrs Woffle and Mr Tumble opened their front doors at the same time.

"Who or what is making that bingybongybangy sound?" they groaned.

Mr and Mrs Stick had been woken up too, as had Mr Mallow.

"I think the BINGYBANGYBONGY noise is coming from the roof," he said. "Follow me."

Up the teeny, tiny staircase went Mrs Woffle, Mr Tumble, and Mr and Mrs Stick.

The more steps they climbed, the darker it got.

And the BING BANG BONG noise got louder and they became quieter and quieter.

"A hundred and four!" whispered Mrs Woffle. "A hundred and four steps we've climbed."

"Sssh!" everyone said.

BING BANG BONG. They all stopped still.

The door on to the roof was open.

Everyone was a little bit scared. Wouldn't you be?

"It could be a very, very big mouse!" said Mr Tumble.

"Or the BING BANG BONG monster," giggled Mr Mallow, who was out on the roof.

"Be careful," they all said. "He might eat you."

Mr Mallow gulped as he heard BING BANG BONG then BUMP BUMP BRUM BRUM BRUM ... followed by a very loud POP.

A voice said, "Pass the spanner." BANG! BANG! "Looks like ... that wobbly widget's fixed."

Mr Mallow rubbed his eyes. Close to the edge of the roof was a spaceship.

"Don't just stand there!" nine alien voices shouted. "Give us a push, please!"

Which he did.

There was a loud WHOOSH! followed by a POP! And then a little beeeeep.

And a very quiet, "Thank you."

"Took your time there!" said Mr Stick. "We thought you'd gone to the moon and back."

"Almost!" said Mr Mallow as he explained that nine aliens had taken the BING BANG BONG monster with them to Planet Zog.

Everyone nodded and said, "We thought as much. Nighty night, then."

And Mr Mallow smiled.

If you enjoyed this story, why not try some of Sue's books:
Danny's Drawing Book and *Cowboy Baby*

HUGO'S EGG | EVA IBBOTSON

I was the youngest in my family and the only boy – and my sisters teased and tormented me from morning to night. They were pretty girls with long blonde hair – but to them I could do nothing right, and sometimes I was so unhappy I just wanted to die.

One morning when my parents had gone out early, my sisters were boiling eggs for breakfast. They took three nice brown eggs out of the carton from the supermarket – and then a fourth, which was a sort of greyish colour with dark patches.

"We'd better throw that one away," said my youngest sister, but the others tittered and said, "That's Hugo's egg."

They boiled the eggs and sliced the top off their eggs and I sliced the top off mine.

It was bad – it was disgusting, filled with a sort of mucky gunge, and it smelled of sulphur.

My sisters thought that was very funny. "You'll have to eat it," they said. "If you don't you'll be sorry."

I picked up my spoon. But when I looked into the depths of the egg, the messy gunge had changed, and rearranged itself. And then I saw an eye … a small claw … a scaly wing…

Now my sisters were white with fear. But I found I knew what to do. I blew softly, then I blew again – and with each breath the creature assembled itself more and more. Then I gave a last blow, and there it stood on the table, growing with every minute: a proper green and golden dragon with fiery nostrils and a curving tail.

"Get on my back," it said – as dragons do.

I did as I was told. It was surprisingly comfortable; there was a hollow between the scales. The French windows were wide open, but first the dragon sent a jet of fire towards each of the girls, and as he did so, their long fair hair shrivelled and sizzled and they became as bald as coots.

Then together we rose up and flew out into the wide world.

I live with my dragon now, in a cave on the side of a beautiful mountain.

I didn't know anybody could be so happy.

If you enjoyed this story, why not try some of Eva's books: *Monster Mission* and *The Secret of Platform 13*

THE SHEEP WHO WALKED ON HIS OWN
KAYE UMANSKY

Little Bo Peep, she lost her sheep. It was all because of a sheep called Barry, who decided to take a walk on his own. He got tired of the other sheep's conversation. Whatever he said, the others would copy him.

"Baaaaaa!" said Barry. And the other sheep would go:

"Baaaaaaa! Baaaaaaa! Baaaaaa!"

"Silly things," said Barry. "They don't have a thought of their own."

One day, he got so tired of this, he decided to take a walk on his own. He pushed open the field gate … squeeeeeek! … and set off down the lane.

Soon, he met a cow peering over the hedge. The cow said:

"Mooooo! Moooooo!

What you gonna do?"

And Barry said:

"Baaaaaaa! I'm Baaarry and I'm going for a walk by myself."

Next, he came to a cockerel sitting on a fence. The cockerel said:

"Cock a doodle doo!

What you gonna do?"

And Barry said:

"Baaaaaaa! I'm Baaarry and I'm going for a walk by myself."

Next, the farm dog came running up. The dog said:

"Bow, wow, wow!

What you doing now?"

And Barry said:

"Baaaaaaa! I'm Baaarry and I'm going for a walk by myself."

Next, he came to a fat white duck swimming on a pond. The duck said:

"Quack, quack, quack!

You'd better go back."

And Barry said:

"Baaaaaaaa! I'm Baaarry and I'm going for a walk by myself."

Next, he came to a horse, standing under a shady tree. The horse said:

"Neigh! Neigh!

Do you know the way?"

And Barry said:

"Baaaaaaa! I'm Baaarry and I'm going for a w – oh dear! I think I'm lost!"

And he was, too.

But just then, along came Little Bo Peep. She said, "Oh, there you are, Barry! I've been looking for you everywhere. Where have you been?"

Barry was just about to explain about going for a walk by himself, when this is what he heard, from behind him:

"Baaaaaa! Baaaaaa! Baaaaaa!"

"Oh my!" said Barry, very surprised. "And there I was thinking I was going for a walk by myself!"

Barry and all the other sheep went back to their field with Little Bo Peep.

AND THEY DIDN'T FORGET TO BRING THEIR TAILS BEHIND THEM.

If you enjoyed this story, why not try some of Kaye's books: *Clover Twig and the Incredible Flying Cottage* and *The Stepsisters' Story*

MAKING FRIENDS | CHRIS HIGGINS

"There's nothing to do here," I complained.

"Go and explore," said Mum. "It's stopped raining." Our holiday home was an old tin-miner's cottage on the Cornish cliff tops. It was dark and dusty and smelled as if it had been shut up for ages.

I headed down the steep path towards the beach. It was deserted and stank of seaweed. I sat on a rock, alone and miserable.

Then I noticed a boy, bare to the waist and so skinny I could count his ribs. He was squatting by a rock pool.

"Aren't you freezing?"

"Don't feel the cold, me." His voice was rough with the Cornish burr. "I like it down here. I hate being cooped up inside."

He held out a grey shell. Inside, thin brown threads waved in the air. I recoiled.

"It's alive!"

He sucked out the contents. "Not any more, it ain't," he said, and we both laughed.

"Look!" He pointed up at the sky.

A bird hovered motionless above us. Suddenly it plummeted like a lift into the sea and came up with a fish in its mouth.

"Gannet," he explained. "Always hungry. Like me."

We clambered over the rocks together and he showed me spiny sea-urchins, shrimps, spider crabs and a creature called a sea hare that has a shell *in* its body. We roamed the beach, sifting through piles of seaweed to find periwinkles and worms and tiny sponges that if you pressed them, squirted water. Down by the shoreline we discovered eels burying themselves in the sand.

Mum called me from the cliff top. "Will? Come and see what I've found!"

"Go you," he said and turned away. At the top I looked back for him, but he'd disappeared. Out on the rocks was a lone grey seal.

Mum had an old book on mining disasters. "There was one here, you know. They'd have been buried alive underground. See this photo? Some of them were only boys."

From the page my new friend grinned at me. I ran back to the beach to find him, but he was nowhere to be seen. As I watched, the seal slipped from the rock and swam gracefully out to sea.

If you enjoyed this story, why not try some of Chris's books:
32C That's Me and *It's a 50/50 Thing*

THE STRIPY KITTEN | JULIA GREEN

Evie's cat had three kittens: one black as night, one grey like a shadow, one teeny stripy one. The little one was Evie's favourite. Two of the kittens had new homes: now only the stripy one was left. Dad called him Scaredy-Cat because he was frightened of EVERYTHING.

Most of the time, Scaredy-Cat hid.

Under Evie's bed.

Behind the sitting-room curtains.

In baskets and boxes.

On Friday, Granny came to tea as usual. She was lonely, living by herself. She told Evie that Fridays were her favourite days. She brought home-made gingerbread stars for Evie's tea.

Granny went home when Dad came back from work. Evie helped wash up. She fed the mother cat. But where was the stripy kitten?

Evie called.

She hunted everywhere.

Under beds, behind curtains, in boxes and baskets. She even looked outside, in case he'd escaped into the garden

The kitten was nowhere to be found.

Evie phoned Granny to tell her. "I've got an idea," Evie said. "Please look in your big squashy bag, just in case Scaredy-Cat hid inside."

Evie waited while Granny went to search. Evie's heart went pitter-patter, extra fast.

She heard Granny pick up the phone again. She heard another sound, like a tractor engine.

"Purrrrr…"

"You were right!" Granny said. "One tiny tabby kitten curled up tight! He must have climbed inside my bag at teatime. I carried him all the way home without knowing he was asleep in there!"

Next morning, Dad drove Evie round to collect the kitten.

"We're best friends already," Granny said, stroking the kitten on her lap. "He watched telly with me last night. He slept on my bed and kept me warm as toast. He had porridge for breakfast. And he's got a new name."

"What's that?" Evie asked.

"Tiger," Granny said. "Because he's stripy and brave like a real big tiger."

Tiger purred.

Evie looked at Dad.

Dad looked at Evie.

"He's happy here," Evie said.

"Much happier," Dad agreed.

"Can he stay?" Granny asked. "You can see him whenever you want."

Evie nodded. Now Granny wouldn't be lonely any more.

Tiger padded over to the back door. There was a whole big jungle out there to explore!

If you enjoyed this story, why not try some of Julia's books:
Over the Edge for younger readers and *Blue Moon* for older readers

FENELLA BUTTS | PAUL HARRISON

There were lots of reasons why Fenella Butts didn't like school. She sat on the bus on the way to Manor Park Primary with that familiar sick feeling in her stomach, and she thought about why she felt that way.

Mainly it was her name that caused her problems. Fenella was a bit different, but *Butts* was worse, much worse. Imagine growing up being called *Butts*. And imagine having parents who thought calling their daughter Fenella would somehow make things better. Her class, year two, teased her about it; in fact, the whole school teased her about it – even Ryan Swales, and he always got chosen last at football. And he picked his nose. And ate it.

Fenella didn't like the head teacher either. He scared her. He had hairy ears and his clothes smelled of biscuits. What's more, he always seemed to catch her when she was late.

"Late again, Butts!" he would bellow as she tried to sneak down the corridor. It was too squeaky, that corridor. No matter how carefully she tried to tiptoe past his office, her shoes would always squeak as loudly as a plague of mice. *And* the corridor smelled funny. It was that peculiar mix of disinfectant and wind – *boy* wind. Probably Jack Potts – he was always at it. He needed to change his diet.

The bus came to a stop and everyone else piled off and charged into school. As usual, Fenella was the last one off the bus. She trudged across the playground, trying not to be noticed, and went straight to the classroom. She put down her bag, looked around at the familiar room, and her heart sank just that little bit more. She knew every inch of the place: its slightly chipped tables; its well-used, dog-eared books; the strange damp patch on the ceiling. She also knew, deep down, what the problem really was. Why it was she didn't like school. You see, everyone else in year two had been at school for three years, but Fenella had been there for twenty. What's more, she looked set to be there for another twenty to come.

The real problem was that Fenella Butts was the teacher.

If you enjoyed this story, why not try some of Paul's books:
The Perfect Prince and *The Dinosaur Spotter's Guide*

WOLFIE! | MARTIN WADDELL

Once there were three little pigs who lived in a house made of brick. They thought all their Big Bad Wolf troubles were over, but...

One day the Big Bad Wolf came jogging out of the forest in his tracksuit.

"Here we go!" groaned the three little pigs, and they bolted the door and shuttered the windows.

"I'll huff and I'll puff and I'll blow your house down!" boasted the wolf. He'd been working out in the gym, and he felt sure he could do it.

"Why?" asked the pigs.

"So I can eat you!" snarled the wolf.

"Well, if you *must*," sighed the pigs. "But you know how upset you got last time."

"A wolf's got to do what a wolf's got to do!" said the wolf, licking his lips.

He huffed and he puffed and blew himself up V-E-R-Y B-I-G, and...

FOOOOOOOOOO, the wolf blew

The pigs' washing line blew away with the washing, but he couldn't blow their house down.

"Nice try, Wolfie!" called the three little pigs out the window, making the wolf really angry.

He huffed and he huffed and blew himself up B-I-G-G-E-R still, and...

FOOOOOOOOOO, the wolf blew.

A flowerpot blew off the veranda, along with three deckchairs the pigs used when they had their pig-brunch in the sun.

"Have another go, Wolfie?" suggested the three little pigs, which made the Big Bad Wolf madder than ever, so…

He HUFFED and PUFFED HIMSELF UP EVER SO BIG, and…

FOOOOOOOOOOOO, the wolf blew.

Nothing stirred, not even a brick.

The Big Bad Wolf broke down in tears, gnashing his teeth.

"Never mind, eh?" called the three little pigs, which totally blew the wolf's brain.

"You've asked for it, piggies!" he sobbed, and…

He HUFFED and he HUFFED and he PUFFED HIMSELF UP EVER SO BIGGER THAN BIG and got ready to puff their house down, but…

One little pig had crept through with a pin, and…

In went the pin.

"OUCH!" went the wolf, and…

FIZZZZOOOOOSSSSH!

The Big Bad Wolf blew away over the forest like a jet plane.

The three little pigs still live in their house, and…

The Big Bad Wolf is back working out at the gym.

If you enjoyed this story, why not try some of Martin's books: *Farmer Duck* and *Owl Babies*

MICKY MURPHY AND THE ACROBAT-APPLE
ELIZABETH ARNOLD

Micky Murphy liked climbing the apple tree. Matt the mongrel liked sleeping under it, except in autumn when apples rained down on his head.

Micky Murphy climbed up into the middle of the tree. "I wish I were you," sighed a big round apple, and down her smooth green face fell a tiny tear. "I want to be an acrobat."

"You are an acrobat," Micky said kindly. "You swing in the air by a tiny stalk. You're an acrobat-apple."

"It's not enough. I want to leap through the air and spin like a top. I'm tired of being stuck up this tree."

Autumn came. Rain fell. The wind blew. Acrobat-apple swung gently in the rising wind. She smiled; she was having some fun at last. Around her apples fell, breaking and bouncing. Acrobat-apple didn't care.

"Don't climb the tree!" Mrs Murphy told Micky when the rain stopped. "The wind is too strong. The branches might break. Apples will fall on your head."

Micky Murphy stared into the tree. Matt the mongrel watched from a distance.

Acrobat-apple swung wildly as the other apples rained down like snow.

The wind grew stronger. Acrobat-apple leapt up and down. She swung round and round. She had never moved so fast before. She laughed happily. "Look at me!"

Micky Murphy laughed and clapped. Matt the mongrel barked and barked. It was lovely to see Acrobat-apple so happy. Suddenly Acrobat-apple spun so wildly she broke her stalk. She was free from her tree at last. She spun in the air. She danced in the wind. She flew like a bird. She felt wonderfully free. She was still singing when she hit the ground.

Micky and Matt raced over to Acrobat-apple. She looked a bit bruised but she smiled happily. "I did it!" she said. "You can eat me now."

"Well done!" Micky Murphy said. "But you're too bruised to eat. I've a better idea. I'll polish you till you shine and later I'll choose a pip so you can live on as a new acrobat tree."

They imagined a tree dancing with apples that swung in the air and blew high and low. It was a beautiful tree, and everyone was happy.

If you enjoyed this story, why not try some of Elizabeth's books: *The Gold-Spectre* and *The Parsley Parcel*

THE DAFFODIL DUCKLING | GWEN GRANT

"That's a funny place for a daffodil," Evie said.

"That's because it's not a daffodil," I told her.

We stared down at the bright splash of yellow lying at the bottom of the lock.

It did look like a daffodil.

A dead one.

"That's a duckling," I said.

Evie got so close to the edge, it's a wonder she didn't fall in.

Then we heard it.

"Cheep! Cheep!"

"It isn't dead, Kate!" Evie cried.

The tiny sound echoed in the huge emptiness of the lock. The canal was being cleaned out, so there was no water in it.

Only mud.

"How did it fall in?" she asked.

"I think I know," I said. "I bet its mum took it from one side of the lock to the other and it got too close to the edge. Just as you are, Evie."

"But I won't fall in," Evie said.

"We should take more care when we change things," I grumbled, "so that nothing gets hurt."

Evie frowned.

"How will it get out?"

"It won't," I told her. "It can't."

The sides of the lock gates were criss-crossed with wooden beams.

"Who do you know who can climb better than me?" Evie asked.

"No one," I said, because it was true.

Evie was like a spider on the climbing wall, her long, thin arms and legs everywhere.

Now she went down the lock gates just like a spider.

I wanted to say, "Don't do that," but Evie would just have said, "Someone's got to do it," and then gone.

At the bottom, she held on with one hand, scooped up the duckling with the other, then climbed back up.

"There's its mum," I nodded.

Evie knelt and let the duckling slip into the canal.

It floated away like a daffodil, passing its mum as she splashed and chuntered towards us.

"Aaah!" Evie said soppily. "She's come to say thank you."

The duck nipped her fingers. Hard.

"Ouch!" she cried. "Hey, I didn't steal your baby."

"She thinks you did," I grinned as the duck waggled crossly away.

There was a red mark on Evie's finger.

"Some thanks," I said.

"Yeah," Evie laughed. "But someone had to do it."

If you enjoyed this story, why not try some of Gwen's books:
Private – Keep Out! and *Race Day*

I HATE THAT BAT | SUSAN GATES

My name is Gift and I live in Africa and this is the story of my pet bat, Levi.

Levi was a giant fruit bat. He lived in our chim – that's our word for toilet. And everyone hated him but me.

"I hate that bat!" said my sister, Anna. "I just went to the chim. When I opened the door he whizzed out! He nearly knocked my head off!"

"I hate that bat!" said Mum. "He's so messy! Besides, we won't need that old chim soon. We're having a fine new one built in our house!"

"But what will happen to our old chim?" I asked her.

"Your dad will knock it down," she told me.

"Oh no!" I cried. "It's Levi's home! He'll fly away."

"Good riddance!" said Mum and Anna.

I went to see Levi in the chim.

He was hanging upside down eating a mango, spitting the skin everywhere.

"Levi," I said sadly. "What shall we do? Soon, you'll have nowhere to live."

Suddenly from outside I heard Anna scream. "Leopard!"

I looked out the chim door. A leopard was slinking out of the bush. He had his eye on our goats.

"Go away!" screamed my sister at the leopard.

She went running towards him.

That crazy, brave girl, she was trying to fight off that leopard with a broom!

The leopard snarled, "Rrrrr!" He got ready to spring.

"Run, Anna!" I yelled.

I went racing out of the chim, shouting. The leopard swung his head round. His golden eyes blazed. He came sprinting to get me instead.

I should have run. But I was frozen with fear.

Then *whoosh*, something came whizzing out of our chim. It shot over the leopard on great clattering wings. It almost knocked its head off!

The leopard spun round. Yowling, it shot back into the bush and disappeared.

Mum and Dad came running. "What happened?" they cried.

"Levi scared off a leopard," said Anna.

"He saved our lives," I told Mum. "He's a hero!"

Mum was so grateful to Levi she let him stay. And Dad never knocked down the old chim.

Levi's in there now. Hanging upside down, eating a mango, spitting the skin everywhere.

If you enjoyed this story, why not try some of Susan's books: *Red Eye* and *Ghost Dogs*

BONGO'S CHANCE | LAURA ADKINS

Here are four important facts to know about me: my name's Bongo. I'm a dog. I like watching television. My favourite thing on television is football.

Television is amazing because there are all these people living inside it. They keep appearing and disappearing. Sometimes they have no legs and sometimes they're just talking heads. But I like it best when they play football. Everyone loves football in our house. I even have an official dog football shirt.

Football is when lots of people are trying very badly to catch a ball. The trouble is (and I reckon this is why it's called football), they keep knocking it away with their feet. No wonder they hardly ever catch it.

"Use your teeth!" I growl. That's what any sensible dog would do with a ball.

One morning I was walking past Pete's school, daydreaming about dog stuff, when I realized I'd forgotten to sniff my favourite tree. I suddenly stopped, but my walker (who's called Mum) kept on walking. The lead jerked, and to her surprise and mine, the collar pulled right over my head.

"Bongo, stay..." Mum warned, but I wasn't going to waste this chance. I was already sniffing around for something to chase. Then my ears shot up. In the field outside Pete's school there were children playing football! I whizzed into that field as fast as four legs could carry me. I was a blur of fur.

"Bongo!" Mum yelled, as I dodged and darted through

children's feet, half-deafened by their shouts. Left a bit, right a bit, I used some nifty nose-action to get the ball under control. I caught it in my mouth and sank my teeth in hard. The ball made a loud and angry *hissssss!* Holding my head up high, I trotted triumphantly back to Mum and dropped the ball at her feet. We both stared silently at the shrivelled thing.

I'd killed it.

The children came chattering to look over the hedge. One of them was our Pete. When he saw Mum and me, I could see he was embarrassed. No wonder. Losing football to a dog less than half his size! Next time he should use his teeth.

If you enjoyed this story, why not try Laura's book:
Ordinary Oscar

WISHES | JIM ELDRIDGE

Once upon a time there was a boy called Eric who loved baked beans. Unfortunately, baked beans made Eric fart. His mother and father told him not to always keep eating beans, as he stank the house out, so Eric usually waited until they were out of the house before indulging.

One day, when his family was out, Eric was in the kitchen opening a very large tin of beans when who should pop out of the tin but a genie, who materialized right beside Eric.

"Who are you?" demanded Eric.

"I am a genie and I have been trapped in that tin of beans for years! To thank you for releasing me, I shall grant you three wishes."

Eric was stunned. Three wishes! Wow! As he emptied the baked beans into a bowl, Eric wracked his brain for what he would wish for. A new bike? A new computer? No, they were all tiny wishes. How about going into outer space?

Eric ate his way through the bowl of beans, thinking the whole time of what he REALLY wanted.

"Come on," said the genie. "I haven't got all day to wait. You've got three wishes."

"I'm thinking about that," said Eric. "I really don't want to waste them on something unimportant."

The genie stood there tapping his foot impatiently as Eric finished the beans. Then they heard the front door open and his mother call out, "Eric! I'm home!" His mother was home early!

Whether it was the shock of so nearly being discovered, or the beans that did it, Eric let out a huge fart.

"Oh no!" he said. "I wish I hadn't eaten those beans!"

"One wish!" shouted the genie.

"No!" groaned Eric. "I wish I hadn't said that!"

"Two wishes!" shouted the genie.

"No!" moaned Eric.

He could hear his mother in the hall. At any second she would open the door to the kitchen and come in and smell the dreadful smell. His only hope was to wish that she hadn't come home yet.

"I wish…" he began.

"Yes?" prompted the genie.

"I wish for 366 more wishes," said Eric. "And the first one is: I wish I hadn't just farted."

If you enjoyed this story, why not try some of Jim's books: *The Trenches* and *Spy Smuggler*

THE LUCKY GUESS | BRIAN SIBLEY

Toby Thurston stared at the big glass jar with the screw top. It was full of sweets of all shapes, sizes and colours: hot reds, sticky yellows and orangey-swirly ones.

Beside the jar stood a notice that read:

> ## HOW MANY SWEETS IN THE JAR?
> Guess the Right Number and Win the Lot!
> 2p a guess or 6 guesses for 10p

There were many stalls at the summer fair and Toby had looked at all of them, but he kept on coming back to this one.

"Go on, sonny!" yelled the woman behind the stall in a loud, booming voice. "Have a guess and try your luck!"

Toby only had tuppence left and, as much as he fancied winning the big jar of sweets, he wasn't sure that he wanted to risk the last of his pocket money.

So, he started, very quietly, counting the sweets: "Three red, two pink, four green and one mauve…" He had just reached twenty-seven when the woman realized what he was doing and turned the jar around.

"It's tuppence if you want to guess!" she bellowed crossly, and Toby was so terrified that he handed over the coin and wrote down his guess on a form: 366.

The woman roared with laughter. "*366?*" she hooted. "You silly little boy! What a waste of tuppence!"

Only then did Toby notice that all the other guesses were a thousand or more.

Toby was still feeling incredibly stupid when his father came over and joined him. Mr Thurston had been entertaining children in a nearby tent, doing conjuring tricks and producing a rabbit out of a top hat.

"Never mind, Toby," said his father, adding mysteriously, "we'll see just how close you were at the end of the afternoon."

Several hours later, when the competition judges got around to counting the number of sweets in the jar, the strangest thing occurred: to everyone's surprise, there were *exactly 366 of them*!

Toby carried his jar home, opened it up and counted the sweets again. *Two thousand, three hundred and seventy-nine!* It was all terribly puzzling.

That was when Toby's father decided it was finally time to start teaching his son the *real* secrets of MAGIC!

If you enjoyed this story, why not try some of Brian's books:
The Frightful Food Feud and *Three Cheers for Pooh*

MONKEY BIRD | CAROL DRINKWATER

Tim gently placed our white dove on the window sill.

"Look – a rainbow!" I cried.

Beyond our orchard with soggy sheep, beyond village and scattering clouds, the coloured arc shimmered. Rain still dripped noisily from the gutters above. It didn't drown out the shouting in the kitchen below.

My big brother and I stood together and watched her snowy head cocked to the sky. I felt such happiness. For as long as I could remember Tim and I had been enemies. Not fighting and hurting one another like our parents, but silent, silent witnesses. Monkey had changed everything.

It began a couple of weeks back when, in the pouring rain, I had visited my patch of garden. I had needed to get out. I was crying about Mum, her bruises, her pain. Then I saw, hunched in a puddle, a white dove. Her left wing was trailing, torn by barbed wire and soaked with mud. I tried to pick her up but she pecked furiously at my hand. It really hurt. Crouching, I stroked the back of her head, until eventually she settled and I managed to get her into the empty rabbit hutch. She would be dry there. I wouldn't tell Tim because he would make fun.

I took her bread, water, but she was not feeding, not getting better. I nicked a sock from Tim's drawer and slipped it over the wing, to keep warm.

That must have been when he took her.

I rushed into his room, furious. "Where's Monkey?"

"What kind of name is that for a bird, Monkey!"

"Give her back!"

He showed me the splint he'd made. How he had folded the cardboard over the wing and taped it, really loving.

"She'll get well if I help. Can I?"

"She's my bird," I insisted.

"Sure. Look, she's eating."

I stared at my brother. I had never seen him so soft, never understood how he cared. Monkey healed under his gentle fingers.

Now, our bird took a sideways step, like Dad when he's been drinking, and then almost before we knew it, she lifted her wings – first the good one, then the damaged – and took off.

"Tim, she's done it, Monkey's flying!"

If you enjoyed this story, why not try some of Carol's books:
My Story: The Hunger and *My Story: Suffragette*

PIGS MIGHT FLY | MICHAEL BOND

One morning Olga was having breakfast when she heard her name being mentioned.

Well, it wasn't exactly her *name*, but Mr Sawdust was looking straight at her when he said: "Pigs might fly!"

"Pigs might fly!" repeated Noel, the cat, when he heard. "No wonder everyone laughed. I mean … can you picture it?"

"Quite easily," said Olga. Munch, munch. "Guinea pigs can do anything if they set their minds to it." And as soon as she was on her own, she decided to show just what she meant.

It was Karen Sawdust who first noticed the strange goings-on as she was leaving for school.

"I don't know what's come over Olga," she said. "She's running round in circles, jumping up and down as though there's no tomorrow. She'll do herself a mischief if she's not careful."

"Oh, dear," said Mrs Sawdust. "Perhaps I'd better take her to the vet?"

Olga stopped in her tracks and closed her eyes as she hid behind the television. Vets stick needles in you!

It wasn't until much later that morning that Noel found her.

"So that's where you've been," he said. "We've been looking for you everywhere!"

"As a matter of fact," said Olga sleepily, "since I last saw you I've been to the moon and back."

Noel stared at her, not knowing whether to believe his ears or not.

"What was it like?" he asked.

"Lovely," said Olga. "There wasn't a cat to be seen for miles around. After that I lay back for a while on a fluffy white cloud and watched the world go by. Then I flew back home in case I was being missed."

"Missed?" repeated Noel. "Missed? Chance would be a fine thing. Meeeeow!"

He was about to leave Olga to it when he paused. "This door's been shut all the morning in case you had to go to the vet," he said. "You couldn't have been anywhere."

"I can make myself very thin when I want to," said Olga. "Thin enough to wiggle under the crack."

"Wheeeee!" she squeaked as Noel stalked out of the room in disgust. "That's another thing about guinea pigs. We're much better than cats at having wonderful dreams."

If you enjoyed this story, why not try some of Michael's books:
The Tales of Olga da Polga and *A Bear Called Paddington*

Charlie's mum was asleep on the sofa. She looked sad and it was all Charlie's fault.

He'd just been nastier than a tummy ache in the night.

Mum had made Charlie scrambled eggs. This was a huge surprise because she hadn't done *anything* except rest for weeks. Hadn't played with Charlie. Walked him to school. Put him to bed. She couldn't. In case Charlie's new baby brother or sister arrived too early.

Ooh! Thinking about this new baby *really* made Charlie hot and angry.

That's why, instead of saying, "Yum. Thanks, Mum," and tucking into lunch, he spat, "Yuck!"

"Char-lie." Mum looked really hurt. "You *love* scrambled eggs. Come on…" She waved the plate under Charlie's mouth.

Charlie glued his lips tight.

"OK." Mum never gave up. "Let's play Magic Mouthful. Remember when you were tiny and didn't like the taste of something I'd say, 'Shut your eyes, open your mouth and pretend this spoonful tastes like strawberry ice cream, or chocolate pudding, or apple crumble with cust—'"

"I'm not a *baby* any more." Charlie scowled at Mum's tummy. "Pretending yuck things taste nice is a stupid game!"

As he yelled, Charlie swept his plate off the table.

*

Although Charlie cleaned up every scrap of egg mess, he wanted to cheer Mum up.

"I know," he decided, spotting an empty mug beside the sofa, "I'll make Mum hot chocolate. Her favourite."

Slight problem, though. Charlie wasn't allowed to use the cooker. He had to make hot chocolate with cold milk.

It had no chocolate powder in it either, or marshmallows, because there was a child lock on the pantry.

And Charlie was too small to reach the shelf where Mum kept the milk frother.

"Never mind. I think my drink *looks* like proper hot chocolate, anyway," decided Charlie. He stirred lots of brown sauce into the cold milk, then made froth by shaking the washing-up liquid. Instead of marshmallows, he sprinkled chunks of bread on top of the mug.

"I'm sorry I was horrible. I *do* want to play Magic Mouthful again," Charlie said, carrying his mug of frothy hot chocolate carefully to the sofa.

"It's your turn to taste and do the pretending, Mum…"

If you enjoyed this story, why not try some of Catherine's books: *Fat Boy Swim* and *Tug of War*

WHY IS A LEAP YEAR CALLED A LEAP YEAR?
DAVID HENRY WILSON

Long ago, in the Year 4, the Greek gods lived on Mount Olympus. (They don't live there now, because they got fed up with all the tourists.) One day in February the chief god Zeus decided they should play some games, on condition that he was allowed to win them all. So the other gods let him win the 100 metres, the 200 metres, the 400 metres, the parking metres, the marathon, the long jump, the high jump, the javelin, the itch (that's been scratched now), the hammer, etc.

The god of sport, who was called Runnamilo, got more and more annoyed at having to let Zeus win, so when they came to the last event, the pole vault, Runnamilo decided that *he* would win it.

Pole-vaulters use a long pole to help them jump over the bar, and so all the other gods crashed into the bar, while Zeus jumped over it. But Runnamilo jumped over it too, which meant they had to raise the bar. Zeus was not very pleased when he knocked it down, but he still thought he'd win – until Runnamilo ran up the track, planted his pole in the box, and soared up higher and higher and higher.

Runnamilo never came down. As soon as Zeus saw what was happening, he produced a magic spell, which left Runnamilo going up and up and up until he bumped his head on the sun, giving it such a knock that it took an extra day to recover.

"I won! I won!" cried Zeus. (To win the pole vault, you must come back down to Earth and collect your medal.) "I won everything! Congratulations to me!"

Runnamilo was never seen again – which is why nobody's ever heard of him – and to mark his own achievements up on Mount Olympus, Zeus ordered that every fourth year there should be an extra day in February, and there should be a competition known as the Olympic Games.

But Aphrodite, the goddess of dates – who had made a date with Runnamilo for that evening – was broken-hearted, and wanted everyone to remember Runnamilo's wonderful jump. So she ordered that every fourth year should be known as a leap year.

If you enjoyed this story, why not try some of David's books:
Triple Trouble With Jeremy James and *Causing Chaos With Jeremy James*

TIGER – THE NO-GOOD GUARD DOG
MALACHY DOYLE

"We need a dog," said Poppa. "We need a guard dog."

So they went to the Dogs' Home and Willow chose a big strong puppy.

"This is the one I want," she said. "I'm going to call him Tiger."

"You can't live in the house," Poppa told him, when they got home. "You have to live outside, and bark when anyone comes."

So Tiger lived outside. And every time someone came to the gate, he charged across the yard. But he didn't bark. And he didn't bite. No, he only wagged his tail and then he licked them.

"I'm sorry, Willow," said Poppa, one day. "But Tiger will have to go, for he's a no-good guard dog."

But that night a burglar came. He climbed over the gate and Tiger didn't hear him. He climbed through the window and Tiger didn't see him. And he stole Momma's gold ring!

"Don't bark," said the burglar, climbing out, for there was Tiger, right below him. "Good dog," he said, as Tiger wagged his tail and licked him.

Tiger followed the burglar, out on to the street. "Go home, dog," said the burglar. But Tiger wouldn't. He followed him home, curled up on the mat outside his house, and waited.

In the morning, back at Willow's house, Poppa woke up. "We've been burgled!" he cried.

"They've taken my ring!" cried Momma.

"They've taken my Tiger, too!" cried Willow. "I can't find him!"

"They can keep him," said Poppa. "I told you he was a no-good guard dog."

Willow was coming home from school that afternoon when she saw a man being followed by a dog. "Tiger!" cried Willow, and the man began to run.

Willow ran fast, but the man ran faster. The man ran fast, but Tiger ran the fastest. He raced past the man, stopped to lick him and tripped him up.

The man flew into the air, and what flew out of his pocket? A shiny gold ring!

"We can keep Tiger now, can't we, Poppa?" said Willow, when they got home. "For he is a good guard dog, isn't he?"

"I suppose he is," said Poppa, as Tiger licked him. "I suppose he must be."

If you enjoyed this story, why not try some of Malachy's books: *Horse* and *Charlie Is My Darling*

THE POSITIVE CHAIR | ANDREW COPE

At Friday teatime, Dad did one of his mad things. He called us over to the new armchair and circled his hands in the air, like he was doing a spell. He said some daft words that made us giggle. Something like, "Hocus pocus, satsumas and pears, make this into a positive chair." It's typical Dad behaviour, so we went along with it. Dad tested the chair, just to check he'd not made it *too* positive. As soon as his bottom touched the seat, he jumped up, punching the air and whooping with energy. I was next. And I am twelve, so you can't trick me. But, do you know what, I actually felt energized as my bottom touched the cushion. My mum and brother were the same. It was really weird. For the next few weeks, the chair settled into its new home, and every time I was stuck with my maths homework I'd sneak a quick sit down.

Uncle Ray and Auntie Ella always come to ours on Boxing Day. Dad calls them "professional grumblers". Auntie Ella wasn't very well. She never is – I think it's to do with being old. She always catches everyone else's germs. And Uncle Ray said how terrible the weather was and how awful the Christmas edition of *Doctor Who* had been. Auntie bought Mummy a bottle of wine that nobody in our house likes. Uncle Ray moved through to the lounge, where I heard him complaining about all the new toys littering the floor. Apparently he didn't get very many presents in his day. And what he did get, he *really* appreciated.

Dad guided Uncle Ray to the new chair. Me and my brother held our breath. This was the ultimate test! He turned around and got ready to plop his bum into the positive chair. His bottom hovered for a second while he looked at our expectant faces. "What?" he asked.

"Nothing!" I blurted.

And his bony bum hit the cushion.

A huge grin spread over Uncle Ray's face. "Is that one of those Nintendo Wii things?" he asked, pointing to where the TV was. And he sat for two hours, playing, laughing and enjoying Boxing Day.

If you enjoyed this story, why not try some of Andrew's books:
The *Spy Dog* series

Ryan picked up the stone. It fitted smoothly into his hand, but it had one jagged edge.

He pressed it against the wall. It made a blue mark. Ryan dragged the stone along the wall, leaving a blue line behind him.

He drew the line along the bakery wall, then along the wall of the police station. He drew it along some backyard walls, then on the wall of a factory that went on for a long time. As long as the stone went on drawing, Ryan wanted to keep going. He imagined drawing the line through grass, on the sides of hills, and even through the air.

Danny was on his way home from school. He was new there and no one seemed to like him. And his teacher had shouted because he'd forgotten his homework. His shoulders were hunched, and his head lowered, so it was some time before he noticed the line.

That's new, he thought. The blue line glowed faintly on the red wall. It looked as though it might lead somewhere. So he followed it.

Past the bakery and the police station, Danny followed the line. Past backyard walls, and a factory wall that went on for a long time. Then the line ended.

There was a space, then a lamp post. On the lamp post was another part of the line. Danny looked at the next lamp post; there was the next part of the line. When he looked closely, Danny thought he could see a line *between* the lamp posts, connecting them.

Where the town ended, there was a field with the blue line cutting through it. Where the field ended, there was nothing. Nothing, except for the blue line, zinging through the empty air. Danny touched it. It felt like a charged wire. He hesitated, then pulled.

All the buildings of the town squeezed together as Danny pulled. The teacher who'd shouted at him, the boys who'd laughed, were yanked together by the blue line. Then they started to unravel.

Danny pulled and pulled, both ways. Finally, at the very end of the line, there was Ryan.

He held the stone out towards Danny.

"Your turn," he said.

If you enjoyed this story, why not try some of Livi's books:
Sky Wolves and *The Angel Stone*

THE MIAMI STICKER | KJARTAN POSKITT

It always rained on concert nights. One other figure was already huddled in the bus shelter when I arrived, clutching my case. I stood looking up the dark road, ignoring him, but knew I was being stared at.

"You got a trumpet in there?" came the old man's voice.

I nodded without looking round. It didn't take a lot of brains to guess there would be a trumpet in a trumpet case. There were large headlights in the distance – I'd soon be on the bus.

"Cairo, Cape Town, Miami, Berlin…"

He was reading the tatty labels stuck on the case. They weren't mine – they were there when I'd got it. The headlights went past. It was a lorry.

"Tell me, is the pearl inlay on the middle valve still chipped?"

This made me look at him. He was wearing an old baseball cap and a shabby overcoat. "How would you know that?" I snapped irritably.

"Sorry!" he grinned. "It's an old friend. I played that trumpet in the Queen's Ballroom, Miami."

"Really?"

"Six of us playing hot jazz for three hours. What a gig – what an audience!"

"Lots of rich people?"

"Nah, it was a real dump. There were just two fat old women with blue hair eating doughnuts. For three hours!"

He chuckled at the memory, and I laughed too.

"Then a month later in Berlin we had two thousand people up dancing. So are you in a band?"

"School concert band. We only play at St Chad's Hall."

"What do you mean *only*? You should put a sticker on that case saying *St Chad's Hall*."

"It'd look a bit naff next to the others."

"Why? So long as you play with pride, there's no such thing as a naff gig. I don't have much in my pockets these days, but thanks to that trumpet I've got a head full of treasures."

There was a swish of tyres on the wet road as the bus arrived. Before I got on, he reached out and stroked the case.

"Take care of my old friend," he said. "And don't forget that sticker. If I put one on for Miami, you can put one on for St Chad's!"

If you enjoyed this story, why not try some of Kjartan's books: The *Urgum the Axeman* series and the *Murderous Maths* series

DRAGONFLIES AND DAMSELFLIES
MICHAEL COX

In the olden days when everyone was really smelly and only ever had a bath on their bathday (or birthday as it's now known), "personal insects" were a big problem. Everything and everybody had their own little swarm of insects which constantly buzzed around them. Horses were haunted by horseflies, fruit was frustrated by fruit flies, houses were harried by houseflies, dragons were demented by dragonflies and, of course, damsels were driven doolally by swarms of damselflies.

"It's no fun living in the olden days!" moaned the disgruntled damsels. "We want discos, romance and designer party frocks. But all we get is flies! Those stupid knights are so busy trying to rescue the dragons from the dragonflies that they ignore us damsels in distress! Come to think of it, they ignore us in *dat dress*, too!"

It was true. The knights were incredibly stupid (partly because knight schools had yet to be invented), so they spent almost all of their time at knight clubs or going out and getting their hair singed so badly by the dragons that they were forced to wear knight caps.

"Let's invite the knights to a huge lakeside picnic!" cried the damsels. "And then, driven mad by our flies, we'll all suddenly jump in the lake. That way those dozy knights will just *have* to rescue us!"

So that is exactly what they did. But when the knights tried to rescue the damsels, they were all drowned. This was because the knights had put on their best suits (of armour) for the picnic, so they sank straight to the bottom of the lake clutching the damsels, who couldn't swim anyway.

The poor dragons were left to get rid of their own flies by breathing fire at them. Sadly, they singed their own skin so badly that they too had to jump into the lake to cool off, so they were all drowned as well.

And that's why when you visit a pond or lake today, you will often see swarms of dragonflies and damselflies hovering just above the surface of the water. They're still waiting for the damsels and dragons to come out so they can torment them a bit more.

If you enjoyed this story, why not try some of Michael's books: *Horribly Famous: Tutankhamun and his Tombful of Treasure* and *Johnny Catbiscuit and the Tentacles of Doom*

A MAMMOTH LEAP | **MATILDA WEBB**

The teacher droned on and on. The class was in the local museum. *Again*. Simon fiddled with his glasses, which had broken for the umpteenth time. He was leaning on a glass case wondering whether he should do up his shoelaces or not. Then he wondered if his mum had put crisps in his packed lunch.

With his glasses back on, the flint spearheads in the case swam into focus. He looked at them properly. Something stirred in his imagination.

All of a sudden he was kneeling on a rock ledge above a mist-filled gorge. Hunters with spears brushed past him as they went swiftly down to the trail. His heartbeat matched the rhythm of their running feet. Soon they were lost to view in the enclosing forest.

He shivered and pulled his wolf fur tighter. He hated being left behind. But the hunters knew he couldn't see far. He was more use joining the elders in doing the close, skilful work of shaping flint into weapons.

But this time he would prove himself! He grabbed a spear and slid down the slope. His breath fogged as he ran along the trail.

Suddenly the forest ahead of him erupted with noise. Trees crashed to the ground. A giant beast trumpeted in fear and fury. Simon stopped dead. He heard panicked shouts. Without warning the beast burst through the trees ahead of him. He knew this was his one chance to prove himself. Prove himself or die in the process.

He took aim at the great grey shape now charging at him, even though it wasn't in focus. He sent his spear flying. The deadly spearhead found its mark. The mammoth crashed to the ground.

The hunters crowded round, shouting and laughing. They looked at Simon with a new respect. Perhaps they'd been wrong to leave him behind all these times.

Someone nudged him. The gorge and all its heart-stopping action vanished. The teacher was moving on. But even though Simon tripped over his shoelaces (sending his glasses flying) and even though there were no crisps in his packed lunch box, he walked with a new confidence. From now on nothing could dismay the great mammoth hunter.

If you enjoyed this story, why not try Matilda's book:
The Ship's Kitten

THE BABYSITTER'S BOTTOM | IAN WHYBROW

Here comes Mrs Featherlegs – peckly speckly, easy squeezy under the gate!

"Come along, chicks, keep up, keep up!"

"Oh, Mum!" cheeped the chicks.

"Why can't we scratch for grubs by the henhouse?"

"Mums get tired of scratching about," said Mrs Featherlegs. "I've got an invitation to the Cock a Doodle Dance! We're off to find you a babysitter, keep up, keep up!"

"Wait!" cheeped the chicks. "You can't let someone *sit* on us!"

But Mum was in a hurry, so she didn't hear.

Here's Miss Saddleback scratching herself against a post.

"Pardon me for interrupting," said Mrs Featherlegs. "But please can you be my babysitter? So I can go to the Cock a Doodle Dance?"

"Snort!" said Miss Saddleback. "I'm so itchy, I *must* go for a mud bath. You'll have to ask Lily the cow. Sorry to muck you about."

"Cheers!" cheeped the chicks. "Thank heaven for that! Her big bottom would have *squashed us flat*!"

Here's Lily the cow in the milking parlour.

"Pardon me for interrupting your flow," said Mrs Featherlegs. "But please could you be my babysitter? So I can go to the Cock a Doodle Dance?"

"Oh noooo!" said Lily. "I always go with the girls after work and chew the cud. Sorry, you'll have to ask somebody else."

"Cheers!" cheeped the chicks. "That cow can't sit on us! Cheep

cheep cheep! Thank goodness for that. Milk in your mash is lovely and creamy – BUT Lily's big bottom would have *squashed us flat*!"

Poor Mrs Featherlegs, what a disappointment.

"You go on without me, girls," she sighed to the other hens. "I can't find a babysitter and I'm all upset."

Hello, who can this be? It's Fluff, the Old English Sheepdog!

"Don't get in a flap, Mrs Featherlegs!" panted Fluff. "Never fear! You *shall* go to the Cock a Doodle Dance because – I shall be your babysitter!"

"Help!" cheeped the chicks. "Oh what shall we do? Fluff's got a GREAT BIG BOTTOM, too!"

Fluff woofed: "Bedtime, chickies! Close your eyes. And you will get a big surprise!"

Then slowly,

slowly,

down came Fluff's enormous great big fat bottom…

"Oh, that's lovely – snuggle up tight! Soft as Mum's bottom! Ahhhmmm! Night night!"

If you enjoyed this story, why not try some of Ian's books:
Harry and the Dinosaurs Make a Splash and *Animal Soup*

ONCE IN A BLUE MOON | CAROLINE PITCHER

High on a church roof stood some statues. There was an angel and an imp, a dragon and a drummer, a jester and a shepherdess with her sheep. On the ledge over the door were the statues of the stonemason and his little apprentice.

One night the apprentice cried, "Look, Master! The moon is blue."

"Then we can all go down into the town," said the stonemason.

The angel reached out her hands for the imp and the jester, the dragon carried the drummer and masons on his back, and down they flew into the square. The shepherdess and her flock ran down the winding steps inside the steeple.

It was a wild, wild night! The dragon lit a fire and roasted chestnuts and potatoes. The drummer played for everyone to dance and sing. The imp undid the lock of the bank with his twisty fingers, took all the money and stuffed it through poor people's letter boxes. The sheep trotted along the lanes, eating the flowers from the gardens. Above the town flew the angel, and all the night birds flew with her.

When the church clock struck seven, the stonemason said, "We must go back. When the sun rises we will be stone again."

"I've lost a lamb," cried the shepherdess.

"I'll find him," said the little apprentice, and off he ran. But when he returned, carrying the lamb, the square was empty and he began to weep.

"Be quick!" cried the statues from the roof. "The moonlight is fading and the townspeople are waking up."

A woman bustled to work with her son, Tommy. He looked up and saw the statues on the roof. The sun shone and the statues turned to stone. Tommy heard weeping and saw the little apprentice in the shadows with the bleating lamb in his arms.

Tommy scooped them up and ran all the way up the steeple steps to set them out on the sunlit ledge.

The little apprentice smiled at Tommy and turned to stone.

"Come on! I'll be late for work," called his mother.

Tommy ran down and took her hand.

He opened his other hand.

It was full of blue teardrops, set like glass.

If you enjoyed this story, why not try some of Caroline's books: *The Shaman Boy* and *The Winter Dragon*

CLEMENTINE | KAREN SAUNDERS

Clementine McKenzie changed my life.

She was new at school, and ended up sitting next to me. Her hair was long, and the front was threaded with indigo beads. She was dressed all in purple – a lilac skirt, a mauve blouse, a plum cardigan and lavender tights.

Clementine explained, "I'm having a purple day."

After the break bell went, Clementine followed me. But I was used to being alone.

"Where are your friends?" Clementine asked.

I didn't answer. Tamara was marching towards us.

"Katie's found a friend," Tamara sneered. "What're you wearing, ugly friend? That's not our uniform."

Clementine just sipped her blackcurrant juice.

"You look stupid," Tamara taunted.

"Shut up, Tamara," I said, then wished I hadn't.

"Nobody likes you," Tamara replied meanly.

"I do," Clementine said. "Why don't *you* shut up and go away?"

Clementine gave her drink carton a squeeze and sprayed juice all over Tamara.

Suddenly, I liked her too.

Clementine became my best friend. She was what Mum called "individual". Clementine called *her* mum Willow. They lived in a B&B, because Willow didn't stay anywhere long. Clementine wove beads into my hair, like hers. When I went round for tea, I ate sweet potatoes, fish fingers and carrots. It was an orange day.

I liked it being just us. Then Clementine suggested making friends with Lottie.

"Why?" I asked.

Nobody talked to Lottie. Tamara had turned on her after she realized she couldn't pick on me any more.

"You know, Katie, you've got to make new friends," Clementine said. "Promise me if I go away you'll make an effort."

"OK," I said. "But I'm happiest being friends with you."

The next day, Clementine told me she was leaving. And by the end of the week, she'd gone. I realized I didn't like being alone any more.

Sighing heavily, I crossed the playground to where Lottie was sitting.

"Hi, Lottie."

Now what? I was hopeless at this.

"I like your hair," Lottie said shyly. "The beads are really pretty."

"I'll do yours if you like?" I offered.

"Thanks!" Lottie said happily.

The bell went. We walked into class together.

"Do you want to sit with me?" I asked. "There's a spare seat."

Karen recommends:
Allie Finkle's Rules for Girls by Meg Cabot and *Goodnight Mister Tom* by Michelle Magorian

THE NEW MASTERS OF THE UNIVERSE
ELEANOR UPDALE

Warning: This poem may get under your skin

I have some small companions
Who live upon my head.
They run and writhe and wriggle
When I am in my bed.
And then, when I am fast asleep,
Their wives start laying eggs.
Each one contains a little louse,
With lots of little legs.
I saw one down a microscope,
His body looked like jelly.
I could even see his poo
Working through his belly.
Six tiny limbs with savage claws
Were clinging to a hair,
And two short pointy aerials
Stood waving in the air.
Their purpose seemed to me to be
To help him feel his way
As he ran up and down my scalp,
Sucking blood, to stay
Alive, and breed more lice,
To bite and suck blood more.

"But why?" I asked my mummy,
"What are these creatures for?
They don't make any honey,
They don't spin any thread,
They can't be sold for money,
You can't eat them with bread."
"I know," she said, "they're useless,
And it's worse than you expected,
They make you itch,
They make you scratch,
Those bites can get infected."
So Mum went mad with chemicals,
With shampoo and a comb,
Till choking cries of agony
Rang through our happy home.
My sister, who has longer hair,
Could only scream and shout
As Mummy brushed and combed and tugged,
To get the head lice out.
But all their eggs were stuck with glue
Extruded from their tummies.
My mum was quite defeated,
And all the other mummies
Were doing just the same as her,
With cursing and with swearing,
And trying other remedies,
One of them even daring

To try to Hoover her kids' heads
To get the bugs away,
But they survived, and left more eggs,
To hatch another day.
Each lady louse lays eighty-three,
And each of them lays more.
There really is no way that we
Can hope to win this war.
Those mighty mites are here to stay,
And size-for-size they're stronger
Than elephants or dinosaurs,
And may survive for longer.
But in the meantime, you should know,
In one way they're quite cool.
'Cause if you show the teachers them,
You get a day off school.

NOW PLEASE STOP SCRATCHING.

If you enjoyed this story, why not try some of Eleanor's books:
The *Montmorency* series

WHAT JACK DID | GUY BASS

The school bell went at 3.40 p.m. As the other children made their way home or waited for the bus, Jack Small walked into the middle of the playing field behind the school. He planted a small pod in the ground. Within seconds, his sling-glider had grown from the soil. Jack jumped in and took to the air, then waited for the vibrations of the glider's wings to open a hop-hole in the sky.

"Here we go again," Jack said to himself. He shot through the hop-hole, emerging amidst the coiled, writhing spires of The Living City. He was met by a barrage of bomb-backed plunder-bunnies. Ghost Rodents! The armies of the *Phantasmagoria Rodentia* had begun their invasion!

"Destroy the city! Death to the living!" cried Bucktooth, the rodent general. His ghostly sky-galleon, powered by its haunted heart, ploughed through the city's living, tendril-like towers. A battalion of tiny sling-gliders weaved and spiralled to avoid the galleon's hamster-cannons and shrew-ghouls.

"Follow me into the city!" cried Jack. The sling-gliders darted through the twisting steeples. The galleon pursued them mercilessly, its heart pumping like a steady drum. On and on they flew, until the city's spires became so dense they began to wrap and coil around the sky-galleon. Soon it was left hanging, suspended like a fly in a web. Jack sped towards it, arming his deus ex machine-gun. He fired on its haunted heart. As the galleon exploded, Jack soared upwards, and saw the three suns rise over the city.

Victory celebrations went on long into the night, but one sling-glider pilot was notably absent. Jack had taken to the air once more. He looked down over The Living City and smiled, then opened a hop-hole and shot through. He appeared above the school just in time to hear the Monday-morning bell chime. He rushed into the classroom and hid himself at the back.

"We shall be starting the week with some creative writing," said his teacher. "Three hundred words entitled 'What I Did This Weekend' … and none of your *silly stories* this time, Jack Small. I want to know what you *really* did."

Jack just shrugged, and wrote a story about going to the zoo.

If you enjoyed this story, why not try one of Guy's books:
Dinkin Dings and the Frightening Things

"Flora! Come inside. I must brush your hair."

Flora's mother stood at the back door to call again. "You'll be late for school. Breakfast is ready! Come in NOW."

Flora bounded in and submitted to her hair being brushed and plaited to keep it tidy all day.

Swish, swoosh went the brush, her head jerking back at each stroke.

"Whatever were you doing outside?"

"Counting flowers. Twenty-three pink tulips, four red ones, and there are six yellow ones beside the rhubarb. There are *hundreds* of white narcissi. They were dancing in the wind and the bluebells ran across to join them. They curtsied to each other and then did a jig, or maybe it was a polka. The blackbirds whistled the tune and the robin kept them in order. He was very bossy.

"When the wind stopped, there was a great hush. That was when the fairy came. It was a very small fairy who slid down a sunbeam and landed with a bump on some daisies. I thought I'd imagined it, but the daisies blushed pink at the edges where he'd bounced. So it must've happened. He was mostly transparent, but rainbow lights shone from his head when he played with the dragonflies beside the pond.

"Suddenly a long single note sounded, so sad and sweet and far away. And the fairy – more of a pixie really; anyway, very very tiny – found a spider's web, thinner than silk, and swung into the cherry blossom. The blue tits flitted around like mad, so I think the fairy flew home with them.

"Then I heard you call, so I came in."

"You do rattle on," said Mum. "Sometimes I wonder if you know what's real and what isn't. You've got a good imagination, anyway. Now have your breakfast. Gran's making the toast."

Flora sat at the table and scratched the left side of her head where her mother had pulled her hair too tightly.

She looked at Grandma, buttering the toast as it popped from the toaster.

"Do *you* believe me?"

Grandma spread honey on the last bit of toast and cut it into four neat triangles before setting them before Flora.

"Every word, darling, every word."

If you enjoyed this story, why not try Margaret's book:
The Cat Who Decided

THE FINAL BATTLE | SEB GOFFE

Lanthir Manablade sheathed his sword, and took a moment to catch his breath. The young hero had survived many trials to get to this point, and now only a door separated him from his goal, the evil Baron Tarsek. He had battled through the depths of the castle dungeons for hours, slaying foe after foe with might and magic. Creatures of ever-increasing power had fallen against his trusty blade and arsenal of spells, from lowly goblins to the ancient red dragon that lay behind him now, thrashing out its death throes on the cold stone floor. Gulping a healing potion, Lanthir pushed open the door and stepped through.

"Your reign of terror ends here, Tarsek!" he shouted as he entered the room.

"I wouldn't be so sure," retorted the baron, rising from his throne of skulls to meet the hero. "You may have beaten my dragon, but I am the most powerful sorcerer this world has ever known! I shall crush you like the insignificant worm that you are!"

With that, the epic battle began. Lanthir fired a bolt of electricity from his fingertips, but the wily baron anticipated it and stepped aside, before twisting one of his many rings of power. Immediately he vanished from sight, and a cackling laugh rang in Lanthir's ears.

"Ha-ha-ha! How are you going to defeat me if you can't even see me?"

Lanthir drew his sword and gripped it tightly, waiting for the baron to reveal himself. He heard footsteps rushing in from his left, and swung his sword towards the sound. It met nothing but air, and the laughter rang out again. Lanthir's senses could feel the swirl of magical energies building, and he began to panic. He swung his blade wildly, hoping to hit the Baron by chance, but then came the inevitable blast of magic. Lanthir screamed as his life left his body. As his vision dimmed and the sounds of battle faded in his ears, he rued his decision not to buy the Gem of Seeing from the old gypsy woman. Then words appeared from the darkness, floating in front of him.

You have been killed by: Baron Tarsek. Do you wish to reload? Yes/No

If you enjoyed this story, why not try some of Seb's books:
The *Stadium School* series (co-authored by Cindy Jeffries)

THE TREASURE CAT | JANE JOHNSON

It's been cold this winter. Every morning the window is veiled with condensation, not only from my breath but from Baraka's too. Baraka is my cat; more accurately, he is the house cat: he came with the house when we moved in. Although I am not supposed to let him in, he knows every cranny of the house and always sneaks inside. I cannot sleep without the sound of his purring, and he enjoys the warmth: it is our bargain, our secret.

Mother says, "We hardly have the money to feed ourselves, let alone a cat. We can barely afford this house as it is."

I know money is tight. We have soup night after night. Baraka doesn't need our soup; he looks after himself. Every morning, even though his patch on the duvet is still warm, I find traces of his hunts downstairs – feathers, a tail; the spurred feet of a lark – always in the same place on the hearth. I clear them away when I make the fire. Even though he is feeding himself, Mother would complain.

Sometimes he lies beside these tokens as if to say, *See how clever I am. I have left the best for you* (a vole's snout, a rabbit's foot, an unidentified gall bladder).

Today there is a mouse, still alive. Its black eyes shine with fear. When Baraka lets it go, it runs straight up the chimney. (I have not yet lit the fire.) Baraka watches me expectantly. I sigh. Poor mouse: it must be saved. Its little heart beats so fast its whole body pulses against the charred stones. I climb on to the stove to fetch it down but when I touch it, it runs into a niche. I reach up, hoping it won't bite me; instead, it runs down my arm, jumps to the ground and runs away. Baraka doesn't seem to care; he gazes at me intently, unblinking. There is something else in the niche: a bag, heavy. It is filthy, but its contents gleam as brightly as Baraka's eyes.

Gold coins: hundreds of them.

Baraka gives me his most enigmatic smile, as if to say, *You certainly took your time working it out.*

If you enjoyed this story, why not try some of Jane's books:
The *Secret Country* trilogy

VICTOR THE VAMPIRE | CHERRY WHYTOCK

Victor thought being a vampire was tough. Having to be weird and spooky could get boring, and going everywhere in the dark sometimes gave him the creeps. And then there was the blood...

"Drink it all up like a good little vampire," said his mum, "or you'll never be huge and horrible like your dad."

"Yuck!" said Victor. Even the sight of the gloopy, oozy red stuff gave him collywobbles. He pushed the bowl away. "Why can't I have sugar puffs like normal people?" he wailed.

"Because you're a vampire," his mum snapped, "and being a vampire is very special and important. It's up to us to give people nightmares and swoop about in the dark making scary noises. You can't do things like that if you don't eat a proper vampire breakfast."

"Humph," said Victor. He pushed his chair away from the table and went out into the yard. His black cloak dragged through the mud behind him. He looked at his reflection in a moonlit puddle. He had white fangs and interesting pale green skin. He was wearing his favourite T-shirt, which said, "BE AFRAID ... BE VERY AFRAID" in luminous orange across the front. He practised his best scary noise: "Whooooooooa!" The sound echoed nicely round the yard. *OK*, thought Victor, *I suppose being a vampire is quite fun ... apart from the blood...*

When Victor had swooped and whooped around the dustbins and tried hanging upside down for a bit, his empty tummy was grumbling loudly. He crept back into the kitchen and found his gigantic dad standing by the fridge tucking into a big bowlful of red stuff.

"Hi, Dad," said Victor.

His dad spun round; his green cheeks went pink as he hid the bowl behind his cloak. "Oh! Hi there, son," he said shakily.

Victor sniffed; he could smell something delicious, which definitely wasn't blood. "I think I can smell strawberry jelly!" he squealed.

His dad brought the bowl out guiltily from under his cloak. "It *is* strawberry jelly," he said. "I just never could stand the taste of blood ... but don't tell your mother, will you?" he begged.

Victor picked up a spoon. "No way, Jose!" he said, smiling happily.

If you enjoyed this story, why not try some of Cherry's books: *Honeysuckle Lovelace, The Dog Walkers' Club* and *Fizzy Pink*

FLOWER OF THE FERN | A LEGEND FROM POLAND RETOLD
BY JAN PIEŃKOWSKI

It is midsummer night, the shortest night of the year. The boys light a bonfire in a forest clearing and compete with daring leaps over the flames. Bartek strides away into the dark woods on a quest.

He hears the laughing girls down by the river. Each girl puts a candle on a piece of bark and floats it. They run along the bank as the current takes the bobbing lights down the river; the one that wins the race brings the promise of marriage. Kasia's mind is on Bartek as she finds a long reed to keep her little craft midstream.

In the heart of the forest a single dazzling flower blooms at midnight. It is said that whoever finds it and picks it before the cock crows at dawn can have great riches. But there is a catch – those riches cannot be shared.

Bartek goes deeper into the forest. Suddenly a white shape glides, silent, across his path; it's only an owl. He hears the howl of wolves. In headlong flight he trips across a fallen tree, tumbling into a bramble thicket. The thorns rip his clothes. A startled snake slithers across his foot. Glow-worms light up a pathway through the mossy undergrowth, guiding him into a glade of ferns. A pulsating blue light draws him towards it. At the centre Bartek sees a beautiful flower, like nothing he has ever seen before. He must have it.

He picks the flower and hides it under his shirt. The cock crows. His torn clothes become magnificent princely garments; he sees jewelled rings on his fingers and a splendid black stallion pawing the ground. Bartek leaps into the saddle and gallops back to his friends.

"Look at me, I'm rich! I can have anything in the world."

Kasia runs up to him, putting her hand on his. "You're hurt, you're bleeding."

Bartek starts to take a jewelled ring off his finger to give her; as he does so, he feels the icy roots of the Fern Flower tighten around his heart. He slips the ring back on, turns and spurs his horse back into the forest.

One day he will return, but that's another story.

If you enjoyed this story, why not try some of Jan's books:
The Thousand Nights and One Night and *The Fairy Tales*

PORKY | K.M. PEYTON

Once upon a time a very small woman had a very big baby. He was very greedy, and although he was so big already, he would not stop eating. He ate and ate, and if there was no more food, he cried and cried. They called him Porky. He kept his little mother very busy running out to the shops all day to buy more food. He ate so much she had to buy a big basket on wheels to put all of him in it. He grew so fast that he burst his buggy when he was six months old and his mother had to buy a huge wheelbarrow to put him in.

"I can't push you! You must learn to walk!"

So Porky learned to walk, although he found it easier to roll. He grew and grew and his legs were like two tree trunks. He ate more and more.

For breakfast he had twenty big pancakes. His mother mixed them in a bucket and served them with lots of sugar. Porky poured a tin of golden syrup over them.

"Lovely! Lovely!" he chortled.

For lunch he had ten sausages and a pile of mash and roly-poly pudding and custard, and for tea a big cream cake and some buns. For supper he had roast beef and Yorkshire pudding and roast potatoes and Brussel sprouts and ice cream and peaches, and before he went to bed he had cheese on toast and six milkshakes.

One evening he went out to the fish and chip shop after his cheese on toast because he was still hungry, and his little mother went to bed, she was so tired with all the cooking. She was nearly asleep when she heard a loud explosion outside. She thought it was a car backfiring. She listened a while but all was silence. So she turned over and went to sleep.

In the morning she went in to Porky and found a tiny little child in bed, smaller than she was.

"Mummy, I exploded," said Porky.

She picked him up and carried him downstairs. She sat him at the table and gave him a glass of water.

"There there," she said.

If you enjoyed this story, why not try some of K.M. Peyton's books: *Minna's Quest* and *No Turning Back*

A LITTLE FRIENDLY SANDCASTLE CONTEST
TERESA COLE

One hot summer day, two families sat together on the beach.

"We're just going shopping, dear," said Sally Jones to her husband, Bill. "Look after the children."

"Make them a sandcastle," said Julie Brown to her husband, Pete.

And off they went.

"We've made a sandcastle," said the children, pointing to a small pile of sand with a flag on top.

"Ah," said Bill. "But we used to make them bigger."

"And mine had towers and arches," said Pete.

"Go on, then," said the children. "Show us."

So Bill made a great big castle with sandpies all around, and was very pleased with it – until he saw Pete's. Pete's castle was smaller, but it had four fine towers and a gatehouse.

Bill frowned. "I'll start on the big one now," he said.

"Yes," said Pete. "But I think I need a stronger spade."

While he'd gone to buy it, Bill made an enormous castle with towers, turrets, arches and battlements. It was as big as a settee and looked wonderful. His face dropped, though, when he saw Pete's perfect model of Windsor Castle, as big as a car and nearly complete.

"Hm," he said. "I'll just fetch something I need."

Chug-chug!

Pete turned to see Bill mixing sand and water in a cement

mixer. His castle was already as big as a garage and just like Buckingham Palace.

"Right," said Pete, "I just need…"

It was as he arrived in a huge mechanical digger that Sally and Julie returned. "What are you doing?" they cried. "You must stop at once!"

"Oh, please don't do that." A fat little man in a plumed hat came puffing up. "Your castle building is famous. People are coming from miles around. I'm the mayor, and I've never seen the town so full. Look. They want you to carry on."

"But it was just a friendly contest."

"Ah, but imagine what you could do if you all worked together. And afterwards we'll have tea in my parlour and a firework display for all."

So together they made the most enormous, magnificent, fantastical sandcastle anyone had ever seen.

"You know," said Bill afterwards, "we probably didn't make them quite that big before."

Teresa recommends:
The Secret Garden by Frances Hodgson Burnett and
The Turf-Cutter's Donkey by Patricia Lynch

"Imagination," said Mrs Grouch. "Who can spell 'imagination'?"

Every hand in the classroom shot up except mine, because I wasn't sure how to spell that word. I hadn't been sure how to spell *any* of the words the teacher read out, and I'd slipped so far down in my seat that I was peeping over the desk.

Spelling is not my best subject in the world.

Mrs Grouch peered through the forest of hands like a beady-eyed bog troll looking for someone to eat for dinner. But instead of choosing one of the kids who was groaning to be seen, she smacked her lips at the one kid who wasn't!

The teacher stomped towards me like a ferocious dragon, snorting black smoke through her enormous scaly nostrils. Then she craned over my desk and began picking her teeth with a long shiny talon.

I quickly sat up straight.

"Imagination!" she squawked, eyes wide and neck extended like a startled hen laying a very large, and possibly square, egg. "You could at least give it a try!" she shrieked, flapping her wings irritably.

"I…" I said.

"Well, that's a promising start," interrupted Mrs Grouch, cackling at her own joke like a demented witch. Then she hopped on her broomstick and glided to the front of the classroom to write "I" on the whiteboard.

"I…" I stammered. "I was going to say that I'm not sure how to spell 'imagination', but I know I have one because I always imagine things are something different."

"Then perhaps you could write a little story to read out loud in class?" Mrs Grouch grinned like a chimpanzee in Bananaland and finished writing "imagination" on the board. "But you must use this word several times and spell it correctly," she added, tapping the whiteboard several times with her banana pen.

"OK," I smiled, because I like writing stories.

And this is the story I wrote to prove to Mrs Grouch that even though I couldn't spell the word, I do *have* an imagination, because I imagined her as a bog troll and a dragon and a hen and a witch and a chimpanzee.

I can't wait to read it to the class!

If you enjoyed this story, why not try some of Michael's books: The *Jake Cake* series and the *Agent Amelia* series

RALPHIE RABBIT AND THE OGRE
JANET BINGHAM

Ralphie Rabbit had just eaten three fat carrots. He was hopping lazily home, when suddenly he was grabbed by the ears and he found himself face-to-face with the local ogre.

"Yum," said the ogre. "A nice rabbit for my supper!"

Ralphie thought quickly. "You look pale," he said. "I think you need vitamins."

"What are vitamins?" said the ogre, who had been feeling poorly since eating a mouldy fish the day before.

"Vitamins are in your food. They do you good," explained Ralphie. "Fruit and vegetables are full of them."

"I don't eat yucky rabbit food," snorted the ogre. "I eat rabbit."

"But I'm a hungry rabbit," lied Ralphie. "If you feed me first, you'll have a healthy vitamin-stuffed rabbit to eat."

"All right," said the ogre. "I'll go and raid the village for some greens."

"Not just greens," said Ralphie. "Get lots of colours. We need variety!"

The ogre grunted. He tied Ralphie to a tree and stomped off to the village.

The villagers were used to the ogre's raids. They went indoors for a cup of tea while he poked about among the market stalls.

Soon the ogre had as much food as he could carry. He hurried back to Ralphie and untied him. "Eat up!" he said. "I'm hungry!"

"Wait!" said the crafty rabbit. "First we have to sort it."

"Sort it?" growled the ogre.

"Vitamins must be eaten right, or they'll do us no good!" fibbed Ralphie. "We have to match up all the fruit and vegetables by colour and shape. See, cabbage goes with lettuce, tomatoes go with plums…"

The ogre picked up a carrot and frowned at it.

Ralphie stretched. "Ouch!" he groaned. "My muscles are stiff. I need to take a run, or I'll be too tough for you to chew."

The ogre hardly heard him – he was still wondering whether to put the carrot with the parsnips or the oranges.

Ralphie tiptoed away and then began to run. Soon he was safely home.

The ogre threw a tantrum when he realized his supper had escaped. But then, because he had no meat to eat, he ate the vegetables and fruit.

And to his surprise, they tasted rather nice.

If you enjoyed this story, why not try some of Janet's books:
My Little Star and *A New Home for Little Fox*

TREMBLE WITH FEAR! | WILL RAWSON

"Tremble with fear, puny earthlings!"

Jamie looked up from his breakfast cereal to see two tiny purple aliens staring at him from the kitchen table. They were both five centimetres tall and stood angrily by the milk jug.

"Take us to your leader!" cried one. "We have come to rule your planet!"

"You're a bit small," said Jamie.

"No we're not," replied the alien.

"Yes you are, you're tiny!"

"We are not small," the alien repeated in a patronizing voice. "We are just standing a long way away."

Jamie snorted. "You'd have to be stood in the next street to look that small!"

The alien frowned. "We're not small; you're just far too big. Look at you, it's perfectly ridiculous being that size." He shook his fists in the air. "For we are Zzyxc and Xthyyz, from the planet Gryyxke. We have journeyed far!"

Jamie sighed. "Why do you aliens always have such silly names?"

"What do you mean?"

"You know," he explained, "in movies and books and ... on the kitchen table, you're always called Xilch or Gryyyk or something daft. Why can't you pick a nice name for once?" Jamie thought for a moment. "Tell you what. I'll take you to my leader..."

"Yes?"

"... if you change the name of your planet to Alan."

"Alan?"

"Yes."

The alien considered this for a moment. "I quite like that."

"Me too," agreed his friend.

"OK," they said.

"Fine," said Jamie. "My leader is my mum and she's upstairs."

"Aha!" the alien shouted. "And she leads your planet?"

"Not yet, no," Jamie admitted.

The alien snorted. "Pah! Then she is useless – foolish child! Come Xthyyz, let us fly back to Planet Alan, and return with a mighty army!"

They jumped off the table and scurried towards the door.

"Maybe," said the other alien, "maybe we should change our names to Alan as well?"

"What, all of us?"

"Yes, then we could all be Alan from Planet Alan."

"I like the sound of that! Let us go!"

Jamie watched as a tiny pink spaceship flew out of the window and headed off to what would soon be the most confusing planet in the universe. Then he had some toast.

Will recommends:
Public Enemy Number Two by Anthony Horowitz and
Mortal Engines by Philip Reeve

READY! | ABIE LONGSTAFF

"Aaarrgh! Look at the time!" says Mum with a mouthful of toast. "We have to leave for school in ten minutes!"

"Get ready, everyone! Quick!" Dad jumps up, flinging the newspaper across the room.

"Huh?" says Joe from the sofa.

"We've got loads of time!" says Emma. She is making a house out of a box.

Baby Tom doesn't say anything. He is too busy chewing his thumb.

Mum and Dad rush up and downstairs finding
books
  and PE kits
    and homework diaries
      and snacks
        and umbrellas
         and sandwiches
          and juice boxes
           and show-and-tell toys.
          Back and forth they run.
           Round and round
            and upside down.

"Joe!" Dad shouts. "Stop watching telly and start getting ready!"

"I am ready!" says Joe. He has put one sock on.

"Emma!" says Dad. "Put your jumper on."

"Yes, Dad," says Emma. She puts glue on the roof.

Mum hops into the kitchen pulling on her tights.

"If you two are not ready in time," she warns. "I'm taking you to school in your pants."

Emma looks at Joe.

Joe looks at Emma ... and

"HURRY!"

they cry.

Joe and Emma pull on trousers and a skirt as fast as they can.

But whoops! Emma is wearing Joe's trousers.

And Joe is wearing Emma's skirt.

"Swap!" they shout. "Quick!"

"Loo, everyone!" yells Dad. "Loo and teeth."

Baby Tom does a poo in his nappy.

"EW!" Mum takes him for a nappy change.

Dad drinks his tea too quickly and spills it on his shirt.

Mum brushes her hair with the house keys.

Emma has her coat done up on the wrong buttons.

Joe has both shoes on but only one sock.

Baby Tom is a little bit sick on his coat.

But at least they are all at the door in their uniforms and work suits.

"Hooray!" says Dad. "We're ready on time!"

"Hooray!" says Mum.

"Um ... Mum?" says Emma.

"Yes?" says Mum.

"It's Saturday today."

"Yippee!" says Joe. "No school!"

"Oh," says Mum.

She sits on the floor.

"It IS Saturday," she laughs. Dad hugs her and starts to laugh …
then he turns pale.

"Saturday!" he says.

"Saturday!" he moans.

"Swimming lessons!"

"Oh no!" says Mum.

"Quick! Everyone! Get ready!"

Abie recommends:

The Black Stallion by Walter Farley and
A Little Princess by Frances Hodgson Burnett

THE FALL OF KING FROGBOTTOM | JULIE SYKES

King Frogbottom was in a very bad mood. He'd broken the handle of his favourite sword.

"Never mind, Dad," said Princess Rose. "The blacksmith can fix that for you."

"Fix it?" roared the king. "I don't want it fixed. It's broken. Get rid of it. I want a new one."

So the sword was thrown in the royal dustbin and the king rode out in his carriage with the princess to buy a new one. Passing the castle gates, the king stopped to yell at the gatekeeper.

"Where's the dragon? Why isn't he protecting my castle?"

"The dragon has a sore throat, Your Majesty," said the gatekeeper. "He'll be back in a day or two."

"That's no good," said the king. "If the dragon can't work, then get rid of him. Get me a new one."

"But—" stammered the gatekeeper.

"But nothing," shouted the king. "I've no time for things that are broken."

The king ordered his carriage on and soon they reached the town. The road was rutted from heavy traffic. Suddenly the carriage lurched sideways and stopped.

"Sorry, Your Majesty, but the wheel's come off," apologized the coachman. "It won't take me long to fix it."

"Pah!" shouted King Frogbottom. "I don't fix things. Get rid of the carriage and get me a new one."

While the coachman was arranging for a new carriage, King

Frogbottom and Princess Rose continued their journey on horseback. The blacksmith was sure he could have mended the broken sword, but the king wouldn't hear of it, saying, "It's in the dustbin. I want a new one."

King Frogbottom was very pleased with his new sword and carried it proudly on the ride home. As they approached the castle gates, a loud roar rent the air.

"Must be the new dragon," said Princess Rose sadly, for she'd been great friends with the old one.

"Aaaaah!" yelled King Frogbottom, as his scared horse jumped sideways and tipped him off.

Slowly the king opened his eyes.

"Ooooh, my leg hurts," he moaned. "I think it's broken. Call for the doctor to fix it for me."

Princess Rose coughed.

"But we don't fix things here," she said delicately. "We get new ones."

If you enjoyed this story, why not try some of Julie's books:
Pirate Small in Big Trouble and *That Pesky Dragon*

BRUNSWICK AND THE ALIENS
JOSH LACEY

BANG!

   CRASH!

   SMASH!

   "Ouch."

Brunswick stood up, holding his head, and said "ouch" again.

He looked around and sighed. He knew already that this wasn't going to be a good day. He had crash-landed on a planet full of loud noises and bad smells. And there were hundreds of people staring at him.

The people looked weird. Their faces weren't green. They didn't have pointy ears. And only a few had rings through their noses.

"I've come from the Intergalactic Marketing Board," said Brunswick. "We're doing a survey of consumer habits on different planets. Could you spare a minute to answer some questions?"

Several people opened their mouths and emitted an ugly noise which sounded like this: "Ha, ha, ha."

This must be a greeting, decided Brunswick. He held up his hand and said, "Ha."

"Ha, ha, ha," shouted the people around him.

"Ha," repeated Brunswick. "Now, who would like to answer my questions?"

But they just kept shouting, "Ha, ha, ha."

Perhaps they can't hear me, thought Brunswick. So he took off his helmet.

When the people saw his green skin, his pointy ears and the ring through his nose, they clapped their hands together. Then they threw small round pieces of silver into his helmet.

One of them was taller than the others. He was wearing a black uniform. He said, "Hello, hello, hello."

"Ha," said Brunswick.

The tall figure said, "Can I see your street entertainer's licence?"

"Ha, ha, ha," said Brunswick.

"I don't want any funny business," said the tall figure. "You had better come with me." He grabbed Brunswick with both hands.

Brunswick didn't like being grabbed. He said, "Spaceship! Get me out of here!"

There was a fizzing sound followed a blinding flash.

The policeman blinked. The crowd burst into applause. Brunswick had disappeared.

Back in his spaceship, Brunswick looked at his list of planets. He drew a line through Earth. The inhabitants were not friendly.

He set the computer's coordinates for the next planet on the list. The computer said, "Estimated distance to destination: eleven hours."

Perfect, thought Brunswick. *Just enough time for a snooze.* As the engines engaged, he lay down on his bunk and closed his eyes.

If you enjoyed this story, why not try some of Josh's books: *Bearkeeper* and *A Dog Called Grk*

"Sit down quickly, please. We've a lot to get through."

The children filed into the assembly hall, chatting and laughing. It was a wet, grey February afternoon, the wind rattling at the frames in the cavernous room, but it was time for their music lesson. The last session on a Monday always lifted their spirits. It meant they could relax, forget about SATs and maths and all the other things they had to fill their minds with throughout the day. All they had to think about was Mrs Oates thumping away on the piano, encouraging them to open their mouths and sing out.

"So what'll we start with today? Come on, your choice."

The children hadn't settled yet. Carrie was whispering to Polly, Jamal and Ned were trading football cards and Billy was finishing a story about a kid who'd eaten six helpings of chocolate pudding with chocolate sauce, a world record he reckoned.

"We need something good and rousing to blow away the cobwebs. Jamal, can you put those cards in your pocket, please, before I confiscate them? What about 'Camptown Races'?"

There were some vague murmurs, but no real takers.

"Oh, all right," she continued. "I know what'll get us all going…"

Mrs Oates began bashing away at the keys, and the first few bars of "Yellow Submarine" started to ring around the hall.

The children soon picked up the tune – one of their favourites – but after the first verse, they could tell something wasn't right. Although she carried on playing, glancing at the sheet music every now and again, Mrs Oates had a puzzled look on her face.

"Keep singing, keep singing," she bellowed after the chorus, emerging from behind her piano, trying to track down the source of the problem. The children continued, but some of them could hear it, too. Yes, there *was* a strange sound coming from somewhere…

Mrs Oates was homing in on Jake Garnett. She stood in front of him, listening intently to the noise coming from his mouth.

"It's you, Jake," she said, her eyebrows arching in disbelief, "isn't it?"

Jake swallowed, opened his mouth to answer, and out hopped a small green frog.

"Ribbit!" it said.

If you enjoyed this story, why not try Damian's book:
Selfish Sophie

THE BABYSITTING BLUES (AND PINKS)
KAREN McCOMBIE

"But I want some!"

"But we don't have any!"

"But I want some, Ruby!"

I glanced down at the very cute, four-year-old butterfly-fairy-princess and wanted to *strangle* her.

Sure, I loved goofing around with my kid sister, putting on pink, glittery face paint and helping her choose the perfect outfit for a butterfly-fairy-princess (wings, pants with "Saturday" written on them and polka-dot wellies), but when she started *whining* ... oh, I wished it was legal and non-cruel to stick her in a soundproof cupboard under the stairs.

"Maisie, I *know* you want yoghurt, but we DO NOT HAVE ANY!!"

I didn't shout that last bit – I just said it in this very firm voice that dog trainers use.

It didn't work.

"But, Ruby, I *really* want..."

Aargh! How did Mum put up with three of us whining in turn like this? Maybe she had developed the superhero power of being selectively *deaf*. A bit like Jake, who never seems to hear Maisie yelling for someone to help play "hostiples" or find her doll's missing *eye* or something.

Whatever, I was hoping Mum's hairdresser was in a mad rush and would send her home early with only half a haircut. Maisie was doing my *head* in.

Ding-dong!!

"*I'll go!*" yelped the butterfly-fairy-princess.

"STAY!" I ordered her. "You are *not* going anywhere in just your pants!"

I must have looked *seriously* grumpy when I answered the door. Ben's eyes widened at the sight of my scowl.

Instantly, I switched the scowl for a smile, in honour of Jake's newest and most gorgeous mate.

"Is Jake in?"

"Sure," I said, trying to sound casual. "Go on up!"

Ben gave me another quick glance before he went.

Wow. Maybe he *liked* me a little bit? I had never let myself think that before.

As I closed the front door, my heart pounding, I quickly and subtly checked in the hall mirror for signs of bad-news blushing.

And saw a glittery pink butterfly face staring back at me – done badly, by a four year old.

"Ruby! Can I have some yoghurt *now*, please?" Maisie suddenly demanded.

Sigh.

If only there were a soundproof cupboard under the stairs for me to crawl into…

If you enjoyed this story, why not try some of Karen's books:
The Seventeen Secrets of the Karma Club and the *Sadie Rocks!* series

IS ANYONE THERE? | GHILLIAN POTTS

Hallo! Sorry! Did I make you jump? You're a bus inspector, aren't you?

That's right. You like it here, son?

Yes, I'm here a lot. I like to watch the buses go in and out and the drivers and the men that fix the engines when they go wrong.

Getting dark now. You scared?

I'm not afraid of the dark. It's only the absence of light. That's what my mum always says. When I was quite small I'd put out all the lights and practise finding my way round the house in the dark. I was never scared. Not ever.

Everyone's scared of something.

Yes, you're right. All right, if you'll tell me what frightens you, I'll tell you what frightens me.

Rats. Can't stand them.

Really? Well, there aren't any here. My best friend, Tommy, had a white rat. He never brought it here, though. I liked it a lot. But it died...

Yeuch!

Oh, I'm sorry. I won't talk about it again, I promise! Please don't go. Please?

That what you're frightened of?

Yes, being left alone. I never minded when Mum went out and left me because I knew she'd always come back in a little while... But now I'm on my own all the time. The bus drivers don't talk to me.

Don't like you, huh?

No, it's not that. They really can't help it. They just don't notice me. And the people who do notice me never stay. I'm the only one who stays. You'll go soon, I expect.

You can come with me.

No, I can't. I promised Mum I'd wait for her, you see. I have to wait *here*, in the bus garage.

How long for?

I've waited a long time... But she'll come. I know she will. She always does. She says that if I'm lost, I should stay where I am and she'll come and find me. So that's what I'm doing.

Oh! Look! Look there! *Mum!* Hey, Mum! Over here! Now I can go. Now people won't say the garage is haunted.

Keep off! Get away from me! You're a ghost! So's she!

Please! Don't be scared. After all, you're a ghost, too.

Didn't you know?

If you enjoyed this story, why not try some of Ghillian's books:
Diary Days and *Sink or Swim*

THE GRAND-CATS AND THEIR GUESTS
BEVERLEY NAIDOO

Do you know grandparents who talk about their grand-cats? I want to tell you about Dennis and Jemima – and what grand cats they are! Jemima is dainty, sleek and velvet black. She is named after Jemima from *Play School* (ask your parents!) although she looks nothing like that Jemima. Dennis is younger, bigger and bossier. He has long black hair like Dennis the Menace's spiky mop. But our Dennis is no scruff! He is very handsome, with a white tuxedo and neat white socks.

Jemima and Dennis live at number 32 in a village close in Devon. A low verge separates their small back garden from a large field. At one end of the verge is an ancient tree stump shaped like a lion. From here, the grand-cats love to spy on the cows, study butterflies and gaze at the moon.

Like good country cats, they make their own entertainment. They invite field mice, baby rabbits and birds to party games in the kitchen at night. Their humans often find leftover guests in the morning, although sometimes they find the game still being played, with the poor guest transfixed by four green eyes. A human hand swoops to the rescue and offers treatment for shock. A tasty dried apricot does wonders to restore a shaken mouse. It seems the apricots are so popular that some guests may be risking these party games to come back for more!

Recently, however, there has been a strange turn of events. A newcomer cat – Ginger Max – has appeared in the garden without invitation. He acts like he is a guest of honour and now it is the grand-cats who are transfixed! They watch Ginger Max step through the cat flap into the kitchen and help himself to their dinner. When the humans find him, they put him out firmly. But each day Ginger Max returns, making himself more at home … first in the sitting room, then in Dennis's special spot at the top of the stairs and, finally, in Jemima's favourite snuggery on the humans' bed! Where will this story end? What's more, two little grey hoodie cats have now appeared on the garden verge and are showing great interest…

If you enjoyed this story, why not try some of Beverley's books: *The Journey to Jo'burg* and *The Great Tug of War*

GET THE MESSAGE? | VINCE CROSS

There was a hole in the bottom of the fence – probably an escape run for rabbits. Rufus scrabbled at the dirt with his gloved hands, desperately trying to scoop away the hard, resisting ground.

"Hopeless," hissed Charlotte. "We'll never get under in a million years. But we could squeeze through there, couldn't we? Look!"

Further along the fence's far side, a notice was nailed high on a tree. *Private. Keep Out! By Order!* it commanded. Underneath, a fence plank was askew. Rufus levered the wood aside, grunting with the effort. The two children slipped through a gap still far too narrow for any grown-up, and made a run for the imposing buildings huddling beyond the trees.

"Oi! You! Can't you read?" a hoarse voice shouted, as they ducked and swerved across beautifully kept lawns. The gardener snatched a walkie-talkie from his belt, barking urgently, "Red alert. Intruders! Repeat. Intruders! Over?"

Rufus and Charlie's flying feet dodged neat green boards whose delicate lettering politely suggested, *Please Keep Off The Grass.* A passing cook tutted, "Can't you read?" adding crossly, "Children these days! No manners. You'd expect better. At least in a place like this!"

A hallway discouraged entry. *Authorized Personnel Only*, the sign above it warned. Rufus and Charlie looked at each other, nodded, and threw themselves up the stairs which rose beyond it.

"Excuse me. And exactly where do you think you're going?" a

dinner-jacketed flunkie yelled at their backs. "Can't you read?"

A self-important door blocked their way. *Office of The Chief Minister. Strictly No Admittance*, it trumpeted. Rufus looked triumphantly at Charlie. She punched the air, mouthed, "Yes!" and then pushed the door with her shoulder.

A startled secretary leapt to her feet. "What on earth…? Didn't you see the notice? Can you *really* not read?" she exclaimed.

But the tall, elegantly suited man standing at her side registered not the slightest flicker of emotion on his oh-so-familiar television face. Charlie thrust her newspaper at him.

"For you, Chief Minister," she said. "*Sir!*"

He studied the headline. "*Global warming confirmed. Millions will starve.*" His voice was smooth. Educated. Reassuring.

"You *read* extremely well, sir," said Rufus. "But why aren't you doing something about it?"

If you enjoyed this story, why not try some of Vince's books: *My Story: Princess of Egypt* and *My Story: Blitz*

THOMAS SPROCKET'S PROBLEM POCKETS

LIZ BROWNLEE

Thomas Sprocket filled his pockets with STUFF. Rubber-band catapults, conkers, bits of wire, treasure maps, gun-shaped sticks and fluffy toffees – he liked to have them all handy just in case.

His mother was not so keen. There had been several washing-machine incidents. Floods, that sort of thing. One day she gave him a friendly warning.

"Tom! *WHY* do you need so much stuff in your pockets? Your underpants have all turned green with felt-tip ink. The filter is clogged with sweet wrappers. Your marbles in the spin have made me deaf in one ear. I am warning you – clear out your pockets or it is cabbage sandwiches for your packed lunch! Now put all these things where I would put them and DO IT NOW!"

So Thomas sadly emptied out his pockets, thought very hard about where to put everything, and then went to school.

Later that day, Tom's mum went shopping. She had to visit the bank first to get some money out. She heaved her heavy handbag on to the counter and looked in, and was horrified to see – a plastic submarine! Her tissues, reading glasses, spare black tights and credit cards were all stuck together with toffee! Her make-up, powder-puff, lipstick, mirror, diary and purse were all covered in Tom's pocket fluff. There was a blob of plasticine squidged in the bristles of her hairbrush. And from right down the bottom, underneath her indigestion tablets and keys, she pulled out a small, realistic automatic gun!

154

She growled loudly, and waved the toy. "I am going to KILL that boy!" she hissed.

The cashier screamed, people all around flung themselves to the ground, and security guards popped out from nowhere to capture her. Aghast and pale, she was handcuffed and carted off to jail in a police car, sirens squealing.

That night Tom used the washing machine on his own. It bounced, it sloshed, it clanked, it groaned, and in a ball of smoke – it broke.

The police soon realized that Tom's mum was innocent. She was so pleased to be free, she even looked forward to washing Tom's clothes.

Tom never put stuff in his pockets again. He bought himself a handbag instead.

Find Liz's poems in:
Let's Recycle Grandad and *There's a Hamster in the Fast Lane*

BUSTER THE FLY | LYNNE RICKARDS

Buster the fly was feeling glum,
and heaving a sigh, he asked his mum,
"Why, oh why was I born a fly?
I want to be noticed when I zoom by –
a glorious,
     beautiful,
          quite indescribable,
               fanciful, danciful bug!"

His mum replied, "Well, pardon me –
a fly is a wonderful thing to be!
You're faster than lightning and clever to boot,
and eat all your vegetables *and* your fruit –
my handsome and capable,
               so unmistakable,
                 truly unbeatable son."

"But, Mum," he said with a tear in his eye,
"I would much rather be a butterfly.
Imagine me batting my fabulous wings,
all stripy and silky with speckles and things –
a ravishing,
     colourful,
          totally wonderful,
               butterfly out of this world!"

"Or maybe a ladybird," Buster said,
"I've always been fond of the colour red.
Most children love the way they're spotted,
and unlike flies, they're never swatted,
those tiny,
    shiny,
        very protectable,
            highly collectable bugs."

Then Buster had another thought –
"A bee is a beautiful bug, is it not?
All yellow and black, with their stripes looking good!
That's just what I'd be, if only I could –
the whizziest,
    busiest,
        fuzziest,
           buzziest
              bumblebee ever there was."

"I might be a dragonfly, down by the pond,
a slender blue stick like a wood fairy's wand.
They hover so wonderfully still in the air,
on transparent wings, and dart here and there,
those delicate,
    elegant,
        truly magnificent
            creatures of beauty and grace."

A grasshopper bounded up out of the grass,
and Buster exclaimed as he watched him pass,
"Now there is a handsome bug, did you see?
He is far more impressive than little old me –
all emerald green
　　　　　and ever so keen,
　　　　　　　　　the greatest high jumper there is!"

"A cricket is something I'd love to have been –
he's so often heard but is seldom seen.
He is chocolate brown, quite small and thin,
with musical legs like a violin,
an almost invisible,
　　　　　magical,
　　　　　　　　　musical
　　　　　　　　　　　　singer of evening songs."

Poor Buster sighed, "Alas, it seems
I'll only be beautiful in my dreams."
His mum replied, "But don't you see,
you're the loveliest bug in the world to me –
a dipping and diving,
　　　　　bobbing and weaving,
　　　　　　　　　aerodynamic,
　　　　　　　　　　　　simply fantastic *fly*!"

If you enjoyed this story, why not try some of Lynne's books:
Pip Likes Snow and *I Win!*

IMAGINE | JULIA DRAPER

Imagine carrying a tray. Imagine carrying a tray with a plate on it. Imagine carrying a tray with a plate on it and on the plate is a big, wobbly jelly. Imagine carrying the tray and the plate and the wobbly jelly (which is pink) and walking at the same time. Imagine the walking and the tray and the plate and the jelly, but this time imagine walking ALONG A TIGHTROPE at the same time. And you're wearing a pointy hat with a bobble on the top, and you have a red nose like a tomato and you've got baggy purple trousers on that flap about when you walk.

Imagine you're walking a tightrope carrying a tray with a wobbly pink jelly on it and you're wearing a tomato nose and baggy trousers and another man's trying to knock you off the tightrope with custard pies and the audience is crying with laughter.

Imagine wobbling your foot a bit. The rope starts to sway back and forth, and the tray starts to wobble and the jelly wobbles even more. The audience is going, "Woooo!"

The audience would love you to fall off the rope. They would LOVE the jelly to go *SPLAT* on the floor and they would love you to hurt yourself because you've got that clown make-up that's sad but also funny at the same time.

Imagine the other man in baggy trousers comes up and pretends to tickle you under the arms. That makes the rope sway even more. He turns to the audience, honks an old-fashioned car hooter in time to his laughing.

"HONK HONK HONK!"

Then at last you really do fall off the rope properly. And guess what, the jelly slides off the tray and off the plate and lands on your face. *SPLAT!* So you sit up with a pink jelly all over your face and the audience is screaming with laughter and you get up, slip on the jelly and fall flat on your back again.

Well, that's what my dad does every night. He's a clown. Sometimes he does it two or three times every day.

One day I'm going to be a clown just like him.

If you enjoyed this story, why not try Julia's book:
A Secret Place

THE MAD HOPPER | RUTH DOWLEY

Dan, Jill and Charlie were mad on football. Mr Jones next door was mad on gardening.

Except for one tree, Dan, Jill and Charlie's garden was grass. That is best for footballers. Mr Jones's garden was vegetables, bushes and flower borders. That is best for gardeners.

Unfortunately, sometimes the ball sailed over the fence. Then Mr Jones got hopping mad. He hopped about, red-faced, shouting.

Dan, Jill and Charlie were scared of him, though Charlie often watched him gardening.

One spring day, Mr Jones planted seeds in rows. Dan let fly with a strike that soared past goal into the vegetable patch.

Mr Jones became the Mad Hopper. "Blooming kids!" he shouted. "Vegetables will come up all over the place!"

Another time, Jill headed the ball. Full-power. It crashed over the fence and broke a branch.

Mr Jones became the Mad Hopper. "Blooming kids! You've wrecked this bush!"

In summer, the footballers practised tackling. Charlie got the ball off Dan. He whacked it into the tree. It rebounded over the fence and hit Mr Jones on the arm.

"Sorry!" called Charlie.

Mr Jones kept weeding.

"May we have our ball back, please?" called Jill.

Mr Jones went in the house. They rang his doorbell. No answer.

They looked over the fence again. Mr Jones came from his shed. The ball had vanished.

"He's hidden it!" whispered Dan.

When Mr Jones went to the shops, they climbed over the fence to search. The ball wasn't in the shed.

But Mr Jones forgot his money and returned. He charged up the path. He became the Mad Hopper.

"We're looking for our ball," said Jill, terrified.

Charlie stared.

"What are you gawking at?" the Mad Hopper roared.

"Your garden. I can see it all from here. It's *blooming brilliant*!"

The Mad Hopper halted mid-hop. "You've the making of a gardener, young man. Perhaps you'd like to help me sometimes. Tidy up if the ball comes over. I've learned that balls don't always go where you aim."

He pointed to the footballers' tree. Caught at the top was their ball!

Mr Jones stopped becoming the Mad Hopper. Friendship grew over the garden fence.

That is best for footballers and gardeners.

If you enjoyed this story, why not try some of Ruth's books:
Top Biker and *Hard Rock*

A WALK IN THE SNOW | ALAN TEMPERLEY

This happened quite a long time ago. Harry had been at school for one term. He was five.

When school started again after the Christmas holiday the snow was deep. School was a mile away but Harry always walked there by himself. It was lovely, making tracks and throwing snowballs.

His class was getting a new teacher. After assembly they all went off with her, but Harry had gone to the cloakroom to get a handkerchief from his raincoat pocket. When he came back everyone had gone.

Where were they? He wandered the school looking into classrooms.

At last, standing on tiptoe to see through a high window, he saw boys and girls he recognized. A thin, bony lady with chopped-off hair was talking to them and waving her arms. Harry didn't like the look of her.

He stood there for ages. Nobody came. What should he do? He thought he would go home.

So he put on his coat, scarf and school cap, and walked away across the playground.

Halfway home there was a stream in a little valley below some allotments. There were minnows in it. He broke the ice with a stick to see them. His coat and cap got in the way so he took them off.

Then he made a snowman.

Then he explored the sheds in the allotments.

At last, feeling hungry, he went home for dinner.

His mum was doing the big Monday wash in the back shed where there was a boiler. Clouds of steam billowed into the air.

"Good gracious," she said. "Where have you been?"

"School."

"Do you know what time it is?"

"Dinner time."

But dinner was still two hours away.

"Where's your coat?" she said. "And your cap? And your scarf?"

This was serious because they hadn't got much money. So Harry walked back with Mum and found them in the snow beside the stream.

When they got home she gave him biscuits and a hot drink by the fire.

After dinner she took him back to school. Harry was a bit scared but the head teacher laughed and took him to meet the thin, bony teacher with chopped-off hair.

She was very nice.

If you enjoyed this story, why not try some more of Alan's books: *Harry and the Treasure of Eddie Carver* and *The Huntress of the Sea*

PUMPKIN | SUE ASHBY

In the sun-warmed greenhouse I sit soft and velvety on the palm of a girl's hand. I am no bigger than her fingernail. She lays me on my side and blankets me with soft earth. Snug in a pot, my seed case swells, then bursts. I shoot two leaves above the pot on a thin, green stalk.

When I grow two more leaves, the girl takes me to the top of the vegetable plot. There she tucks me into a big pile of rich, crumbly compost. Every day I stretch a little further: the delicate lobes of my leaves reach up towards the sun, my thirsty roots wriggle down to drink the water below. At night, in the light of a full moon, a family of mice nibbles my stalks; a slug slithers slimily under my foliage. But still I prosper and grow.

Under the scorching sun my vines spread out like the tentacles of an octopus. They lurk in the lettuces, rampage through the radishes, tumble over tomatoes and spill out on to the lawn. My male and female flowers bud yellow and spiky. Their faces beckon the bees to mix their pollen and make my fruits grow.

Mist hangs cobwebs in the morning air. My flowers have shrivelled and died. In their place small pumpkins, round as the globe, grow amid the artichokes, between the broccoli, beneath the beans.

The world turns. In the ever-shortening hours of daylight my plump pumpkins, fleshy, fat and orange, dwarf the leaves that are already fading away.

Dusk falls on the night of the year when pumpkins everywhere are destined to become lanterns. The girl comes and cuts my biggest, heaviest pumpkin free. She struggles to the house with it in her arms. In the kitchen she saws off the top of its head, scoops out its seed-brains and carves a scary mask into its face.

In her bedroom window my pumpkin's warm light glows, keeping her safe from the hidden dangers of the night.

The apple tree bends in the wind. Ice stretches tight as a drum over the garden pond. In the garden shed, seeds from my Halloween pumpkin wait patiently for their turn to grow.

Sue recommends:
Catcall by Linda Newbery and *Abela: The Girl Who Saw Lions* by Berlie Doherty

THE BIT OF EVERYTHING DOG | CAROLINE PITCHER

When we went to the Dogs' Home, I asked my mum, "What kind of dog is *that*?"

"He's a bit of everything," she said.

The Bit of Everything Dog came to live with us. He was fluffy black with ginger legs like boots, and so we called him Wellie. He loved to swim. His fur was as thick as sheep's wool. Wellie was waterproof! He loved to dig. Earth flew everywhere when he buried his treasures. In his dreams he raced, chasing rabbits. He played football with his nose.

Once he burst the ball.

"That dog is a disaster," groaned my dad.

Wellie was my friend. He was *always* pleased to see me.

One day we all went walking by the river. The air smelled of bluebells. The river flowed fast with spring rain. Wellie barked for me to throw a stick but Mum said, "No, Beth, it's too deep for him today."

My little brother Tom slipped on the mud. He let go of his teddy. The teddy bobbed away downstream and Tom began to cry.

SPLASH! Wellie dived down off the bank. Sleek as a seal he swam and grabbed the teddy. He turned to swim against the flow. The water swept above his head, but Wellie would not let go until he struggled up the bank and dropped the teddy at Tom's feet.

He barked *and barked* and shook himself from his nose down to his tail. A thousand drops of water flew like little rainbows as

Wellie pranced in triumph.

"That dog is a hero!" cried my dad.

The years went by. The teddy lost an ear and sat on the window sill all day.

Tom and I grew tall, but we still took Wellie walking by the river.

Then came *that* day. Wellie wouldn't get out of his basket. His eyes looked far away. His paws were cold and still.

Wellie left us.

Whenever I walk by the river now, I think I see a black dog running on the bank. I see him prance in triumph, just as he did that day, and I hear his joyful barking.

And I remember Wellie, the Bit of Everything Dog. Wellie the hero!

If you enjoyed this story, why not try some more of Caroline's books:

The Snow Whale and *The Gods Are Watching*

ROMAN GLADIATORS | **KATHRYN WHITE**

Jojo grasped the Roman vase.

His knuckles glowed white.

The wonky vase went from his chin to his droopy trousers.

Jojo staggered from Chestnut class down the school corridor behind Harriet.

They were taking the vase to the hall for the Roman Relic competition.

Jojo thought the vase was boring; even the Roman stick men painted around it made it look sad.

Jojo wanted dinosaurs instead, but Mrs Baxter had said, "No."

Harriet opened the door.

Jojo struggled through and wondered why his nose always felt itchy when he couldn't scratch it.

Breathless, Jojo stopped in the corridor and put the monster vase down.

As Jojo scratched, he decided that dinosaurs definitely would have looked better. But, if his class was to win the competition for most authentic relic, Wormley Archaeological Society would give them book vouchers – neat.

"Hurry up," said Harriet. She sighed, her hand perched delicately on the door handle.

The bell rang for break.

The doors burst open.

Harriet was swept behind the shatterproof door, her nose flattened to the glass.

Jojo looked in terror as a herd of wild, unruly children charged at him.

Jojo stopped breathing. He grabbed the mighty vase in trembling hands and clutched it to his quivering body. He had to protect it. He had to save it. He had to … scratch his nose.

Jojo keeled over.

Bravely, he hugged the Roman vase as if it was his secret teddy bear, Mr Flumps.

He lay helpless, staring up at the dead flies trapped inside the dull light shade above him, still clutching the vase.

He whimpered as the galloping herd flowed around him like a tidal wave.

Sometime later, Harriet pulled Jojo to his feet.

Their anxious eyes carefully inspected the vase.

Yes. What a Roman gladiator he was; he had saved it.

Jojo punched the air.

Together, they marched on victorious and reached the hall.

Harriet opened the door.

Jojo stepped in with a joyful smile and … tripped over Harriet's foot.

The vase crashed.

Their dreams shattered.

But Mrs Baxter soon glued all the pieces together again.

A week later, Jojo and Harriet stuck up the hall notice, "Winners are: Chestnut class – for most authentic *Mosaic* Vase."

If you enjoyed this story, why not try some of Kathryn's books: *Here Comes the Crocodile!* and *The Nutty Nut Chase*

A HOUSE FOR A MOUSE | LYNNE RICKARDS

There once was a mouse
with a very fine house.

It was shiny and black
with a door at the back
and a little front gate
with a big number 8.

Well, a few years went by,
and the wee mouse did sigh,
"Life's becoming a squeeze –
barely room for the fleas!"

Said the mouse, "This won't do –
I can't live in a shoe!
I must find a new place
with a little more space."

Off he set with his sack
that he'd packed on his back.
Far and wide he did roam
as he searched for a home.

Well, the first thing he found
was a hole in the ground,

so he wriggled right down
and got looking around.

It was lovely and roomy
but also quite gloomy –
then, to his surprise,
he saw four gleaming eyes...

Said the mousie, "Oh, dear, dear –
there are two snakes in here!"
So he clambered back out
with a squeak and a shout.

At that moment he heard
the "peep-peep" of a bird,
from the top of a tree,
so he climbed up to see.

Said the mouse, "Me oh my –
this is ever so high!"
But he liked what he found
in that nest off the ground.

It was comfy and dry,
a twig house in the sky.
"This is just what it takes
to be safe from those snakes."

But the bird flapped her wings,
shedding feathers and things,
and she squawked, "My tree house
is no place for a mouse!"

So the mouse looked instead
in an old garden shed.
Said the mouse, "Stars above –
here's a house I could love!

In a corner there lay
something furry and grey...
It was sleepy and fat –
a great huge purring cat!

Said the mouse, "Goodness me –
this is no place to be!"
and he scampered so fast
that he whizzed straight on past

the grey cat as it purred ...
the big tree with the bird ...
and the hole that he'd found
with two snakes underground...

Then he spotted a gate
with a big number 8...

Said the mouse, "Glory be –
This is perfect for me!"
So he shut the back door
and went wandering no more.

If you enjoyed this story, why not try some of Lynne's books:
Pink! and *Jack's Bed*

THE GREATEST SAGE OF UNYUN

KJARTAN POSKITT

Gelgar the sage looked around at the empty shelves in her cave on the mountain top. For many years the villagers of Unyun had climbed up to ask her advice. In return for her great wisdom, they would leave offerings of money, woolly socks or funny-shaped vegetables.

"Why do they no longer come?" she asked Dood, her faithful servant.

"They go to the Oracle of Yesno now," replied the hippie.

"But why? I am the Greatest Sage of Unyun."

"Not any more, you're not."

"But that so-called oracle is nothing more than an enchanted talking statue. Boring!"

"Maybe, but it gives better answers," said Dood. "Like when they asked you if it was rude to eat fish with a spoon, you replied, '*The fish still dreams of water*'."

"See? I'm brilliant," said Gelgar. "So what did this oracle say?"

"It just said NO. And then they asked if it was unlucky to stand under a giraffe in a storm."

"I said, '*The rain will seek you out*'."

"The oracle just said YES," said Dood.

"Is that all it says, YES or NO?"

"Direct answers, that's what people want. Not your rubbish."

"Oh, really?" said Gelgar. "We'll see about that!"

Gelgar put on her cloak and walked all the way down the

mountain to the oracle. When she got there she found herself waiting at the back of a long queue. One by one the villagers approached the statue and whispered into the stone ear. The hole in the mouth would then utter one word – YES or NO. Eventually her turn came.

"What is she doing here?" gasped a woman.

"I thought she knew everything," said another.

"Maybe she can't understand her own answers!" laughed a third.

Gelgar ignored them – instead she whispered her question and stood back. At first the oracle made no sound, but then with a ghastly creak the head turned to face her.

"Oo-er!" went the crowd.

"ARGHHHH!" screamed the statue.

BARR-A-POOSH! The statue exploded into a cloud of dust.

"There!" cried Gelgar triumphantly. "That proves that I am the Greatest Sage of Unyun."

"But what dreadful thing did you ask?" the crowd demanded.

Gelgar grinned. "Is the answer to my question no?"

If you enjoyed this story, why not try some of Kjartan's books: *The Gobsmacking Galaxy* and *Dead Famous: Isaac Newton and His Apple*

MUD EGGS | NICKI CORNWELL

Once upon a time there was a hen called Poppy who couldn't lay eggs. Whenever she heard the proud *cluck cluck cluck* of a hen who had just laid an egg, she felt sad. She decided to make herself an egg out of mud and leaves.

"Call that an egg?" said the hens. "Eggs do not have bits sticking out of them!"

And they all laughed at her.

Poppy thought they were being mean. She threw away her egg and tried again. This time she broke up the leaves so that the egg was ever so smooth, and she made it into a perfect egg shape.

"Well, how about this one?" she said.

But the hens burst out laughing. "Eggs are not mud coloured!" they cried.

"I'll show them!" Poppy said to herself. This time she made an egg that was the perfect shape and size, and she painted it a creamy white colour. Trembling with excitement, she cried, "Come and look at this one!"

The hens gasped with astonishment. Then one of them said, "But that doesn't count! It hasn't been laid!"

And they turned their backs on poor Poppy.

That night, Poppy sat on her perch thinking sad thoughts. In the morning she was just about to throw away her egg when she cried, "Hang on just a minute! Why am I trying to copy *their* eggs? This is a Mud Egg, not a Hen's Egg. I could paint it yellow or red or blue. I could put patterns on it, or pictures. I could make big ones and little ones. And they'd all be different. Hen's eggs are BORING: they all look the same!"

Poppy began to make Mud Eggs. She made small ones and big ones. She painted them all in different colours. She got paint all over her feathers, but she didn't care!

"I am an artist! That is what I am!" she cried. "I am a Mud Egg Artist!"

Poppy has been making Mud Eggs ever since. At night she sleeps on top of the pile. At the last count she had six hundred and forty-two eggs. Sometimes she gives one away, but only if she *really* likes someone.

If you enjoyed this story, why not try Nicki's book:
Christophe's Story

PRINCESS POPPY AND THE POP STAR PRINCE | PAMELA OLDFIELD

"It is time you were married, Poppy," the king told his daughter. "We want you to meet Prince Ferdinand, who lives beyond the dark forest."

"Oh no!" Princess Poppy shook her golden curls. "Prince Ferdinand is so sad. They say he has no friends. Anyway, I want to marry a pop star."

The queen laughed at the very idea.

"I do!" cried the princess.

But the king and queen insisted that she should ride her white horse through the dark forest to meet Prince Ferdinand.

"You might change your mind," said the queen hopefully.

The sun shone down as Princess Poppy rode through the dark forest, but she was soon lost. It was dark when she stopped at the house of a woodcutter to ask directions.

"Why do you want to meet sad Prince Ferdinand?" asked the woodcutter's wife. "They say the poor young man has no friends."

"I must see for myself," she told him, so the woodcutter pointed out the path that she should take and the princess rode on.

Next morning, when she arrived, she jumped down from her horse and went inside the palace to find the prince. He was alone in the throne room playing his guitar. When he had finished, he looked up and saw Princess Poppy.

She asked him, "Why do you have no friends?"

"I'm too busy writing my pop music," he said sadly.

"The tune is very catchy," said the princess.

"I wrote it myself – but unfortunately I don't have any words to go with it."

"I could write some words for you," she told him eagerly. "You could become a pop star!"

"I have an idea!" At last the prince was smiling. "You could marry me," he said. "We could write our own songs and go on stage together!"

But then Princess Poppy had another idea. "After the wedding we will give a free pop concert in the palace grounds! That will make us famous!"

The wedding day arrived and hundreds of people came and the sun shone down. After the wedding, the concert began. The music went on and on and the people danced and sang until it was dark.

At last everyone was happy.

If you enjoyed this story, why not try some of Pamela's books: *The Terribly Plain Princess* and *My Story: The Great Plague*

DO NOT READ THIS | JON SCIESZKA

You are not going to believe this. I don't know if I even believe it.

Three hundred and sixty-six. It burns my brain. It will burn yours.

Forget it.

Stop reading.

Right now.

I don't want to be responsible for dragging anyone else into this. I can't. I won't.

Look away. If someone is reading this to you, plug your ears.

Pretend you are listening. But don't listen. It's your only hope.

It's too late for me. But not too late for you.

Oh, man.

Why? Why? Why?

Why would someone design a scheme like this? So terrible. So final.

But seeming like something so good.

Let's put together something for the kids. Something short.

Something punchy. Something everyone will think is just a fun read.

But then…

Oh yes, but then…

Something so bad yet so simple that it can be done in exactly three hundred and sixty-six words.

You think that's an accident? A coincidence? A number pulled out of a hat? Of course it isn't. Think about it. How many days in a year?

Add one for leap year. What do you have? Oh yes.

Why are you still reading? They can do it, you know. It will happen, you know. You are rushing towards it, you know.

I thought I could outsmart them too. I didn't think there was any way it could be done. Something like that has to take way more than three hundred and sixty-six words.

Doesn't it?

No, it does not.

It takes three hundred and sixty-six words exactly. And guess where you are? Two hundred and sixty-six.

I am sure you have seen that movie where the scary video makes bad things happen. Now there is one where a mobile phone call does the same thing.

But this makes those movies look like a kid's birthday party.

So get away while you still can. It is almost too late.

You will not feel it at first. But it will be planted. It will be there.

Because see, the thing is, at exactly word number three hundred and sixty-six, that is when it happens, and then there is no saving you.

Because the second you read that, you

If you enjoyed this story, why not try some of Jon's books:
The Stinky Cheese Man and Other Fairly Stupid Tales and *Knucklehead: Tall Tales and Almost True Stories of Growing Up Scieszka*

NIGHT FLIGHT | SIOBHAN PARKINSON

Everyone told Ludo it was nonsense. Beds can't fly, they said. And neither can you.

What do they know? thought Ludo. Nothing at all.

Look! they said, when they made the bed. There are no wings. No propellers. Not even an engine. Just a nice neat little bed, with its feet on the ground.

Feet! thought Ludo. Who ever heard of a bed with feet. Huh!

They stretched out his cool white sheet, and they fluffed up his soft white duvet, and they plumped up his two plump pillows till they were plumper than plump.

Now, they said. That's a nice, safe, cosy little bed. No more talk about flying in the night, right?

Wrong, thought Ludo.

This bed flew.
He knew it flew.
It flew, he knew.

When the night-time came, and the curtains were drawn, and the lights went out, and Ludo lay back on his two plump pillows that were plumper than plump under his fluffed-up duvet, over his cool white sheet, with his eyes closed … there came a most tremendous whooshing sound, and Ludo's tightly drawn curtains flew back, and Ludo's tightly closed windows flew open, and Ludo's neatly made bed flew up into the air and out of the window and up and up and when …

Into the starred and velvet sky
and Ludo's heart sang out:
I can fly, I can fly, I can fly!

He flew to a star.
It was blue.
It was bright.
On he flew.

He flew to the moon.
It was cold.
It was gold.
On he flew.

And then morning came,
pink and soft and grey and light.

Must fly, said Ludo. Toodleoo, moon. Stars, bye-bye.

But the moon and the stars and the velvet night sky had faded away, faded away, faded away.

And Ludo flew back home, right in through his window, where the curtains flapped in the cool morning breeze. And his neat little bed settled right down with its feet on the floor.

Nonsense, they said. Beds don't fly, they said. And neither can you.

But they do.
And he could.
And he knew that they do.
And he knew that he could.

And he would, he would, he *would.*

If you enjoyed this story, why not try some of Siobhan's books:
Blue Like Friday and *Something Invisible*

LUCKILY UNLUCKILY | COLIN McNAUGHTON

Tiger was out hunting in Africa one day.

(Yes, I know there are no tigers in Africa – this one was on holiday, OK?)

Young Elephant was eating his lunch.
(TIMBER! Munch! Chomp! Burp!)

Suddenly! Tiger saw Young Elephant!
(An elephant eating a tree is hard to miss!)

"Grrrowl, snarrrl!" said Tiger.
(Which roughly translates as "Yum, yum!")

Luckily – Young Elephant saw Tiger coming.
(Which, as he was bright yellow with black stripes, was hardly surprising.)

***Un*luckily** – tigers are much faster than elephants.
Tiger *ROARRRRRRED* and leaped magnificently through the air.
(Tigers are very good at being magnificent.)

Luckily – Young Elephant escaped!
("Hurray for 'Monkey Hairyplanes!'")

***Un*luckily** – Young Elephant fell from the Hairyplane.

(Loop the looping hairy aeroplanes are difficult things to hang on to!)

Luckily – it was a lovely day.
(Young Elephant was trying to look on the bright side of things.)

Unluckily – Young Elephant wasn't wearing a parachute.
(Well, why would he be?)

Luckily – Young Elephant had big flappy ears.
(So that's what elephants' ears are for!)

Unluckily – he weighed two tons.
(Going down!)

Luckily – he had a splendid view of the countryside.
(The animals on the ground looked like ants.)

Unluckily – the countryside was rushing up to meet him.
("Oh no, those are ants!")

Luckily – there was a big haystack right underneath him.
(Strange, but true.)

Unluckily – there was a needle in the haystack.
(Isn't it always the way?)

Luckily – he missed the needle.
(*Well, they* are *hard to find.*)

Unluckily – he also missed the haystack.
(*Now, that really* was *careless!*)

Luckily – he landed on something soft.
(*Phew!*)

"**Unluckily**, that something soft was *me*,"
said Tiger in a flat voice.

"Lucky me!" said Young Elephant.
And he lumbered off to eat some more trees.
(Which was unlucky for the trees, I suppose.)

The end.

(By the way, in case you were worried about Tiger, well, don't
be. They posted him back to India in a big flat envelope where,
with the help of his mum, some chicken soup and a bicycle pump,
he is recovering nicely.)

THE END.

Silly me, I forgot to tell you the moral of this story:

"Travel broadens the mind."

(*Or, in this case, flattens it completely*.)

DEFINITELY THE END!

If you enjoyed this story, why not try some of Colin's books:
Suddenly! and *Captain Abdul's Pirate School*

COME BACK, WIGOTHY! | DAWN McNIFF

Laurie had a kitten called Wigothy.

Wigothy had fuzzy black fur and a very loud purr. He was small and soft, and smelt of soil and sunshine.

Laurie and Wigothy were big friends.

Laurie shared his fish fingers with Wigothy, and made him paper aeroplanes to chase. At night Wigothy curled up under Laurie's duvet and purred.

Everyone loved Wigothy except Granny.

"That blooming cat … ATISHOOOOOOO! … gets up my nose," said Granny, when she visited.

"Oh dear," said Mum. "Wigothy makes Granny sneeze."

"The furball needs to go!" said Granny. "ATISHOOOOOOO!"

But Laurie was firm.

"Wigothy is staying," he said.

Then one day Wigothy *was* gone. Just gone.

He didn't come in at breakfast. Or at tea time. Everyone searched. Everyone called. But Wigothy was lost.

Laurie cried and cried.

"He's only a baby," he said. "He'll be scared."

Laurie put some fish fingers on the doorstep for Wigothy.

"Come back, Wigothy!" he called.

But Wigothy didn't come.

Laurie got a tummy ache. He didn't want his tea. At bedtime Laurie couldn't sleep. He threw a paper aeroplane out into the black night.

"Come back, Wigothy!" he called.

But Wigothy didn't come.

"I'm sorry I called him a furball," said Granny the next day. She helped Laurie make a poster. It said: LOST KITTEN. REWARD FOR FINDER. They stuck it on a lamp post.

Laurie sat on the doormat all day, waiting and waiting.

"Come back, Wigothy!" he called through the cat flap.

But Wigothy didn't come.

That evening Laurie lay alone in his bed. He felt cold without Wigothy. He thought about the dark night. He thought about big foxes. He thought about little Wigothy, and he cried.

Then suddenly he heard Granny downstairs…

"ATISHOOOOOO! ATISHOOOOOO!"

"It must be Wigothy!" cried Laurie.

And there he was – all dusty and covered in cobwebs.

"Oh, thank goodness!" said Mum. "Maybe he got locked in someone's shed."

"ATISHOOOOOO!" said Granny. "ATISHOOOOOO!"

Mum sighed. "But, oh dear, what about poor Granny?"

"Not to worry," said Granny. She pulled a package from her bag. It was some medicine to stop her sneezing.

"Wigothy is staying," she said firmly.

"Staying for ever!" sang Laurie.

And he gave Granny a big hug.

Dawn recommends:
Triple Trouble With Jeremy James by David Henry Wilson and *Clever Polly and the Stupid Wolf* by Catherine Storr

A LEAPING HEART | TOM BECKERLEGGE

There was once a boy who was unlucky enough to fall in love with a girl who appeared only once every four years, and then only for a day. She came out of thin air one morning as he was stuffing dirty socks into the washing machine. The boy was so surprised that his jaw dangled uselessly open for twenty-four hours. As the girl began to vanish, she told him she would return in four years, and gave him a smile that kept him warm for months.

Determined not to repeat his mistake, the boy bought fifty parrots, and spent the next four years in his bedroom scribbling down all the things he wanted to tell the girl, while the birds flapped around his head and squawked back all the phrases he read aloud. But when the girl reappeared, the boy stammered and stumbled over his words, until all the syllables crashed into one another. The girl smiled politely but couldn't understand him. As she disappeared, the boy opened the window to let the parrots fly free, and swore never to speak to anyone again.

Enrolling in a monastery, the boy scratched at his itchy robe and decided that actions spoke louder than words. He silently resolved to win the girl's heart by learning to juggle with fire. After four years of singed hands and soot-filled nostrils, he could keep ten brands in the air at once, and make fire somersault across the sky. But when he saw the girl again, his steady hands trembled, and he set his itchy robe on fire. He was still trying to douse the flames as the girl waved goodbye.

By now the boy had been waiting for twelve years, and had lost all hope. He left the monastery, and built a factory with furnaces fuelled by wheelbarrows of love letters. When the girl reappeared, he pretended to be too busy to notice her. But at the last second, as she was fading away, the boy panicked and shouted that he loved her. The girl opened her mouth to reply, and promptly vanished. With a sigh, the boy turned off the furnaces and settled down to wait for her answer…

If you enjoyed this story, why not try some of Tom's books under the name Tom Becker:

Darkside and *Darkside: Lifeblood*

FREEWHEELING | JOANNA CAREY

It was my birthday. I got up early, dressed and crept downstairs to check: yes – a nice big parcel, and lots of cards on the breakfast table. Mum was still asleep – I'd have to wait, so I went outside.

We haven't lived here long. There's no garden, but there's an alley right outside our back door where people often dump things – shopping trolleys and stuff. I always look to see what's new and that morning there was a pram, a broken chair, a microwave oven and, behind a disgusting old mattress, there was a bike. It didn't look too bad – not the usual rubbish. Why was that dumped? Perhaps it was stolen! I walked on, kicking an old football, and thinking… Then I went back and had another look. It was a bit beaten up but the tyres were good, and after glancing furtively around me, I hauled it out on to the road. Most of the boys in my class had bikes. It seemed silly not to try it out. So I set off – not stealing it, *obviously*, just testing.

It felt good. I couldn't help smiling as I freewheeled down the hill to the corner shop. A crowd of older kids had left their bikes outside, so I did the same. In the shop, I spent ages trying find the 50p I *thought* was in my pocket. I couldn't find it, and when I came out, the bike had gone.

Vanished. Nicked.

I had to run home (uphill). Mum was waiting. I opened my birthday present; it was a cycle helmet.

"Surprise!" said Mum. "I've got you a bike! Only second-hand, but I think you'll like it. Go out and look – Bill at the bike shop said he'd deliver it very early this morning. He's checked it out, it's ready to ride and he promised to tuck it away out of sight in the alley. Let's go and find it! But hurry – you mustn't be late for school."

It wasn't a happy birthday.

Next day some boys turned up at Bill's shop trying to sell the bike. Bill recognized it, and telephoned my mum.

"Blooming kids," he said. "You can't trust anyone these days."

If you enjoyed this story, why not try some of Joanna's books:
In You Go, Joe and *Horace in Hospital*

THE MESSAGE | ELEN CALDECOTT

"We'll never get through," Gwennan said when she saw it. The wall was a cliff stretching for miles in both directions. "We'll never get past the soldiers. We'll never deliver the message."

"'Course we will," Heulwen answered. "They're Romans, not gods. Father trusted us with this because we're smart. We'll find a way. Come on."

Gwennan followed her sister. The wall marked the border between the Roman world and the barbarian, so the Romans said. But it was built right in the middle of the Brythonic lands and her father was thane on both sides of it. It shouldn't be here! It wasn't right! They had to deliver the message to the warriors beyond it. It all depended on them getting past soldiers.

"We can't just stroll through. The Romans won't let us. They've got swords. And archers. And spears."

Heulwen grinned. "Well, we know the land. They don't. I've got an idea." She crouched low, searching the damp earth. "Here. This is going to hurt."

Gwennan nodded slowly. Heulwen stood by a nettle patch; she grabbed one firmly, then drew it slowly across her own cheeks. Then it was Gwennan's turn. The sting was instant. A burning, itching pain, swelling her face like a natterjack toad's.

Heulwen grinned through her tears. "Come on, let's get through the gate."

There was a narrow causeway over the deep ditch. The wall loomed high above it. Two soldiers guarded the entrance, with more stationed nearby.

"Halt! What is your business in Caledonia?"

"Sir, we are ill," Gwennan said, her voice barely a whisper. "The swelling boils. We must get to the sacred grove to pray for a cure."

The soldier took a step backwards.

Heulwen stepped forward. "Will you let us pass, sir?"

The soldier nodded urgently. "Take your pestilence north. Let us see how the Caledonians welcome it." The second guard sniggered.

Gwennan grabbed Heulwen's hand and ran under the arch, ranks of heavy stone flashed passed. Then they were through. They kept running until the wall was far behind them. Their kinsmen were waiting for the message. But they would see the Romans again soon. And next time there would be a Brythonic army beside them.

Elen recommends:

The Thieves of Ostia by Caroline Lawrence and *Here Lies Arthur* by Philip Reeve

THE OLD, OLD SNAIL | TERRY JONES

There was once an old, old snail who had lived so long he could remember the time before snails had their own houses to live in.

"We used to crawl around afraid of the sky," he'd say. "For out of the sky would come birds – swooping down on us and snapping us up as easily as a drop of rain falls off a leaf."

And when he told them this, his grandchildren would shudder in their shells.

"In the days before we had our own houses, each snail would have to seek its own shelter for the long winter nights. Sometimes you'd find an empty peanut shell, but that was always small and tight and you'd wake up with terrible cramps. Sometimes you'd make your home in a hollow log, but that was always too big and heavy to carry around, and you could never take it to the Snails' Ball."

"Oh, Grandfather!" his grandchildren would say. "We're glad we live now!"

"Yes," Grandfather Snail would reply, swivelling his horns around and about, "life is much more comfortable today. But there's something I miss."

"Whatever can that be, Grandfather?" his grandchildren would say.

"I miss…" the old, old snail would reply, "I miss … the exploring!"

"The exploring?" his grandchildren would all exclaim together.

"Yes. You see, in those days, we weren't such stay-at-homes. Us snails would be off, climbing the mountains of the world, sailing across the seven seas and even flying to the moon!"

"Flying to the moon?!" his grandchildren would exclaim. "Surely you can't mean that!"

"Oh yes," the old, old snail would say. "In those days we thought nothing of flying at the speed of light. Us snails could turn water into liquid gold and make forests rise up into the sky so that we could slide beneath them without scraping ourselves on the rough bark of trees. In those days, snails ruled the world! And every other living thing lived in fear of us snails!"

"Gosh!" the young snails would say.

"But that's all gone," the old, old snail would sigh. "And you know what? I prefer it like this, because no matter where we wander, us snails are always at home."

If you enjoyed this story, why not try some of Terry's books: *Fairy Tales* and *The Saga of Erik the Viking*

COSIES | D.J. SAVAGE

When her parents died, Emma was adopted by her Aunt Olga. Aunt Olga spent most of her time knitting.

The weirdest things she knitted were webs for the house spiders.

"I feel sorry for them having to spin their webs all by themselves," she said. "They're so small, and must get very tired."

So she'd spend hours knitting brightly coloured webs for all the spiders. You could see the woollen webs stretching across the corners of the ceiling, and in the dark nooks and crannies of the house that spiders like.

Because wool wasn't sticky, however, the webs were quite incapable of catching flies, so Aunt Olga made Emma go round the house twice a day, using stepladders to reach the high webs, and personally feed flies to the spiders with her own two hands.

"Aunt Olga, you must stop knitting webs for spiders!" Emma said.

Unfortunately, Aunt Olga listened to her.

She started knitting cosies instead.

Cosies, as you probably know, are woolly coverings, used to keep something warm – like a tea cosy, to place over your teapot. But Olga knitted a fridge cosy, a phone cosy, and an oven cosy.

Emma had enjoyed practising on the piano in the living room, but that soon disappeared under a piano cosy. When Aunt Olga covered the TV with a TV cosy, she could no longer watch her favourite programmes.

Day after day, more pieces of furniture disappeared under cosies, never to be seen again. All Emma had to do each night was listen to the clicking of Aunt Olga's knitting needles.

One evening, Emma was worried to see, Aunt Olga had almost completed a little-girl cosy. It was exactly the size and shape of Emma.

She snuck downstairs in the middle of the night when Olga was in bed, and unravelled it. The next morning, Aunt Olga had to start all over again.

All day Aunt Olga would sit knitting a new little-girl cosy. Each night, Emma would sneak down to unravel it.

But one night, Emma fell asleep before she could sneak down.

The next morning, Aunt Olga had something scary to tell her.

"Emma, dear," she said. "I have a lovely present for you."

D.J. recommends:
Through the Looking Glass by Lewis Carroll and *King of Shadows* by Susan Cooper

DEAR GEORGE | VIVIAN FRENCH

Dear George,

Hope you're well. You know I said I couldn't come to your party because Ma and Pa were dragging me away on my Very First Royal Tour? ("SUCH good experience for you, Freddie darling!") Good news – I can come after all. Are you still having a picnic on Alligator Island? I do hope so. I can't wait to see those alligators!

Bet you're wondering what happened. You might want to take notes. I know your parents don't do much touring, but sooner or later they'll be off. And it won't be a tea party, believe you me. You'll find yourself bowing all over the place, and waving from coach windows, and having to SMILE until your teeth hurt. That's what happened to me. And by the second day I was so bored I'd starting counting flies for fun. So I thought, "Right! They keep telling me to be polite. They keep telling me to be charming. That's OK – I'll be the politest, most charming prince in the history of the universe." So I was. I didn't just smile, George, I shook hands. And I INSISTED on stopping the coach to kiss old ladies. (Don't ask.) And I hugged every single baby in every single crowd. You'd be surprised how many babies there are in a crowd, George. You should see the gooey biscuit on my velvet coat.

At first Ma and Pa were THRILLED. They said I showed Enthusiasm and Commitment, and they were proud of me. That lasted until lunchtime. After lunch, they began to mutter a bit. "No need to be QUITE so enthusiastic, Freddie. We DO have another

202

twenty miles to go…"

So that was when I started offering lifts. "Oh, MA! Just LOOK at that poor woman and her three little children and her pig and the twenty-seven cabbages. STOP THE COACH! They must ride with us. No, I won't accept a refusal. Those cabbages are HEAVY. The pig? It's no problem. Pop it in my seat. I'll walk … I'd be DELIGHTED!"

Third day? They sent me home. They said it was for the best.

I think it was the pig that did it, George.

See you at your party!

If you enjoyed this story, why not try some of Vivian's books:
Tiara Club: Butterfly Ball and *Draglins: Draglins Escape!*

THE OLD TIN | JUDITH HENEGHAN

Jem found the old tin. It lay half-buried in the pebbles by the shore. He picked it up. It wasn't heavy, though when he shook it he felt something shift.

The tin was round, sealed up with tape. The picture on the lid was scratched and worn. Jem wiped it with his sleeve. It might have been a compass, or the moon.

He took the tin home.

"Open it!" said his brother.

"Let me!" said his sister.

"No," said his mother, who had to find ways to feed her children. "We shall hold a raffle!"

Everyone in the village bought a ticket for the raffle. They knew that objects salvaged from the sea were almost always worth something.

When the day of the raffle arrived, the villagers gathered on the quay. The tin was passed around for each person to examine.

Mrs May, the baker, was first. She wrinkled up her nose. "It stinks of seaweed!"

"Not seaweed," said her son, sniffing. "I smell tar – and nutmeg!"

"It's heavy!" said Old Mack, a fisherman. "Coins?"

"Too light for coins," said the postman's wife, weighing the tin in her hands. "Buttons, I reckon!"

The postman's daughter gave it a shake. "More rustle than rattle. Feathers, perhaps? Or love letters?"

"Or empty," grunted the postman, though everyone knew that a tin washed up on the shore must surely contain something.

And so it went on.

Finally it was Jem's turn. He held the tin in his hands and shut his eyes tight. He wanted it to be so many things – treasure and glory and promises and adventure. Yet most of all he wanted to hold on to the hope that such things existed.

He was still clutching the tin when his mother drew the winning ticket.

It was his.

"Open it!" cried Mrs May.

"Quick!" shouted Old Mack.

But Jem didn't open it.

The villagers felt cheated for a day or two. Then they forgot about the tin. Only Jem remembered. When a month had passed he took it back to the shore and laid it carefully on the pebbles, where the tide could take it.

That night he dreamed of treasure and glory and promises and adventure.

If you enjoyed this story, why not try Judith's book:
Stonecipher

IT'S WAR IN THE PLAYGROUND
GILLIAN ROGERSON

Miss Pearson secured the helmet on to her head. She checked that her knee pads were in place. She called out, "OK, Mrs Clarke, I'm ready."

Mrs Clarke rang the bell for playtime.

There was a noise like thunder as feet thumped across the hall. Miss Pearson flattened herself against the wall as the children ran into the playground. Miss Pearson followed them and was immediately hit by a football. It bounced off her helmet.

"Who did that?" cried Miss Pearson.

There was no reply.

"Miss! Miss!" Jessie tugged at Miss Pearson's coat. "Sam Smith bit me."

Miss Pearson walked over to the year-one boy and said, "Did you bite Jessie?"

"No, I did not!" Sam was outraged. "I missed."

Miss Pearson sighed. "We don't bite people, or even try to bite them."

A football hit Miss Pearson on the shoulder. "Who did that?" she yelled.

"It was those year-four boys," said Sam. "Shall I bite them?"

"No!"

"Shall I bite the football?"

"No. Go and play, Sam."

"Miss! I need the toilet!"

"Off you go, then," said Miss Pearson.

"Can I go, miss? I'm desperate."

"OK, but no messing about," said Miss Pearson.

"Miss! I have to go as well."

"No, you can wait, Tim. You can't all go at once."

"It's not fair. You let those two go. I really need to go," said Tim.

"No."

Tim looked down at his wet trousers. "It's too late now, miss."

Miss Pearson sighed. "Go inside and get cleaned up."

The football hit Miss Pearson on the nose. "That is it! I'm keeping the ball!"

"It's not fair!" the year-four boys shouted.

Miss Pearson looked at her watch. Five minutes left.

"Miss! Lucy won't play with me!"

"Miss! I've hurt my knee!"

"Miss! Sam Smith just licked my cheek!"

"I didn't bite him," Sam said with a smile.

I've got a headache, thought Miss Pearson. She checked her watch, smiled and then blew the whistle.

"It's not fair," the children grumbled as they trudged back inside.

Mrs Clarke was waiting for Miss Pearson. "Mr Stevens has phoned in sick. You'll have to do afternoon playtime as well."

Miss Pearson stamped her feet and said, "It's not fair."

If you enjoyed this story, why not try some of Gillian's books:
The Teddy Bear Scare! and *The Smallest Hero*

The family (Dad, Mum, Richard, Matthew, Dominic and Lizzie) were going to Granny and Grandpa's for three days over Christmas. There was a light dusting of snow on the ground and the air was icy cold.

"Can I take Timmy with me?" asked Lizzie. Timmy was her hamster.

"I'm sorry," said Dad, "but there's no room on the car what with all the family and the presents."

"Please," pleaded Lizzie.

"I'm sorry, Lizzie," Dad said. "He can't come with us. He'll have plenty of food and water and we will only be gone for a few days."

So Timmy was left in his cage in the porch.

Lizzie was very quiet on the journey thinking about her hamster, and on Christmas morning before she opened her presents, Lizzie said, "I hope Timmy is all right."

"He'll be fine," said Dad.

But Timmy was not fine. When we arrived home after Christmas, we found the little creature curled up in the corner of his cage, lifeless and cold.

Dad put Timmy in a small cardboard box. "We'll bury him in the garden underneath the willow tree," he said glumly. Lizzie held the box in her cold little fingers. She cried and cried as Dad hacked away at the hard earth with a spade.

The next door neighbour, Mr Gomersall, looked over the fence. "It's a bit cold for gardening, isn't it?" he asked.

Dad explained about the hamster. "We found him curled up in the corner of his cage when we got back," he said sadly.

"Are you sure he's dead?" asked Mr Gomersall.

"I'm afraid so," said Dad.

"May I look?" said the neighbour. "Hamsters like to sleep deeply when it gets cold."

Lizzie passed the box over the fence. Mr Gomersall cradled Timmy in his warm and wrinkled hands and stroked the little furry body. Amazingly, astonishingly, miraculously, Timmy's tiny paws moved and he opened his eyes.

"See," said Mr Gomersall, "he's not dead. See him stir. Your hamster was just sleeping deeply."

Lizzie screamed with delight. Gently, she put Timmy back in his cage amongst the straw.

Mr Gomersall smiled. "All he wanted was a little extra love and warmth – like all of us, really."

If you enjoyed this story, why not try some of Gervase's books: *Dominic's Discovery* and *What's the Matter, Royston Knapper?*

THE FOOTSTEPS | ECHO FREER

There they were again: left, right, left, right, going across the ceiling above his bed; footsteps walking from his doorway to the opposite wall.

It was the same every night at eleven o'clock.

"You should be asleep," his mother said.

"An overactive imagination," dismissed his dad.

"Probably a ghoooooooost!" teased Frankie, his brother. They shared a bedroom and Frankie had never heard the footsteps.

"They're real," Charlie protested. But no one believed him.

He could hear the clock chiming downstairs: one, two … ten, eleven … there they were again, always going one way – never coming back.

His parents had a rule that the boys must never to go up into the attic. It was dangerous, because the house was old and the timbers in the loft were worn. Charlie didn't believe them. Maybe his parents were hiding someone up there – a spy, or an escaped criminal? Or perhaps an animal had got stuck?

One thing Charlie knew was that he was determined to solve the mystery.

The next night he was wide awake. He could hear the TV downstairs.

Then the clock began to chime.

Bong…

Quickly, Charlie sneaked out of bed and put on his slippers.

Bong…

He took a torch and tiptoed out of the bedroom to the door on the landing that was kept locked.

Bong…

By reaching up he could just touch the bolt and draw it back.

Bong…

Stealthily he climbed the stairs.

Bong…

A sticky cobweb caught his face.

Bong…

Yuck! He wiped it away.

Bong … bong…

He'd reached the top of the stairs.

He waited.

Bong … bong … bong!

This was it!

He held his breath. But there was nothing.

He shone the torch around but he couldn't see anyone – or anything!

Slowly, he began to walk across the floor above his bedroom. There was nothing up there. Not even a trapped squirrel. By the time he got to other side, he felt very disappointed.

He turned to go back, but the wooden floorboards under his foot crumbled and gave way. Suddenly, he was falling through the ceiling.

"Aaaaagh!"

He sat up in bed, shivering. What happened?

Frankie glared at him. "Another stupid nightmare?"

"Suppose so," yawned Charlie.

…Or was it?

If you enjoyed this story, why not try some of Echo's books:
Mimosa Fortune and *Magenta Sings the Blues*

POLLY — PROBLEM PRINCESS | ALEX T. SMITH

Polly was a princess.

She had the crown and seventeen pink royal ponies to prove it.

Here is what she DID like about being a princess: the castle, the personal indoor lagoon, her pampered pooch Percy.

Here is what she DIDN'T like about being a princess: everything else!

The problem was that she was always being bossed about.

"Polly!" the queen would cry. "Stop climbing that tree immediately! Your dress will be filthy and the Evil Baron's coming for tea in a minute!"

"Polly!" shouted the king. "Stop welding saucepans to the Royal Yacht! You will scuff your shoes, and what on earth will my Knights of the Occasional Table think?"

The bossiest person of all had to be her fairy godmother, Miss Pinch. She was a miserable woman who looked like a toad wrapped in chiffon.

"Polly! Stop shampooing the Royal Elephant and come and kiss these frogs!" she would holler.

"Polly! Stop sharpening your crayons with that sword and see if you can feel the pea I've hidden under your mattress!" she would snap.

"Polly!" Miss Pinch would scream. "Stop waving my knickers out the window and come here NOW! I want you to prick your finger on this spinning wheel so I can see what happens!"

If Polly didn't arrive quickly enough, she and Percy would get whacked on the head with Miss Pinch's wand.

"I've had enough of this, Percy," complained Polly after a particularly trying day. "I'm fed up of all this bossing! I wish we could be all by ourselves somewhere marvellous."

Polly pursed her lips and Percy pursed his too.

Then Polly had an idea…

"Miss Pinch!" cried Polly. "The magic mirror just said you weren't the cleverest lady in the land!"

Miss Pinch burst into Polly's bedroom, red-faced with panic. Whilst she bashed and shook the mirror, Polly swiped the magic wand!

"I wish we could be all by ourselves somewhere else," Polly whispered, and she shook the wand above herself and Percy.

They closed their eyes.

There was a flash.

Slowly Polly and Percy reopened their eyes. They were on their own desert island, miles away from everyone.

"Perfect!" laughed Polly and she splashed into the sea.

If you enjoyed this story, why not try some of Alex's books:
Eliot Jones, Midnight Superhero and *Home*

THE INCREDIBLE MR EGIL | NICK ARNOLD

My knowledge of science dated to 1935 and I hadn't been to school for ages, but that didn't bother Mr Egil.

"Tom," he would say, "science has moved on. There's so much to learn – the universe is teeming with beauty. I wish you could see the explosions around a black hole, the flash of an exploding star, the ice fields of Pluto…"

"I don't s'pose I ever will," I said doubtfully.

"Never say never," said Mr Egil mysteriously, and he flicked his blue tongue in a way that upset some of the younger kids.

With Mr Egil I felt as if I could travel to the stars, but all my dreams came to nothing. One day during a science test, a silly girl in our class called Layla asked Mr Egil whether the moon was a planet.

Mr Egil was having a tough day, and when he got cross, he would glow red hot. This time he began to change colour and blast out heat right away. And it was then that I recognized the stink that had been hanging about the science lab all day. It was gas. There was a leak somewhere.

"GET OUT! GET OUT!" I was screaming. As usual, everyone stared right through me, and that's when a horrible thing happened. Mr Egil's face sagged and seemed to unzip and his whole body peeled apart like a banana and something hot and buzzing and slimy wriggled out. A thing with bulging eyes and jointed jaws that dribbled blue drool and rubbery black tentacles that sprouted from its shoulders.

The class emptied in two seconds, and it was only just in time. With a wall of flame and a BANG so loud I heard nothing, the entire science block blasted apart. And that was the end of Mr Egil – no one found any trace of him, and if they had, they wouldn't have made much sense of his body.

As for me – I bet you think that I got killed. But you'd be wrong. You can't die twice, and that's the point of my story. I never minded that Mr Egil was an alien because he never minded that I was a ghost.

If you enjoyed this story, why not try some of Nick's books:
Horrible Science: Blood, Bones and Body Bits and *Horrible Science: Evil Inventions*

SEARCH FOR SUPPER | SHEILA MAY BIRD

Deep in the darkest wood lived a witch.

Deeper in the darkest wood lived a bear.

One day the witch had nothing to eat, so she went into the dark wood to search for supper.

It just so happened that same day the bear had nothing to eat, so he went into the wood to search for supper.

And so it was that they met.

"Aha," cackled the witch. "A bear. Now that would make a great number of suppers."

"Mmm," said the bear. "A witch. Now she would be enough for a meal or two."

The witch raised her wand.

"Stop right there," she said. "I'm going to have you for my supper!"

The bear raised his claws.

"I don't think so," he said. "I am going to have *you* for *my* supper!"

They stared at each other. The bear scratched his head in a perplexed manner. The witch lowered her wand and sat down heavily on a rock. The bear sat beside her.

"Well," said the witch eventually. "I can't be your supper if you're to be mine."

"I know what you mean," said the bear. "It just wouldn't work, you eating me and me eating you."

As they sat, wondering how to solve the problem, a cart

passed, pulled by a man riding a horse.

The bear smacked his lips greedily. The witch drooled noisily.

"Now there's a meal or two," said the bear, rising to his feet.

"Oh yes," agreed the witch. "Two of my very favourites."

The man and his horse saw the bear and the witch. The man was struck rigid with fear. The horse, however, having far more sense, broke loose from the cart and galloped away at great speed.

The witch and the bear didn't mind. It wasn't the man or the horse that took their fancy. The man was a baker and his cart was laden with pies and puddings, cakes and croissants.

"Honey cake!" the bear mumbled, spraying crumbs in every direction. "My favourite." And he shovelled in the cake with no thought of table manners.

"Flapjacks and doughnuts!" sprayed the witch, as raspberry jam trickled down her pointed chin and dripped on to her lap.

If you enjoyed this story, why not try some of Sheila's books:
Sam, the Big, Bad Cat and *My Auntie Susan*

THE FROG IN THE SWAMP | LOU KUENZLER

It was Princess Tallulah's twenty-first birthday.

"You must marry by midnight," reminded the king, "or the Wicked Fairy's curse will come true. You'll sleep for a hundred years."

"I don't want to sleep!" said Tallulah. "I want to party!"

"Then, find yourself a prince to marry," urged the king.

Unfortunately, all the princes had ridden off to a half-price-armour sale.

"I'll have to try the swamp," sighed Tallulah.

Bob the frog was sitting in the mud.

SPLUG! went his toes.

BUZZ! went a fly.

FLIP! went his long, sticky tongue.

Bob the frog was happy.

Until…

Princess Tallulah puckered up her lips.

"Muwahhhh!"

She kissed Bob's slimy green head.

POW!

Bob the frog turned into a prince.

He stuck out his new, short, royal tongue. He tried to catch a fly.

"Useless!" groaned Bob.

"Don't be disgusting," said Tallulah. "You can't eat flies. You're a prince now!"

"But I don't want to be a prince," said Bob. "I was happy as a frog."

"Too bad," said Tallulah. "Now, hurry up and ask me to marry you."

"*Marry you?*" said Bob.

"Yes. Or I'll have to sleep for a hundred years," said Tallulah.

"I can't marry you," said Bob. "We're not in love!"

"IN LOVE!" Tallulah stamped her foot. "What's love got to do with anything?"

"Everything!" said Bob.

But Tallulah stamped her foot again. She stamped so hard, she woke the Wicked Fairy, who was sleeping in a nearby tree.

"Who woke me?" screeched the fairy. "I've got a curse to put on today. It's exhausting being wicked."

"Sorry," quaked Bob and Tallulah.

"I should send you straight to sleep for a hundred years," hissed the fairy. "But I'm so tired, I'll save that spell for myself."

She waved her wand. "I'll turn you both to frogs!"

ZAP!

It was done.

Bob the frog was happy again.

And, strange to say, Tallulah was happy too.

She liked swimming in the pond.

She liked the SPLUG of the mud.

She even liked eating flies.

But, most of all, she liked Bob. And, now that she was a frog, Bob liked Tallulah, too.

Together, they hopped happily ever after and hatched a

hundred tiny tadpoles the next spring.

Lou recommends:
Bob and the House Elves by Emily Rodda and *The Shrimp* by Emily Smith

FANCY DRESS | RACHEL BILLINGTON

Poppy Dix twirled in the middle of the room. "Look at me!" she called out.

"Ugh," responded her best friend, Leonie Twill. "You can't go out like that."

"Why ever not?" Poppy pointed her toe. She was wearing ballet shoes.

"Then I'll have to walk on the other side of the road."

Poppy's brother, Nimrod, looked up from his computer. "Yellow," he said glumly. "Like sick."

"I hate you both!" screamed Poppy.

Mrs Dix came into the room. As usual, she was carrying baby Sylvia. "Oh dear." She stared at Poppy. "What are you supposed to be?"

"A daffodil!" shrieked Poppy. "Why else would I wear a frilly yellow skirt and a green petal top with matching cap?"

"I think I'll make a cup of tea," said her mum. She heaved Sylvia across her shoulder and went out again.

"Your mum hated it too." Leonie smiled.

"Less like a flower fairy, more like a banana," said Nimrod.

"I made it all myself," said Poppy, trying not to cry, "out of crêpe paper."

"My bluebell dress was hired from a professional costumer."

"Actually, you're most like a parsnip," said Nimrod.

Poppy tore at her costume, which fell in tatters on the floor. She only stopped when Mrs Dix returned. Instead of a baby or a cup of tea, she carried a large white box.

"Why didn't you tell me it was a fancy dress party?"

Poppy looked down at her bare legs. She muttered, "You were busy."

"With Sylvia, you mean." Mrs Dix frowned. "New babies take up a lot of time." Then she smiled and held out the box. "Open it, darling."

The box was tied with a silk cord. Inside there were sheets of white tissue paper. Very carefully, Poppy lifted out a dress as light as gossamer. Every bit was covered with embroidered flowers, and on the sleeves were lacy butterflies.

"My grandmother made it for me when I was a little girl and my mum was busy all the time." She took Poppy's hand. "Now you can enjoy it too."

"It's the most beautiful dress I've ever seen!" cried Poppy, and she hugged Mrs Dix so hard that they both nearly fell over.

If you enjoyed this story, why not try some of Rachel's books: *There's More to Life* and *Far Out!*

THREE GIRLS, ONE TRACTOR | RODDY DOYLE

There was once a little girl called Mary.

Actually, there was twice a little girl called Mary. You see, Mary had a twin sister. And they looked the same. Exactly the same. They were identical. They were like two legs on a pair of jeans.

But the other girl wasn't called Mary. She was Margaret. And, by the way, she had another twin sister – not Mary. So the three girls were twins and a half. Or triplets.

The other girl was called Megan and she was even more identical than the other two. Everybody said it. "That little girl looks very like herself," they said. And they were right. Mary and Margaret looked alike, and Megan looked even more alike.

Sometimes this mattered and sometimes it didn't matter.

But it mattered now. Because Mary was in jail even though it was Megan who stole the tractor. Or maybe it was Margaret.

Oh no, I've given away a big part of the story before I've even started.

Anyway, Megan, or Margaret, didn't really rob the tractor. She, or she, just borrowed it. And she, or she, was bringing it back when the farmer caught her – or her.

But the farmer didn't really catch her. She jumped out of the tractor and ran home. The farmer ran after her. But he'd only just finished his dinner: half a big chicken, spuds and two helpings of red jelly. So he was a bit slow and sweaty and, by the time he got to Megan, Margaret and Mary's house, the three little girls were standing in a row, and he didn't know which of the little girls had robbed his tractor.

Until he saw the oil on Mary's hands.

"Aha," said the farmer. "Gotcha."

But the oil on Mary's hands hadn't come from the tractor, even though the tractor was very oily. The oil on Mary's hands had come from the helicopter that Margaret, or Megan, stole the day before Megan, or Margaret, borrowed the tractor.

It's getting a bit confusing, so I'll start again before I run out of words. Lucky it's a leap year, so I've got an extra word.

There was once a little girl called – oops!

If you enjoyed this story, why not try some of Roddy's books: *The Giggler Treatment* and *Wilderness*

WITCHES' KNICKERS | GHILLIAN POTTS

A plastic bag blew along the street and up into a tree.

"Hey, witches' knickers!" said Freddie.

"What? Where?" said Megan.

"There! In the tree. Look!"

Megan looked up. In the top of the tree was an orange plastic bag. The wind tugged at it.

"That's not knickers!" Megan told him. "That's a bag. From the supermarket."

"No, it's some witch's knickers. See, they swoop down on their broomsticks and they don't see the tree in the dark till the last minute and the tree grabs their knickers as they swoosh past and – no knickers!"

Hamid came along. "What're you looking at?" he asked.

"Witches' knickers," said Freddie, pointing.

"Oh, right." Hamid nodded.

The bag fought the tree. The wind pulled. The bag puffed up.

Megan sniffed. "So why would a witch be wearing a plastic bag for knickers, anyway?"

"Ah!" said Freddie. "Plastic bags are windproof, OK? And when the witch flies around on her broomstick, it's windy, OK? And the wind is cold. So to stop the wind making her bum cold, she pulls a bag on over her real knickers!"

"Freddie," said Hamid. "Nobody could wear a plastic bag. Where would you put your legs?"

"Umm. Through the handles?" Freddie grinned.

"Don't be daft," Megan told him. "That wouldn't work."

"Yes, it would! Witches have awfully thin legs," said Freddie.

"Rubbish!" Megan sniffed. "What you would have to do is cut the two bottom corners off and put your legs through the holes. Then you could put some string through the handles and tie it around your waist."

Freddie shrugged. "OK, so that's what they do."

The bag filled with the wind and jerked at the tree.

"I bet the witch's come back and she's tugging it," said Freddie.

The bag pulled free and whirled up and up.

"It's escaped!" shouted Hamid. "Go, bag, go!"

"And it wasn't a witch's knickers," said Megan, "because there weren't any holes in the bottom. So there!"

That night, Megan put on her black robe and her black cloak and tied her pointy black hat tightly under her chin.

Then she put on her orange plastic-bag knickers, got on her broomstick and flew out of the window.

If you enjoyed this story, why not try Ghillian's book:
A Witch in the Classroom

227

NIGHT MARE | KATE CANN

It was all right before Red got a moped. Before, the shoving and sneering and jeering was all kept at school and in the streets nearby, and there was usually someone around to stop it before it got critical.

But now – now Red could get further. Now Red could follow Jasper home.

All the way home, Chris Newberry riding pillion on the back, both of them shouting, "Oi, gippo! Where d'you live? Where's your caravan?"

Jasper loved where he lived. So far along the country road it was tarry pitch-black at night, apart from the bright prickling of the stars. But it got him hassle at school. They said he slept in a ditch.

Red had followed his bus, circling like a jackal. Jasper sat still, mouth dry, full of dread. When it was his stop he jumped off and darted into the woods at the road's edge. He could hear the moped behind him, wheels grinding against mud. Then silence. Then pounding feet. They had dumped the moped; they were coming after him on foot.

It was winter, dark early, and in the trees it was very gloomy. "There is nowhere to run, gippo!" yelled Red.

Jasper ran on.

And then, as he knew he would, he hit the fence. He froze. The bony trees shielded him. He could hear Red and Chris searching and swearing, calling his name as they trampled the undergrowth.

He kept still.

Then he heard heavy plodding on the other side of the fence. A horse, a big hunter, was coming to investigate. Jasper put out his hand, patted the side of her huge head.

"Is that him, over there?" Red called.

"It's too big!" Chris snapped. They sounded scared. A mist was falling, and the moon rose. The woods were creepy now, unearthly. Jasper kept still, and the bullies came closer, right up to him …

… and in the blackness, the great horse shifted, twigs snapping around her, and exhaled. Hugely. A great *heuuuugh* of air.

"Come and get me!" roared Jasper.

The bullies fled, terrified, no idea what had terrified them. Jasper stepped out from the trees, and the moon shone down on him, and filled him with light.

If you enjoyed this story, why not try some of Kate's books for older readers:

Leaving Poppy and *Possessing Rayne*

DENNIS THE LIBRARY CAT | MICHAELA MORGAN

Dennis was a scruffy little street cat.

Nothing special.

But he did LOVE stories.

Sometimes other cats told him stories. But often they were too busy.

"Owwwhhhh!" Dennis would sigh. He was STARVING for stories.

Then one day Dennis slid through an open door and found a place that was stuffed full of stories.

It was a library.

It was peaceful. Perfect for snoozing. All around him people were reading stories. Mums and dads read them to children. Children read them to each other.

Dennis snoozed in a patch of sunlight. All day long stories tiptoed into his dreams.

I'll come here again, thought Dennis. And he did. Often.

But one day he woke from a lovely library snooze and ... he was locked in!

Oh no!

And the library was closed for the Christmas holidays!!

Dennis didn't panic.

He was warm. There were mice to catch. There was water to drink. This was almost everything he needed to be perfectly content.

But after a while he got bored.

He stared at the books.

How do you get the story out of them? Dennis wondered.

He tried licking a book to see if he could get the taste of a story.

Then he tried chewing a book to see if he could get the flavour of a story.

Then he stared and stared and waited for the story to move so that he could pounce on it and capture it like a mouse.

But the book just lay still and quiet.

"Owwwwwhhh…" Dennis sighed. It was a sigh so deep that it made a page turn over.

Dennis turned the *next* page with a careful paw…

Hours passed …

   … days passed …

   … nights passed …

    and

… picture by picture …

   … sound by sound …

     … guess by guess …

… it all started to make sense.

There was no stopping him.

He read *The Cat in the Hat*.

He read *Puss in Boots*.

He devoured stories.

Finally, the library reopened, and Dennis went to find the other cats. Now he could tell *them* stories.

He could tell fairy stories.

He could tell scary stories.

He could tell funny stories!
Dennis was now a very SPECIAL cat indeed.
He was The Cat Who Learnt to Read.

If you enjoyed this story, why not try some of Michaela's books:
Dear Bunny and *The Thing in the Basement*

"Dennis the Library Cat" © Michaela Morgan, 2008, is an adaptation of the Collins Big Cat guided reading books for ages 4-7 entitled *Tiger's Tales,* written by Michaela Morgan and illustrated by Debbie Moon, first published by Harper Collins in 2005.

THE TALE OF BOO-BOO MAGEE AND THE LOUDEST DRAGON IN THE WORLD |

ALEX WILLIAMS

Long ago in the village of Trembleton people huddled under their beds all day and all night. They ate their breakfasts, lunches and dinners there with trembling fingers and spent the rest of the time staring at one another with fearful eyes.

They lived liked this because a thunderous, petrifying roar boomed out across the village from the mouth of a cave on the hillside.

The villagers whispered to one another in the darkness under their beds, trying to guess what terrible beast was making the din.

"It's a dragon," hissed the mayor, trying not to sneeze despite the fluff under the bed wafting up his nose.

"I bet it's a big green one with purple wings and fiery eyes," added his wife.

"It's certainly the loudest dragon in the world," the mayor groaned, clamping his hands over his ears.

The mayor's young son, Boo-boo Magee, was getting bored with lying under his bed all the time. On top of that he was missing his cat, Mumbles, who had disappeared a short time before the roaring had begun.

So he crawled out and stood up.

"What are you doing, Boo-boo?" his papa whispered fiercely.

"Get back under your bed, Boo-boo, this instant!" his mama ordered, almost forgetting to whisper.

"But we can't stay under our beds for ever. It's really very dull," Boo-boo replied. "I'm going to see what's making all that noise."

"But it's a *dragon*!" his father exclaimed. "With great hairy nostrils and teeth like pitchforks!"

Boo-boo put on a pair of earmuffs so he could hear himself think over the roaring.

"As long as we're lying here, we could imagine it to be anything, Papa," he replied.

As the boy walked through the town towards the cave on the hillside, trembling eyes peered out at him.

The boy's mad, they all thought.

Into the dark cave went Boo-boo Magee – through tunnels that twisted round and round like the inside of an enormous seashell. At the centre he found … not a dragon, but … Mumbles, his cat, crying because he was lost, his plaintive calls magnified by the cave into the loudest roar in the world.

So Boo-boo picked up his cat and went home.

If you enjoyed this story, why not try some of Alex's books:
The Talent Thief and *The Storm Maker*

HAIRY STICKY TAPE | MARIAM VOSSOUGH

I'm looking for dog hairs. They're usually all over our house, but Mum just hoovered and I can't find any.

I start breathing really quickly. I can feel myself getting upset. I'm not going to cry, though. Mandy, my big sister, hasn't stop crying since it happened.

At last I see some near the bottom of the sofa. That's Spotty's spot when we're watching telly. I kneel down and pull ten short black hairs out of the faded blue cover. I lay them carefully on the floor and slowly attach them, one by one, to a piece of sticky tape.

I fold the tape over on itself to make sure the hairs don't fall off. Then I put the hairy sticky tape into one of my best pink envelopes. I write "Spotty" on the front as neatly as I can, but it comes out all wobbly.

I hug the envelope tight. This is going in my special box for ever and ever.

I remember the night we got him. Dad brought him home as a surprise. It was snowing and he had little white frozen dots on his little black puppy nose. That's why we called him Spotty.

Before, when Dad still lived here, him and Mum used to argue loads. I would hide under the table hugging Spotty, and cry into his soft warm coat. Sometimes he'd get really soggy, but he always stayed with me. That's why I won't cry now, because I need him here.

It's those stupid boys' fault. Mum stormed outside to stop them kicking their ball against our fence. But she didn't shut the front door properly and Spotty ran out. We can't let him outside without a lead, though. He just runs away.

I chased him, but he was already on the road. That's when the car hit him.

He wasn't moving when Mum picked him up.

The phone rings. I feel sick. I know it's her.

I let Mandy answer it. I can't listen … I won't listen…

Mandy taps me on the shoulder, but I want to hide inside my head. She pulls my fingers out of my ears and tells me to open my eyes.

She's smiling…

Mariam recommends:
The Secret Garden by Frances Hodgson Burnett and *Swallows and Amazons* by Arthur Ransome

THE NIGHT ORPHANS | TOM BECKERLEGGE

In the gaps between the shifting worlds of a million different dreams, a group of children wander through a land of perpetual darkness, their footsteps crunching upon stony ground. How long they have been travelling, none of them could say: without the rise and fall of a sun, they have no way to measure time. The direction in which they are headed is also a mystery: the night discourages curiosity by keeping the vast landscape around them a secret.

Though their little group is all they have in the world, none of the children know what the word "family" means. They do not bother with names, identifying each other by the smell of their breath and pitch of their voice. They are not even sure how many their group numbers. Lying, stealing and cheating are commonplace – it is easier to commit such crimes when no one can see your face.

As they trudge on, the children tell each other endless stories to ward off loneliness: jokes without punchlines; silly poems; long, rambling tales that trail off into the darkness. Even those who have never learnt how to form words take their turn, clicks and grunts tumbling from their mouths until their lips are dry and throats sore.

When their feet begin to ache, and their limbs grow heavy, the children sit down to rest. Some seize the opportunity to huddle together for warmth. Under the cover of darkness, small hands fold over one another, and lips map faces with kisses.

Despite such brief comforts, in the land of perpetual night it is easy to lose hope. Luckily, although the children can never fall asleep, they can still dream. All have heard the elder children whisper hoarsely about the existence of light, a magical substance that illuminates other worlds. In the privacy of their imaginations, the children try to imagine what such a thing could feel like: a riotous explosion; a stinging pain in the eyes; a cool, soothing breeze.

No matter what sensation they conjure up, the night orphans would eagerly kill to experience light, if only for a fleeting second, if only for long enough to blink and see the faces of those around them…

If you enjoyed this story, why not try another of Tom's books under the name Tom Becker:

Darkside: Nighttrap

Charlie's on his way home from school. It's raining. Charlie hates getting wet; in fact, he hates everything.

ESPECIALLY:

- Being eight years old.
- Having to leave his old home and move down south with his mum to live with his grandpa, because his dad's gone to live with someone else.
- The scary tree that taps on his bedroom window every night.
- Most of all, he hates his new school. The other kids laugh at the way he talks, he's the only one not in a secret gang, and he's the only boy in the class without a nickname.

When he gets home, his mum isn't there – she's at college, learning to be a teacher. Grandpa's there, though, and he hugs Charlie and doesn't tell him off for making muddy footprints on the kitchen floor. He makes Charlie hot chocolate and buttered toast; Charlie's feeling a bit better about everything when Grandpa asks him how things are going at school and he starts feeling bad again.

He gives Grandpa the note about the school Christmas party. It says: INCLUDES HARRY POTTER LOOKALIKE COMPETITION!!!

Grandpa looks thoughtfully at Charlie. "Hmm… Prepared to put in a bit of work, m'boy?"

Charlie blinks. Then nods. Hard.

"Got an old box of tricks in the attic. Let's go!"

They practise every night for three weeks.

On the afternoon of the party, Charlie puts on a special cloak his mum's made, and Grandpa's spare spectacles. Draws a lightning-bolt scar on his forehead.

When the judging starts, he whips out his wand (made with a twig from the scary tree, which isn't really scary at all!) and performs the brilliant tricks he's learned.

SHAZZAM!! He produces giant lollipops from three boys' ears.
Amazement!!

SHAZZAM!! He pulls bright handkerchiefs from another's trainers, and turns them into a rainbow.
Delight!!

SHAZZAM!! He coaxes a bunch of pink roses from his teacher's handbag, and turns them to silver confetti with a wave of his wand.
Laughter!!

Finally, SHAZZAM!! He conjures a string of pork sausages from a girl's pocket, and makes them dance a rumba before they vanish.
APPLAUSE!!

Charlie wins the competition – and his new friends give him a nickname.

Guess what?

Yes!!

It's "Magic"!!

Rosie recommends:
Matilda by Roald Dahl and *Harry and the Wrinklies* by Alan Temperley

PICK UP A PENGUIN

STEVE BARLOW & STEVE SKIDMORE

Things just seem to happen to Eddie Johnson. Take the other day.

It was a boring Saturday and I was heading home across the park, when I saw Eddie mooching across the grass. The thing is, there were six penguins trotting along behind him. Yes, you heard right. Six black and white penguins waddling along like a bunch of ETs in dinner jackets.

"Eddie!" I shouted.

He gave me a gloomy look. "Hi."

"Squawk," squawked one of the penguins.

"Squawk," agreed the other five.

I was gobsmacked. "Eddie, I know you've got a label on your head saying 'brains not included', but even you should have noticed that there are six penguins following you."

"Oh, those things." He shrugged. "I found them in our front garden this morning. They've been following me all day. I reckon they must think I'm their mum or dad. Perhaps they're wanting me to feed them."

"Or maybe," I said, sarky-like, "they're hiding from polar bears."

"Oh, no," said Eddie seriously, "polar bears don't eat penguins."

"Why?" I said. "Can't they get the wrappers off?"

He looked blank. "No. It's because polar bears live at the North Pole, you see, and penguins live at the South Pole."

I don't really know why I waste my comic genius on Eddie. "Well, what are you going to do with them?"

He shrugged. "Dunno."

"But you can't walk around town with six penguins following you," I pointed out. "It's not natural. You should take them to the zoo."

He brightened. "That *is* a good idea. I'll do that."

He turned and walked off – the penguins lolloping anxiously after him like a line of waiters at a posh restaurant.

Next day I was back in the park. I couldn't believe my eyes. Eddie was back and so were the penguins! I blinked. They were all wearing sunglasses and carrying plastic buckets and spades (a tricky thing to do with wings).

"Oi, Eddie!" I yelled. "What are you doing with those penguins? I thought you were going to take them to the zoo."

Eddie gave me a miserable look. "I did. They had such a good time, today they're making me take them to the beach!"

If you enjoyed this story, why not try more of Eddie Johnson's adventures:
Stone Me! and *Don't Look Back!*

DRAGON | ADÈLE GERAS

When I was a little girl, I lived for a couple of years in North Borneo, in a town called Jesselton. I loved living there. We had a beach just outside our house and the weather was always perfect, though sometimes it did rain as though it never wanted to stop and the roads turned into mini-rivers.

One day, when I went into my bedroom, there was a dragon curled up on my bed. It was blue and scaly and had very sharp teeth. Did I scream? Of course I did. The creature looked up, as if I'd disturbed him in the middle of a sleep, which I suppose I had, if you looked at it from the dragon's point of view.

"There's really no need to scream," he said. "I'm not going to hurt you. This is a nice shady room and I'm simply having a rest on your bed. It's a very pleasant bed."

"Thank you," I said. It *was* a pleasant bed. I liked it very much myself, but I didn't know how I was ever going to sleep in it again after this visit. Perhaps the dragon would leave slime on the sheets? Were dragons slimy? I had no idea and I didn't want to find out.

"Are you going to stay long?" I asked.

"No, I'm on my way home now," said the dragon. "And I'll reward you for your kindness, never fear."

The next thing I remember is my mother coming to see why I was screaming.

"There was a dragon on my bed," I said.

"Such an imagination!" My mother smiled. "But that reminds

243

me: I was at the shop today and I bought you a lovely dressing gown. Come and see."

I followed my mother into her bedroom. The dressing gown had a dragon embroidered on the back in blue silk. I recognized *my* dragon at once. I think he winked at me. How did he get to be on my bed one minute and then on my dressing gown? I have no idea, but he managed it. Have a look at the dressing gown if you don't believe me. I've kept it for more than fifty years.

If you enjoyed this story, why not try some of Adèle's books: *Troy* and *Ithaka*

SCORPION COUNTRY | CHRIS POWLING

We were camping in scorpion country.

How did I know?

Because my big brother told me, that's how. He told me over and over again – usually adding an extra detail to wind me up. This morning, as we crawled out of our sleeping bags, he gave me my usual reminder. "Nasty little beggars, scorpions. If you're lucky, their sting is no worse than you get from a wasp. If you're unlucky, it feels like a nail banged right through your foot."

I looked at my boots. Chet looked at them, too. He was waiting to see if I remembered the drill. Remembered it? How could I possibly forget it in scorpion country? I picked up my right boot by its toe and knocked it sharply on the ground with its opening facing away from me. To my relief, nothing came scuttling out. There was nothing inside my left boot, either. Chet gave me an approving nod as he reached for his own boot. "Well done, Ned," he winked. "You've got the hang of scorpion country, all right."

"How about you, Chet?"

"What?"

"You forgot to do your own check," I said.

Chet stared down at his half-on boot, his face suddenly as yellow as the rocks and sand surrounding our tent. "Ned, there's something coiled up against my foot," he whispered. "I can feel it by my ankle."

"Is it a scorpion, Chet?"

"What else could it be?"

Slowly, tremblingly, millimetre by millimetre, my big brother eased off his boot. At any moment we expected the shock of a wasp-sting if he was lucky or a nail banged right through his foot if he wasn't. Instead, what we got was the flop of leather against leather as Chet freed the bootlace from inside his boot.

The bootlace?

I've got to admit, he recovered brilliantly. "Just testing, Ned!" he said airily as he knocked his other boot against the ground. "Nothing works better than a bit of drama, you know. There's no chance you'll forget the drill now!"

"Neither will you, Chet," I said, hoarsely.

For out of his second boot scuttled something tiny, coiled and eight-legged which vanished through the tent flap, off into scorpion country.

If you enjoyed this story, why not try some of Chris's books:
The Mustang Machine and *Thing*

HOW I DONE IT IN 366 WORDS
RAYMOND BRIGGS

Once upon a time, last week, there was this old bloke and a Big Fat Book Publisher told him to write a story with only 366 words. Not one word more and not one word less. This old bloke didn't know what to do. The Big Fat Book Publisher said the story had to be for children. What children? the old bloke said. I don't know any children. They may be soppy children, daft children. I don't want to waste my time writing a story for soppy children or daft children. I know what I will do: I'll just write about the problem of writing with only 366 words. It will be called "How I Done It In 366 Words". I wonder how many words I've used already? I'd better have a count up. Bum. 134 already!

This is getting boring and I haven't even started the story yet. Now you have got to have a hero in a story … but I don't know any heroes. Well, make one up… What about this heroic old bloke who's being tormented by a BFBP? She is making him write a story with only 366 words. The heroic old bloke bashes on, writing line after line of tripe, searching for a story. What do children like nowadays? Sweets? Chocolate? Burgers, chips? You can't write a story about burgers and chips, can you? What about the boy who ate 366 burgers in 366 minutes? Or what about the girl who ate 366 chocolates in 366 seconds (a world record)? Now we have a hero and a heroine. The only trouble is they both died by being so silly. So it was a sad ending. Endings should say, "And they lived happily ever after, surrounded by mountains of chips, lorry loads of burgers and metric tons of chocolates".

I wonder if the BFBP weighs 366 kilos. I hope she comes to a sad ending. I don't want her going on tormenting old blokes with her 366 words. I hope she suffers 366 torments. Serve her right. HAR HAR. THE END.

345. Just counted. It's still too short! Bum again. So now I've got to get to THE END again, then when

If you enjoyed this story, why not try some of Raymond's books: *The Snowman* and *Fungus the Bogeyman*

HOW TO FIND GOLD | **VIVIANE SCHWARZ**

The most important thing about finding gold is that no one else must know what you are doing. If anybody finds out, they might get to the gold before you do.

Be silent. Practise always making the same face. A frown is easiest. Start frowning now and check every time you see a mirror.

Next, you must learn how to sleep with your eyes open. You will find this very useful once you have found gold and need to guard it.

Get yourself a pet that will surprise you at night. Crocodiles are ideal.

Carry one with you wherever you go to build up your strength. Start with a young crocodile. It will grow.

Most gold is no heavier than a fully-grown crocodile, so carrying one will make you strong enough to carry the gold.

Many treasure hunters make the mistake of choosing a pet that is too light, like a parrot. This is utterly useless.

Work hard. Be strong. Then the time will come to find gold.

Hidden gold will be either buried or sunk.

To find buried gold, you need an old map with a cross on it. The cross marks the gold. An old map without a cross is no good, even if you draw one on.

If you know someone who has an old map with a cross on it, go and ask them for it. Don't forget to take the crocodile. Chances are they will hand it over.

Failing that, look for sunken gold.

To find sunken gold, you must learn of the hidden mountains under the sea, the lair of the kraken, and the paths of the great storms. They all wreck ships and leave gold on the seabed. Read up about them in books. Practise holding your breath while you read. Then take a boat and strong rope, and dive in the right place.

Once you have found the gold, hide it. Do not spend any of it or people will take notice. Hide the crocodile with the gold. Draw a map with a cross, then hide the map and forget all about it.

Now stop frowning. No one will ever find it.

The gold is yours for ever.

If you enjoyed this story, why not try some of Viviane's books: *Timothy and the Strong Pyjamas* and *There Are Cats In This Book*

GRANDDAD'S SLIPPERS | VAL TYLER

"You all right, Granddad?"

"Just a little tired, Princess."

"Shall I get your slippers?"

"Thank you." Granddad smiled. "I can't get comfortable without them."

"Tea's ready!" Mum called.

"I'm just getting Granddad's slippers."

I ran into his bedroom. "Granddad, they're not under your bed!"

"Try the bathroom." Mum sounded irritated.

I checked the bathroom. "They're not there."

"I can't think where they'd be," Granddad said, scratching his bald head. He looked tired. "Have you tried the back door?" Then he smiled. "You are good to me."

"That's because you're a good granddad," I said, blowing him a kiss. Granddad pretended to catch it.

I went into the kitchen. Granddad's wellies were next to mine by the back door, but no slippers.

I went to tell him, but he had fallen asleep.

After tea, Granddad was still asleep.

Mum rested her hand on his old wrinkled one. A strange expression crossed her face as she leant over and kissed him on the forehead.

"Shall I find his slippers?"

"No," Mum said. Her voice sounded shaky.

"What's wrong?"

Mum took me into the kitchen. "You know Granddad's very old."

Of course I did.

"And old people sometimes die."

I suddenly realized what Mum was going to say. "No," I cried, pulling away.

"Yes," Mum said, gently holding me.

"But he's not wearing his slippers! He can't get comfortable without them."

On the day of the funeral, I was looking for my best shoes. You have to wear your best shoes to a funeral, but I couldn't work out where they were.

And then I remembered.

Granddad and I had been in the shed. We were going to plant some seeds and he'd told me to take off my shoes and put on my wellies. I told him to put on his, and so he'd taken off his slippers and I'd taken off my shoes and we'd both put on our wellies.

I went out to the shed and found Granddad's slippers. They were old and worn out, a bit like Granddad.

"Come on," Mum said, opening the front door. "What are you doing with those slippers?"

"Taking them to Granddad," I said. "He can't get comfortable without them."

If you enjoyed this story, why not try some of Val's books:
The Time Apprentice and *The Time Wreccas*

ONCE UPON A TIME... | KAY WOODWARD

Once upon a time, there was a princess who lived in a deep, dark, scary wood. She was probably beautiful. She was definitely poor. And her grandmother had *very* big teeth.

Oh no, she didn't.

She most certainly did. Shall we get on?

The poor princess lived in a very small house made of straw. Or was it wood? It could even have been brick. Yes, it must have been brick to withstand the very strong winds around those parts. Sometimes, it could blow so hard that it would blow your house down, you know.

This princess had a wicked stepmother. They always do, don't they? You never find a nice stepmother in a fairy story. This particular stepmother was a jealous old hag with a hooked nose, two ugly daughters, a magical mirror and an orchard full of delicious, ripe, rosy-red apples.

Mmmm...

They were poisonous, of course. Really quite deadly.

But back to the princess. Or was she a poor mermaid? I forget. Anyway, she had a fairy godmother. She was lucky that way. And the fairy godmother was always on the lookout for sharp needles and glass slippers. And pumpkins. We mustn't forget those.

What about the prince? He was charming, obviously. Tall, dark, handsome? Check. And he was a dab hand at rescuing damsels, distressed or otherwise.

Have we forgotten anyone? Dwarfs? Seven, please. Pipers? Just the one. Shoe-making elves? Marvellous.

So, the princess. You remember her. The one with the wicked stepmother and the fairy godmother and the dashing prince?

That's the one.

Well, our princess wasn't terribly fortunate. Downright unlucky, actually. Her porridge was never hot enough and her bed never comfy enough – well, it wouldn't be with that pea underneath, would it? And she had an awful habit of falling asleep for a hundred years. And whenever she fell asleep, wouldn't you just know it? A huge prickly forest would spring up around the castle. No, hang on. Was it a staggeringly tall tower without a staircase? A marzipan cottage?

Who can say?

Probably a fairy-tale castle. They're always popular.

Anyway, once upon a time, there was a beautiful princess—

Oops, no room here.

That'll be another story then.

If you enjoyed this story, why not try some of Kay's books:
The Dahlmanac and the *My Secret World* series

THE FUNNY DADDY | WENDY COPE

Once upon a time there was a funny daddy. He could do funny dancing and he was always telling jokes. He had two children: Louise and Callum.

"Mum," said Callum one day. "Do you think Dad is the best joker in the world? I do."

"I'm not sure," said Mum. "But I'm glad you think so."

Louise, who was six years older than Callum, just rolled her eyes. Just then Dad came in.

"Hello, son. What colour is a burp?"

"Burple!" replied Callum.

"What did the banana say when the elephant stepped on it?"

"Don't know that one." Callum thought hard.

"Give up?"

Callum nodded.

"Nothing. Bananas can't talk!"

Callum laughed. Then Mum asked Dad how his day had been and the jokes were over for a while.

At school Callum had a friend called Terry. He asked Mum if Terry could come and play after school. On Wednesday, she came and fetched them both and took them to Callum's house. Dad was home.

"Hello, Dad. This is Terry. Terry, this is my dad. He's the best joker in the world. Tell us a joke, Dad."

Callum and Terry stood and looked at Dad. And do you know what happened? Dad forgot all his jokes and couldn't think of a thing to say. Poor Dad. Poor Callum.

"Sorry, son. Can't think of one just now. Later, eh?"

"Yeah. That's fine, Dad. " He tried not to look upset.

They boys went upstairs to Callum's room and began to build a castle out of Lego.

After a while they heard Mum call, "Anyone hungry?"

"Yes!"

They abandoned their castle and ran downstairs. Loud music was coming from the living room, so they looked through the door. And there was Dad, doing his funny dancing: swinging his hips, waving his arms, pointing to the ceiling, with a sort of pouting expression on his face. Terry had never seen anything quite like it. He laughed and laughed until Callum thought he might choke. Callum was laughing too. Dad saw them and waved.

"How do you make a bandstand?" he yelled above the music.

The boys shook their heads.

"Take their chairs away," he shouted, and kept right on dancing.

If you enjoyed this story, why not try some of Wendy's books: *Twiddling Your Thumbs* and *Another Day on Your Foot and I Would Have Died*

THE NOT-SO-BAD WOLF | TONY ALLAN

The truth is, I was never big and I wasn't often bad either. Sometimes, maybe, if I happened to find myself unexpectedly in a chicken coop, or if I got a chance to scare someone of a nervous disposition. Most people, though, thought I was rather small as wolves go. As for my pack-mates – well, they often used to comment on my friendly nature. But then, what could I expect once my name got into the newspapers? No one was going to get excited by a story about a short, smiley wolf. A big bad wolf I had to be.

Actually, the size thing was an issue for me. If you're a wolf, you want to be big. Small, and people reckon you're harmless, even some sort of pet. Sometimes they mistake you for an Alsatian dog, for heaven's sake. That really happened, a couple of times when I was young. You can imagine how that made me feel. Terrible.

So that's why I want to tell you about the Little Red Riding Hood thing. You see, I never meant to harm the girl. And as for dressing up in Grandma's clothing – well, that never happened. You just can't believe all the things you read in the papers.

The fact was, I didn't want to hurt anyone. I just went to the cottage looking for food. The scraps people leave out – you'd be surprised what you can find in dustbins.

So there I was, scavenging. And everything would have been fine if it hadn't been for the old lady. She spotted me straight away. I could see her behind the curtains. If she'd had an ounce of sense, she'd have stayed where she was, safe and sound. But she didn't.

She came out the front door. I tried snarling at her, which usually works, but she didn't seem scared at all. Instead, she just looked at me, and she was smiling. That just wasn't right.

Then she did something really bad. Something no self-respecting wolf could put up with.

She called me "Wolfie".

"Wolfie," she said. "Are you a hungry wolfie? Does wolfikins want something nice for supper?"

And that was when I ate her up.

If you enjoyed this story, why not try some of Tony's books:
The Symbol Detective and *Tales of Mystery and Imagination*

NARINDER'S MOUSE | SALLY NICHOLLS

He was small and pink-eyed, with white fur and a pink tail that curled around Narinder's coloured pencils. Narinder pushed the lid of her pencil case open. The girls squealed.

"Look at his little nose."

"What's his name?"

"Where'd you get him?"

"Can I hold him?"

"His name's Snowy," said Narinder. "I got him for my birthday." She picked him out of her pencil case and dropped him gently into Alice's hands. Alice squeaked.

"He's *gorgeous*."

Narinder watched silently. She's a bit of a mouse herself, Narinder. She's got brown eyes and long, soft hair, the sort that doesn't get mussed up even on windy days. She's got a big brother, Ranjit, who plays football with my brother. I saw him once, yelling at Narinder about something. Narinder just walked along, head bent, not saying anything.

"I wish I had a mouse," said Alice. Snowy's eyes darted back and forward. He looked terrified.

"My brother's going to kill him," said Narinder.

We stared.

"*Kill* him?"

Narinder's dark head was bent over the mouse.

"He's going to flush him down the toilet. He said so." She touched Snowy's head. "He's always doing stuff like that."

"You're making it up," said Laura, but the rest of us were silent. I remembered Ranjit's angry face, grabbing Narinder's arm. I believed her.

"Listen," said Alice urgently. "I'll have him. Let me have him. My mum won't mind. Then Ranjit won't be able to do anything to him."

"He was my birthday present," said Narinder. Her eyes never left Snowy.

"You can have my Christmas money," said Alice. "Fifteen pounds. You can say he escaped. You can come and visit him. Oh, please."

For a long moment, Narinder was quiet. Then she nodded, and turned away.

I have badminton on Thursdays, so I don't get home till after five. My brother was eating cake in the kitchen in his football kit.

"... lost four-nil. Ranjit was rubbish. Mooning over Rex."

"Rex?" Mum was saying.

"His mouse. He's vanished. Ranjit thinks the cat's got him. He's a right softy, Ranjit."

I stopped. "*Ranjit's* mouse?"

"Yeah." My brother turned. "He'll be all right," he said. "Don't worry. They can look after themselves, mice can."

If you enjoyed this story, why not try Sally's book:
Ways to Live Forever

THE BOY WHO TURNED INTO A TELEVISION
DAVID BELBIN

Tom watched a lot of TV. In bed. On his computer. Whatever he could, whenever he could.

His parents became so worried, they took his TV away. They got rid of their other TVs, too. They even disconnected the aerial and the Internet.

"Get a life!" they told him.

"It's not fair!" Tom replied. "What's wrong with TV?"

Tom sulked. He wouldn't read books, see friends, or play on his computer. His big sister, Beth, sulked too.

"My friends want to talk about TV shows," she complained. "I hate missing things."

Tom yawned. "Me too."

"Hang on!" Beth said. "Keep your mouth open! I can see something."

"What?"

"Open and close! Again!"

"What is it?"

"There's a TV playing in your throat. Open again!"

"Why?" Tom asked.

"I'm changing channels. *Emmerdale's* on in a minute!"

Tom's parents were frantic. They took Tom to the doctor. She said nothing could be done.

"Your son has got televisionitis. There's an epidemic at the moment. If you hadn't brought him in, he would have grown TVs all over his body."

"Is there a cure?" Mum asked.

"No. I can give him a pill to stop it getting worse."

"He keeps opening his mouth. It is very distracting!"

"I suggest you do what most people do when this happens. Leave him in a corner and ignore him."

Beth took Tom to the dentist.

"This is the worst case I've ever seen," the dentist said. "I can't cure him. I can make the picture smaller."

"If you can't get rid of the screen," Beth said, "could you at least turn up the sound? It's hard to hear."

Time passed. Tom bought a shaving mirror for when he wanted to watch TV. He could never get the angle right. And it was tiring, keeping his mouth open all the time. If he closed for a rest, he couldn't find the station again. When Beth wanted to watch her soaps, she had to prop his mouth open with toothpicks.

After six months, Mum and Dad gave in. They reconnected everything and bought new TVs. Tom learnt to ignore the TV in his mouth. But he became very popular whenever there was a power cut.

If you enjoyed this story, why not try some of David's books:
The Right Moment and *Boy King*

BANANA TIME | CINDY JEFFERIES

A loaf and six bananas. That was what Sam's mum asked him to buy. He carried the shopping carefully until he came to a tramp sitting on a low wall. Sam looked at his bananas, and then at the tramp.

"Would you like a banana?" he asked.

"Thank you very much!" said the tramp. "You are kind."

Sam went on a bit further, until he came to two young children. They were pushing and shoving each other, until one of them nearly fell into the road.

"Don't do that!" said Sam. "It's dangerous! Have a banana instead."

Just outside his front gate, there was a bus stop. And at the bus stop were a mother and toddler. The toddler was crying.

"Why is she crying?" asked Sam, who rather liked toddlers.

"She's tired," said the mother. "And it's past her teatime, and the bus is late."

"Would she like a banana?" asked Sam.

"I'm sure she'd love that," said the mother. "Can you spare one?" As soon as Sam handed her a banana, the toddler stopped crying and started to smile instead. He waved goodbye and went indoors.

In the kitchen, Sam's mum was waiting for the shopping. "Where are all the bananas?" she said. "I asked you to buy six, but you've only got two!"

Then Sam explained about the tramp, and the children, and the toddler, and Sam's mum laughed. "I was going to make a banana cake for our tea," she told him. "But there aren't quite enough to do that now."

"Oh dear," said Sam, who was very fond of banana cake.

"Never mind," said his mum. "We've got plenty of bread. Let's have Banana Sandwich Experiment instead."

And so, while Sam buttered some bread, his mum mashed the last two bananas. She spread the mashed banana on to four slices of bread. Then she drizzled honey on to one, chopped crystallized ginger on to another, scattered brown sugar on the third one, and added chocolate sprinkles to the last slice.

Then Sam and his mum sat down and enjoyed their tea. They decided that Banana Sandwich Experiment was just as tasty as banana cake, and twice as much fun to make!

If you enjoyed this story, why not try some of Cindy's books:
The *Fame School* series and the *Stadium School* series

GHOST STORY, TRUE STORY | M.G. HARRIS

This happened to Jennifer. She babysat me thirty years ago.

Jennifer was disorganized, especially about cars. Driving through the countryside one night, her car slowed to a halt – out of petrol.

In the middle of nowhere.

Outside it was pitch-black. No moon, no street lamps. Velvety darkness. The narrow road cut through a little wood. Between the trees Jennifer spotted a light burning.

A house.

Jennifer was young enough to have the Hansel and Gretel story in her head but too busy being cool to remember. So she forgot to be scared.

A little old lady opened the door. Slowly. She looked surprised to see Jennifer. But then a smile spread over her face. She had a kind face, soft pink-and-white cheeks like a fuzzy peach. There was something about that smile ... but Jennifer couldn't put her finger on it.

The air smelled rich, sweet, of caramel. Treacle tart, the old lady said. "Can I use your phone?" Jennifer said. Another smile, this time sad.

"Doesn't work... There's something wrong with the electricity."

She sliced buttery chunks of warm, gooey treacle tart, heaped whipped cream on top. She poured tea from a pot in a cosy. Jennifer became so comfy she didn't want to leave.

So she stayed. Not a hard decision. Cold car versus warm bed.

And as much pie as she could eat.

Next morning Jennifer woke to the smell of frying sausages and tomatoes. That old lady took great care of my babysitter.

Jennifer set off for the nearest village, four miles away. At a pub, she begged someone to sell her a gallon of petrol. Jennifer described where she'd left the car.

What house in the woods? What old lady?

From the back of the pub, an elderly voice said, "I know the house. Ain't no one lived there for years. Ten, at least."

A villager drove Jennifer back to her car. The house was there – but empty.

"It was a fire. Bad electrics, burned out. Mrs Adams she was, that died. Relatives couldn't sell the house. Cursed – so they say."

Stunned, Jennifer wracked her brain. Had she dreamt it?

Yet the taste of that treacle tart stayed with her. For years.

If you enjoyed this story, why not try M.G.'s book:
The Joshua Files: Invisible City

HUXLEY BEAR'S HONEY HUNT | CLAIRE FREEDMAN

Huxley Bear woke up with a tickly prickly feeling in his nose.

"I smell honey in the air!" he sniffed. And lickety-licking his lips, he set off to find it.

"Hello, Huxley!" called Twitchy Rabbit. "You're up early."

"I'm honey hunting," Huxley said.

"Can *I* come?" Twitchy asked eagerly.

"Finding honey is a job for big bears – all by themselves!" Huxley said.

"Please!" begged Twitchy. "I can distract the bees for you. I'll make sure you don't fall from the honey tree."

"I *never* fall from trees!" sighed Huxley.

"There's always a first time!" Twitchy laughed.

So Huxley followed his tickly prickly nose, and Twitchy Rabbit followed Huxley Bear.

"Morning!" called Squeaky Mouse. "Where are you two going?"

"*I'm* on a honey trail," said Huxley.

"Need any help?" asked Squeaky.

"Finding honey is a job for big bears – all by themselves," Huxley sighed.

"I could carry the honeycomb back home," offered Squeaky.

So Huxley followed his tickly prickly nose. Twitchy Rabbit followed Huxley Bear, and Squeaky Mouse followed Twitchy Rabbit.

Sniff, sniff!

"Up in that tree!" whispered Huxley, suddenly stopping. "HONEY!"

"Hooray, yummy honey!" sang Twitchy at the top of his voice. "Am I distracting the bees enough, Huxley?"

"Sshh!" said Huxley crossly. "You've made so much noise, now the bees know we are here!"

He began to climb the tree anyway.

"Ouch!" cried Huxley as something jabbed him in the bottom.

"Sorry – only me!" called Twitchy excitedly. "I'm right behind you in case you fall!"

C-R-E-A-K! The branch swung dangerously as Huxley reached inside the tree hollow to pull out a big dripping honeycomb.

C-R-E-E-E-E-A-K!

"Get back, Twitchy!" cried Huxley. "This branch can't hold BOTH our weights!"

SNAP! The branch broke.

THUD! Down Huxley fell.

"Look out!" gasped Squeaky. "The bees are after you, Huxley. And they don't look friendly!"

The bees followed Huxley. Huxley followed Squeaky. Squeaky followed Twitchy.

PHEW! They made it back home safely!

Huxley's tummy rumbled loudly.

"At least we got ourselves some yummy honey!" he grinned.

"Oh dear!" squeaked Squeaky. "I knew there was something I'd left behind!"

"But you are right about one thing, Huxley!" giggled Twitchy. "Finding honey IS a job for big bears. All by themselves!"

If you enjoyed this story, why not try some of Claire's books:
Follow That Bear If You Dare and *The Monster of the Wood*

CHELSEA AND THE BABY BIRDS | ALEX HERRING

Chelsea loves everything about school except one big thing. She hates having lunch there.

When Chelsea is at home, she can have the food she likes, sausages and crisps. Mrs Pike, her teacher, does not like sausages and crisps and sends a note home.

"All food in the lunch boxes has to be healthy."

Every day Chelsea opens her lunch box. There are no crisps or sausages now. Her mum gives her cheese sandwiches and an apple. Chelsea doesn't like cheese or apples.

"Perhaps you will learn to like them," says Mum.

"I won't," says Chelsea. She eats the bread.

In the playground is a tree with a nest in it. Chelsea can see the baby birds. They are always hungry. She can see their yellow beaks open and hear their cries. They want their mother to bring back food.

"Perhaps they want my cheese and my apple," Chelsea says. "I don't want them."

A clown comes to the school and gives all the children a balloon. At lunch time Chelsea holds her balloon while she watches the baby birds in the tree. They are very hungry today and Chelsea wants to help them. She gets her cheese and ties it to the balloon. Then she lets the balloon go. It rises up, up, until it is as high as the nest. Then it sticks in the branches. Chelsea feels very happy. The baby birds can eat her cheese. But later she wants her balloon back. She climbs the tree, up, up, until she reaches the balloon. She can see the baby birds in their nest. They cry to her: "Kee, kee."

Chelsea takes the cheese from her balloon and gives it to the birds but they don't want it. Then she looks down. It is a long way to the ground. Chelsea can't move. Maybe she will have to stay in the tree all night. She starts to cry.

"Look!" says a boy. "Chelsea is up the tree."

Mrs Pike gets a ladder and helps Chelsea down.

"What a silly thing to do," she says.

Chelsea doesn't care. She has seen the baby birds and they don't like cheese either. She clutches her beautiful balloon.

Alex recommends:
Stargirl by Jerry Spinelli and *Ways to Live Forever* by Sally Nicholls

GREGOR THE UGLY | P.R. MORRISON

Gregor the Ugly Giant was sitting by the side of a forest combing the dirt out of his long black hair. He was complaining to himself and crying out in pain whenever the comb became entangled in a knot. Which was often.

An inquisitive fawn heard his cries and came wandering out of the trees. "That Ugly Giant looks unhappy," it said, and because it was full of the joys of youth, decided to cheer him up. "Good morning, Mr Ugly Giant."

The giant stopped complaining and peered out from behind his matted hair. His eyes were bloodshot and his filthy red face was covered in warts. On one side of his hooked nose was a strange growth the size and colour of a plum. He was the ugliest giant the little fawn had ever seen, but he hid his fear because his mother often told him, "Never judge a creature by its appearance."

The fawn blinked his big beautiful eyes and in a sweet voice said, "I can see that you are a very unhappy giant, but it is no good just sitting there complaining. You must find a way to help yourself."

The Ugly Giant put his comb down on the grass. His hands were as big as puffball mushrooms and his nails were as black as the earth he sat upon. He considered the little fawn's advice and then nodded. "Yes," he growled. "What you say is true. I must help myself."

"Is there anything I can do?" asked the little fawn, because his mother had also advised him to be kind to those less fortunate than himself.

Quick as a flash, the giant grabbed the fawn, popped him in his mouth and swallowed him in one bite. The Ugly Giant licked his lips and smiled. "My stomach is full. *Now* I am happy again. Thank you, little fawn." Then he picked up his comb and went back to disentangling his hair.

As for the unfortunate little fawn? Well, it would have done well to remember another piece of its mother's advice. "Never, ever, speak to giants. Particularly hungry ones."

PS The ugly giant had a very bad tummy ache for five days.

If you enjoyed this story, why not try P.R.'s book:
The Wave Traveller

Karam was going to like this school. He was sure of it. He was new to this city, to this country. He wanted to make friends. And everyone was so friendly.

Everyone except Alex.

Alex was not nice. First day in the playground he thumped Karam. Blood everywhere.

"Beware of Alex," Paul told him. "He used to be nice; then about four years ago, he changed. Now he is evil."

Every day after that, Alex went after Karam. If only someone could help him. But who?

Then, one day as he was walking home, blood dripping from his nose, Karam heard the whisper of a voice in his ear.

"Karam, I can help you."

Karam turned round quickly. "Who said that?"

But there was no one there. Only the icy breath of the February wind.

Karam ran all the way home. But the voice followed him.

"Karam. Karam."

He had never been so afraid.

Yet as he lay in bed that night, the voice soothed him. "Karam, Karam, my name is Jenny and I can help you."

In his dreams he asked, "How?"

And Jenny told him.

Karam went to school the next day with a spring in his step.

When Alex rushed towards him, Karam said softly, "Remember

Jenny, Alex? She remembers you."

Alex's face paled to grey. He remembered Jenny. "Jenny …
came to you?" he asked.

Karam nodded. "She says that she is my friend now."

To Karam's surprise, Alex smiled. "I am free," he said.

Karam didn't understand.

Alex explained. "Four years ago, Jenny said she was my friend.
But she's not, Karam. She makes you do bad things."

"You're lying," Karam said.

Just then, Paul appeared. Karam felt a tug on his hand. It folded
into a fist and punched Paul right on the nose. Karam tried to say
he was sorry. But the words wouldn't come.

It was Alex who helped Paul to his feet.

Karam felt himself change. He was angry. He wanted to fight.
What was happening to him?

And the winter breath of her blew in his ear. "For the next four
years, you are mine, Karam. This is a leap year … and you are
Jenny's Choice."

If you enjoyed this story, why not try some of Catherine's books:
The *Nemesis* series and *Tribes*

MISSION ACCOMPLISHED | TOM EASTON

Captain Jack stood on the uneven surface, inspecting the laser gun. It looked OK, but rattled when he shook it. The mission depended on him opening it.

Spacegirl Maisie lunged for the gun. "Let me see," she said. Jack turned away and she bounced off him and fell. Tears. Maisie had been crying most of the day, since she'd lost her favourite pink hairclip.

"Shh," said Jack. "You'll attract attention."

Too late.

"What's going on?" the alien queen shouted from below. Jack put his finger to his lips. Maisie sniffled.

"Be nice to your sister, Jack! Don't make me come up."

"Spacegirls don't cry," Jack lectured once the alien had gone quiet. "Especially when they're on a dangerous alien planet." He peered at the gun. If he could just remove the back section…

"Let me see that thing," Maisie said, bouncing up.

"No!" Jack said, swinging away again. This time he accidentally hit Maisie in the head and she disappeared off the bed. Thump.

More tears. Captain Jack rolled his eyes. How was he supposed to accomplish the mission with all this fuss? The alien queen bolted in, seized Spacegirl Maisie and looked like she was about to shoot lasers from her eyes.

"What happened?" she said. "Why are you being so horrible to your sister?"

Jack tried unsuccessfully to hide the gun.

"What are you doing with my hairdryer? Give it here!"

He couldn't let it go. The mission depended on it. The alien dropped Maisie and came for him. Jack dodged out of the way and leapt for the door. Unfortunately the alien snapped out a tentacle and grabbed his ankle. He went down and the gun flew out of his hand, cracked into a wall and broke into pieces.

"Right! You're going to your room till Daddy gets home!"

Maisie toddled towards the broken gun. As Jack was carried away, he peered over the alien's shoulder to see Maisie inspecting the wreckage. She pulled out a small pink object – the hairclip she'd lost earlier by poking it through a hole at the back of the gun.

Captain Jack winked at his little sister as the alien carried him off. Maisie smiled.

Mission accomplished.

Tom recommends:

Northern Lights by Philip Pullman and *The Hobbit* by J.R.R. Tolkien

BEN'S ADVENTURE | MARGARET FORRESTER

"Come here, Skye. We'll be late for breakfast!"

Ben called in vain. Skye had found a rabbit burrow which had to be explored. As Ben scrambled up the slope, he worried about his problem. It was Mum's birthday, and he had nothing to give her. He had saved some money from doing little jobs, but not enough.

"Darling, I don't want anything. Make me a card; I'd like that."

But Ben wanted to give her something special.

Near the top of the slope, he saw Skye pulling at something in the burrow. Exasperated, Ben tried to grab the exuberant puppy. At his feet lay a small muddy box. Curious, Ben pressed the catch and gasped. Inside was a brooch of watery brilliance, a hundred iridescent colours making tiny rainbows of light.

"Thanks, Skye." He clapped the joyful mongrel affectionately. "You've found Mum's birthday present!"

At tea time, Mum opened her presents – a silk scarf from her sister in Canada and an azalea plant from her neighbour.

"I've kept the best till last," said Mum as she opened the hand-made card leaning against the box. "I wonder what it can be…" Her voice trailed off as she saw the brooch winking in the lamplight. "Ben, where did you get this?"

The whole story came out.

"I can't keep it. It may be valuable and someone will be looking for it."

"I found it. If it *is* valuable and they lost it, they should take more care."

And Ben burst into tears with disappointment.

Next day the police arrived. Ben retold the story and with Skye, took them to where he had found the brooch. "Good work, young man," said the policeman. "This is the lead we've been looking for. Well done!"

Some weeks later, Ben received a letter. Most of the stolen jewellery had been recovered. With the letter was a cheque.

"I can buy you a brooch now!" cried Ben in delight.

"Most of this will go into your savings account," said Mum. "But come Saturday, we shall do some shopping. A small brooch for me, maybe. And how about a collar for Skye?" She paused and smiled. "And maybe a bicycle for my wonderful Ben."

Margaret recommends:
The Paper Bag Princess by Robert Munsch and *The Mousehole Cat* by Antonia Barber

THE JOY OF SNAILS | KAREN McCOMBIE

I have this thing about snails.

It's gross, I know.

But I love hunkering down on the grass and watching them *oozing* their way around the garden, all serene and calm.

"Mollie!! Come in here *now*!"

That's Mum shouting. But I'm going to ignore her. I don't want to go indoors, 'cause she's going to go nuts at me about the mess in the kitchen.

I didn't *mean* to knock over that big jar of dried pasta all over the floor. I was only reaching over to see what was in the shopping bags she'd just dumped on the kitchen cabinets.

"*Mollie!* I *know* you're out there!" Mum shouts again, sounding weary with me. She gets weary with me a *lot*.

I hunker down some more, so I'm hidden behind the rhododendron bush.

Down here, I get a great view of snails. It's a favourite spot of theirs, 'cause it's kind of rocky, and they like gliding behind the rocks when they're done with *oozing* around the garden.

And, oh – here comes my favourite snail right now! It's not like I can recognize *all* the snails in the garden – but this one's different. It's really old. Maybe as old as *me* (eight).

I know this 'cause it's *massive* compared to the others and has a really thick whorl of a shell with these amazing patterns on it. (Alex says garden snails can live to be ten years old. I believe him, though sometimes he tells me fibs for fun. I can tell when he's lying 'cause he'll finish his story with, "It's absolutely *true*!")

"Alex! Can you go and get Mollie *now*!"

Uh-oh. Alex is in trouble, 'cause he's meant to be looking after me.

Uh-oh again – I can see him looking out his bedroom window, which means *he* can see *me*.

"Mollie!" he shouts, but he's grinning, so that's OK. Still, how come he's holding that toy of mine like he's going to drop it?

I get up, lick my favourite snail goodbye, and head off to see what Alex is up to.

"Here, Mollie!" calls Alex, dropping my toy.

With a quick leap, I catch the squeaky hamburger in my mouth, my tail wagging…

If you enjoyed this story, why not try some more of Karen's books:
The *Indie Kidd* series

COPPER | EMILY SMITH

Uncle had worn the green amulet as long as Tara could remember. It was round and flat, and hung round his neck on a leather thong. Sometimes he took it off so she could gaze at the green swirling bands. But not for long. "It brings me luck," he said. "It brings us all luck."

For a long time it seemed the malachite amulet did bring luck to the people of the Green Caves. The hunting parties did well. The rains came on time.

But one year, the luck seemed to turn. Their best hunter was killed. The roots seemed fewer and thinner. Everyone was hungry.

One autumn day, Uncle set off with two other men to go to a settlement in the next valley. They hoped to exchange some skins for food.

Tara watched him tie the bundle of skins to his back. He suddenly looked old.

Uncle turned to her, holding something out. "Take this. It will bring you luck."

Tara started forward – then saw what he was holding out. "The amulet?" she cried. "But it's yours!"

Uncle placed the amulet over her neck. "It's yours now."

"You'll need it! On your journey!"

Uncle smiled sadly. "I prefer it to be here. At the Green Caves. With you."

Tara turned to see the old woman watching. She thought the old woman would say *she* should have the amulet. But she said nothing.

perstitious. Not like my sister, who never walks

n cracks in pavements.

I've done is, if I want something to happen, I

site.

upport Wolverhampton Wanderers. Sorry about

always took me to Molineux, since I was about

died a year ago, my big brother, Kevin, took me,

as with his mates and I knew he'd have a better

re.

y is, we're playing Scunthorpe, home, we should

us talk, as far as I'm concerned.

horpe thrashing *us* 6 – 0, and when we win, nice

al fluky own goal in the very last minute, I think:

did that, because I thought of the worst thing.

s didn't work, and it was the worst possible time.

none call, and I could hear Mum talking in that

s way, saying, "Not Kevin! His car? How bad?"

ay at home while they went to the hospital, but

ght, *He needs my help.*

give it. In the car on the way, try as I might, I

ture him hurt in some horrible accident.

n't do it. I *wouldn't*. I refused to imagine it.

got to the hospital, all I could think was how

had to do was picture something, and his life

Every day they [...]
night Tara piled so[...]
the skins beside th[...]

In the morning, [...]

It was not there.

Suddenly Tara re[...]
as she bent over th[...]

There was some[...]
the amulet. Or if it [...]
flat bone, and dug [...]

She stared.

It was like gold...

Tara looked up.

The old woman [...]
gleaming metal. "It [...]
changed."

If you enjoyed this st[...]
A Stain on the Stone[...]

I've never been su[...]
under ladders or [...]

The only thing [...]
imagine the oppo[...]

For instance, I s[...]
that. It's just, Dad[...]
five. And when he [...]
even though he v[...]
time if I wasn't th[...]

What they all s[...]
thrash them.

That's dangero[...]

I imagine Scum[...]
and easy, our usu[...]
That was me tha[...]

But one day th[...]

There was a p[...]
horrible bad-nev[...]

I was told to s[...]
I wouldn't. I thou[...]

But I couldn'[...]
couldn't do it, p[...]

No. Not *coul*[...]

And when w[...]
selfish I was; all[...]

would be saved.

We walked along the corridor. *This is his last chance*, I thought. *Just do it! One little picture of the worst that could happen. That's all.*

I couldn't.

Sorry, Kevin.

We reached the ward he was in. He was sitting up. He had a big bruise on his forehead. That was all. Nothing broken at all. He grinned at us.

I couldn't believe it. Everyone was so happy while I stood there in a state of shock.

Next Saturday he and I went to Molineux. Coventry. Easy game. We lost 4 – 1.

If you enjoyed this story, why not try Neil's book:
Pickers and Stealers: A Beadle's Tale

SONG OF THE RAIN | ALAN JAMES BROWN

The Music Man drummed the rain *rat-a-tat*, *rat-a-tat* on the windowpane. He drummed worms of water on to the window sill. He drummed *drip, drip, drip* on to the soft soil of the garden.

The rain said, "Play me home, Music Man, play the song of the rain."

The Music Man played a stream on his flute, rushing higgledy-piggledy down the mountain. It leaped and laughed from the craggy rocks to the valley below. Silver fishes flashed as they dashed and darted and leaped the rushing rapids.

He played a river on his fiddle, twisting and turning, twirling and swirling across the low lands. The boats on the water bib-bobbed and in their rigging was the jingle of cymbals.

The Music Man played the water all the way to the foaming swishy-swashy sea. When he struck his guitar, waves crashed and gulls screamed. Whales slapped their huge tails and boomed the horns of their spouts.

Then he played very gently on his big double bass. The whales groaned, deep, deep and sorrowful. Ships hooted in the mist as water rose with a sigh from its home in the sea. It made dark clouds that floated high in the ocean of sky.

The Music Man played a wind on his harp. It was a lifting wind, sharp with the salt of the sea. The wind carried the clouds over the ships and the whales towards the land. It carried the clouds over the twisting river with boats bib-bobbing, over the tumbling stream with fishes dashing and darting, to the gaping tops of the snaggle-toothed mountains.

Then on his piano he played a fierce storm. The sky was as black as night, the wind howled and the Music Man crashed thunder, *ca-boom! ca-boom!*

Rain began to fall. It tumbled down the mountain in torrents. It rattled on the Music Man's windowpane, *rat-a-tat, rat-a-tat*. It ran in worms on to the window sill and *drip, drip, dripped* on to the soft soil of the garden.

The Music Man threw his window wide and breathed the fresh washed air. In the sunshine he sang an arch of glowing colour from craggy mountain top to swishy-swashy sea. He sang a rainbow.

If you enjoyed this story, why not try some of Alan's books:
Michael and the Monkey King and *Billy the Hero*

A TALE OF TWO BIRTHDAYS | NINA BAWDEN

Lots of stories start *Once upon a time*. But this story is about one particularly special January day in the lives of two people who lived opposite each other in the same narrow street in North London. One was a very old lady celebrating her eightieth birthday, the other a little girl who was just one year old.

The old lady had quite a nice birthday. Her daughter cooked a roast chicken for lunch and her son and her brother and sister came to her party. They brought her presents: a bottle of scent, and a silk scarf, and a box of chocolates. But when they had all gone home and the old lady went to draw the curtains against the evening dark, she looked out of her window at the house opposite and saw that it was covered with balloons, pink ones and purple ones, fluttering and bouncing and beautiful. *How perfect for a birthday party*, she thought and then, quite suddenly, felt jealous and grumpy.

She thought for a minute. Then she remembered she had a drawer of presents she kept for her grandchildren when they came to visit her. She found a fat squeaky duck that a one-year-old person might like to play with at bath time. She found a pretty card and wrote on it. *Happy birthday. You are very lucky to have all those lovely balloons. I am eighty years old today and I wish someone had given me one!*

And she packed up the squeaky duck in some fancy paper, stuck the card on the outside and took it across the road and posted it through the letter box. Then she went home and made herself a cup of tea, and sat in a chair, still feeling jealous and grumpy. She turned on the television but there was nothing that she wanted to watch. And she had finished the book she was reading. Then she heard the letter box bang.

It was a letter from the house opposite. It said, *I hope you had a happy birthday, too. Next year you must come to my party and you can share my balloons.*

And the old lady went to bed happy.

If you enjoyed this story, why not try some of Nina's books:
The Peppermint Pig and *The Finding*

LADYBIRD, LADYBIRD | GILL VICKERY

"It's not fair!" Archie said. "Why do I always have to look after the twins?"

"I've got to take these cakes to the fête. Dad's in the garden if you need him," Mum said and whirled out, her arms full of tins filled with delicious cakes nestling moist and sweet inside. That was the good part of the village fête – the food, and Mum's cakes in particular. The rubbish part was looking after the twins. They were dressed as ladybirds for the dance they were going to do at the fete with all the other little girls from Miss Katherine's Dance Academy.

"These costumes are stupid," Molly said. (You could tell it was Molly because she had a sprinkle of freckles across her nose.)

"We want to be pink ladybirds," Polly said. "Pink is cool."

"Ladybirds are always red," Archie said.

"Make us pink," Molly insisted.

"No!" Archie said.

The twins' eyes filled with tears. Archie was alarmed: that always happened before his sisters lost their tempers and got him into trouble.

"All right," Archie sighed.

In no time at all the twins had changed into their pink tights, their pink T-shirts and their pink skirts. Archie drew big fat spots in black marker pen on the back of the T-shirts and the skirts. Then he unpinned the net wings from the red costumes and pinned them under the twins' pink arms. Finally, he jammed the little black caps with antennae on to their heads.

"Cool!" Molly and Polly chimed.

"You're in trouble," Dad said when he came in from the garden. He was right. Mum wasn't too pleased when Dad turned up at the fête with two pink ladybirds.

I'm not getting any cake today, Archie thought sadly.

Miss Katherine and the other mums weren't pleased either because when the ladybirds did their dance, everyone noticed the pink ones.

"Adorable!"

"So cute!"

"Little stars!"

Mum smiled. She ignored all the cross mums and gave Archie an especially large piece of Victoria sponge filled with her best butter icing. *Life isn't bad after all*, thought Archie, munching away. And he had really enjoyed drawing those big black spots on the twins' costumes – he'd always hated pink.

If you enjoyed this story, why not try Gill's book:
The Ivy Crown

THE NEW BIKE | ANN RUFFELL

Toby wanted a bike, but they didn't have much money. His dad liked making things, so they went to the scrapyard and found bits of bike to make into a whole new one. Dad polished it and painted it and by the time he had finished, it looked as cool as a shop-bought new one.

Kevin Povey and his gang met Toby on his way to the park

"New bike, eh?" said Kevin with a gleam in his eye. "Give us a go."

"No," said Toby. His dad said he had to stand up to bullies. But Kevin Povey was bigger, taller and stronger. And he had four mates. It didn't take long for the bike to pass from its first owner to the next.

"Watch me!" yelled Kevin Povey, steaming off down into the park. He did a crazy emergency stop by the miniature railway.

That's my tyres gone, thought Toby.

But as the bike stopped, the saddle went on, taking Kevin Povey with it. He missed the glass of the tropical plant house by inches. His gang guffawed, but stopped quickly when Kevin glared at them from painful asphalt.

"Think you're clever, eh?" he sneered. He wiped the blood from his elbow and jumped on to the pedals.

Kevin started to do wheelies, lifting the front wheel high. He managed about five before the front wheel decided it had had enough and wheelied off by itself.

"What's this, a circus bike?" mocked Kevin. His gang cheered when he rode it standing on the back wheel. He was brilliant at it until the handlebars came off.

Then the chain made a noise like the last bit of Coke when you're drinking it through a straw. The pedals fell off first, then the back wheel came apart from the frame.

It was a pity Kevin Povey had decided to do his circus act right by the boating lake. His gang carried him home dripping.

Toby collected up all the bits of his bike and took them home.

"I forgot to tighten the bolts after I painted it," said Dad, looking a bit grey. "Are you OK?"

"That was the best bike in the world," grinned Toby.

If you enjoyed this story, why not try some of Ann's books:
The Kings' Castle and *Mr. Wellington Boots: Three Magical Cat Stories*

THE TREE AND THE RIVER | NICK GARLICK

One day a river stopped to talk to a tree growing on its bank.

"You're not very important," said the river.

"Why?" asked the tree.

"Because there's millions of trees," the river replied, "and you all look alike. Nobody knows who you are. But there's only one of me and I've got my very own name. *Everybody* knows who *I* am."

"I know somebody who knows who I am," said the tree.

"Who?"

"A little boy called Emil. He comes to play every week and he sits on those two flat branches near the top of my trunk."

"How dull!" sneered the river. "I can stop all that!"

It promptly flooded its banks, washed all the earth away from the roots of the tree and bore it off towards the sea.

"Now you're just another piece of wood," said the river. "And I'm still the river."

But when it burst its banks, the river made a big hole where the tree had stood and the rest of the water gurgling along behind it poured through the gap and drained away into the fields. All that was left of the river was the part that was carrying off the tree. When it reached the sea, the waves chopped it up into tiny little bits and swirled them away to the far distant reaches of the world. Soon everyone forgot it had ever existed.

The tree drifted slowly along through the night and the day, the summer and winter, from ocean to ocean throughout the years. Its bark grew brown. It was battered and beaten by storms. But its trunk stayed the same and the two flat branches at the top were never worn away.

One day, many years later, a storm washed the tree up on to a beach. It lay in the sun, getting warm. An old man was strolling along the sands and he stopped when he saw it. He peered at it closely and poked at the two flat branches with his walking stick.

"Well, well, well," he said. "Good gracious me! *I* remember *you*!"

He took off his hat and patted the trunk.

"Hello, old friend," he said.

"Hello, Emil," said the tree.

Nick recommends:
How Tom Beat Captain Najork and His Hired Sportsmen by Russell Hoban and *Howl's Moving Castle* by Diana Wynne Jones

ALL I SAID WAS... | MICHAEL MORPURGO

I looked up from my book, and saw a pigeon on my window sill. All I said was: "Hi there, pigeon. You know what I'd like? I'd like to be you. I'd like to be able to fly off to anywhere I liked. That would be so good."

And he said: "Fine with me. Just open the window and I'll come inside. I'll lie there on your bed and read a book. I've always wanted to read a book." So in he hopped, and off I flew, out over the rooftops, and down towards the sea.

I was thinking: *Wings are best, wings are really great. This flying lark is amazing. I want to be a pigeon all my life.*

But then, as I was skimming low over the beach, the gulls came after me, squadrons of them, all out to get me. So I flew inland, over the rivers and fields. And what happened? The crows started mobbing me. So I landed in a cornfield to hide. And what happened? A farmer started shooting at me. I don't know how I got out of there, but I did.

I'd had quite enough of all this by now. I was thinking: *Books are better, a whole lot better. In future I'll just read about being a bird, I'll just imagine it. Safer that way, I'll live longer.*

I flew back to town and landed on my window sill, and there he was, lying cross-legged on my bed, reading my book. Only the strange thing was, he didn't look like a pigeon at all any more. He looked more like me! Then I saw myself in the window. I was still a pigeon! I tapped on the window with my pigeon's beak. He looked up at me.

"Hi there, pigeon," he said. "You know what? This is a great story I'm reading. It's all about a boy like me who wants to be a pigeon like you. So he does a life-swap, and becomes a pigeon. Trouble is, it turns out that he doesn't like it that much after all. That's when he finds out he can't change back, that he's a pigeon for life. Shame, eh?"

If you enjoyed this story, why not try some of Michael's books: *War Horse* and *Kensuke's Kingdom*

MAKING A SPLASH | NIGEL HINTON

Ellie wrapped the towel round herself and sat on the bench. She closed her eyes and concentrated.

She pictured the dive. She saw herself on the top board. Saw the blue water below. Saw the graceful spins and rolls she would perform. Saw her legs held dead straight as the water closed over her without a splash. Heard the applause that would tell her that all the training had paid off and she had won the competition.

There was a tap on her shoulder and she looked up.

"Better go poolside – your category is next," Mum said. She smiled and patted Ellie's shoulder. But there was something in her eyes.

"What's up?" Ellie asked.

Mum sighed. "Your father is here."

There was a jolt in Ellie's heart. Dad!

Even after six years he could still make her wish and hope – but for only a moment.

Then she would remember.

Remember how he had walked out on Mum and Davey and her. Remember how he only bothered to turn up when he could boast about his clever kids – at school plays, and football games and diving competitions.

Remember how cruel he could be if they failed. The time he had made little Davey cry after a match because he'd missed a penalty. The time he'd laughed at her art display.

So she'd better win today.

She followed Mum across the tiled floor and out on to the poolside. She sat waiting her turn. She saw nothing – just thought about her dive.

Then her name was called.

She climbed the steps and looked down from the top board.

There he was – in the front row of chairs on the very edge of the pool. Of course! Ready to stand up and applaud when she won.

This one's for you, Dad, she thought. And dived.

It was perfect. Perfect spins and rolls. Perfect. Then, as she hit the water, she deliberately flipped her legs to the left.

When she surfaced again, Dad was standing there, a shocked look on his face. His clothes were soaked and his hair was dripping.

She waved at him and swam to where Mum was waiting, like she always was, to help her out.

If you enjoyed this story, why not try some of Nigel's books:
Beaver Towers and *Buddy*

PANCAKE FACE | GEORGIA BYNG

Alice Peasbody lived in Victorian times. Her nickname was "Pancake Face". She didn't have a nose.

No nose might have been bearable if it hadn't been for the pointing, the sniggering, the looks of horror. Alice began to wear a hood and keep away from people.

One day she asked the doctor for a pretend nose.

The false nose was attached to a pair of spectacles. It was a clever contraption. The moulded, ceramic protuberance rubbed uncomfortably on her flat face, but with it on, at least Alice felt more normal, so she wore it.

At sixteen, Alice went to work as a secretary in a city. Life was better. No one knew about her noselessness. She chose the dark corner desk and kept herself to herself.

The office building had a roof garden where birds would come to sing. Only they knew Alice's secret, for, alone in the sun, she would remove her spectacles and so, her nose.

Five years passed.

One day, a handsome, sunny-natured man called Alex Crane came to work in the office. He made everyone laugh, but Alice kept to the shadows, lest he should see her false nose.

Then she grew very unhappy. Who would ever love a Pancake Face?

More and more the only things that made her happy were overhearing Mr Crane or being on the roof with the birds.

Then one bright summer evening, she found herself on the roof with the birds, surprised by *Mr Crane*.

What was more, her spectacles were on the bench! As Mr Crane walked towards her she reached for them, and, knocked, they clattered to the floor.

"It's lovely in the sun, isn't it?" said Mr Crane, joining her on the bench opposite.

"Lovely," agreed Alice. "ATISHOOOO!" She pretended to sneeze, holding a handkerchief to her face.

Mr Crane rubbed his eye. Then, to Alice's amazement, he pulled it *out of its socket*!

"They used to call me Cyclops," he said, his single eye twinkling. "What about you?"

"P-Pancake Face," Alice stuttered.

Alex and Alice Crane began a toy company a year later. Disguises For Fun, it was called. As for their own disguises, they decided never to wear them again.

If you enjoyed this story, why not try some of Georgia's books: *Molly Moon's Incredible Book of Hypnotism* (the first in the series) and *Molly Moon, Micky Minus and the Mind Machine* (the latest instalment)

MR PEPPER'S PERSONAL ASSISTANT
A traditional tale retold by SEAN TAYLOR

Mr Pepper was a very busy businessman. Every day he had papers to tidy. He had letters to type. He had clients around the world to speak to on the telephone. And one morning Mr Pepper said, "I'm getting so terribly busy I'm going to need a PERSONAL ASSISTANT."

So he put a notice in the window.

> PERSONAL ASSISTANT REQUIRED
> *Must be very good at tidying papers.*
> *Must be able to type letters.*
> *Must speak another language.*

Mr Pepper sat down on his revolving chair, feeling pleased. And he was even more pleased when there was a knock at the door.

"You've come for the job, I expect," he smiled, opening the door.

In walked a dog.

"Dogs are not allowed in my office!" said Mr Pepper. "I'm a very busy man. Shoo!"

But the dog did not go away. In fact, it raised a paw and pointed to the notice in the window.

"I'm not looking for a *dog*!" said Mr Pepper. "I'm looking for a PERSONAL ASSISTANT."

The dog nodded.

"Well, I'm sorry," said Mr Pepper, "but it says quite clearly: *Must be very good at tidying papers.*"

The dog raised its eyebrows. Then it jumped on to Mr Pepper's revolving chair and started tidying his papers. First it put all the notes, letters, reports and bills into neat piles. Then it put the neat piles into colour-coded cardboard folders. Mr Pepper had never seen his office look so tidy.

"Thank you very much," he said, "but I'm sorry. It also says quite clearly: *Must be able to type letters.*"

The dog raised its eyebrows. Then it switched on Mr Pepper's computer and started typing so quickly that its paws were just a blur. In fact, it was so good at typing that it could look out the window and whistle at the same time.

Moments later the printer gave a whirr and out came a perfectly typed letter.

"I see," coughed Mr Pepper. "That's … er … very impressive. But I'm sorry. I simply cannot give the job to a *dog*. If you look at the notice, it says: *Must speak another language.*"

The dog looked Mr Pepper straight in the eye. Then it said, "*Miaow.*"

If you enjoyed this story, why not try some of Sean's books:
When a Monster Is Born and *The Bopping Big Band*

THE MIRACULOUS BLISTER
LINDA BUCKLEY-ARCHER

Long, long ago in a country of mountains and sheep and biting winds, a shepherd's daughter, after many days of helping her father with the lambing, limped back home complaining of a sore toe. The mother settled her in front of the smoking fire amongst her younger brothers and sisters.

"Well, that's a beauty and no mistake!" exclaimed the mother as she pulled off her daughter's clogs and examined the large, grape-like swelling at the tip of her big toe. "It needs lancing, and the sooner the better."

The girl cried out as the mother cut through her skin and watched in amazement as out slipped a spherical object, blood-streaked and curiously luminous. Ignoring her daughter's tears, the mother spat on it and rubbed it on her skirts.

"Bless me! It's a pearl! The biggest I've ever seen!"

The family had full bellies for the rest of the year on the proceeds of the daughter's miraculous blister. By the time it was the lambing season again, the money was running out. The mother's heart leapt with joy as she saw the girl returning from her annual labours in the mountains, for she was wincing with every step that she took. And, sure enough, the oozing blister delivered forth another pearl, even larger than the first.

From then on the girl was sent on extremely long errands with the flimsiest of excuses and, in consequence, the shepherd's family grew very rich indeed. Fearful of their precious daughter being kidnapped, the family told no one of their secret and let it be known that a distant relative had bequeathed them a legacy. Although the girl was not particularly comely, the family's newfound prosperity ensured that she was overwhelmed with offers of marriage. Rubbing their hands at the prospect of a wealthy son-in-law, it was a doctor's hand that was finally accepted.

Weddings being a costly business, the parents rode in a carriage whilst insisting their daughter walk the fifteen miles to the church. It was a decision they were to regret, for the doctor, distressed on their wedding night to see such a thing, performed the operation that cured for ever his bride's toe and her parents' greed.

If you enjoyed this story, why not try some of Linda's books:
Gideon the Cutpurse (Part One of the *Timequake* trilogy)
and *The Tar Man* (Part Two of the *Timequake* trilogy)

DEAR GOD | VIC ROTHWELL

Dear God,

Thank you for looking after Johnny and keeping him in heaven where people are kind to him and there are angels. I didn't get to say goodbye because he fell asleep and didn't wake up and was buried when I was on holiday in Devon. I miss cuddling up with him and I love him lots and lots. I thought about him every day when I was on holiday even when I played football with my new friend Travis. Please can Johnny have a happy birthday it's his birthday tomorrow and he would like a big chocolate cake with lots of candles. Please can Johnny go snowboarding and have his favourite music. His favourite type band is heavy metal it makes his ears prick up. Can you tell him I think of him every minute and I'll never have another hamster because he was the best.

Sorry I am a chatterbox I know I am a chatterbox because Auntie Pauline says so.

Can I have a word about our house? Mum says we're going to a new bigger house but I don't want to. It's miles away and all my friends are here and it's not fair. I promise I'll be good and even sleep in Sam's room instead and he can have mine. Then we don't need to go. Please can you explain to Mum she doesn't listen to me.

Because I cut my hand and it was bandaged my teacher Mrs Jones put in my writing book "Very Good With a Bandaged Hand" but I didn't even try. I promise to try really really hard if we stay in the house because I will be good.

Please can you make Grandpa better he has a tickly cough.

God bless Mum and Dad and Auntie Pauline and Johnny and Grandpa and Travis.

God bless my brother Sam even though I don't like him.

God bless anyone I've forgotten.

The end.

Love Katie, aged 7 3/4

PS It isn't my fault my bedroom window got broken it was Sam he is a pest. We were playing cricket. Can you tell Mum she says we're both as bad as each other and it's not fair.

Vic recommends:
Utterly Me, Clarice Bean by Lauren Child and *Charlotte's Web* by E.B. White

TURTLE SOUP | SHEILA MAY BIRD

Turtle was somewhat surprised when a net fished him from the sea. One minute he was swimming, the next he was going for a ride in a boat. It was quite exciting for a lonely turtle who'd never been anywhere before.

From the boat, Turtle went in a lorry. From the lorry to a plane and finally a truck that delivered him to "Carlo's Restaurant". Turtle enjoyed his adventure and was none the wiser about what lay in store when he was handed over to Carlo himself.

"Tonight my customers will dine on turtle soup for the first time in their lives," said Carlo, as he placed Turtle in a large pot of cold water.

Turtle was relieved to be in water again, even if he couldn't swim far.

Gradually the water became uncomfortably hot. So much so that Turtle, with all his might, heaved himself out of the pot and paddled, as fast as he could, under a cupboard.

From his hideaway, Turtle watched Carlo with interest as he went about preparing tasty dishes for his customers. After a while Carlo inspected the large, now steaming pot.

Carlo had never cooked a turtle before. He wasn't sure whether they turned to mush or fell apart in boiling water. He didn't expect it to disappear altogether.

"Goodness, the turtle has dissolved," he said, taking a spoonful of the water to taste.

"Turtles have little flavour," he decided, and to improve the taste of his soup, he added an onion.

Several tastes later, culminating in the addition of carrots, beans, potatoes, lentils, mushrooms, herbs and garlic, Carlo was satisfied that his turtle soup was ready to be served.

The soup was a great success!

Much later, while delighted Carlo was washing up, he noticed Turtle.

"Well, I owe you a great deal, little fellow," he said, picking Turtle up and putting him in a sink to swim.

And so, Turtle and Carlo became the best of friends. To make his turtle soup, Carlo popped Turtle into the cold water at the start of cooking, but before it got warm, he took him out again.

Carlo became rich and famous, and neither of them told anyone their secret.

If you enjoyed this story, why not try another of Sheila's books:
Doctor Witch's Animal Hospital

HOW TO STICK OUT YOUR TONGUE A REALLY LONG WAY | FIONA DUNBAR

The Louisiana Leapfrog Academy is the best school ever, because there you actually *win prizes* for sticking out your tongue. Yes, really! Oh, but you have to be a frog to go there. You're probably not a frog; sorry.

Sticking out your tongue is a pretty essential life skill if you are a frog, because that's how you catch flies. If you can't do it, you starve.

Nathan can't do it.

Nathan can leap, swim, croak, make his eyes disappear when he swallows … pretty much everything, except fly-catching. This means he always has to eat flies caught by other frogs, which is frankly not brilliant either for Nathan (yucky saliva from other mouths) or for other frogs (all work, no reward!).

Eventually, the Louisiana Leapfrog Academy have had enough. "Nathan," they tell him, "we're sending you off alone into the Massive Muddy Meandering Mississippi River. You get hungry enough, you'll find a way to catch those flies."

At first, Nathan feels pretty good. He leaps, he swims. He croaks with joy. Oh, the freedom! But then he gets a tummy-grumble like not-so-distant thunder. He meets a gaggle of Creole toads. "Will you catch something for me?" he asks. But they just spit at him and say, "Allay, you ugly gren-wee vert!" This is how Louisiana Creole toads always speak.

Nathan is furious; no one has ever been so rude to him! Nor

has Nathan ever been rude himself – not since he was a tadpole and didn't know any better. Nathan does a big, angry "GWOOOORK!" at the Creole toads, but they just laugh their smug toady laughs at him.

So Nathan draws himself up, gathering all the saliva he can muster, and – SPLOOTCH! Out comes a ball of spittle. And with it – his tongue! Swift as an arrow, and long as a Louisiana multicentimillipede. Which is *long*. Long enough to catch a very delicious damselfly that happens to be passing at that moment. Nathan's eyes pop up with froggy surprise. He pulls back his tongue, and *gulp!* he swallows it. It is the yummiest damselfly Nathan has ever tasted.

Result: three slimy, embarrassed Creole toads. Also, before long, the Louisiana Leapfrog Academy Fly-Catching Award for Nathan!

If you enjoyed this story, why not try some of Fiona's books:
Pink Chameleon and *Blue Gene Baby*

BEWARE! | FRANCES THOMAS

A tiger is on the prowl
in the hills tonight.
Beware! Beware!

The long long grass she's flattening
her yellow eyes aflare
and the monkeys stop their chattering
to see her there.

The grass is all ashiver
and all the trees are bare
and there's not a place to hide from her.
Beware! Beware!

The grey wolf stops her hunting
to sniff the air.
Her babies all are sleeping
curled up in their lair.
But till she's safely home with them
they must all
beware.

The snake lifts up her head
and stares her emerald stare.
She's not afraid! *She* doesn't care!

(But she slips into the bushes,
it's safer there.)

The birds send out a warning.
It clatters through the air.
It's not safe until the morning.
Beware! Beware!

The antelope stands frozen.
It is more than he can bear.
If he's the one who's chosen
there's no safety anywhere.

She's looking out for something
with her yellow yellow glare,
she's looking out for some*one*.
But where? But where?

Through the dark dark village
she pads, as light as air,
past the shuttered, silent houses
and the boy who isn't sleeping
sees her passing there.
Beware! Beware!

She's stalked throughout his nightmares,
her name he'll scarcely dare

to whisper to the forest…
And now – she's there!

If he called now – they'd come running
with guns and knives to snare.
If he called now, there'd be gunshots
resounding through the air.
She's a menace – she's a danger.
And yet he cannot bear
to see her torn and dead and bleeding
with her velvet coat so rare.
So he watches, and he watches.
And soon she isn't there.

In the morning he'll remember.
It is a tale he cannot share
of her fierce and scary beauty
how she passed beneath the moonlight,
and of all the sleeping village
only he could see her there.

There's a long way to go,
and the stars are everywhere,
but her paws are soft as velvet
and her breath comes quiet as air.

Till she slips between the rocks

to the secret cavern where
tired and cold and hungry
and starting to despair
little ones are waiting.
She's there! She's there!

If you enjoyed this story, why not try some of Frances's books:
Supposing… and *Megan the Detective*

BACK TO SQUARE ONE | ROB CHILDS

I jump out of my sports car and gaze at the little football pitch. This is where it all began, my soccer career, and I've not seen it since the day I left school.

I cross the playground and stroll into the building through the main entrance, something I'd never done before. Us kids always had to use a side door.

The head, Mrs Parker, greets me.

"So glad you could come today, Mr Castle," she says. "Or may I call you Conrad?"

I nod. "Prefer it to Connie – my nickname here. Short for unconscious," I explain. "'Fraid I was a bit of a daydreamer in class."

"But not in games," she smiles. "The children are really looking forward to meeting our most famous old boy, who's now captain of England."

"Feels so strange to be here again after all these years," I admit.

"It must bring back many memories. Happy ones, I hope."

"Sure," I lie, grinning.

She leads me along the corridor towards the hall and I stop as we reach *Scruffy's* old room. It's empty, but I see the floor is still covered with large black and white tiles, making it look like a giant chessboard.

Scruffy Scrivens!

I can picture him now in his tatty cardigan, crumpled shirt and food-stained tie.

I stare at the black square in the far corner of the room where I spent most of my time in his class – in the *bad-boy* chair with its little wobbly desk.

Square one, he called it.

"Go back to square one, Connie. That's where the black castle sits in chess," he'd say, making a double pun on my name and colour. "Out of trouble."

Not that I minded. There was a good view of the playing field.

"I remember *this* room well," I mutter, pulling a face. "Used to be…"

I nearly say *Scruffy's*.

Then the weirdest thing happens. I see a shadowy image of old *Scruffy* sitting in my corner and glaring towards me.

"Mr Scrivens' room," says the head, perhaps thinking I'd forgotten his name. "I'm afraid the poor man died exactly a year ago today. He was found slumped at a desk over there by the window…"

If you enjoyed this story, why not try some of Rob's books:
Black and White and *B.A.S.E. Camp*

CHERRY BLOSSOM | KAREN WALLACE

When Cherry Blossom was born she was tiny and wrinkled and nobody thought she would grow. Poor Mrs Blossom didn't know what to do.

"Put her out in the garden," said Mr Blossom. "She needs sunshine and somewhere warm to sleep. Soon she'll be strong and lovely."

The next day Mrs Blossom wrapped her daughter in a white quilt and pushed her pram under the cherry tree. But even though she was warm and there was lots of sunshine, Cherry Blossom didn't grow.

One day a green bird stuck a bunch of cherries on top of the pram. They sparkled like rubies in the sunshine.

"Can I build my nest in your pram?" she asked.

Cherry Blossom nodded and that moment she decided to grow. Mr and Mrs Blossom couldn't believe their eyes. Everyone thought it was a miracle.

When Cherry Blossom was too old to sleep in her pram, she played in it. Sometimes it was a castle and sometimes it was a ship. But she always left room for the green bird to make her nest.

Winter came. Cherry Blossom knitted tiny sweaters with her mother. She painted the pram with her father. Because Mrs Blossom was going to have another baby and Cherry Blossom wanted a brother or a sister more than anything else in the world.

When Charlie Blossom was born, he was tiny and wrinkled. But Mr and Mrs Blossom didn't worry. They wrapped him in a white quilt and put him in his pram under the cherry tree.

Spring turned to summer. The blossom turned to cherries. But Charlie Blossom still didn't grow.

One night Cherry Blossom dreamed she was a baby again. She remembered the green bird and the shiny cherries and the moment she decided to grow.

So Cherry Blossom picked a bunch of cherries and hung them from the top of Charlie's pram. The sun was shining and the cherries sparkled like rubies. That moment, Charlie Blossom decided to grow. At first, no one could believe their eyes. Everyone thought it was a miracle.

And maybe it was.

Cherry Blossom loved her brother more than anyone else in the whole wide world.

And love can make anything happen.

If you enjoyed this story, why not try some more of Karen's books: *The Diamond Takers* and *The Man With Tiger Eyes*

A COW CALLED CAITLIN | SIAN PRICE

Zac's wearing eight jumpers; he can hardly bend his arms. Mark's walking backwards and nearly fell in the school pond! Phoebe's doing a sponsored hop, but mine is the best plan of all. *I'm* going to sit in a bath of beans! Well, I'm going to stand in a bin of beans because we don't have any baths at school. I bet you're wondering why I'd do such a thing.

It all started when Mrs Jenkins showed us a video. It was of an orphan school in Africa. The children were so poor that most of them didn't even have a pencil to write with.

"Couldn't we do something to help?" I asked. "Could we send them books or a computer?"

Mrs Jenkins smiled. "That's an excellent suggestion, Caitlin."

She told us about a charity that helps people in Africa by buying them the things they need like books, crops or even animals like goats and cows.

"It costs eight pounds for two books," said Mrs Jenkins.

"We could raise more than that," said Zac.

"Easily!" shouted Mark. "Let's buy them a cow."

Everyone agreed. And that's how I came up with the bath idea.

My brother's lent me his wetsuit. He asked me to wash the beans off afterwards, and I'm wearing my swimming goggles in case a bean hits me in the eye when I jump in. As I walk towards the bin in the playground, I'm feeling a bit nervous, but I just picture the orphans on the video and leap right in. It's not as bad as I thought.

The beans are cold and feel funny under my toes, but it's worth it when everyone claps. I stay in the bin for a whole hour and Zac says, "Caitlin's one of the bravest people I've ever met."

Mrs Jenkins came into class looking very excited today. "Class eight, I have a special letter to share with you." It was from the school in Africa. Phoebe cried when Mrs Jenkins showed us the picture of the orphans with their cow. I felt a bit emotional myself. And guess what? They've asked us to name it. I wonder how everyone would feel about Caitlin.

Sian recommends:
Sticky Beak by Morris Gleitzman and *Love That Dog* by Sharon Creech

THE PORTAL | ADRIENNE KRESS

Before I tell you I've found a portal to another world, can I begin by saying it really is no big deal? Don't get all, "You have a portal to another world in your bedroom! That is so cool!" Because it really isn't. See? There you go, even after I just – like this second – just said not to think anything of it, you're still getting excited.

You won't be excited when you have to crawl under my bed and up between two springs in the mattress to get there. It really hurts. It does. OK, and don't ask how I found the portal in the first place, because the answer is just embarrassing.

And you so won't be excited when you meet Stan. Who is Stan? Didn't I already tell you? Well, Stan is the sole inhabitant of my other world. The only single other creature there aside from when I go and visit. Yeah. My best friend, Harvey? He gets to lead armies in his world. And his sister? Well, she is the queen of an entire island. A really big one. Then there is my cousin Todd, who discovered that, through the trapdoor in his basement, there exists a world which only he can save by bringing some magical amulet or something across several mountain ranges, an enchanted forest, and a desert. It's OK, he has a wizard and an elf helping him. He's been gone for two weeks now. Got to miss the maths test. So not fair.

But me? My world? It can hardly be called a world. It's a room. A bare room with no door or anything, and no windows. Only Stan. He is this troll-like goblin-thing. Kind of grey. Snot-coloured, you know? And all he does is sit and read yesterday's paper. It's always yesterday's paper. And he only shares the financial section with me. Even when he's done with the comics, he just sits on that part of the paper to make sure that I can't grab them from him. But, I mean, he's already read them!

So OK, I'll take you through the portal, but don't get all excited and ... stuff.

...

...

What do you mean, "It's cool!"?

If you enjoyed this story, why not try Adrienne's book:
Alex and the Wigpowder Treasure

THE MAGICAL SNOWMAN | EMMA MURRAY

"Wait, please wait," Charlie cried as he ran after the bus. He ran and ran but it was no good.

For weeks he had been dreaming about the trip to the funfair with his class. Roller coasters, waltzers and – his favourite – the biggest slide in the world. Now he was going to miss it all. Shoving his hands in his pockets, he stomped on the snow as he walked home – crunch, crunch, crunch.

As he reached his street, he almost tripped on a big orange carrot lying in the snow. Puzzled, he picked it up. Then he saw the sight ahead and it all became clear.

It was a snowman. The biggest one he had ever seen. But when he went closer, he saw the poor snowman had no mouth, no nose and only one eye. Looking at the carrot, Charlie knew he could fix the nose, but what about the rest?

He ran into his house and hurriedly explained everything to his mother. She went and fetched a bag of raisins.

"This will put a smile back on the snowman's face," she said.

Charlie carefully put the raisins on the snowman. Then he found an acorn for the eye. Finally he gave the snowman his nose.

"There you go, Mr Snowman," Charlie said, placing his hand on the snowman's icy shoulder.

Then something strange happened. His hand felt odd, sort of numb and tingly. As he shook it, there was a giant flash of light, so bright that he had to shut his eyes tightly.

When he opened them, he saw a huge slide made of ice, all the colours of the rainbow, stretching high into the sky. He looked at his hand, then the snowman. It was magic!

Charlie ran over to the slide and *whoosh*! He slid all the way down, tumbling into the soft snowdrift at the bottom.

When his classmates came back from the fair, they played on it too. Everyone agreed that Charlie's slide was the best they had ever seen.

The next day, the sun came out. Both the slide and snowman had disappeared. Charlie was sad, but happy that he had something even more amazing to dream about.

Emma recommends:
The Very Hungry Caterpillar by Eric Carle and *Superfudge* by Judy Blume

ALIEN WELCOME STOMP | DINAH CAPPARUCCI

The astronauts went to Planet Mars and came back again. They were sorry to say that it was mostly red dust and not really worth the trip. What they did not say was that they had stopped off at another planet on the way back, which is camouflaged and not visible from Planet Earth. This planet had been a lot better, with proper green aliens that waggled octopus-like arms, and skinny ones with leaf-shaped, slanty eyes, and some other well-known types.

As the astronauts parked their spaceship on the invisible planet, the aliens cheered and waved and threw their hats in the air.

The astronauts were invited to a special alien welcome dance and (kind of) enjoyed a concert of native alien music. There was a barbecue in their honour, on a beach of green dust where the water was red and yellow stripes. Later they went for a paddle and the aliens stole their trousers, for "a laugh".

When, finally, the astronauts were tired, they lazed on gnodlibooms[1], watching the planets spin and sparky silver stars whizz across a violet sky.

Basically the astronauts were fooled into a false sense of security.

The aliens were in their "costumes", which were disguises they knew the astronauts would like. Their real bodies were oozing and repulsive, but invisible to the astronauts because they appeared at a very high light frequency and showed elsewhere in the cosmos (shocking some microscopic life forms into premature extinction).

That night, when the astronauts were sleeping in the alien pyjamas which they'd borrowed, the aliens stole their helmets and jumpers to add to the trousers.

And this is what the aliens wore when they landed on Planet Earth.

The humans waved and cheered as the astronauts walked down the ladder from the spaceship. Beaming officials escorted the astronauts into the changing rooms. One asked, "Would you like me to help get your helmet off?"

"No," said the astronaut.

The aliens locked the door of the changing rooms and dumped their astronaut clothes on the floor. Then, disguised as human traffic wardens, they began the invasion of Planet Earth. If you see one, you must stamp on the squashy tentacle inside its boot.

If you enjoyed this story, why not try Dinah's book:
Aliens Don't Eat Dog Food

[1] Gnodlibooms, from the Alienize. No equivalent translation.

THE JEWEL OF THE NIGHT | P.R. MORRISON

On a clear winter night many, many years ago, a shooting star swept across the sky. It travelled from north to south and then east to west, trailing an arc of golden stardust.

"Look at me!" it called out. "I am the brightest and most beautiful star in the sky. See how I shine!"

The other stars soon grew tired of its boasts.

"It takes more than one star to light up the sky," they said, but the shooting star would not listen.

"You are jealous of my beauty," it replied. "You will never shine as brilliantly as me. I light up the darkness. I am the jewel of the night." And off it sped again, pushing the smaller stars aside in its haste.

"Slow down. Don't be in such a hurry," they pleaded, but the shooting star laughed and travelled faster still. "How can I slow down when all the sky needs my glorious light?"

The vain and selfish shooting star was so dazzled by its own beauty that it failed to see it was on a collision course with Earth. It was travelling so fast and so blindly, it had no time to change direction, and it crashed in a spectacular shower of glittering sparks that flickered and died. Its golden glow was no more.

The shooting star looked around at the cold dark mountain top it now lay upon and asked, "What will the night sky do without me now?" But when it looked upwards, to its surprise it saw millions of twinkling stars, and all of them were just as bright and just as beautiful as it had once been.

"It takes more than one star to light up the sky," it said sadly.

The star had learned its lesson, but it was too late. It could never return to the sky. Instead it would have to lie alone for ever on that bleak mountain top, an ordinary lump of grey rock that not even the sun's rays could make beautiful. But on clear nights, when all the stars came out and the full moon bathed the mountain in its silvery light, the star imagined it was a sparkling jewel once again.

If you enjoyed this story, why not try another of P.R.'s books:
The Wind Tamer

No matter how hard Darren worked, he could not get ahead. Although he worked hard at school, he was always bottom of the class. And after twenty years with an international company, he was still dusting desks and sweeping floors.

"This is terrible," he said despairingly. "I've got to get ahead."

"There's a shop in Brumwich selling them," said his wife.

So Darren went to Brumwich.

"I've got to get ahead," he said to the salesman.

"Yes, I can see that, sir." The salesman looked at him with pity. "We have a marvellous selection here. May I suggest the ever-popular David Beckham model," he said, taking it from the shelf.

As soon as he tried it on, Darren knew it was for him. And just as he had expected, when his wife saw it, she wanted to get ahead too. So she went to Brumwich and came back looking like Victoria Beckham.

From that moment, everything went brilliantly for Darren. He got a new job and made huge amounts of money. He moved to a big house and drove a Rolls Royce.

But then something terrible happened. As he was exercising in his private gym, his head fell off and shattered.

"I'm sorry, sir," said the salesman in Brumwich when Darren showed him David Beckham's head in pieces, "we don't have any more like that. The fashion today is for the ugly look: piggy eyes, big red nose, warts – just like the head you used to have."

Darren was desolate. He couldn't go back to his job and his wife with his old head. His life was in ruins.

And then he had a brilliant idea.

"Give me a cat's head," he said. "One with a first-class pedigree?"

"May I suggest this beautiful Persian cat, sir," said the salesman. "And the body to go with it."

"Excellent," purred Darren.

In time he became the pampered pet of the Duchess of Dewdrop. And since he was extraordinarily beautiful, he appeared in TV advertisements for cat food and kitty litter.

He never saw his wife again, but he heard that her head had also fallen off – and she had become a handsome little corgi adopted by the queen.

If you enjoyed this story, why not try some of Bowering Sivers' books:

The *Jammy Dodgers* series

The queen checked the king's diary. "Aargh!"

The king slunk away, his buttons done up wrongly, torn slipper flapping and crown over one eye.

"What's up, Your Majesty?" asked her maid, Tally.

"The king's mother's coming on a state visit," moaned the queen. "The clot didn't tell me!"

"So what's wrong?"

"She's Empress of the Seven Islands. She has seven palaces and seven hundred servants dressed in white!" The queen pulled chunks of her hair loose. "The king will go mad if we don't impress his mother."

"But the palace is perfect," said Tally.

"It's not the palace!" said the queen. "It's you lot! All you servants look as if you've just tobogganed through a hedge!'

Hark who's talking, Tally thought.

The queen ordered new uniforms, which arrived the day before the visit. Tally gave everyone a sharp haircut.

But next morning, the queen exploded when she saw her servants. "You're all crumpled and rumpled! You didn't hang up your uniforms! You haven't brushed your hair! The empress will arrive in *one hour*!"

"Calm down, Your Majesty," said Tally. "Edna," she said to the head housemaid, "fetch soap and cloth and get scrubbing."

"Scrubbing what?" said Edna.

"Faces."

Tally fetched the ironing board and said, "When your faces are clean, iron your uniforms. Do it properly or I'll iron them with you inside!"

She stuffed cotton wool in both ears and whipped out a large comb. "Then I'll get your knots out," she said, "and I won't hear any screams!"

When everyone was smart and sparkling, Tally beckoned to the queen. "Your turn now!"

Minutes later, everyone lined up outside to greet the Empress of the Seven Islands. The queen held out her hand. "Welcome, Empress."

"Where's my son?" demanded the empress.

The king bounded out. "Here, Mummy!"

The empress gasped. "What *do* you look like!"

As usual, the king's crown was wonky and his hair stuck out in tufts. He had egg on his chin *and* waistcoat, his shoelaces were undone and his trousers torn.

Tally bit her lip and whispered to the queen, "We made everyone perfect for the visit, but—"

The queen nodded and, just before she fainted, said, "We forgot the king!"

If you enjoyed this story, why not try some of Valerie's books:
The *Toby Tucker* series and *The Princess Files*

FROM: peterpiper@aob.net
TO: support@mooresstores.com

I placed an online order with you last week for a 6-volt Handi Shinybrite torch. It arrived this morning. Unfortunately, it is sealed inside tough, see-through plastic packaging, which I can't get into. Any suggestions?

FROM: support@mooresstores.com
TO: peterpiper@aob.net

Thank you for contacting the support team. Your custom is very important to us.

We are sorry to learn you have had difficulty with the packaging on your Handi Shinybrite torch. Have you tried scissors?

FROM: peterpiper@aob.net
TO: support@mooresstores.com

My scissors are somewhere at the back of a deep, dark cupboard. That is why I need the torch.

I have tried to get into the packaging using a nail file, a barbecue fork, a kitchen knife and my teeth. So far this has resulted in a trip to Accident and Emergency because the knife slipped, and one to the dentist because I broke a tooth.

FROM: support@mooresstores.com
TO: peterpiper@aob.net

Thank you for contacting the support team. Your custom is very important to us.

We are sorry that you are experiencing ongoing problems. Our packaging is designed to protect our products so that they always reach you in perfect condition.

FROM: peterpiper@aob.net
TO: support@mooresstores.com

That's all very well – the torch IS, I believe, in perfect condition, which is more than I am since I started to open the packaging. I have a flesh wound that required stitching and a gap in my front teeth. I also have a broken nail file, a bent knife and a barbecue fork with one prong missing.

Why can't you people put your stuff in packaging that normal people can open without sophisticated cutting equipment?

FROM: support@mooresstores.com
TO: peterpiper@aob.net

Thank you for contacting the support team. Your custom is very important to us.

Extensive market research with focus groups indicates that our customers demand robust packaging. However, we have noted your comments.

Maybe you should consider buying some new scissors.

FROM: peterpiper@aob.net
TO: support@mooresstores.com

Thank you for your suggestion. I have bought some new scissors to open the packaging around the torch that I bought to find my old scissors in the first place.

The new scissors are sealed inside tough, see-through plastic packaging, which I can't get into…

If you enjoyed this story, why not try some of the two Steves' books:
Mind the Door! and *Star Bores*

KATE AND THE ALIEN | MATTHEW BRADLEY

Kate met an alien in the street.

The alien looked very like Kate. She had two arms, two legs, one head with long brown hair, and two blue eyes. She was wearing a school uniform, but Kate knew that she was an alien because she had big green teeth!

"Hello," Kate said to the alien.

"Hello," the alien said. "I'm Jay."

"What are you doing here on Planet Earth?" Kate asked.

"I'm waiting for my dad," Jay said. "He's late!"

"You can come and wait at my house if you like," Kate said. "We've never had an alien round before."

"Thanks," said Jay.

"Keep your mouth closed in front of Mum, though," Kate said. "If she sees your teeth, she might go crazy and call the police!"

Mum was in the kitchen.

"This is Jay," Kate said.

"Hello, Jay," Mum said.

Jay shut her mouth. Tight.

"Is she all right?" Mum asked.

"She's fine!" Kate said. "But her mouth hurts. She burnt her tongue on some hot peas at lunch time."

They went upstairs to Kate's bedroom. Kate showed Jay her teddy bear, Oscar.

"Urgh!" Jay said. "He's weird. I have bears, but they've got two heads, five eyes, eleven paws with claws, and big green teeth!"

"Your bears sound scary," Kate said.

"No!" Jay said. "They're cute." She picked up a pair of purple mouse slippers. "I like these," she said. "My pet mice are purple."

"Your planet sounds strange," Kate said.

They went into the garden. Kate showed Jay how to cartwheel across the lawn. Jay showed Kate how to bite with big green teeth. Jay bit a hole in the garden fence.

Then…

The sky went dark and the sun disappeared. A flying saucer flew right over the house!

"What on earth is that noise?" Mum called.

"Nothing!" Kate shouted. "It's just Mr Thompson's lawnmower!"

"It's my dad," Jay whispered. "I've got to go."

The flying saucer was parked in the street.

"Goodbye," Jay said. "You should visit my planet. I think you'll really like it. But you'll have to keep your mouth shut."

"Why?" Kate asked.

Jay grinned. "Because if you don't, they'll see your big white teeth and call the police!"

Matthew recommends:
Woof! by Fritz Wegner and Allen Ahlberg and *The Scarecrow and His Servant* by Philip Pullman

A TASTELESS TALE | KATE O'HEARN

Hannibal wasn't like any other caterpillar in the world. He hated eating leaves.

Crawling beside his friend Cecil, he asked why they didn't eat meat.

"Simple," Cecil explained. "We don't have teeth. Besides, we're supposed to eat leaves."

"But I hate them," Hannibal complained.

"Well, that's all there is for us."

Hannibal wasn't satisfied with this. Leaving Cecil, he went looking for other things to eat. Soon he came across a grazing cow. *People eat cows*, he thought. *So will I.*

Crawling up the cow's leg, he reached its back and tried to take a bite. But like Cecil said, he didn't have the teeth for it.

Hmmm, thought Hannibal. *Maybe I can't eat a cow. But I'll find something else.*

As he continued searching, a large bird suddenly swooped out of the sky and landed on the ground before him. Pecking at a bunch of leaves, it caught Cecil in its sharp beak and swallowed him whole.

"Good heavens!" cried Hannibal. "That bird just ate Cecil! I think I should eat him."

Racing as fast as his many short legs could carry him, Hannibal ran up behind the bird and pounced on its foot. Opening his mouth extra wide, he tried to take a big bite.

"What are you doing down there?" the bird asked curiously.

"Eating you," Hannibal answered. "You ate Cecil, now I'm eating you."

"Don't be silly," laughed the bird. "I'm supposed to eat caterpillars. You're supposed to eat leaves."

"I hate leaves," complained Hannibal. "I want to eat meat."

"Well then, have you tried caterpillars? They're awfully good."

Hannibal paused from his chewing. "No. But it wouldn't be right. I know everyone around here."

"Suit yourself," said the bird casually. "But if you ask me, there's nothing nicer!" Flicking Hannibal off his foot, he flew away.

Left alone, Hannibal wondered how a caterpillar might taste. Knowing he could never eat a friend, he looked down at his back foot and decided to take a little bite.

"Ouch!" he howled.

When the pain faded, Hannibal realized that caterpillar tasted awful. Sighing, he limped over to some greenery. Liking them or not, he finally agreed that caterpillars were indeed meant to eat leaves.

If you enjoyed this story, why not try one of Kate's books:
Shadow of the Dragon, Part One: Kira

THE LOST TICKLE | ENID RICHEMONT

"I've got a new game," said Lucy. "It's called PASS THE TICKLE."

She gave Mum a tickle and Mum wriggled and giggled.

"Now you've got to pass it on," Lucy told her. "That's how you play."

Mum gave Fred a tickle and Fred hooted and tooted.

"Go on. Pass it on now," Lucy told Fred.

Fred gave Sarah a tickle and she chuckled and squealed.

"Pass it on now," Lucy told her. "You could give it back to me."

So Sarah gave Lucy the tickle, and Lucy squeaked and jumped about.

Then Lucy passed the tickle on to Auntie Pam.

But Auntie Pam didn't wriggle or squiggle or giggle.

"Oh dear, I think I've lost my tickle," Auntie Pam cried.

Lucy started looking for Auntie Pam's tickle.

She looked into drawers and under tables.

She looked behind cushions.

She looked inside the fridge.

She looked in the dustbin and she looked in the shed.

She looked behind the flowerpots, but the tickle wasn't there.

Lucy asked Cleo the cat.

"Have you got my Auntie Pam's tickle?"

But Cleo rolled over. "Got my own tickle," she purred. "Try it. It's right here on my tummy."

Lucy asked Maisie the hen.

"Have you got my Auntie Pam's tickle?"

But Maisie just poked under her wing with her beak. "I've got a flea," she squawked. "So who needs tickles?"

Lucy tried Wendy the goat.

"Have you got my Auntie Pam's tickle?"

"I've got this thistle," munched Wendy. "I don't need a tickle."

Lucy tried Oscar the gerbil.

"Have you got my Auntie Pam's tickle?"

"I'm making this wheel go round," puffed Oscar. "I'm too busy for tickles."

Then Lucy heard chuckles.

They came from inside the carrycot.

She ran over to check.

Her baby brother, Tim, was chuckling and gurgling, and there, on his tummy, sat Auntie Pam's tickle.

"Found it!" cried Lucy.

Auntie Pam came running.

She picked it up. "Yes, that's my tickle!" she cried.

Auntie Pam smiled.

Then she giggled.

She just couldn't stop laughing.

And baby Tim just went on gurgling and chuckling.

"He's got his own tickle," said Lucy. "So he can play, too. Come on." She tickled Mum. "Let's start all over again!"

If you enjoyed this story, why not try some of Enid's books:
Plop City and *Billy and the Wizard*

PROMISE | THOMAS BLOOR

The old woman woke with a start. The fox was there. He was down at the end of the garden. His coat was of pale rust and his eyes were amber, and utterly inhuman.

The old woman stamped, shook her fist and made an angry hissing sound. But the fox would not scare. He got to his feet, slowly, and disappeared through a hole in the fence.

The old woman ate a slice of bread for lunch. In the afternoon she slept in her chair again. She dreamt of years ago, when she was a young woman. She dreamt of the last time she saw John.

He stood by the window in his uniform, looking out into the garden. It was the day before his unit left for service overseas.

"I know what you're thinking," John said. "You're thinking, 'What if he never comes home?'"

She said nothing. But it was true. He always knew.

"I will come home," he said. "I promise you. One way or another and no matter how long it takes."

Again, the old woman woke up suddenly, her heart pounding and the blood singing in her ears. The fox was outside. He was looking in at the window, up on his haunches, his black forepaws resting on the sill.

The old woman turned her back and went into the kitchen. She made herself a cup of tea, rattling the kettle and slamming the sugar bowl. When she came back, the fox had gone.

That night she couldn't sleep. She remembered playing the piano, many years before, with John sitting nearby, listening.

"Do you suppose we'll sit here together when we're old?" she said.

"Of course," said John. "We'll sit by the fire and dream."

In the morning the old woman undid the latch on the window and opened it wide, as far it would go. She turned on the television and sat nodding in her chair.

When she awoke, the fox was there. He lay at her feet, stretched out in front of the fire. His black paws twitched and his whiskers flickered as he dreamt his fox dreams.

The old woman smiled, closed her eyes, and fell back to sleep.

If you enjoyed this story, why not try some of Thomas's books:
The *Worm in the Blood* trilogy

ALICE | GRAHAM MARKS

The small boy reached up and took his mother's hand as they began to climb up the steps which led to the dark red front door of the biggest, strangest, oldest house he'd seen in his whole life. He was going to visit his grandfather and great-aunt; he had been before and knew that while they weren't exactly big, they were the strangest, oldest *people* he'd ever seen, too.

Inside this house it was always quiet, and quite unlike any other house he'd been into. Everything was dark – the heavy swoop of velvet curtains, the carpets covered with patterned, tasselled rugs, the ornate furniture and the wallpaper – and when shafts of sunlight did break through, like golden swords, they were always full of a swirling ballet of dust motes.

Somewhere, he knew, his grandfather would be waiting; he always had to go and shake hands with the tall, thin, white-haired man who would stand looking down at him through dusty gold-rimmed spectacles. Once he'd seen his grandfather, his mother would then take him to be inspected by his great-aunt, who was in another room, somewhere else in the house. But today was different.

"She's not well," his mother told him as she took him through the museum silence of the dining room and into the sunny warmth of the morning room, which smelled delicious.

"Time for tea!" beamed Alice, who was small and round, like a country loaf of bread; he often wondered why his grandfather and great-aunt made someone so nice live downstairs.

They sat at a table Alice had laid especially for them, and he ate freshly made scones, home-made strawberry jam, and honey that had crystallized, all of which Alice had brought up from the kitchen; he didn't drink tea, but what his mother called milk-and-a-dash (although he did have it in a proper cup and saucer), and the tall brown chairs scratched the backs of his legs. He'd been told this was because they were stuffed with horsehair, and he did wonder why they hadn't used something softer.

When they left to go home it was Alice, from the kitchen, underneath the stairs, who waved them goodbye at the front door, smiling.

If you enjoyed this story, why not try some of Graham's books: *Omega Place* and *Kaï-ro*

CUDDLES COST NOTHING | KES GRAY

Danny had gone to the toy shop with 50p to spend.

"How much is that remote control car?" asked Danny.

"40 pounds," said the toy shop owner.

"Oh," said Danny.

"How much is that stunt kite?" asked Danny.

"19.95," said the toy shop owner.

"Oh," said Danny.

"How much are those bongos?" asked Danny.

"9.99," said the toy shop owner.

"Oh," said Danny.

"How much is that puppet?" asked Danny.

"20 pounds," said the toy shop owner.

"Oh," said Danny.

"How much is that Toxic Volcano Kit?" asked Danny.

"24.99," said the toy shop owner.

"Oh," said Danny.

"How much is that laser sword?" asked Danny.

"5.99," said the toy shop owner.

"Oh," said Danny.

Danny placed his 50p back in his pocket and looked sadly at all the shelves of toys.

"How much money have you got to spend?" asked the toy shop owner.

"It doesn't matter," sighed Danny, closing the toy shop door behind him.

When Danny got home he walked quietly upstairs to his bedroom and sat miserably down on his bed.

"What's the matter, sweetheart?" said Danny's mum, walking into his room.

Danny sighed and then covered up his eyes.

"It just isn't fair," he sobbed. "I went to the toy shop to spend my 50p but I couldn't afford anything I saw. Everything I wanted was too much money, or loads of money, or even more money than that. It is so unfair. All the best things in the world cost so much money to buy. I never have enough for anything special."

Danny's mum sat down beside him on the bed.

"Is there anything special that I can do?" asked his mum.

"No," sniffed Danny.

"I think that there is," smiled Danny's mum.

Danny's mum put both her arms around Danny and gave him the biggest cuddle in the world.

Danny's heart raced like a racing car, soared like a stunt kite, beat like bongo, fizzed like a volcano, danced like a puppet, and shone like a laser.

"How was that?" smiled Danny's mum.

Danny wiped the tears from his cheeks and smiled.

"Better," he beamed.

"Good," said his mum.

"And guess what!" beamed Danny. "And I've still got 50p left!"

If you enjoyed this story, why not try some of Kes's books:
Eat Your Peas and *Billy's Bucket*

THE OVERCOAT | FRANK RODGERS

It was a bright, cold winter afternoon a long time ago. On our village street, the bare trees stood shivering on their patches of frozen grass.

I was seven and my sister Rosie was nine. Wrapped up in coats and scarves, we were playing on the pavement outside our house.

An old man slowly came towards us. We knew everyone in our little village, but this person was a stranger. We were curious. We wondered where he had come from and where he was going.

As he came nearer, we noticed how thin he looked. His big bony head stuck out of his threadbare jacket like a turnip on a stick. His watery eyes were fixed on the ground ahead of him. He was trembling.

Rosie and I stood aside to let him pass. But just as he drew level, his legs seemed to give way, and he slowly fell to the ground.

Alarmed, we fetched Mum and Dad. They helped the old man to his feet and brought him into our kitchen. Mum and Dad made him strong, sweet tea, bacon and eggs, baked beans and buttered toast. It was just what he needed.

He told us he had walked twenty miles that day and had twenty more to go. Without a penny to his name, he was walking to the city to find his long-lost sister.

Dad gave the old man five shillings for his bus fares, although I knew he couldn't really afford it. He also gave the old man his overcoat.

The old man thanked Mum and Dad for their kindness and shook hands.

We all walked with him to the bus stop and waved goodbye.

We never saw him again.

Six weeks later Mum and Dad received a parcel. Inside was Dad's coat. In the pocket was five shillings and a letter from the old man's sister.

She said her brother had died the previous week. But he had died contented. If it hadn't been for us, she said, they would never have found each other again.

I'm an old man myself now. My mum and dad and Rosie are gone.

But I'm still here.

And I still have the overcoat.

If you enjoyed this story, why not try some of Frank's books:
Mr Croc Rocks and *Eyetooth*

A SMELLY STORY | MARGARET McALLISTER

The kitchen bin was overflowing, and beginning to smell nasty. Potato peelings and half-eaten slices of pizza were pushing the lid off. Somebody took the rubbish out and put it in the dustbin. It was a hot summer, and getting hotter every day.

That dustbin was getting dangerous. Mouldy bread and rotting peaches lurked at the bottom. There were plate scrapings, bad bananas, fish scraps, meat bones, sour yoghurt, and a sock. There was an old egg in there, a nappy, and something unpleasant that had died under the sink. The summer grew hotter, and the smell grew into a slinking, slithering stink. Fumes crept down the path. Soon it was powerful enough to heave the lid right off the dustbin and escape. By this time the pong was even stronger, a looming, lingering, long pong, spreading across the garden. It was a King Kong of a pong.

Flowers wilted and died. Earwigs rolled on their backs with their legs in the air. Hedgehogs curled up. So did the nettles. The people in the house kept the windows closed. The cat refused to go through the cat flap and the man next door collapsed.

Summer days passed. The King Kong pong knocked sparrows out of the trees and pigeons off the roof. The postman no longer came to the door. He threw the letters over the wall and ran. The frogs left the garden and complained to the council. The fence dug itself up and escaped. The gnomes packed up their fishing rods and wheelbarrows and moved three streets away.

Along came a bin man with broad shoulders, hairy arms, and

gloves thicker than a fireman's boots. "This one is a bit niffy," he said as he picked up the dustbin and emptied it into the bin lorry.

The air became clean. There was no smell any more except the scent of roses and honeysuckle. The hedgehogs uncurled. The birds and frogs returned. So did the gnomes. The cat came out and the man next door came home from hospital. The dustbin was washed with bleach. The bin man was awarded a medal.

In the kitchen, on a hot day, somebody scraped plates into the bin...

If you enjoyed this story, why not try some of Margaret's books: *Never Wash Your Hair* and *The Worst of the Vikings*

"Look what I've got!" Emma called to Joe.

Joe stuck his head through the gap in the hedge between their gardens. He peered at the ball of fluff in Emma's hands.

"What is it?" asked Joe.

"My new pet mouse," said Emma. She stroked the soft grey fur. It wiggled and Emma grinned. "I've got the best mouse in the world."

Joe shrugged. "I've a better mouse."

"No you haven't."

"I've had a mouse for ages and ages," said Joe.

Emma shook her head. "Prove it!"

Joe turned towards his back door. "Follow me."

Emma twisted through the gap in the hedge and followed Joe inside. Joe ran up the stairs to his room. Emma went more slowly, careful not to frighten her mouse.

Joe pointed to the desk in his room. "There's my mouse."

"Huh!" Emma snorted. "That's silly. A computer mouse isn't a proper mouse."

"My computer mouse is better than your furry mouse," said Joe.

"Prove it!" said Emma.

"My computer mouse doesn't need feeding," said Joe.

"I like feeding my mouse," said Emma.

"My mouse doesn't pee or poo. It doesn't smell," said Joe. He held his nose. "Pooh!"

Emma sighed. "OK, so cleaning out its cage isn't fun. But my furry mouse can make cute little squeaking noises."

"My computer mouse can click," said Joe.

"I can cuddle and talk to my furry mouse," said Emma.

"So what?" said Joe. "Your mouse can't understand you."

"How do you know?" asked Emma.

Joe laughed. "Its brain isn't big enough."

"Well, at least it has a brain. Your computer mouse is just a lump of boring plastic."

Joe gave Emma a hard stare. "With my mouse I can play games and discover all about the world. Your furry mouse doesn't even know what a computer is."

"I bet it does," said Emma.

"Prove it!" said Joe.

Emma carefully put her little mouse on the desk. With tiny black eyes it stared at Emma and twitched its nose. Then the furry mouse scuttled on to the keyboard. It jumped and somersaulted over the keys. Tap, tap, tap… Words appeared on the computer screen.

Reel ferry mice r BEST!

"Your mouse can't spell," said Joe.

If you enjoyed this story, why not try one of Paeony's books:
No More Yawning!

THE UGLY COW | LOU KUENZLER

There was once a gentle brown cow named Daisy.

She produced plenty of thick, creamy milk. And NEVER kicked the farmer when he milked her.

But the farmer did not appreciate Daisy.

His name was Sid. And he was grumpy and mean. He teased Daisy because she had one rumpled, crumpled ear, which looked a bit like a cauliflower.

"You're an ugly old cow, Daisy!" he said. "I ought to take you to market and sell you."

So, Sid tied a rope around Daisy's neck and led her down the road.

Around the first bend, he came upon a little old lady with warts on her nose.

"She's uglier than you are, Daisy!" giggled Sid.

But the old lady looked up at Daisy and smiled.

"That's a fine cow you have there, farmer," she said.

"An ugly cow!" scoffed Sid. "I'm taking her to market to sell."

"I'll buy her off you now," said the old lady. "I'll give you three beans."

"Three beans!" Sid was about to tell the old woman to stuff the beans up her ugly, old nose, when he remembered something…

Of course! There was a story his mother had told him when he was just a lad.

I know how this works, thought Sid. *I give the old lady the cow. She gives me the beans. But they are magic beans. I plant the beans.*

And a tall beanstalk grows. I climb the beanstalk, kill the giant who lives at the top and steal his all gold. Then, I WILL BE RICH! RICH! RICH!

"It's a deal!" said Sid. "You can have the ugly cow!" He grabbed the beans and ran home.

In time, a beanstalk *did* grow … slowly! It grew about as tall as Farmer Sid's waist. It had six broad bean pods on it. The beans made a nice enough stew – but there was nothing magic in them.

Unlike Daisy!

As the old woman led her round the corner, Daisy turned as pink as a pomegranate and flew up to the sky. Gold coins rained down while Daisy turned somersaults in the clouds.

"Yippee!" cried the little old woman. "A magic cow! And all for three beans! Fancy that!"

Lou recommends:
The Last Polar Bears by Harry Horse and *The Stone Mouse* by Jenny Nimmo

THE TRUE ORIGINS OF KING KONG
JEREMY STRONG

Everyone has a mother and King Kong was no exception. His parents were Mr and Mrs Kong, naturally. Mr and Mrs Kong were big, BAD gorillas. They lived on the planet Threa, which is like Earth, but bigger. Everything on Threa is bigger, especially gorillas and stories.

Animals rule Threa and humans are used as pets, though they are very difficult to house-train and not at all obedient. They interfere with things and mess everywhere and won't clean up after themselves. (Not much different from Earth, then.) Mr and Mrs Kong didn't like this, and they preferred to play with Barbie dolls instead. (Giant Barbies.)

They liked these dolls so much they would steal them from shops, and soon they had a collection of hundreds. But of course eventually they were caught. As punishment, they were banished from Threa for ever. This meant they were forced into a space pod, stuck inside an asteroid and blasted into space. Tough.

The asteroid hurtled through space until it hit Earth's atmosphere, where it burst apart. The gigantic asteroid pieces fell on Siberia in 1908. (It's true – look it up.) Meanwhile the space pod carried on until it landed in the Pacific Ocean, near an island.

The Kongs – and by the way, Mrs Kong (also known as Queenie) was pregnant – waded ashore. They had been allowed just one Barbie between them. They made their nest on the island, and that is where Baby Kong was born. He wasn't called

King Kong until he was grown up. King Kong and the Barbie doll were inseparable. But one dreadful day it was stolen by a passing bird. (A roc – the same bird that kidnapped Sinbad – what a rascal!) King Kong was absolutely gutted to lose his Barbie doll.

This was soon followed by another terrible tragedy. His parents died. And so he grew up all alone. Then, one day, visitors came to the island, humans. King Kong didn't like them much, but one of them, a woman, looked just like his Barbie doll. He'd found his Barbie! He was overjoyed and immediately set out to steal her. And that's how the whole thing started. You know the rest of the story.

If you enjoyed this story, why not try some of Jeremy's books: *My Brother's Famous Bottom Gets Pinched* and *Beware! Killer Tomatoes*

THE PARACHUTING FROG | NICK GARLICK

One day, a frog called Max found a toy parachute beside his pond.

"Let's go for a ride!" he said to his friends.

"Frogs don't fly," his friends replied. "Stay here. We're going to have worms for supper. And flies for pudding!"

But Max didn't listen. He wanted an adventure. So he climbed into the harness and waited for a gust of wind to pluck the parachute into the sky. When it did, he flew right over the houses, past the trees and all the way up to the clouds.

Window cleaners gasped. Birds skidded to a halt. The pilots of passing planes scratched their heads in amazement. Max waved politely to them all as he drifted over the city.

Soon everyone was watching the sky, and by the time he eventually dropped back to earth, huge crowds were waiting to greet him. His picture was in all the papers. TV stations queued up for interviews. The prime minister paid a visit, and even the queen telephoned to offer congratulations. Soon there wasn't anyone in the world who hadn't heard about the parachuting frog.

Reporters begged to write his biography. He was offered his own chat show. Film stars argued about who would play him in the film being planned.

But Max missed his friends. He missed his pond and the mud at the bottom he curled up in for a nap after lunch. He missed going for a swim whenever he felt like it. The carpet in his hotel room was dry. He couldn't reach the taps in the shower to turn on the water. Room service didn't even serve worms or flies.

He said he wanted to go home.

"No!" gasped the reporters.

"You can't!" cried the prime minister.

"Think what it will do to your career!" pleaded the film stars.

Everyone was shouting and telling him what to do, so he hopped off to his room for some peace.

That's when he saw the parachute, still lying on a chair. Soon he was floating happily over the city, back to the pond, where his friends welcomed him home with wet, squelchy hugs.

And they all had worms for supper and flies for pudding.

Nick recommends:

The Phantom Tollbooth by Norton Juster and *The Voyage of the Dawn Treader* by C.S. Lewis

JITTERY JEEPERS | CHAE AND EILIDH STRATHIE

Once upon a time there were two little ghosts – Jeepers and Creepers.

Creepers loved scaring people.

He scared boys, he scared girls, he scared mums, he scared dads, he scared dogs and he scared cats. He even scared goldfish right out of their bowls.

But Jeepers didn't like scaring anything. In fact, he was a bit frightened of boys, girls, mums, dads, dogs, cats and even goldfish.

But the thing he was most scared of was … the dark.

He always slept with the light on.

The other ghosts made fun of Jeepers. They called him Jittery Jeepers.

One night Jeepers and Creepers were floating round town when suddenly Creepers spotted a dark doorway.

"Let's go in and find someone to scare," he said.

"No way!" said Jeepers. "It's far too dark."

Creepers started laughing. "Ha ha! Jittery Jeepers! What a scaredy-ghost."

Jeepers was so embarrassed that, even though he was terrified, he followed Creepers into the dark building.

They couldn't see much, but before long they came to a big red curtain. Creepers stuck his head through and took a peek.

"Wow!" he said. "There are loads of people on the other side. I am going to give them the biggest fright ever."

Then he put on his most horrifying face and took a deep breath, ready to shout "BOO!"

But before he could do anything the curtains lifted up by themselves and a bright spotlight shone on to the two little ghosts.

They were on a stage in a theatre – slap bang in the middle of a fabulous show!

Creepers got the fright of his life. He screamed, burst into tears and flew right out of the door!

But Jeepers was in his element – he loved bright lights, after all.

He laughed with delight and did a loop-the-loop above the stage. The audience began clapping and cheering. They had never seen such amazing special effects.

"Pssst!" said the theatre manager. "Little ghost, I'll put your name up in lights if you come back and perform every night."

And from that day on Jeepers was a star.

The other ghosts didn't make fun of him any more – and they never called him Jittery Jeepers ever again.

If you enjoyed this story, why not try some of Chae's books:
The Tickle Tree and *My Dad!*

COYOTE AND THE FIRE WITCH | TAFFY THOMAS

The people of the tribe were freezing. They were freezing because they didn't have any fire. The only fire in the land was at the top of the mountain and was owned by the Fire Witch. She guarded it jealously.

The chief of the tribe sent Coyote to steal the fire. Now, Coyote was a bit like Daddy Fox; he was crafty. He took some friends with him on the mission and set off up the mountain with Chipmunk, Frog and Brown Bird. They crept up on the Fire Witch's teepee.

Coyote seized a brand of fire and set off down the mountain, pursued by the witch. As the witch caught up with Coyote, he tossed the fire to Chipmunk. Chipmunk bravely caught the fire, but it lashed across his back, burning three or four black and white scars. To this day you can still see three or four black and white stripes across the back of every chipmunk. Even baby chipmunks don't know why they're there, but we do.

Chipmunk scuttled down the mountain with the Fire Witch close behind. As the witch caught up with Chipmunk, he tossed the fire to Frog. However, frogs are notoriously bad at catching, and the fire landed on the frog's tail, burning it clean off. So to this day, no matter where you travel in the world, you will never find an adult frog with a tail.

Frog hopped down the mountain with the Fire Witch close behind. As she caught up with Frog, he tossed the fire to the last of his friends. Brown Bird caught the fire under one wing and flew in a circle. The fire was so hot it scorched his breast, burning it bright red. Ever since that day he has been called Robin Redbreast and he lives on both sides of the Atlantic.

Robin tossed the fire back to Coyote, who bravely carried it into the middle of the village and presented it to the chief of the tribe. He set the fire in the middle of the village, and from that day, not just that tribe but all the tribes of the world have had warmth, hot food, music and stories.

If you enjoyed this story, why not try some of Taffy's books: *Farmer Merryweather's Cow* and *A Fearsome Giant*

YELLOW RABBIT | TERESA FLAVIN

On the way to Madrid airport, Ashley said, "I left my yellow rabbit at the hotel!"

"We can't go back or we'll miss our plane," answered Daddy. "I'll phone the hotel later."

Ashley pouted, and when they got home she made Daddy call the hotel in Spain. He asked the manager to find Yellow Rabbit and to call him back.

"Don't get too hopeful, Ashley," said Daddy. "But maybe we'll be lucky."

Ashley hugged her teddy and wondered sadly where Yellow Rabbit was.

In the hotel, Maria the cleaner found Yellow Rabbit. When she finished working, she sat the rabbit on the table in the staffroom as she left. Nobody paid it any attention except for Ramon the handyman.

I'll have some fun, he thought.

When Maria, Ana and Beatriz arrived for work in the morning, Yellow Rabbit wore a top hat made from a cork.

"That rabbit is no boy!" said Ana. She made a dress from a plastic bag and tied it around Yellow Rabbit.

"She needs a tiara," said Beatriz, and she pulled a pink scrunchie on to Yellow Rabbit's head.

"And jewellery," added Maria. She tied a sparkly earring around its neck.

The next day Ramon made a tiny sombrero and string sandals

for Yellow Rabbit. Beatriz crocheted a frilly flamenco dress. Ana tied bracelets of silver elastic around its arms.

Soon they had made Yellow Rabbit lots of outfits, including a swimsuit and a fur coat.

Every day Ashley asked if the hotel had called. Every day Daddy hugged her and said no. Ashley imagined her rabbit in a skip somewhere and cried into her teddy's fur.

One day a Christmas card arrived from the hotel. In the photo the cleaners posed around a yellow rabbit in an elf suit. Daddy hurried to phone the hotel.

A week later a parcel came for Ashley. Yellow Rabbit was inside, lying on top of a cereal-box wardrobe full of outfits. It wore a raincoat over its flamenco dress and held a paper umbrella and a note.

Ashley kissed Yellow Rabbit and read the note out loud. "Thank you for letting your rabbit stay with us. She missed you! Love, Maria, Ana, Beatriz, Ramon."

If you enjoyed this story, why not try some of the books Teresa's illustrated:
Fly High! The Story of Bessie Coleman and *Pushing Up the Sky*

THAT'S WHAT I WANT | CAROLINE PITCHER

When Ruby put her bike back in the shed, she noticed a gap in the fence.

Through the gap she saw a cage and in the cage was a white rabbit, with eyes as pink as pomegranate seeds and ears like ice-cream scoops.

"Oh," she cried. "You're gorgeous!"

Ruby asked her mum if *she* could have a rabbit.

"No. They scratch and poo," said Mum. "A rabbit is a real responsibility."

"That's what I want," said Ruby.

The rabbit was always in the cage.

"They never let you out," whispered Ruby. "If you were *my* rabbit I'd give you a parsnip."

One night, the wind roared around, banging things together. Tiles flew off the roof. Branches snapped off trees and sailed across the garden.

When Ruby went to fetch her bike, she heard scrabbling in the corner of the shed. Behind a sack of compost was the rabbit with eyes of pomegranate pink. She was trembling and her whiskers flickered.

"I'll get you food and water," said Ruby resolutely. "I shan't give you a name, Raquel, because you're not mine."

So Raquel Rabbit lived in the shed. They played on the grass in the glorious summer days. Ruby had to stop Raquel eating the best plants.

On Saturday, Ruby's dad headed for the shed for his lawnmower. There was a silence, then a roar.

"Ruby! That's next door's rabbit, not yours!"

Soon the doorbell rang. There was another mum and girl on the doorstep.

"It was the storm," said Ruby. "If you don't want the rabbit—"

"It's ours," said the other mum.

But the other girl said, "Auntie gave it me. I don't want it." She pointed at Ruby's pink plastic beauty salon and whispered, "That's what *I* want."

"There's lipsticks missing," admitted Ruby, "and the straighteners are bent."

"It's still what I want," said the girl.

"And the rabbit's what *I* want," cried Ruby. "Swap you?"

"Done!" cried the girl, and they shook hands.

"You can't do that," said the mums.

But neither of them could think why not.

So the girl, whose name was Paige, had the make-up salon and Ruby had Raquel Rabbit.

Both of them were happy, and sometimes they played together.

If you enjoyed this story, why not try some of Caroline's books:
The Littlest Owl and *Mariana and the Merchild*

THE FAIRY CUPBOARD | MARIAM VOSSOUGH

Guess what? I'm locked in a cupboard! Don't worry, no one's actually locked me in here. The door's stuck. My dad's gone to fetch his tools. Crazy, eh?

I've got this big cupboard in my bedroom that goes right underneath the loft stairs. It's cool 'cause it has a tiny little door, so it's kind of hidden away. My mum's been super nagging me to tidy it up. Now she says I can't go to the cinema unless I de-junk it.

This is so embarrassing, but I used to think that fairies lived in here. Stop laughing, I was only five!

At night, I'd lay out my flowery tea set for them. It'd take me for ever to get all the knives and forks straight. Now, this was the tricky bit, I'd take one cup at a time and tiptoe to the bathroom. I'd fill it with water and try to sneak back without spilling any. Then I'd carefully break a piece of my bedtime biscuit on to each plate. Sometimes I'd get the furniture out of my doll's house so they'd have comfy seats to sit on. Totally mad?!

No way ... I think I can see a tea set back there. Hold on...

Yep, it's the same one! There are still crumbs on the plates!!!

I used to write notes to them as well (why am I telling you this?). It must have been my mum who wrote back, but she'd never admit it.

News alert! I've found a note in the tea set. This is super-cringey. Listen...

dear fairees
I carnt find my favorit wand cud u help luv rose

And underneath it says...

Dear Rose,
Your wand is in your dressing-up box. Please write again if you need help with anything.
Love,
The Cupboard Fairies

Well, fairies, I need help getting out of your blooming cupboard!
YOU. WILL. NOT. BELIEVE. THIS. The door has just opened! All by itself. My dad's not here or nothing. This is seriously spooky.
It can't have been. No way.
Right, I'm not going to think about it. I'll just get on with sorting this mess out.
I think I'll keep the tea set, though. Just in case...

Mariam recommends:
The Hobbit by J.R.R. Tolkien and *Fungus the Bogeyman* by Raymond Briggs

ESSA AND THE MARSH-HORSE | KATY MORAN

Essa drew in his breath when he saw the new marsh-stallion: milk white he was, and full of fire, standing a little apart from the mares. They let men ride on their backs and the stallion was not sure if they were true horse-folk, or something else. He stood still, frozen, ears flattened, when Essa came near. Here was one of those cruel two-legged beasts who had roped him in, snatched him from the wide marshlands. He had kicked hard at them, towering on his hind legs, biting, afraid and desolate. He would serve this one just the same if it came any nearer.

Essa climbed up the wooden fence, leaning in, calling with all his heart to the stallion, *Come, friend. Oh, I'm sorrowing for you. I know how it is not to be free.*

Back in the village, they said the new stallion was unbreakable, his spirit too wild. They said it would be better to spill his blood at midsummer, turn the horse over to the gods and let Loki ride him across the night.

Fools, Essa thought. *It's not breaking: it's knowing.*

The sun sank, spreading fire where the land met the sky. It shaded the web of cloud pale gold, shadowing a thicket of hawthorns. Essa's hair blew back from his face but he barely felt the chill. In one swift move, he sprang over the fence and stood within the corral. The mares lifted their heads and gazed, impassive, but the marsh-stallion wheeled away, mane flying, paler than the foam on the crest of a wave.

Easy, my friend, easy. Essa held out his hands, head lowered, and in that moment, Essa's spirit flew free from his body, like water spilling from a fallen cup. He was the horse: the stallion's fear and anger rushed through him, sour and festering. Essa felt the wild heat of the stallion's spirit flickering all around as though he were bathed in flames.

We shall be friends, brothers, you and I.

And Essa was standing by the fence once more, just a boy. But the marsh-horse had come closer. Right up to Essa, he walked, the fire of him burning steady now, burning peacefully.

If you enjoyed this story, why not try Katy's book:
Bloodline

LEAP DAY | CECI JENKINSON

When the world was young, a wizard looked after Time for the First King. They understood that sometimes days are fast and sometimes slow and that the less you fiddled with Time, the more you would have.

But when the First King died, the New King wanted Change. He summoned the wizard and said, "Every day must contain exactly twenty-four hours."

"Why?" asked the wizard.

"It is tidier. Take these Time-clippers and go."

The wizard hovered above the year and told the months what the New King had said.

"I will come round now and trim all your days," he said.

"Not *my* days!" cried January. "I am the first month. My days should be the longest."

"Your days, too," the wizard told January.

"Not *my* days!" shrieked March. "I am the New King's favourite month. My days should be the longest."

"Your days, too," the wizard and January both told March.

The wizard flew down and started clipping. January and March screamed when their days were trimmed and, once the wizard was past May, began to squabble. Poor February, stuck between them, was pulled back and forth until a whole day was torn off at either end. When the wizard reached the gap between December and January, he put down his basket of clippings and went to comfort February.

Now, in March there lived a hare. "I want those clippings," whispered March to the hare. "Creep the long way round to the basket, pick it up and leap back here over January and February. Your leap will be admired by everyone and I will become the longest month."

So the hare crept to the end of December, picked up the basket and leapt. But when his long shadow passed over February, the wizard looked up and saw him. At a snap of the wizard's fingers, the hare came crashing down in the middle of February.

While the hare limped home in shame, the wizard gathered the pieces of Time and counted them.

"There are enough for one day," he said, "but only every four years. It will be February's day, so that every four years March will have to wait an extra day to begin."

If you enjoyed this story, why not try Ceci's book:
The Mum Shop

KNIGHT OF OLD | JANE CLARKE

Sir Rusty Creakalot was watching young knights getting knocked off their horses.

"I'll show you how to do it!" he muttered.

"Grandpa!" Princess Wimple shrieked. "You can't joust! You're much too old!" She led him into Old Castle to join the feast.

After the tournament, the young knights drank their mead and fell asleep.

"I'll show you how to do it," Sir Rusty mumbled.

"Grandpa!" said Princess Wimple. "You can't stay up late! You're much too old!" She tucked him in bed and read him a story from the *Knightly News* about a dragon sighting near New Castle.

"I could hunt that dragon," Sir Rusty told her.

"You can't hunt dragons at your age!" said Princess Wimple. "You're much too old!" and she blew out the candle and went downstairs.

"I'll show you I'm not too old!" Sir Rusty muttered, picking up his old lance. "I'm going to New Castle to hunt that dragon!"

He crept down the winding stairs of the turret, tiptoed past the feasting hall where Princess Wimple was eating up the leftovers, and headed for the stables. There, he clambered up on his old horse, and slowly, very slowly, they rode out of the castle.

"Watch out, dragon!" he shouted. "Here comes a Knight of Old!"

*

Dawn was breaking when Sir Rusty arrived at New Castle. The dragon was in the courtyard, chasing round the squealing young knights.

"I'll show you how to vanquish dragons!" Sir Rusty tilted his lance towards the dragon.

The dragon's eyes glittered and it bared its fearful fangs. There was a terrible shriek.

"Grandpa!" Princess Wimple galloped up. "You can't fight dragons at your age…"

Too late. The dragon opened its huge mouth and swallowed Sir Rusty.

"*Yuck!*" the dragon spluttered, spitting him out. "This knight is stale. I can't eat him, he's much too old!"

The dragon flew away in disgust.

Sir Rusty picked himself up and shook himself down.

"Grandpa!" Princess Wimple threw her arms round him. "You're much too old to be eaten by a dragon."

"You may be right." Sir Rusty grinned at Princess Wimple and the new knights. "But I got rid of that dragon. I showed you how to do it!"

If you enjoyed this story, why not try some of Jane's books: *Gilbert in Deep* and *Stuck in the Mud*

PET PAINT | PAEONY LEWIS

Poppy stared at her birthday present.

"I hope you like the paints," said Dad.

"Yes, thank you," said Poppy. Although Poppy felt like saying, *I wish you'd bought me a pet, like you'd promised*. But she didn't.

Poppy went to her room and opened her new paints. The bright greens and reds shone and gave her an idea. Poppy painted a pet. A parrot.

Suddenly Poppy heard, "Smelly parrot! Squawk!"

Poppy stared at her picture. It didn't move.

"Smelly parrot. Squawk!" said the voice, and that's when Poppy saw a red and green parrot fly through her open window!

Poppy rushed to find Dad.

"Look! I painted a pet and now it's real."

Dad shook his head and nodded to the lady at the front door. "Sorry," said the lady. "The parrot belongs to me. I've been chasing him down the road and I saw him fly in your window."

So Poppy painted another pet. She used three shades of soft brown.

Before the paint had dried, Poppy heard Dad yell. She ran to find him, and that's when Poppy saw the monkey. It swung from the lamp and was three shades of soft brown.

"That's my pet!" said Poppy, waving her painting.

"No," said Dad. He pointed at the headline in his newspaper: "Monkey Missing From Zoo".

Poppy groaned. Dad went to telephone the zoo and Poppy

returned to her paints.

This time Poppy painted an ordinary black and white pet. Then she used the finest brush to paint a name and a number in bright purple. "Now you're definitely mine," she whispered.

Poppy waited to see what would happen. She waited all morning. She waited all afternoon, until finally Dad peeped in her room and said, "Happy birthday!"

He grinned and held out a black and white puppy with big ears, just like in Poppy's painting.

"It's Suki!" squealed Poppy.

"How did you know her name?" asked Dad. "This was meant to be a surprise."

Poppy cuddled Suki. "I just knew." Just like Poppy knew that the collar tag had Suki's name in bright purple, and their telephone number too.

She tickled Suki's ears. "Maybe one day I'll paint you some kittens," whispered Poppy.

If you enjoyed this story, why not try another of Paeony's books: *Best Friends or Not?*

BEWARE THE LURKER-SNATCHER | MIRIAM MOSS

Ploops are small, soft and as silky as seals. They live in burrows on the banks of streams and have unusual musical powers.

"I'm going swimming on my own!" announced Plip one evening.

"You know small ploops don't swim alone," said Ripple, his mother. "You might get caught by the great, green, pike-toothed lurker-snatcher. It is as long as your father and deadly dangerous."

"Let's make a den outside instead," his sister Hum suggested.

"Good idea," said Ripple, sliding a pondweed pie into the oven. "But remember, when you hear my harpsireed, it's time for supper."

Plip waited until Hum wasn't watching, then he slid down the velvety mud of the bank and disappeared underwater with a neat *plop*. He skimmed in and out of the drifting pondweed, watched rainbow-fish dance to his wife, showered under a small waterfall and then climbed on to a lily pad for a rest. He didn't notice the heron-bird freeze in the shallows and the ducks hurry away to safety as the great, green lurker-snatcher eased its way downstream towards him.

From the bough of the weeping tree, blue-flash bird watched Hum searching desperately up and down the river for her brother.

"Have you seen my brother?" Hum asked anxiously. Blue-flash bird arrowed downriver, in a line of electric blue, and hovered above Plip asleep on the lily pad. Hum rushed downstream – but then stopped dead when she saw the dreadful lurker-snatcher slide into the deep green shadow under her brother.

Suddenly the river filled with soft music. It was Ripple playing her harpsireed, calling them in for supper. Hum knew what to do. She would do what she did best. She started to hum, and skilfully wove a sleep-spell in and out of her mother's music.

Soon the lurker-snatcher's eyelids drooped and a line of snore bubbles flowed to the surface. Quietly Hum lifted Plip off the lily pad and took him home.

Moonlight woke the puzzled lurker-snatcher. Sour-faced, it slid off downstream to where the dark waters tumble into white. The Ploops ate their supper, safe in their warm burrow, and, as the moon rose over the misting river, they fell fast asleep in a happy Ploopish pile.

If you enjoyed this story, why not try some of Miriam's books:
Scritch Scratch and *Bare Bear*

MUG'S NEW TEETH | CHAD PIRANHA

One day Mug the caveman was trying to eat a mammoth when his friend Den popped in.

"Enjoying your supper?" said Den.

"No!" said Mug. "It's as tough as old boots and hurting my teeth something rotten!"

"Why don't you cook it?" said Den.

"What a good idea!" said Mug.

"And why not kill it, too?" said Den.

"Shuckth!" said Mug. "I hadn't thought of that!"

But it was too late. The mammoth had broken all of Mug's teeth.

"No matter!" He shrugged. "I'll juth grow me thum more! Teethy come, teethy go!"

"No need!" said Den, offering Mug a new set of gnashers.

"By gum!" said Mug. "Where did you get them?"

"To tell the tooth," said Den, "I found them in a giraffe's bottom. Try them!"

Mug put in the teeth.

"How do they feel?" said Den.

"Snarty glob lobble!" said Mug.

"Excellent!" said Den. "That will be five million shiny pebbles! I'll see you again in six months."

"What's a month?" said Mug.

Sadly, Mug soon became fed up to the back teeth with his new gnashers. For starters, they kept falling out when he was chasing mammoths. And there is nothing worse than squabbling teeth. Unkind people also called him "Goofy". And when he was wearing the teeth, they called him even worse!

One day Mug met a sabretooth tiger who was looking very down-in-the-mouth because it had left its teeth embedded in a giraffe's bottom.

"Here, have mine!" said Mug, taking pity on the tiger as it gave his leg a vicious suck.

The tiger was delighted. The teeth couldn't stop grinning either.

When Mug got home, Den was waiting for him with a new set of teeth which he'd just chiselled from the finest flint.

Mug put them in, then snapped playfully at Den's left elbow.

"Owch!" said Den.

It was love at first bite.

The teeth lasted Mug for ages. And after he was finally eaten by that extremely ungrateful sabretooth tiger, they lasted for lots more ages: the Stone Age, the Bronze Age, the Iron Age...

Nowadays, they're displayed in the Britsh Museum, next to the mammoth-hair chest wigs, the clam-shell hearing aids and the fish-scale contact lenses.

Chad recommends:
Dead Famous: Leonardo Da Vinci and His Super-Brain and *Johnny Catbiscuit and the Abominable Snotmen*, both by Michael Cox

LUTHER'S POT | CHARLOTTE HAPTIE

Once upon a time there was a boy sitting at the back of the art class, working very hard, making a pot.

His name was Luther.

Luther didn't talk to anyone, he didn't look at anyone, he just kept shaping and smoothing the clay, making sure there were no cracks.

Everyone else went home.

Luther made two handles for his pot. It was almost round, like a pumpkin with a hole in the top.

"Time to go now," said Mr Watkins, the art teacher. "Is this a special pot?"

"It's a present for my sister," said Luther. "She's a baby. She was born and she came home and then she had to go back into the hospital. She's in the hospital now."

"I'll be very careful with it," said Mr Watkins. "I'll fire it in the kiln over the weekend. You come back on Monday morning."

"Thanks," said Luther.

He checked the pot all over again. Then he went home.

Luther's mum and dad were both at the hospital all weekend visiting the baby. His big brother made the dinners, but Luther wasn't hungry. When he went back to school on Monday, he was wearing his pyjama top under his sweater by mistake.

"I'm not surprised," said Mr Watkins. "You're so worried about your baby sister. Even your pot knows all about it. Look—"

Luther couldn't believe his eyes. The pot was rocking and

jiggling by itself.

Mr Watkins picked it up and it almost bounced right out of his hands.

"Don't drop it!" cried Luther.

Very slowly, Mr Watkins tipped it upside down.

Luther gasped in amazement.

All sorts of noises were pouring out of the pot.

…A baby crying, doors banging, an ambulance siren, hospital machines buzzing and beeping…

All mixed together and pouring out of the pot in a horrible, churning whirlpool of sound.

At last, everything went quiet.

"What a lot of worry," sighed Mr Watkins. "Now, let's hear what else this very special pot has to say…"

He held the pot to Luther's ear.

Luther waited. Then he heard breathing.

Very gentle, soft breathing.

"She's sleeping," whispered Luther.

And he knew, for certain, that everything was going to be all right.

If you enjoyed this story, why not try some of Charlotte's books: *Otto and the Flying Twins* and *Otto in the Time of the Warrior*

ON A LEAP DAY | DAVID SEBASTIAN

Adam was twelve, and bored. Bored, bored, bored. When Adam was bored, Adam was odd, and when Adam was odd, he'd have a bath. In the bath, he'd wish he were a fish, or a frog, or a crocodile, or a snake, sssSSSSSsss. It was February 29th, a leap day. Nobody saw Adam again. His parents didn't see or hear anything, except strange gurgling sounds. Nobody knew what happened to him. Adam had shut the window and door as he always did. There were no signs of intruders, and there were no horrible secrets that would make him run away. The police said, "It's a mystery," and employed experts of every kind. Men in white suits who shone blue lights on things, dusted for fingerprints, and crawled around on hands and knees looking for clues. They brought in sniffer dogs that could smell boys, even clean boys, three miles away. But the dogs just barked and licked dripping drops from the taps. The best detective in the land said, "I've never seen anything like it," and cried. A strange woman, wearing strange clothes, had strange dreams in which dead people sang, "Amphibian, amphibian, amphibian." A priest prayed, and said, "Don't give up hope," but after three years, the police suspended the case. Adam's family were very sad, sold their house, and moved away.

Another family moved in. They didn't know about Adam, did lots of DIY, made his old house their new home, but kept the bath. "It's lovely," Katy, the daughter, said. She loved having baths, and she liked watching the whirling, gurgling water spiral down the plughole. On this leap day, four years later, as a full moon shone magic through the window, as the final trickles of water twirled away, Katy saw two eyes peering through the overflow. Then heard a strange voice. "I don't want to live in drains any more," it spurgled[1], and a snake person squeezed out the plughole and into the bath. It wriggled and writhed, and turned into a boy who said, "Hello, I'm Adam the Amphibian."

David recommends:
The BFG by Roald Dahl and *The Boy in the Striped Pyjamas* by John Boyne (for older readers)

---

[1] Spurgle: the sound made by people talking underwater. (On leap days in leap years, it's OK to make up new words.)

ERIC SEES SENSE | JUSTIN ELLIOTT

Eric was quite ginger. But that was all right – better ginger than tabby, as the old cat saying went. Like most brawlers, he had a torn ear, but that was all right, too, because the other moggies said that it made him look tough, a bit like Bruce Willis. Cats watch a lot of TV, these days, and are particularly impressed by action heroes.

But anyway, Eric was mostly a quite normal cat – he slept a lot, he ate a lot. From time to time he would venture outside, sniff around a bit, and generally ensure that none of the local birds were getting too uppity. The usual stuff.

But Eric had a secret. His mean stare came not so much from his toughness as the fact that he was becoming increasingly short-sighted. Frankly, he needed glasses.

Now, cats, as everyone knows, are incredibly vain. Eric was not sure that glasses would fit his image.

On the other hand, the Hawthorne Avenue Feline Olympics were just around the corner, and he was due to take part in the cross-street-glare-off. And he could hardly compete if he could not see his opponent.

There was nothing else for it – he would have to pay a visit to Ronnie, the most notorious magpie in the area.

"I need a pair of glasses," said Eric.

"I might have something like that," Ronnie answered as he surveyed his stash. "But what's in it for me?"

"I will promise not to eat you," Eric replied.

"Deal," said Ronnie.

So, a pair of opera glasses balanced precariously on his nose, Eric made his way to the Olympic venue. He could hear the other cats sniggering at him, but he did not care. He saw nothing but his opponent, Siamese Sam.

Sam's sarcastic smile soon faded when he saw how hard Eric was glaring at him.

And after that? Well, Eric easily progressed to the final, where he won on points against Miguel, a tough Mexican Hairless.

Eric was never ashamed of wearing his glasses after that. He did, however, give serious thought to the notion of asking Ronnie to supply him with a set of contact lenses. You know what cats are like.

Justin recommends:
The Hobbit by J.R.R. Tolkien and *The Owl Service* by Alan Garner

THE PASSENGER | JACKIE ANDREWS

Lieutenant Jack Tate was in deep trouble. His spaceship had blown up under rebel fire and he had only just managed to get himself and his passenger safely into the remaining shuttle before the shockwave sent it hurtling through space completely out of control. "Lieutenant Tate, do you need any help?"

Tate closed his eyes for a second, considering the silly question. And in that moment two things happened at once: enemy fire screamed past the window, and the cockpit door slammed open against the bulkhead.

Ambassador Sula strapped herself in the co-pilot's seat and wordlessly laid a hand over Tate's as he struggled with the joystick. His fury at her intrusion died as he felt the craft respond immediately without his help. The shuttle went into some heart-stopping turns and dives that miraculously dodged all the enemy missiles.

Their relief was short-lived. The rest of the rebel fleet suddenly popped into their space, leaving them only one place to go. To Tate's horror, he saw ahead the deadly turbulence of a black hole.

Desperately, he reached for the joystick in the ambassador's iron grip. "*Turn!* You're going to kill us both!"

"No, lieutenant. Trust me. I know what I am doing."

Tate stared at her. His mission was to keep this woman out of rebel hands. Clearly she thought death was a better option. Frozen with terror, he watched the black hole coming up fast …

… and a lifetime later he opened his eyes to see the green

planet, Solace, filling his screen.

"My home," said the ambassador, smiling. "Thank you for delivering me safely, lieutenant."

Mission over, Jack Tate stepped out of the cramped cockpit of the flight simulator, into a room full of Admiralty staff examiners.

"Well done, lieutenant. That was an excellent demonstration of piloting and discretionary decision-making." The chief examiner shook his hand. "I am pleased to tell you you've passed, captain."

"Thank you, sir," Tate grasped his hand, still reeling and disoriented. "I couldn't have done it without my holographic passenger, though."

"Holographic passenger?" The examiner looked puzzled.

"You know, the ambassador."

"But that was just your *mission*, Tate. There was no passenger. Besides, these old flight simulators can't create holograms."

If you enjoyed this story, why not try some of Jackie's books:
Blood Feud and *Deadly Encounters*

VOICE OF HER PEOPLE | PATRICK CAVE

Silva was royalty amongst the other ponies, iron grey, strong as an oak. Anyone could see. It was right that he should be for Keppar, princess of her people. It was the way of things. And why should Lilo complain? She was allowed to comb out the tangles of his muddy coat until he was velvet and calm, to bring him scraps of root that made his teeth strong, even to ride him to Keppar when she sent her royal word.

Everyone knew who the better rider was. Silva knew it best of all. He had thrown his mistress three times in as many moons!

"Proud young pup!" came a deep voice.

Lilo started, but the voice was not directed at her. She wormed deeper into the herd and listened.

"We are a proud people. Our princes have been ever thus," a second man said mildly.

They were discussing Keppar!

"Aye. But to fight the Red Crests. Is she mad? She is too young to understand, *too* young to know her own mind."

"Or knows her mind *too* well! Like her royal father before her, until those red devils did for him."

The first man spat. "Enough. It's done anyway. The princess has been taken. We had to bind her. She scratched me, see? Young vixen!"

"And will the Red Crests allow us peace? What will they ask in return?"

"Whatever they ask, we will give it. I will ride to meet them. I am next in the royal house. I will make peace…"

The voices faded. Lilo was shaking. She felt sick. Poor Keppar! What had they done to her? It was an outrage! Despite the harshness of her years serving the princess, Lilo felt sorry for the other girl. She'd always done her best for the tribe. It was *right* to send the Red Crests packing.

Lilo hung on to Silva. "What should I do?"

By the time the mists had burnt away, a lone figure was riding over the downland. She sat proudly and rode the snorting royal pony easily. She wore the clothes of a princess.

When she entered the Red Crests' camp, they could see what her answer would be.

If you enjoyed this story, why not try some of Patrick's books: *Sharp North* (for older readers) and *Number 99*

WALKING SYZYGY | KJARTAN POSKITT

"BEWARE – TREACHEROUS CURRENTS". I smiled up at the battered old sign. It was an early March morning and the freak low tide had left the end of the pier surrounded by dry sand. This spot would be twenty feet deep by lunch time, and it might be years before anybody could walk here again.

Something was swinging beneath the sign. It was an old dog collar and lead tied up among the manky seaweed clinging to the pier support. Being curious, I unknotted it, and saw the collar had a disc engraved with the word "Syzygy". I walked off along the water's edge, swinging the lead and wondering what such a strange name could mean.

Behind me the hazy sun was rising through the ruins of the abbey on the cliff top. For a moment my shadow stretched before me and then, just as it faded, a second smaller dark shape moved up beside it. I turned to see who had followed me, but there were just my own footprints leading back to the pier end.

Far away off towards the beach huts Mrs Thompson was walking her white terrier. As always, Dusty came scampering madly towards me. I bent to say hello, but then he stopped and growled in alarm. There was a clumsy splashing noise in the shallows behind me. Dusty turned and bolted. I looked round to see a few fading ripples, and then suddenly the old dog lead twitched in my hand. Something was tugging it out to sea. I snatched it back and it fell free. Enough! I swung it around my head and hurled it right away across the water and turned towards the shore. Behind me I heard the distant splash, but then there were more splashes. Little waves or something, whatever. I'd had enough of the tricks this freak tide was playing on my imagination.

I walked directly back to the slipway. It wasn't until my feet were on solid paving stones that I turned and looked back. The tide was already lapping the pier as once again I wondered about Syzygy.

Then I heard a clink at my feet. The wet lead was lying across my shoes.

If you enjoyed this story, why not try some of Kjartan's books: *Pantsacadabra!* and *Pantology: A Brief History of Pants*

Art galleries are yawn, yawn, boring, tedious, pointless and stupid, thought Matilda as she trailed behind her mum.

"Come on!" said Mum. "It's a room of paintings – why look so glum?"

Because I'm missing TV, thought Matilda, as Mum stopped at the first painting. A sulky boy looked out from it and Mum looked back – for ages. Eventually she moved on to the next one.

Matilda groaned. With several more rooms to go, they'd be here all day. She plodded off by herself. She passed the painting of the sulky boy again, and Mum was only on the third painting.

Booooor-*ring*.

"Boring, is it?" said a voice behind her.

Matilda spun round. There was nobody there.

"It's all right for you," said the voice. "You can walk around and then go. I have to sit here all day, every day looking at people looking at me."

Matilda gasped. Had the sulky boy in the painting just spoken to her?

"That's right," he said. "It's much more boring being in a painting than looking at one."

Matilda hurried on.

The next painting showed an iced lake with children skating. "Whee! Isn't this fun? Shame you can't join us. It's great in here – much better than out there!"

It did look fun. Matilda watched everyone whizzing round until she was laughing with them.

"What are you laughing at?"

The voice came from the next painting. A stern woman in a red dress frowned at Matilda. "Can't those skaters keep the noise down? I have a very important pose to keep."

Matilda moved on.

"Don't talk to me, I'm reading," said the next lady, from behind her book.

The next man asked Matilda to tell his son to be careful on the ice. A smiling woman asked what the weather was like outside. Some people were so busy arguing they didn't notice her watching. Horses neighed, babies wailed, dogs barked, children played and people sang. It took ages to see all the paintings.

"Finished at last?"

She spun round to see her mother standing behind her. "The paintings spoke to me."

"Oh good, I hoped they would," said Mum. "Shall we see what's in the next room?"

"Yes, please!"

Jackie recommends:
Journey to the River Sea by Eva Ibbotson and *The Kite Rider* by Geraldine McCaughrean

AN EASY CURE FOR INSOMNIA

PRATIMA MITCHELL

Grandfather Singh hadn't slept properly for days.

He complained, "I just nodded off when an ambulance went by!"

"Dee daw dee daw," sang six-year-old Baba.

"It got worse…"

"Cats?" asked Minnie, Baba's sister.

Grandfather sighed. "And that party down the street – people shouting, doors slamming. Then the dawn chorus started…"

"Better consult the doctor," said Minnie's mum, hurrying the children to school.

"Never," replied Grandfather. "He'll just give me sleeping pills."

A week later, Grandfather's eyes had sunk into their sockets. He felt exhausted.

"A prize to anyone who comes up with a cure for my insomnia," he announced. "Anything you want," he added recklessly. "Any treat that lasts a day."

"Like the zoo?" Baba asked.

"The zoo with ice creams and a bar of chocolate each," said Minnie, who had bargaining power.

"The zoo and London Eye. No, no! Wembley and the big match," shouted Baba.

Minnie suggested roller skating in the park. "We'd need to buy Rollerblades."

"Just come up with the goods," Grandfather grumbled.

*

Baba and Minnie tried lots of cures – evening massage, which didn't work; hot milk with honey at night; a tape of the sea. Nothing did the trick.

Finally Minnie got Mum to invite Mrs Chatterjee to supper.

Mrs Chatterjee was the most boring person they knew. Her voice was like a hornet droning … or a tropical frog. She talked and talked but never said anything interesting.

When Grandfather heard, he said he would eat in his own room.

"She will be very offended," said Minnie's mum.

Mrs Chatterjee came to supper. Mum made biryani rice with lamb, cauliflower-potato, dal and carrot halvah with vanilla ice cream.

Mrs Chatterjee talked non-stop for three hours.

She talked about her five grandchildren. She talked about her new kitchen. She talked in great detail about how she had booked a holiday. Even Minnie's eyes were closing.

Grandfather was nodding; his face was nearly in the pudding bowl. Minnie and Baba led him to his bedroom. Minnie took off his slippers, and tucked him up. He murmured, "In all my life, I've never felt so tired – or so bored…"

Of course he slept like a little baby, and Minnie and Baba got their Rollerblades.

If you enjoyed this story, why not try some of Pratima's books: *Petar's Song* and *My Story: Indian Mutiny*

FATIMA'S WISH | DIANA GITTINS

"I don't want to go to school!"

"Don't shout at me, Fatima! You *have* to go to school!"

"It's the *fifth* time I've done the Romans!"

"I know it's hard, but you know our work means we have to move a lot."

The cat swished in. Mum scooped it up in her arms and stroked it.

"I wish I was a cat," Fatima said as she went out the door.

"Be careful what you wish—"

Fatima didn't hear the rest. She stomped off and bumped into a lamp post. She felt dizzy, but walked on, getting to school in half the usual time.

Kids swarmed round her.

"Well *hello*!" said the girl who had tripped her up on her first day.

"What is your name, gorgeous?" said the girl who had stolen her pen.

Why had everyone changed so much?

"Oi, you – out!" said the head teacher as Fatima went inside. "You can't come in here!"

"I can't?"

"Get out!" He kicked her in the bum.

"OWW! You're not allowwwwed—!" Her words came out as yowls as she flew through the air. Landing on all fours, Fatima realized that her wish had come true.

She swished her striped tail, twitched her whiskers and strutted off. She was free! She could do *exactly* what she wanted!

A Rottweiler appeared and began chasing her. She dashed across the street. Horns beeped, brakes screeched. Fatima almost got run over. The dog chased her down alleys until she scrabbled up the drainpipe of an Indian restaurant, where she fell asleep on the roof.

Later, the smell of curry woke her up. She was starving and wanted to go home. Kicked by a shopkeeper, tail pulled by a toddler, Fatima arrived home to find the door shut. She jumped on the window sill.

"Mummmm!" she yowled.

"Shoo!" Mum opened the window and dumped a pan of cold water on her.

Fatima slunk into the garden, crying and shivering. "Oh, how I wish I was a girl again!"

"Darling, why are you sleeping in the garden?" Mum scooped her up in her arms.

Fatima started to purr, but instead it came out as words.

"Oh Mum, am I glad to see you!"

If you enjoyed this story, why not try one of Diana's books:
Dance of the Sheet

PLOP | RONDA ARMITAGE

Two rabbits lived on the shores of Lake Worrabop.

One day the rabbits were nibbling the grass when a big, ripe fruit dropped PLOP into Lake Worrabop.

The rabbits were terrified when they heard the enormous PLOP.

"Whatever is that?" asked the small rabbit.

"It's a Plop," said the big rabbit. "It might want to eat us."

The rabbits ran into the forest as fast as their legs would carry them.

Three foxes saw them fleeing. "Why are you running?" they asked.

"A big Plop is coming from Lake Worrabop. It might want to eat us," said the rabbits.

The foxes were frightened, so they ran too.

They met four monkeys. "Why are you running?" they asked.

"A huge Plop is coming from Lake Worrabop," said the foxes. "It's going to eat us."

So the monkeys ran with the rabbits and the foxes.

They met five deer. "Why are you running so fast?" they asked.

"An enormous Plop is coming from Lake Worrabop," said the monkeys. "It wants to gobble us up."

So the deer fled with the monkeys, foxes and rabbits.

Soon they reached the foot of a mountain, where a lion lay in the sun.

"Stop," he roared, and all the animals stopped.

The lion rose to his feet.

"My friends," he asked. "Why are you running so fast?"

"Plop's coming," said the deer.

"Who's Plop?" asked the lion.

"We don't know," said the deer.

"Then why are you running?" asked the lion. "Who told you about Plop?"

"The monkeys told us," said the deer.

"The foxes told us," said the monkeys.

"The rabbits told us," said the foxes.

"We heard this Plop with our very own ears," said the rabbits. "He lives in Lake Worrabop. He's very fierce and he wants to eat us."

"Show me," said the lion. So the lion followed the deer, who followed the monkeys, who followed the foxes, who followed the rabbits until they reached the shores of Lake Worrabop.

Just then another ripe fruit fell into the lake.

PLOP.

The lion roared with laughter.

"So that's your PLOP," he said. "A big fruit dropping into Lake Worrabop."

And the animals never ran away from a Plop again.

If you enjoyed this story, why not try some of Ronda's books: *The Lighthouse Keeper's New Friend* and *Small Knight and George*

THE EMERALD POOL | JANE GRELL

The football team was short of equipment.

"A sponsored walk!" agreed everyone.

"Great!" said Darren, their coach. "Could we make it an unusual one?"

"Cool. We'll walk to the Emerald Pool," decided Ruby.

"Why the Emerald Pool?" quizzed their grandmother.

"Yeah, why the Emerald Pool?" chipped in her twin brother, Roy.

"I hear it is haunted, you know," said Grandma.

"Haunted?" Roy was suddenly interested.

"Yes," said Grandma. "By some strange woman."

"What woman?" asked Ruby.

"There have been sightings of her by hunters, woodcutters and suchlike."

"Who is she, Gran?" asked Roy.

"Well, people say she's Mama Glo, a mermaid who comes to bathe and comb her long black hair with a golden comb. Usually at sunrise. I would stay away from the Emerald Pool, if I were you."

That night, Roy and Ruby planned a secret visit to the pool, but Roy was not happy about deceiving their grandmother.

"This mysterious lady comes out only at sunrise, right?" argued Ruby.

"Yes, but…" said Roy.

"So it is still sort of dark while she's about, right?"

"I guess so," replied Roy.

"Well then," continued Ruby, "we'll walk to the pool in broad daylight, so what's the problem?"

As soon as their grandmother had gone into town the next day, Roy and Ruby set off for the Emerald Pool. Once in the forest, they zigzagged their way down a winding track, ending where a skinny waterfall trickled into a crystal pool.

"Is that it?" said Roy, disappointed. "Titchy, man!"

"Spooky, though," said Ruby.

"Let's get out of here," said Roy with a shiver.

"Come on, let's at least have a paddle," said Ruby, pulling off her socks and trainers.

"Look what I found," shouted Roy, waving something glittery.

Ruby went over. "It looks like a comb's tooth."

"Yeah, Mama Glo's comb," said Roy quietly.

"MAMA GLO'S COMB!" they shouted together.

"I'm out of here!" said Roy, stumbling up the track.

"Wait for me!" cried Ruby, hurriedly pulling her socks over her wet feet and following her brother.

Hot and breathless, they neared the top. A looming shadow blocked their path. Roy and Ruby looked up slowly and fearfully to meet ... the disapproving gaze of their gran.

If you enjoyed this story, why not try some of Jane's books:
Doctor Knickerbocker and Other Poems and *Let the Children Dance*

DENNIS | IAIN McLAUGHLIN

"You want to read a book?" Dennis the Menace's dad sounded shocked. In fact, he didn't just sound shocked. With his jaw hanging slack and his eyes as wide as soup plates, he *looked* shocked as well.

Dennis reached over and pushed his dad's jaw upwards till his mouth closed. A fly was buzzing about, and he didn't want anything bad to happen to the poor fly.

"Yep," he answered. "I want to read a book."

Dad's brain struggled to make sense of this turn of events. You could almost hear the whirring and clunking of the gears in his brain working. "You want ..." he said slowly, "... to read a book."

"Yes," Dennis replied in a surprising show of patience. "I think we've got that worked out – I want to read a book."

A huge grin spread across Dad's face, and he struggled to keep a tear from his eye. At last, his son, the world's most famous menace, was going to do something that didn't include menacing, naughtiness or mayhem. His lip managed to quiver and tremble at the same time so that it looked like a particularly wobbly jelly. Dennis handed him a handkerchief. Not out of kindness – he just hated seeing a grown man being such a wimp.

"Aaaanyway," Dennis said, trying to pull Dad back on topic. "Me and books?"

"Oh, yes," Dad agreed brightly. "Now, what do you want to read?"

"Something old," Dennis replied.

"History?" Dad's mood brightened even more. "Educational, too."

"History?" Dennis answered thoughtfully. "That could be interesting … all that plague, torture, mayhem and stuff."

"Why would you want to read about that?" Dad asked.

Dennis just raised his eyebrows like he'd heard the stupidest question ever – which he had. "Because I'm Dennis the Menace and I like plague, torture, mayhem and stuff?"

"Forget I said anything," Dad said quickly.

"Usually do," Dennis agreed breezily. "Anyway, I don't want a history book. But I do want something educational."

Dad beamed. "Such as?"

"Such as …" Dennis's expression turned crafty. "… your school report booklet. Gran said you were almost as big a menace as me when you were young, and I want to read about it."

"Oh," said Dad. "Bum!"

Iain recommends:
The BFG by Roald Dahl and *The Princess Bride* by William Goldman

THE SURLY BIRD | PATRICE LAWRENCE

Unca Slipfoot was a placid pigeon. He worked from the annex to the surgery by the park. His job was to supervise the early breakfast worm shift. Every morning he perched on the gutter, watching the small brown birds tap delicately at the earth, their wriggling meal interrupted by a cheerful Alsatian running to catch a stick. The birds rose giggling in the air, fluttered, then landed again, resuming their worm hunt until the dog charged again. At 8.30, the small brown birds swooped off to hang out in the playground, and the fat crows stalked in, pecking at the soil and watching each other suspiciously. Unca loved his job. But it wasn't always easy.

"Hey! Unca!" Pendle was a loud-beaked crow with an enormous appetite and a serious attitude problem. "Standards are slipping here. This ground's as hard as rock. My worms keep snapping."

Unca said nothing – just pointed to his calendar. Three days later, like every other year, the trailers came, and the marquees and the fast rides. Hundreds of people trudged through the park, making the ground soft and rutted. Pickings were easy and the crows ate plenty. The day the fair left, there was a squawk under the gutter.

"Hey! Unca!" A fat worm dangled from Pendle's beak. "This bumpy ground is no good. I keep falling in puddles."

Unca said nothing – just pointed to the sky. First came the smell of bonfires and the squeal of fireworks. Then the sun turned pale and a frost sealed the puddles in ice.

"Hey! Unca!" It was only 8.15. Pendle stamped his feet and glowered at the small brown birds chipping away at the hard ground. "See these guys? We're getting their leftovers! We should go first! They're small. We're big!"

Unca said nothing. He didn't even point. Pendle turned around slowly. The Alsatian had put down its stick and was looking the fat crow over. Its yellow canines hovered way above Pendle's head. Dog-slaver dripped from its jaws.

"I'm big too," growled the dog, licking its lips. "I would *love* an early breakfast."

Pendle shot squawking to a high-up branch.

"Don't worry," he flapped towards Unca. "I think I'm due for a diet!"

Patrice recommends:
The Wishing Chair by Enid Blyton and *The Secret Garden* by Frances Hodgson Burnett

LOOK AFTER THE PENNIES | GEORGE LAYTON

It's about half a mile from my school to Dyson's Toy Shop. I was puffed out. I'd run all the way and today my schoolbag was heavier than ever.

I looked in the shop window and it was still there, thank goodness. I'd been saving up for ages; I wanted it for my granddad. For his birthday. It was a statue of this runner on a stand, holding the Olympic torch, and on it was a badge that said:

London Olympics
1948

It cost £1/10/6d, the last one in the shop. He was a good runner, my granddad, he used to run for Yorkshire, and he was going to be seventy on the twenty-ninth of July, the day the Olympic games started. I was so worried that old Dyson would sell it before I'd saved all the money, I'd asked him to put it on one side for me.

"Sorry, lad, first come, first served. I don't want to be stuck with that thing once this Olympics palaver is over with."

"But I want it for my granddad, he's going to be seventy on the day the Olympic games start."

"Then you'd better start saving. Look after the pennies and the pounds'll look after themselves. You'd better be quick, mind, it's the last one I've got!"

He's mean, old Dyson; he could have put it on one side for me.

I had nearly fifteen shillings in my post office savings book from Christmas and birthdays, and I got two shillings a week from my paper round, so I started saving the rest by doing errands for people. I got threepence from Mrs Bastow for getting her shopping from Killerby's. My Auntie Doreen gave me sixpence for cutting her grass and sweeping the backyard. And even though I always peeled the potatoes for my mum, she started giving me a penny for doing it. And every day I checked it was still in Dyson's window.

"I've got it, Mr Dyson!"

I took the bag of money out of my schoolbag and put it on the counter.

"I did what you told me, Mr Dyson."

And I watched him count the £1/10/6d – all in pennies. 366 of them.

If you enjoyed this story, why not try some of George's books:
The Fib and Other Stories and *The Swap and Other Stories*

GHOST HUNT | LOUISE ARNOLD

Tom Golden, legendary Tom Golden, He-Who-Can-See-Ghosts, stood alone in the grounds of the castle. The sky was an ugly mess of grey, smeared with dark clouds. Rain peppered the air, a fine mist that didn't so much fall as loiter, soaking through Tom's coat to the school uniform beneath. Tom looked around warily, straining to hear any sound against the backdrop of wind and distant tides.

Nothing.

"Where are you?" he muttered, heart racing, eyes frantically searching. He knew, beyond a shadow of a doubt, that the ghost was nearby: watching, waiting, biding his time until the right moment to strike.

Tom just had to hope he found him before then.

Something stirred behind Tom, and he spun around, only to see the empty courtyard. Ghostly laughter floated on the air, echoing off the crumbling stonework. Tom scowled. The wind picked up, tugging at Tom's scarf, buffeting colour into his cheeks, howling mournfully through the nooks and crannies of Thorbleton Castle.

Another sound, and Tom turned just in time to see a flurry of movement, a blur of grey, emerge from within a pile of crumbled masonry and dash across the cobbled stones. Instinctively he gave chase. The ghost spotted Tom, and laughed again, the wind catching the sound and throwing it towards Tom, twisted and muffled by the blanket of rain. It spurred Tom on, and he surged forward, gaining ground.

It wasn't going to be enough, though. Even as Tom ran, eyeing the twisted yew tree looming up ahead, he knew that he wouldn't make it in time.

He knew it was all over.

"*Forty forty save all!*" yelled Grey Arthur triumphantly as he touched the tree. Tom staggered to a halt, nursing a stitch in his side.

"You can't do that," he complained. "That's cheating."

"What is?"

"Hiding *in* a pile of stones."

"Aw, come on. Don't be a spoilsport. I won fair and square."

Tom didn't happen to believe there was anything fair, or square, about being able to hide inside a pile of stones. That's ghosts for you, though. Having a best friend who was … *supernaturally inclined* … had certain advantages, but finding games you could both play wasn't one of them.

If you enjoyed this story, why not try some of Louise's books: *Ghost School* and *The Invisible Friend*

MY BABY BROTHER | KIM DONOVAN

The nurse said that 366 babies were born in the hospital in May, but my baby brother, James, came out top for crying.

I bet it was unbelievably scary for him, being pushed out of his little, windowless home inside Mum's belly, into a bright white bedroom that smelled of bubble bath and coffee. A machine beeped, Dad went out of the door, banging it shut behind him, and a doctor with a stethoscope draped around his neck talked to Mum in a foreign accent. James must have thought that someone had turned the volume right up to max. Poor little squirt.

He started to cry so loudly in his see-through plastic cot that I thought my eardrums would burst. It didn't take a rocket scientist to work out that he was completely freaked out by it all.

James stretched out his chubby legs.

I brought my face close to his. "If you were still inside Mum's belly, you wouldn't be able to do that," I said. "There wasn't enough room, remember?"

For half a second, James stopped crying, but then the nurse went and picked him up and he was off again.

"My goodness, you've got a pair of lungs on you," she said as she bundled him up in the soft knitted blanket that had once belonged to me. I wasn't so sure that I wanted him to have my old blanky, but I couldn't think of a good excuse why not.

"What you need is a cuddle," the nurse went on.

James screwed up his face, turned the colour of a raspberry and let out an almighty wail, as if he was about to be murdered.

"Why don't you see what you can do," the nurse said to me.

I stared at her open-mouthed. I wasn't exactly Supernanny.

But before I knew it, James was plonked in my arms, still screeching, and I was rocking him, at the same time looking desperately around for someone to pass him to.

"I'm your big sister," I said in a shaky voice. "And I'm going to take care of you."

James stopped crying.

Maybe it was OK for him to have my old blanky after all.

Kim recommends:
Utterly Me, Clarice Bean by Lauren Child and *The Suitcase Kid* by Jacqueline Wilson

GORMY RUCKLES, MONSTER BOY | GUY BASS

Gormy Ruckles, the monster boy, asked his father a question. It was the same question he had asked every night.

"Can I go outside and monster?"

"Not until you're older," replied his father. It was, not by coincidence, the same answer he gave every day.

But Gormy kept asking the question. For twelve hundred and twelve nights, he asked his father:

"Can I go outside and monster?"

And twelve hundred and twelve times, he got the same answer:

"Not until you're older."

Then, one dark and windswept night in Maytober, Gormy asked the question for the twelve hundred and thirteenth time:

"Can I go outside and monster?"

And (eventually) his father replied:

"Yes, if you like."

Gormy couldn't believe it! He was going outside! He was going to be a proper monster, tearing across the whole valley and roaring at and/or stomping on everything that moved.

He ran to the door and opened it. A chill wind swept in and made his hairs (all 7,000,000 of them) stand on end. The sky was black and filled with bright stars which seemed to stare at him like a million beady eyes. Gnarled, twisted trees creaked and groaned in the darkness, and their branches reached out at Gormy like claws. And, in the distance, he could hear the low growl of thunder. Outside wasn't *at all* like he had imagined.

"What are you waiting for?" said Gormy's father. "A world of monstering awaits you! Unless…"

"Unless what?" said Gormy.

"Well, the thing is, I was just about to sit by the fire with a nice, hot cup of goat juice. There's plenty for both of us … but I suppose you'll want to be off," said Gormy's father. And with that, he poured himself a cup of goat juice and settled down in front of the fire.

Gormy thought for a moment, then closed the door.

"Maybe I'll have some goat juice today, and then go monstering tomorrow," he said.

"You know what they say," said his father. "Tomorrow is another day to monster."

And so Gormy and his father drank goat juice in front of the fire, and the valley was safe from monsters for one more day.

If you enjoyed this story, why not try some more of Guy's books: *Gormy Ruckles, Monster Boy* and *Gormy Ruckles, Monster Mischief*

FREE RANGE | ALLY KENNEN

"Hurry."

Frankie trailed behind her mother, dragging her feet over the grubby supermarket floor.

"Nearly beaten my record," sang Mum, lobbing three boxes of cornflakes into the trolley. "A weekly shop in under ten minutes."

Frankie heard a rustling, and she saw a mouse peeping out of a box of muesli. Startled, they eyeballed each other.

"Mum!"

But she was already running into the next aisle.

"Mum, I saw a mouse!" panted Frankie as she caught up.

"Come *on*."

Frankie was wondering what to do when she heard crunching. The shelf next to her was packed with nuts: peanuts, pistachios, cashews, all sorts. She shrieked as a grey, furry creature scurried down the aisle, tail bobbing.

"I just saw a squirrel…"

But her mother was already out of earshot.

Frankie shook herself a little, then ran after her.

"Forgot the tomatoes." Mum flew past.

In the salad aisle, Mum hurled mixed leaves and courgettes into the trolley. Frankie heard a wet, munching noise, and there, right by her ear, a beady eye watched her.

"Jeepers." Frankie leapt back. It was a rabbit nibbling the cabbages. It had ears and everything.

"Mum, you *have* to see this…"

Frankie ducked as something brushed the top of her head. A hawk landed on top of the aisle and eyed up the rabbit menacingly.

"No!" screamed Frankie. She flapped at the bird and it swooped off.

"Only five minutes left," gasped Mum, sprinting for the checkout. "I'm going to make it, by heck."

But now Frankie had noticed a small boy enraptured by a hedgehog, which was covered in cream and rooting in the cake counter.

Frankie thought they were supposed to be nocturnal.

At the checkout, Frankie spoke to the cashier. "Your shop is full of animals."

"Tell me about it," said the cashier wearily.

"Frankie, focus, we've only got three minutes." Mum threw the shopping into bags. "The clock stops ticking when I touch the car," she said.

"Mum, please…"

"One minute…" Mum paid the cashier and charged out of the shop, passing a fox slinking in.

Mum slapped the car. "I BEAT MY BEST TIME BY THREE SECONDS." She smiled at Frankie. "Now let's have an adventure."

If you enjoyed this story, why not try some of Ally's books: *Beast* and *Berserk*

Danny lived with his mum in a small room, at the top of a tall tower block, in the middle of a big busy city.

More than anything else in the big busy city, or the big busy world, or the big busy universe, Danny wanted a dog.

"*Please* can we have a dog, Mum?"

"I'm sorry," said Mum, "this city's too busy; there's no space for a dog to run and play."

So, every night, Danny looked out at the twinkling stars and wished for a dog.

One night, when he'd wished *really* hard, the stars began to change shape!

There were fish-shaped stars, boat-shaped stars, bird-shaped stars, and best of all, there was a twinkling dog-shaped star!

The dog-shaped star ran across the night sky, in through Danny's window, and into Danny's arms.

"I'll call you Dog Star," whispered Danny, and Dog Star licked Danny's face.

Suddenly, Danny was flying out into the big night sky with Dog Star!

They flew high above the big busy city, and landed on a big desert island in the middle of the ocean. The island was different from the big busy city because it had plenty of space to run and play.

Dog Star and Danny loved their island. They rolled and they splashed and they chased and they dug, all night long.

When morning came, they flew back home to Danny's bed, and Dog Star hid under the covers.

That day, Danny had to go to school. Afterwards, he rushed back to look for Dog Star ... but Dog Star wasn't hiding in the bed!

"WHERE'S MY DOG STAR?" cried Danny.

"WOOF! WOOF!"

Danny looked up and saw that Mum was hugging Dog Star.

"Look who I found when you were at school!" she said.

"Please, *please* can he stay?" said Danny, and Dog Star licked Mum's face.

"Yes!" laughed Mum. "I think he can."

So now, whenever they want, Mum and Dog Star and Danny can fly away to their desert island, where they run and they play, and they jump and they splash.

And that makes Danny the happiest boy in the big busy city, and the big busy world, and the big busy universe!

Emma recommends:

The Mousehole Cat by Antonia Barber and *Something Else* by Kathryn Cave

MONKEY MAGIC | BARRY HUTCHISON

It's not every day your brother turns into a monkey. Mine did last Tuesday, and it is fair to say it took us by surprise.

It happened at breakfast, halfway through his third slice of toast. One minute he looked like himself, the next minute… Well, he still looked like himself, only more squashed and a bit hairier.

Then, in less time than it was taking for Dad's Egg-O-Matic invention to boil my eggs, my brother was gone. In his place sat a brown, fuzzy-faced creature with long, spindly arms. His wide eyes blinked twice, slowly.

"Is it my imagination," he began, "or have I just turned into a monkey?"

I nodded. There were no two ways about it. He was as monkey-like as monkeys can be.

"A talking monkey, though," I said, looking on the bright side. "At least that's something."

"Suppose," he nodded. He scratched his chest where the hair burst through his pyjamas. A tiny flea leapt off and landed with a plop in my orange juice. "I wonder what Mum will say."

"'Why's there a monkey at the breakfast table?' probably," I guessed. Mum was always in a rush in the mornings, and I doubted she'd be impressed by this turn of events.

"How could this happen?" my brother sighed. He had crawled up on to the back of his chair, and was balancing there on one foot. "It's not normal, is it?"

"Has anything unusual happened recently?" I asked, watching

him leap into the air. "Get off the light shade, Mum'll kill you!"

"Anything unusual?" he snorted, swinging back into his seat. "What, besides turning into a monkey?"

"Before that, I mean. Have you done anything different lately?"

"Not really," he grunted. "Although I did have a sneaky drink of that milkshake in Dad's lab last night."

"What," I began, scratching an itch which had appeared behind my ear, "the banana milkshake? In the test tube?"

"Yep."

"The one that tasted like banana ice cream – that milkshake?"

"That's the one."

I reached for a spoon and stared at my reflection in it. An upside-down monkey face stared back.

"Oh dear," I sighed. "Mum isn't going to like this one little bit!"

If you enjoyed this story, why not try some of Barry's books:
Tiger Terror and *Spider Swat*

THE BOY WHO CRIED ALIENS!
by TOM FLETCHER of McFLY

There once was a boy who lived out in the countryside, far away from his school and his friends. In the summer holidays he would get very bored and lonely and would sometimes get up to no good. One hot, sunny day he was walking past a farm that had a large field of crops. The farmer was an old man, and the boy thought it would be funny to play a joke.

He hopped over the fence and started stomping on all the crops. He stomped and stomped in a huge circle, round and round the field, and by the time he finished stomping, he'd made an enormous crop circle.

"Aliens! Aliens!" the boy cried, and the old farmer came hobbling out of the barn as fast as he could, but when he got there he saw there were no aliens at all.

"You were too slow," laughed the boy. "The aliens flew away!"

The next afternoon, the boy thought he'd pull the prank again. He hopped over the farmer's fence and stomped an even bigger crop circle in the field.

"Aliens! Aliens! They're back!" he bellowed, and the old farmer came hobbling out and once again found no aliens in his field.

What fun the boy was having! So on the third day he climbed over the fence and ran to the farmer's field, only to find there was already a new crop circle.

Who made this? thought the boy, when suddenly a humungous spaceship burst out of the sky. It zoomed down and hovered over the field. The boy was so scared he wet himself.

"Aliens! Aliens!" the boy screamed in terror, but the old farmer did not come this time. "Aliens! They're really here!" he shouted again, but still no one came.

Just then, a door in the spaceship opened and a bright green laser beam shot out. It zapped the boy and he floated up into the air and inside the silvery ship. The door closed behind him and the spaceship shot off into the sky.

The old farmer heard the noise and hobbled outside, but by the time he got there, the spaceship and the boy were gone for ever.

Tom recommends:
The *Harry Potter* series by J.K. Rowling and the *His Dark Materials* trilogy by Philip Pullman

A traditional tale retold by JUDY PATERSON

Tortoise believed he was the most splendid creature in the forest and he never tired of pointing this out to the other animals. He boasted about his smooth, shiny shell and he bragged about his great age.

One day Tortoise was boasting and bragging as usual when a cheeky monkey laughed and challenged Tortoise, "I bet you can't ride an elephant!"

The other animals laughed, and that made Tortoise very cross.

"Of course I can! I shall ride an elephant into the village market tomorrow."

Next morning Tortoise set off into the forest, and soon he found an elephant uprooting young trees to eat.

Tortoise shook his head. "No wonder you are cross! No wonder you are smashing up the forest! If I were you I'd be cross too!"

The elephant was puzzled. "What do you mean?"

"Well," said Tortoise, "the other animals think you are a coward, and that is why you never visit the village on market day."

"What is market day and why would I want to go the village?" demanded the elephant.

"Market day is when the people lay out a huge feast ... wonderful things to eat: pineapples, mangoes, bananas..." Tortoise sighed.

"Huuuruumph!" snorted the elephant. "I am no coward, and I want to go to this feast, so please show me the way."

"Follow me," said Tortoise, "but we should hurry, because the feast has started."

Tortoise plodded along in front of the elephant.

"Hurry up, Tortoise, or there will be nothing left for me!" said the elephant impatiently.

"I am going as fast as I can. I can't walk any faster!" panted Tortoise.

"Well," the elephant decided, "if I lift you up on my back, you could tell me where to go and we'll get there faster."

"How clever you are!" said Tortoise.

And so it was that Tortoise rode the elephant into the marketplace.

The people screamed and rushed about as the clumsy elephant knocked over tables and trampled the fruit.

And in the middle of the mayhem, Tortoise tumbled from the elephant's back, landing upside down on his shell.

So from that day to this, tortoises no longer have smooth, shiny shells, and neither do they ride elephants.

Judy recommends:
Fairy Tales and Fantastic Stories by Terry Jones and *The Tiger Who Came to Tea* by Judith Kerr

THE DANGEROUS APPLE PIE | WENDY NEWSHAM

My great granddad is very old and loves to tell us all the exciting things he has done in his life, and especially when he has been in danger.

He was a soldier, called a Desert Rat, and fought in the desert of North Africa.

He was blown up by a landmine and lost the top of his thumb and the top of two fingers; he ran about clutching his hand in pain and had to be stopped before he set off any more landmines.

He was in hospital and it was attacked, but Great Granddad escaped on a train. Then the train broke down and he spent a week in the desert, cold and hungry, before he was rescued.

At the end of the war, Great Granddad had a lucky escape, as the aeroplane he was due to fly on crashed.

He eventually got home by boat and surprised his mum and dad, who had not seen him for five years, on Christmas morning.

After the war, Great Granddad worked in a coal mine and was hit by a runaway coal wagon that came off the rails and broke his leg.

After that, he drove a van for a builder and bought a large apple pie from the corner shop to eat after his sandwiches at lunch time every day.

Great Granddad gained a lot of weight; he got fatter and fatter. Great Grandma could not understand why, and put him on a diet, but Great Granddad carried on secretly eating apple pies and got so big he really was in danger. Eventually he had a heart attack and nearly died.

At the hospital they said he must not eat too much fat, and that eating a large apple pie every day was dangerous, as pastry is full of fat.

Great Granddad came home from hospital, and Great Grandma fussed in the kitchen making cups of tea. They put a tune called "Amazing Grace" on the record player, and the family and all the neighbours celebrated that Great Granddad was out of danger. And Great Granddad promised never ever again to eat a whole large apple pie every day! They really are much too dangerous!

If you enjoyed this story, why not try some of Wendy's books: *The Birthday Party* and *At the Seaside*

ZACH'S MONSTER | TITANIA KRIMPAS

My little brother, Zach, is very noisy. He always wakes up in the middle of the night, and his room is just below mine.

"Mum, Mum!" he cries, until she comes to settle him with her soft, sleepy voice, "Shh, shh now, Zach."

"Dad! Dad!" he yells, until *he* goes downstairs with his, "Get back to bed now, Zach, it's nearly morning."

I keep telling them they need to leave a light on – but they want him to learn to go to sleep in the dark without being frightened.

The thing is, Zach thinks there's a monster who comes into his room when it is dark. When I asked him what the monster looks like, he said, "Black, like night."

When I asked him what the monster sounds like, he said, "Quiet, a bit like Granny."

When I asked him who the monster reminded him of, he said, "No one; he's a monster, not a person."

Sometimes Zach can be quite funny. If you play his favourite game, he laughs the happiest laugh.

He likes you to be the monster, and he hides and hides. He usually wants to play for hours. You count to ten and he disappears into hiding places – not usually surprising ones. He stands flat behind the curtains, lies under the sofa cushions with his chubby legs sticking out, or curls up under the kitchen table into a little ball.

Mum was playing with him yesterday but she had a cold and got fed up. "The monster's got to go and blow her nose," she said, but I know she just wanted to have a nice cup of tea and a Jaffa cake. Mum's always saying she has to go and do something else when really all she wants is a cup of tea and a Jaffa cake.

At night Zach dreams of monsters, and sometimes Mum and Dad are too asleep to hear his cries. Then I go and talk to him. I say, "Don't worry, Zach, it's me, Maya. Not a monster."

I think Zach's monster is Mister Nobody. He's just afraid of being left alone in the dark. I used to be when I was as little as him.

Titania recommends:
Crummy Mummy and Me by Anne Fine and *The Suitcase Kid* by Jacqueline Wilson

BOY KING REX | **THOMAS BLOOR**

It was the boy king's first day at school.

"I've never been before," he told Janie. "Kings don't go to school."

Janie pulled a wobbly curtsy. "Welcome to Level Street Primary, Your Majesty," she said.

Asma poked Janie in the ribs. "Don't encourage him!" she said. "He's not a king any more. Not since they had a revolution in his country. His name may be Rex, but he's no better than us. And he'd better get used to it."

But the boy king didn't get used to it. On Tuesday he arrived at the school gates in a golden coach pulled by six white horses. It caused a traffic jam, and the van delivering custard to the school kitchens couldn't get in. No one was pleased.

On Wednesday he asked for quails' eggs and caviar in the canteen.

"We haven't got any of that," said the dinner lady. "Have some treacle tart."

"Any custard?" said Rex.

Someone threw a sausage. It bounced off the back of his head.

On Thursday he flew into a rage when a boy dripped paint on his royal trainers.

"Guards!" he cried. "Take him away and throw him in the deepest, darkest dungeon!"

Everyone just laughed. Rex went red in the face.

"Don't get upset," said Janie.

"I told you," said Asma. "He has to get used to not being king."

"But I grew up believing I was born to rule!" Rex said.

"Well, you'll have to forget all that."

The boy king sniffed. "All right," he said. "I'll try."

It was seven days before he stopped asking the school keeper to salute him. And it was three weeks before he stopped wearing his crown to school when it was a bit chilly, instead of a woolly hat like everyone else. It was a month before he stopped ordering his classmates to solve his maths problems for him. And it took him two terms before he stopped waving at passers-by from the window of the school bus.

But in the end Rex wasn't so bad.

"Remember when you used to be a boy king?" Janie said to him, one lunch break.

"Do you know," he said, "I don't think I do."

If you enjoyed this story, why not try another of Thomas's books:
Bomber Boys

HARRY AND KATE AT THE BOOK MUSEUM
SOPHIE McKENZIE

Mum, Harry and Kate arrived at the book museum.

"These books are really rare and valuable," Mum said. "This is going to be interesting."

Harry looked round. The museum was full of old glass cases. The books inside were dusty. Even the security guard was snoring in the corner.

Harry was bored.

Then Harry watched a man hang his jacket over the security camera on the wall. Now the camera was covered. The man went over to a glass case containing a rare, valuable book. He took a metal lever from his pocket and forced open the case.

The security guard still snored in the corner.

Mum was examining a book on the other side of the room.

"Look, Kate," said Harry.

Kate looked. The man took the rare, valuable book out of the case. He put it in his pocket and walked through a door marked *Private*.

"Let's follow him," Kate said.

"And catch him," said Harry.

They followed the thief through the door, down a corridor, round a corner, then along another corridor.

Soon they were going down the first corridor again.

The thief stopped. Behind him, Harry and Kate stopped too. They were standing by a sign that pointed to a door. It said:

STOREROOM THIS WAY.

"I think he's lost," Kate whispered.

The thief turned. He saw them. *Oh, no!* Now he was walking towards them. Harry's heart thumped. Where could they run?

"Oi, kids," the thief snapped. "D'you know the way out?"

Harry looked at the sign behind the thief saying: *STOREROOM THIS WAY*. He looked at the thief. He pointed to the storeroom.

"That's the way out," he said. "Through there."

The thief walked into the storeroom.

Harry slammed the door shut. Kate turned the key in the lock.

"We've caught him!" said Harry.

"Hurray!" said Kate.

Harry and Kate went back to the museum. Mum was still looking at books. They told her how they'd captured the thief. Then Mum told the security guard, who rang the police, who arrested the thief.

"Well, that visit didn't turn out like I expected," Mum said, as they went home.

"You were right about one thing, though." Harry grinned. "It *was* interesting!"

If you enjoyed this story, why not try some of Sophie's books: *Girl, Missing* and *Blood Ties*

CINDIE WELLA | LINDA STRACHAN

Cindie Wella stomped her heavy boots on the kitchen floor. "No, I will not wear that dress. I don't even want to go to the stupid ball!"

Felicity Sparkle, her fairy godmother, fluttered her dainty wings and made the glittery dress disappear. *Oh dear*, she thought, *what am I going to do? If Cindie doesn't go to the ball, she won't marry the prince, and the entire world of Fairytale will disappear in a puff of fairy dust.*

"I refuse to go about looking as silly as those two nitwits upstairs. Not for you or any old prince."

Felicity Sparkle frowned. "I thought you liked him."

"I suppose he's OK –" Cindie gave a little grin – "when he's being normal, not being a prince, I mean. But why do I have to wear a silly dress; why can't I just wear this?"

Felicity Sparkle looked at the chunky boots, scruffy jeans and the comfy jumper. She had to admit that Cindie did look quite good in it.

Felicity disappeared in a flash.

"I hate it when she does that," murmured Cindie.

"Ouch!" yelped Prince Charmer as his tailor stuck a pin in him. "No way! This fancy outfit is too fussy. I look like a frilly pig!"

"Not at all, Your Highness. It is the height of fashion."

The prince sighed and squinted at the mirror again. It had gone misty, and words began to appear in squiggly writing. Felicity

Sparkle was having trouble controlling her magic writing wand.

BARN DANCE

She hoped the prince could read it. She wasn't actually his fairy godmother, so this was bending the rules a bit.

"BARN DANCE?" Prince Charmer, who wasn't very bright, looked puzzled. "Barn dance? Why would the mirror say that?"

Felicity rolled her eyes in despair, but the tailor, who was a very clever man, said, "I think it is suggesting that you hold a barn dance instead of a ball."

"What a clever idea. I could wear exactly what I wanted!"

"Yes!" Felicity Sparkle squeaked from behind him.

"Did you hear that?" Prince Charmer asked.

And that's how Cindie Wella went to the barn dance and met her prince. The rest is all happily ever afters.

If you enjoyed this story, why not try some of Linda's books: *Hamish McHaggis and the Lost Prince* and *Spider*

RUBBISH! | HELEN FRANCES

One night, a boy called Adam lay awake in bed. He just could not get to sleep. He peeked under the curtains, down into the yard. There he saw a fox rooting around in the black rubbish bags, pawing at old pizzas. He watched her for ages.

He began to watch out for the fox every night.

Late one evening, the fox visited the bins with her new cubs – two red and one white.

Adam wrote a story about it in school. "Rubbish!" said his teacher. "Foxes are *always* red!"

That night Adam watched the cubs play chase with an empty tin can. Someone in a leather jacket stood in the shadows; when they took photos, the foxes ran away.

Next day it was in the papers.

And then local radio interviewed a vet.

A TV camera crew staked out the street with see-in-the-dark cameras; they wore dark green fleeces. That night, only Adam saw the foxes.

Next night, Mum sent Adam down to the chippy for supper. He got fish and chips and a polystyrene tub of tomato ketchup. It was dark; Adam took his usual short cut home through the yard. He spotted someone at the other end of the street – one, two, three people in white overalls. Scientists. Hunting the white cub.

He looked down.

And he could just see the tip of a white fox nose peeking out from under an old pizza box.

He held his breath.

Two snowy paws appeared.

Adam stood very still. Slowly the box slid backwards, and now he could see the fox's whole face...

The white cub's yellow eyes stared into Adam's eyes, stared at his hand holding the bag with tomato ketchup, stared back up at Adam. Carefully, Adam knelt on the uneven ground, undid the ketchup container and tipped red sauce on to the cub's white fur. It promptly rolled over and over in the dirt, sprang up, and slunk off into the shadows, a dark red streak.

"Have *you* seen this white fox, then?" the scientists asked Adam.

"Nah," he said, "it's all rubbish! My teacher said so!" and he went straight indoors, and for supper they ate fish and chips *without* ketchup.

Helen recommends:

Black Beauty by Anna Sewell and *Prince Caspian* by C.S. Lewis

STATING THE OBVIOUS | **SARAH BURTON**

I do hate it when people state the obvious. When someone says, "It's a lovely day," I don't mind. They're sharing something with you. It's the other kind of obvious I dislike. Like that woman today.

I knew I'd have to leave the old house one day, and that day had come. I'd lived there all my life, first with my parents and my brothers and sisters, then with my own wife and family. Now they were all gone, I was alone, and it was time to go. I was pleased another family was going to be living there. That house needed a family.

I've always been very shy. Of course, we'd all been brought up to be well-behaved, and my mother thought the safest way to get through life was not to attract too much attention. "He who no one notices has no enemies," she used to say to us. She may have been right. I have no enemies. But I also have no friends. As it was my last day in the house, I made a momentous decision.

I made up my mind, just this once, to overcome all my natural instincts. *I will go right up to the new people and say hello,* I thought. *I will welcome them to their new home. If I don't do that, I shall always regret it,* I thought. But it's one thing thinking about being brave, and quite another actually going through with it. I lay awake all night, worrying about it, but in the morning I was determined.

As soon as it was light I got up and started practising. *I will wait right inside the door, and greet them the minute they walk in*, I thought. *Then again, perhaps it would be better if I let them have a few moments to themselves before introducing myself.* As I was debating with myself, I heard the key turn in the door.

The woman screamed the minute she saw me. All my good intentions evaporated in that instant. I shot past her and raced away down the path.

"What was it?" I heard her husband ask.

"A mouse!" she shrieked.

Honestly, talk about stating the obvious.

If you enjoyed this story, why not try Sarah's book:
The Miracle in Bethlehem: A Storyteller's Tale

ELVIS | PIE CORBETT

It was dark. Elvis chucked his homework on to the floor. Maths! Finished, at last.

It was Thursday, so his mum would be late. The first of her nights down the pub. They'd only moved into the flat to be nearer her friends. Most of their stuff was in packing cases. His footsteps echoed.

Tugging a pizza from the freezer, Elvis switched on the microwave. It purred reassuringly.

The TV blared out the *Hollyoaks* tune. That was when he saw the cat freeze and arch her back, hissing and spitting like a savage – at nothing.

Then she shot under the sofa. In the silence that followed, Elvis felt the hairs on his neck tingle.

Crouching down, he tried to coax her out. "There's nothing here," his words echoed. At that moment, he heard a cold voice from behind him.

"Hello, Elvis. We've been waiting."

He spun round.

Of course.

It was the TV.

But had it used his name?

Maybe not.

Calm down.

Get a grip.

His heart thudded.

The screen flickered. A film began. Elvis settled down, forcing himself to watch. He was letting the emptiness of the flat get to him. The strangeness. His mum had asked if he minded being left...

He glanced at the clock on the mantelpiece. *7.05 p.m.* But as he stared at it, the numbers flickered. Rearranged. Till it read: *ELVIS.* Then a moment later, *7.06 p.m.*

Elvis's skin crawled. Fear. He could feel it. Something watching. Something waiting. He shot out of the sitting room.

Slamming the bedroom door, he shoved his chair under the handle. As he turned round, the computer flickered. A red eye appeared. It blinked. Elvis froze.

At that moment, the flat door opened. Elvis screamed!

Twenty minutes later, his mum was still trying to calm him down. "Good thing I came back early," she said soothingly. "You and your imagination. Too many horror films – you will be telling me you've seen Dracula next!"

She laughed as she turned on the kettle. But what she did not see behind her was the radio dial gently turning, the sandwich grill glowing or the electronic carving knife beginning to shudder into life, cutting slices of air...

If you enjoyed this story, why not try Pie's book:
Write Your Own...Chillers

THE PRINCESS AND THE DRAGON
CALLUM HEITLER

The dragon was already flying when it heard the cry. It rang out across the land like a call to arms, and the message was clear.

"Innocent princess in peril – brave men wanted – heroes and sharp weapons designed for messy limb removal and body-mangling preferable."

It was the cry of a princess in distress. If there is one thing a princess can do when trouble comes, it is scream until trouble runs away. Unfortunately, the dragon didn't know this, so when it heard the cry, it decided to investigate. With a giant flap of its wings, it swooped round and tore across the sky. Up, down, up, down – the wings moved like colossal pistons. Below, trees swayed in the downdraught while small animals clung for dear life…

It was a typical village. Mud was the décor, and this went for the people as well as the houses. Tied to a wooden post was a young woman wearing a crown who looked as if she would rather be somewhere else. Her clothes, which may have been white once, were now ripped and muddy. She looked as if she'd been dragged from her bed and pulled through a swamp. She slumped against the ropes – the scream hadn't had the desired effect. No one had come to rescue her and she wasn't able to rescue herself.

And then she heard something. It was the sound of drums. It came quietly at first, barely a whisper on the edge of hearing, but getting louder, and quicker, and closer, and then –

– it stopped.

A prince stood before her.

"Are you here to save me?" the princess cried, staring at the prince in hope.

The only answer she received was the sight of the vampire prince's pointy teeth.

She closed her eyes.

WHUMP!! There was a short scream.

When she opened her eyes, the dragon stood before her. A shred of the prince's cloak hung from the corner of his mouth.

"Are *you* here to save me?" she croaked.

As if in answer, the dragon leaned down and plucked her from her ropes. Behind them the villagers started shouting, "Oi! That was our sacrifice! Bring her back!!"

But they were already gone.

Callum recommends:
The Bromeliad Trilogy by Terry Pratchett and *The Edge Chronicles* by Chris Riddell and Paul Stewart

HANDS UP! | ANNA MAGNUSSON

One day the teacher asked two pupils to bring something old and wrinkled from home which demonstrated a natural process. Erica brought a squishy, blackened banana and droned on about fungi and decomposition. It was very dull, except when she pressed the banana too hard and it split and oozed like snot all over the teacher's desk.

Next, George stepped forward and announced, "My show-and-tell is waiting outside." He called out, "You can come in now." An old woman with short white hair, wearing a dark blue, baggy tracksuit and clean white trainers, walked smartly into the classroom. She had more wrinkles and lines on her face than a plate of spaghetti.

"Hello, everyone," she said with a smile. "I'm George's grandma."

A few girls giggled, and George – who was a rather serious boy – glared at them. "Grandma, please tell the class how old you are."

"Well, I'm as old as my nose and a little bit older than my teeth." Everyone laughed, except George.

"Grandma," he warned.

"I'm 82. And I can play the mouth organ." More laughter, so George said quickly, "I will now demonstrate that when someone gets old, their skin gets thinner, and how blood flows round the body. Grandma, show everyone your hands."

Grandma held out her hands, palms down, and the class crowded round. The veins wound over the back of her hands like blue ropes, like ranges of hills. They snaked over the bones and bulged between her knuckles. Her skin was dry and rough and covered in brown marks, like coffee stains. Erica gently touched the ancient, rumpled hands with her soft fingers.

"Grandma!" shouted George, and everyone jumped. "Hands up!"

Grandma raised her hands obediently above her head. After about twenty seconds, George burst out, in great excitement, "Quick, that's enough. Show us!"

She brought down her arms. The hands were transformed. The lumpy veins had subsided to faint blue shadows under the skin. Then, as they watched, slowly the snakes fattened and rose again between the knuckles and the bones, filled with the blood flowing back to the hands. It was like magic.

Grandma smiled. "Now, who wants to hear a tune on the mouth organ?"

Anna recommends:
Five on Kirrin Island Again by Enid Blyton and *The Wind in the Willows* by Kenneth Grahame

SOMETHING THERE | IAN BECK

"Brush your teeth," Timmy's aunt said cheerily. "This was your cousin Sally's bedroom once."

Timmy was already in his pyjamas; a quick noisy brush under the running tap and he was soon back in the strange pink-painted room.

"Night-night," she said.

She switched the light out and shut the door firmly with a soft click, leaving Timmy in the dark on his own.

In a strange room.

All on his own.

He hid himself under the covers. He often imagined himself as a submarine commander safely surrounded by a strong iron hull. The feeling of safety soon wore off. He was sure he heard a noise. There was something in the room. He pulled his head out of the covers and looked into the darkness. Well, he would have looked if he dared to open his eyes. He listened hard. He could hear the television from downstairs, he could hear the sea in the distance, but he thought there was something else as well. No, he was imagining it. He dared to open his eyes. "Submarine commander," he whispered, "scanning the sea." His eyes got used to the low light from the window. He looked up to the ceiling. "Air attack coming in at two o'clock," he said, losing himself in his game. He tumbled out of bed and landed on the rug. He made a machine-gun noise, and then turned his head and looked under the bed. Two dark eyes stared back at him. He leapt back on to the bed.

There *was* something there.

He waited in the dark. After a minute he leaned down over the edge of the bed and looked under. The two eyes stared back at him. He sat up quickly. He'd never sleep now. After a minute, he looked again. He bravely stared at the eyes. They didn't move. He dared to reach his hand into the space. He felt something soft and still. He pulled out the little creature from the darkness. It felt furry, and he could feel the padded paws of a teddy bear. He pulled it up into the bed with him. It had a friendly face. Perhaps he would get to sleep after all?

If you enjoyed this story, why not try some of Ian's books:
The Secret History of Tom Trueheart, *Boy Adventurer* and *Tom Trueheart and the Land of Dark Stories*

THE LOST DAY | WENDY COOLING

I didn't much like school. I was always in trouble because I talked so much, though I never understood why that was such a bad thing. English lessons were good, though; I loved the words, I loved the music in them. I quite liked geography. The words again – I always wanted to see Babylon, Buenos Aires and Bulawayo, not to mention Madagascar, Merryville and Mevagissey, or Zambezi, Zolatkova and… But anyway, it's geography – not all those enticingly named places – I'm talking about. I really only concentrated when we were studying distant lands and how people far away lived their lives. It was geography – and words – that made me a traveller and caused me to lose a day.

Geography, as everyone knows, is about much more than other places, but sadly my mind wandered when it was time to think climate, night and day, time, tides, the movement of the Earth and the sun. These regular and giant lapses of concentration have resulted in my worrying about that missing day ever since I lost it.

I was on my way to New Zealand on the voyage of a lifetime by way of Tilbury, Tahiti and Tonga, when it happened. The time kept changing; watches had to be adjusted by an hour or so quite often as we moved across and down the world. This didn't bother me, but when we were told that a whole day would disappear as we crossed the International Date Line, I did worry. We went to our cabins as usual on the Wednesday night, but when we got up next morning, it was Friday. Thursday just hadn't happened – I had lost it and, as far as I know, I have never had a day twice, so I've never got that lost day back.

It is not just the feeling of being cheated but a niggling worry at the back of my mind about what might have happened on that lost Thursday. Did I miss meeting someone who would have been really important in my life? Did I miss the biggest and most unimaginable adventure? I suppose I could have fallen overboard and been eaten by a shark, but I shall never know.

Wendy recommends:
The Snail and the Whale by Julia Donaldson and *Anne of Green Gables* by L.M. Montgomery

THE PRINCESS AND THE WEE | HILDA PARKIN

Far away and long, long ago…

The kingdom of Splod's in a terrible mess –
it's lost Lucinda, its princess!
The reason for this nasty hitch?
She were stolen, aged two, by a wicked witch.

Thirteen years later the heralds shout,
"We need a princess! We're all out!"
And every lass in the land says, "Ee!
Diamonds? Palaces? Sounds like me!"

So into Splod stream two thousand lasses
in teams, and ranks, and squads, and masses
and they stand and scream at the palace gate,
"I were nicked by a witch! O cruel fate!"

The king calls his guards, and says, "Eh, boys.
I can't be having with all this noise.
Either chase them away with a knotty stick
or find me the real princess right quick."

As it happened, Lucinda were there in the throng
eating an ice cream, and eating it wrong
so it dribbled, and made a right mess of her skirt.

She said, "Someone will wash it off. A splash won't hurt."

(Some princesses are daft, and others are dafter
but all of 'em are used to being *cleaned up after*.)

The trumpets sounded, the heralds roared,
the king stuck his head out, looking bored.
He said, "We'll find out who plays the princess best
by letting you all take a tiny wee test."

At supper that night every mother's daughter
was compelled to drink four jugs of water
then given a lovely bedroom to be in
but without a sign of a lav to wee in.

In the middle of the night they were half insane
running in the corridors roarin' with pain
"It's a lovely bed and I mustna spoil it!"
cried the would-be princesses. "Where's the toilet?"

In all this racket, one girl lay still;
Lucinda, the princess, had drunk her fill.
Now she lay in a pool of wee
thinking, *Someone will come and clean up after me.*

Next morning, the king cried, "Lucinda, my pippin!"
"That's me," said Lucinda, standing there dripping.

"Ey up, I seem to be soaking wet.
Well, someone will come and dry me, I bet."

"The real thing!" cried the king, through his happy tears
and they both lived happily for years and years.

Hilda recommends:
Little Darlings and *Abbot Dagger's Academy and the Quest for the Holy Grail*, both by Sam Llewellyn

DEAR QUEEN JOLLITY-ANN | VIVIAN FRENCH

Dear Queen Jollity-Ann,

My mum says I've got to write and apologize, so I am.
Sorry.

I don't think George thought I spoilt his birthday picnic, though. We had a lot of fun when we were on our way to the island. I bet you didn't know how good I was at rowing, even if it did make Princess Fiona feel sick. George hardly had to bail out any water at all. I know Princess Fiona made a fuss, but the water never ever got higher than her socks. And there was NO danger we were going to sink. Not once. Boats like that are built to rock to and fro a lot.

Also George didn't mind a bit when the alligator ate his cake. It made him laugh. And by the way, how was I to know you'd hidden a real gold coin inside his slice? It didn't say, "WARNING! Gold coin in this piece" anywhere. If people are going to hide birthday surprises in food I'd say it would be sensible to warn the other eaters. I mean, one of us could have choked on it. The alligator did. If I hadn't held it upside down and banged it on the back it might have choked to death. That wouldn't have been a very good end to the party at all. And I saw exactly where the coin fell in the lake when the alligator spat it out, so I'm sure you could send someone to dive down and fetch it. I could come and show you if you like. I'm not very good at swimming or I'd fetch it myself. Also the alligator might remember me. I don't mind about that, but its mother didn't look too happy. Actually, if you don't mind my asking, do you think it is wise to have alligators in your Royal Lake? I mean, it wasn't that difficult to get the alligator over the barrier. One sniff of George's cake, and there it was. I hardly had to help it at all. And I DID put it back. So I don't really see why I have to say sorry, but Mum says I do.

Sorry.
Love, Freddie

If you enjoyed this story, why not try another of Vivian's books:
The Robe of Skulls

THE SONG OF THE SKYLARK | KENNETH STEVEN

A man called Sorley lived far out in the west. His island home had no trees, just bare rocks and moorland. The man was a woodcarver, and every morning when it grew light he trailed along the shore searching for wood washed in from America, the Arctic, and even Africa. The wood was polished by the sea, dark brown or deep red or gold. He returned home with the finest pieces and carved beautiful violins.

Sorley knew every bird and animal. He knew where the otters slid down to the rock pools and where the seals gathered to be dried by the sun. He knew and loved them all.

One midsummer morning the sea was calm as glass. Sorley decided to walk over to the village to visit an old friend. There was no wood for carving because there were no waves to wash it in.

Sorley set off on to the moors. He heard dragonflies in the heather and the humming of bees. He felt completely content. Suddenly a tiny skylark landed right in the middle of his boot. He stopped in his tracks with surprise. The lark looked right up at him as if asking for help. Sorley gazed at the sky. There was a kestrel, searching for small birds to kill and eat, and at once Sorley understood the lark's fear. He crouched down, shielding it so the kestrel's sharp eyes wouldn't see the frightened bird. He stayed like that five whole minutes until the kestrel gave up and flew off. When Sorley stood up, the lark rose into the sky singing a song of thanks, for the bird knew its life had been saved.

As Sorley was about to walk on, he noticed something in the

heather. It was a great piece of bogwood, smooth and black with age.

This would make the most beautiful fiddle! Sorley thought, and instead of going on, he decided to turn and go home to set to work right away. His fingers trembled with excitement.

All that day and into the night he worked, and at dawn he was done. Outside in the morning light he played the fiddle. He played the song of the skylark.

If you enjoyed this story, why not try some of Kenneth's books:
The Sea Mice and the Stars and *The Dragon Kite*

PIRATES | DAN GREEN

"Why don't we ever DO anything?" said George Junior. But no one was listening. This was the seventh or eighth time he'd said pretty much the same thing.

He had said, "I'm bored."

He had said, "Who wants to play a game?"

When nobody replied, he had said, "I'll sword-fight every last man of you. To the death! Arrr."

(That one gave him a little thrilling shiver.)

But none of them took any notice.

So George Junior lay on his front and glowered at his family. An occasional cluck of exasperation came from Mrs Junior, frowning stiffly into her Sunday newspaper. Mr Junior, suffering another bout of fatigue, sat slumped with a warm flannel over his eyes. George shot his sister, Lizzie, his most withering look. But Lizzie didn't burst into flames. She just carried on humming and crayoning. They all seemed to be wishing he'd shut up, or maybe they were thinking, *Only boring people get bored*. Perhaps they desperately longed for adventure too, but they mostly showed no sign of thinking ANYTHING at all.

George Junior looked at the rain outside and felt like he'd done nothing exciting all year.

That night, he slipped out of the bathroom window (a trick pioneered and perfected a year beforehand). Turning his face to the wind, George Junior headed for the low hill above the houses, shops and streets of his neighbourhood. The rain had stopped, leaving the air fresh. It felt alive and almost warm on his face.

As he climbed, his mind raced ahead of him, tumbling through the grass with the breeze. The grass shuddered and complained in the wind, making a sound like the sea. Close by, a chorus of frogs erupted with eerie whoops. The night breathed with strange calls that didn't belong to George Junior's normal life.

Cresting the hill, beyond the town's orange glow, he found himself overlooking a lagoon. A ship bristling with cannons lay at anchor in the moonlight.

"Pirates!" George whispered.

A whaleboat moved soundlessly to the shore. In the prow, a dark figure stood motionless, scanning the beach. George Junior knew this was his only chance. He swallowed hard and started down towards the sandy shore.

Dan recommends:
Emil in the Soup Tureen by Astrid Lindgren and *The Magic Pudding* by Norman Lindsay

GRANNY TOOTLING'S UMBRELLA | ROS ASQUITH

Granny Tootling was always losing umbrellas.

Monday, she left her pink umbrella in the café.

Tuesday, she left her red umbrella on the tube.

Wednesday, she left her yellow umbrella decorated with ducks at the baker's.

Thursday, she left her spotty umbrella on a park bench.

Friday, she left her smart green umbrella patterned with purple hearts at the circus.

By Saturday she had only one umbrella left.

Tsk, this dull old black umbrella doesn't go with any of my outfits, thought Granny Tootling. *I'll ring the lost property office to see if anyone has found my other umbrellas*.

"Yes," said the man at the lost property office. "We have five umbrellas. One red, one pink, one yellow with ducks, one spotty and one green, with purple hearts. Are any of those yours?"

"Yes! All of them," said Granny Tootling, thrilled.

Wearing her pink coat, her red scarf, her yellow hat decorated with ducks, her spotty stockings, her smart green boots patterned with purple hearts, she hopped on to the bus carrying her dull old black umbrella, in case of rain.

BUT – just as the bus arrived at the lost property office, a large stern lady in a large orange hat jumped up from her seat, grabbed the dull old black umbrella and pulled it from Granny Tootling's grasp.

"MINE, I THINK!" squawked the large stern orange lady.

"Oh, so sorry," said Granny Tootling, feeling flustered. "I'm afraid I picked up yours by mistake. These dull old black umbrellas all look the same, don't they? I'm not an umbrella thief, I assure you." She gave the umbrella back to the stern orange lady, picked up her own umbrella and hopped off the bus and into the lost property office.

Inside were all her lovely bright umbrellas. Granny Tootling celebrated with an iced cake at Mrs Munchie's coffee shop.

Half an hour later she crossed the road to take the bus home.

And guess what? As she hopped on to the bus with her six umbrellas, she saw the very same stern orange lady glaring at her.

"Had a good day, I see," said the stern orange lady beadily.

And what could Granny Tootling do but blush?

If you enjoyed this story, why not try some of Ros's books:
The *Trixie* series and the *Girl Writer* series

ALLY'S (SMALLER) WORLD | KAREN McCOMBIE

My name is Ally Love, and I am five.

My big sister is called Linnhe, and she is grumpy.

"Urgh ... what's *that*?" asks Linnhe, pointing at the thing next to me on the sofa.

"It's my hamster," I say, stroking the potato that is my pretend pet. "We're watching Scooby-Doo."

I *badly* want a real pet, but Dad says we can't get one till our house is all fixed up. Only no fixing-up ever seems to happen, so it's not looking too good.

"Gross. It looks like a *poo*," Linnhe growls at me and my potato as she walks away.

Mum says that one side of your brain is all arty, and one side is sort of smart and tidy. She says Linnhe's got more of a smart-and-tidy kind of brain, which explains why she gets stressed about living in the mess and muddle of our house (and us), and goes crazy if we touch any of her ultra-organized stuff.

My middle sister (Rowan) says that Linnhe is just the Grouch Queen and that's that.

But I do feel sorry for Linnhe. Dad's job is mending bikes, so there are often wheels and tools and mystery greasy bits of metal at home to trip over.

And Mum is an artist, which isn't the *tidiest* job to have. Just last week Linnhe got papier mâché *gloop* and some bent chicken wire stuck in her ponytail. (Oops.)

Then there's Rowan ... she's always gluing sequins or pink

feathers or something *on to* something. Usually our sofa, or the door handles.

Anyway, 'cause I sort of feel sorry for Linnhe, I have a surprise for her; I snuck five leftover Chocolate Buttons into her school bag, which is hanging off the radiator in the kitchen. She will find them when she gets her homework out.

She will be very pleased and touched, and then I'll tell her *I* did it and she'll think I'm the best sister *ever* and stop being a grouch (for a bit).

"*Yuck!!* What is all this *melted*… Who *DID* this?!" Linnhe yells from the kitchen.

Hmm. Maybe I should've thought about the radiator more.

I grab my potato hamster and tiptoe silently up the stairs…

If you enjoyed this story, why not try some more of Karen's books: *Marshmallow Magic and the Wild Rose Rouge* and the *Ally's World* series

FREDDY AND THE PIG | CHARLIE HIGSON

Freddy Wilberforce hated school. "It's boring and a waste of time," he told his teachers. "I'm going to spend the rest of my life playing Xbox, so what use is learning all this rubbish?"

One day he hit on a clever plan and sent a pig to school in his place. He dressed it in his school uniform and gave it an old pair of his glasses. Freddy was not a thin boy, so the uniform fitted rather well.

The pig was very happy at school. It sat in class and grunted. Which is more than Freddy had ever done. The teacher was very pleased with him, but when she handed out worksheets, the pig ate his and did a wee on the floor. Meanwhile Freddy ate everything in the fridge and sat on the sofa all day playing his favourite shoot-'em-up, *Total Death War*. He was very happy, and when the pig came home at the end of the day he seemed happy too.

The next day Freddy sent the pig in again. The pig spent the morning rolling in a puddle, but in the afternoon got full marks in a maths test, so nobody minded. In fact, the pig enjoyed himself more and more each day he went in. Soon he was sticking his trotter up in class and he even joined the football team. In his first match he scored two goals and ate the ball at half time. He was in heaven. Freddy was in heaven too; he was ranked "Top Gun" on *Total Death War*.

The only problem was that Freddy's mum couldn't tell the difference between Freddy and the pig. Freddy had grown very fat and round, his arms and legs had shrunk from lack of use and he could only talk in grunts. The pig seemed brighter and was more helpful around the house, so she sold Freddy to a local farm and sent the pig to university, where he did Mud Studies.

The pig went on to found his own very successful mud pie business, and even got elected to Parliament. Freddy was eventually adopted by a family of vegetarians, but they never let him in the house.

If you enjoyed this story, why not try some of Charlie's books:
The *Young Bond* series

ALL THAT GLITTERS | FRANCES HARDINGE

That December the magpies started to think big.

No more buttons and tinfoil scraps. Instead they stole wing-mirrors, chandeliers, motorcycles. When the vast Christmas tree in the market square went missing, the local paper finally took notice. They blamed the thefts on local travellers.

Ted knew better. His walk to school passed near the woods, so he often saw gangs of magpies flying off over the trees with bike lights or shiny bollards. He was an easy-going, muffin-faced boy, but too smart to try telling people that the magpies were working together.

He almost tried, though, when his three-year-old sister Gwen got the part of an angel in the nativity play, and his mother went crazy with the tinsel.

"Can't we make her less … shiny?" he suggested, as his mother cut a dress from shimmery fabric and covered Gwen's face with glitter. His mother wouldn't listen.

During the play, Ted could hear wing-flutters behind him in the darkened hall. Halfway through "Silent Night", the magpies struck. They whirled on to the stage like a gustful of black and white leaves. A moment later they were gone, and so was Gwen.

Confusion followed. The police were called, but nobody agreed on what had happened. Ted's parents made pleas on local radio. And Ted, unnoticed, crept home, changed into dark clothes, then headed to the woods.

Ted slipped between the trees, following a chittering-chattering-fluttering sound deep into the woodlands. There he found a clearing where mirrors, glitterballs, candelabras and spangly dresses were heaped around the stolen Christmas tree. Under it sat a tearful Gwen. The magpies seemed to be arguing about whether to put her on the top of the tree.

When the magpies saw Ted, they flurried around him, pecking at his face. He flicked on his torch, and the attack stopped. A thousand tiny eyes admired the glitter of the hoard in the torchlight. A palpitation of wings, and the magpies were bringing Ted more torches, all lifeless.

"Batteries! I'll be back with batteries!"

The magpies seemed to understand, and let Ted lead Gwen from the clearing. There were many things you could do with a beak and claws, but changing batteries wasn't one of them.

If you enjoyed this story, why not try some of Frances's books: *Fly By Night* and *Verdigris Deep*

DANGER – CHILDREN AT PLAY | DAVID KLASS

The fight broke out on a sunny spring day, twenty minutes after school ended. Two boys circled each other at the far end of the yard, near the kindergarten playground. Swings blew in the breeze, and sunlight reflected off the slide and made a stripe on the sandbox.

It seemed strange to Justin that such a battle was going on where small children played. Justin was a third year, and he had seen his share of pushing and bullying since he moved to this town. But these were two fifth years, big and athletic, and they really knew how to box.

A crowd of boys quickly formed around the two combatants, ringing them in. All around Justin, excited boys called out advice: "Punch him, Mike." "Take him down, Tom!"

Justin was surprised to hear himself shout: "Hit him, Tom!"

The fight went to the ground. Mike got on top of him. Tom rolled over and covered up.

Finally Mike got off. "Had enough, loser?" he asked. He walked away with his hands raised in the air.

The ring of boys quickly melted away.

Justin was tempted to leave. But there were now just two of them in the schoolyard, and the boy lying on the ground was crying. What if he was really hurt?

Justin walked over to him. "Are you OK?"

Tom slowly uncovered his face. He blinked away tears and took a few breaths.

"Do you need a doctor?" Justin asked. "Should I get a teacher? Can you talk?"

Tom looked up at him and held up his right arm. Justin took it, to haul him up. Instead, Tom pulled Justin down.

In a second, Tom had climbed on top of Justin. He punched him in the stomach.

Justin started crying. "Why?" he asked. "I was trying to help you."

Tom grinned slightly as he climbed off. "Had enough?" he asked, looking and sounding much better.

"Yes," Justin said. "Enough. I give up. I'm sorry."

"That's right, loser." Tom raised his hands high and walked away.

Justin lay on the tarmac, blinking away tears, and watched the swings blow in the breeze. A sign on a post nearby said, "Drive carefully. Children at play."

If you enjoyed this story, why not try some of David's books: *You Don't Know Me* and *Firestorm*

"Oooh, another one!" cried the fairy called Clover as yet another human child's face appeared, looming large through the mountain pool.

The fairies dived into the otter hole. Clover peeked out: the girl's blue eyes glittered as she stared into the water. Clover liked her freckles and smile.

She heard the girl call to her parents. "I can see fairy jewels!"

The words bubbled through the water.

"There's no such thing as fairies or fairy jewels – they'll just be stones," they replied.

The girl looked sad.

And Clover felt sad.

"Wouldn't it be nice," Clover said to the older fairy, Rose, "if they believed!"

"Nonsense! Then we wouldn't be safe at all!" Rose replied, wagging her finger at Clover and telling her again how many more people were coming here since "The Fairy Pools" had been listed in the humans' local tourist guide, as a pixie had told them.

"Yes, but why don't we just find somewhere else to live?"

Rose told her a thousand and one reasons why they'd be better staying put – hiding.

Clover kicked a pebble.

She watched as the girl turned around and jumped up. And then Clover saw that the girl had fairy wings!

Quick as a blink, Clover darted upstream. She flew up the

waterfall, through deep green-blue pools and up high. Yes! No mistake: fairy wings fluttered in the breeze!

Clover secretly flew after the girl with her toy wings and her parents as they hiked up the mountain, higher and higher till the air felt fresh, and she trembled with excitement.

And that was when Clover saw the crack in the rock. Bluebells peeked out, beckoning her in. It was heaven! A mountain stream bubbled down, surrounded by bluebells and snowdrops and wild garlic flowers, covered in delicious dew. It was the perfect new home! Safe and quiet and far from harm.

Clover darted back to tell the others.

But first, she flew right up to the little girl who stood, open-mouthed, as Clover smiled at her, kissed her on the cheek, and then flew away.

"I've seen a fairy!" the little girl cried.

And Clover smiled when she heard the reply: "There's no such thing as fairies."

Liz recommends:

Inkheart by Cornelia Funke and *Cloud Busting* by Malorie Blackman

THE SURPRISE | STELLA GURNEY

When I heard Mum scream, my stomach flipped. I honestly didn't know she'd react like that. Not that she was ever supposed to find Terry.

Sorry, you don't know what I'm on about, do you?

It started a few months ago, when I turned nine. I got some brilliant stuff. And then I got two gerbils, which was a surprise (but not THE surprise – I'll come to that). It was really good of Mum – I'd wanted a pet for ages. They were OK. They ran around and looked fluffy. Mum said they were both boys, which was good, because gerbils breed like rabbits.

So it was a bit of a surprise (but not THE surprise) when I came home from school a few weeks later to find a pile of little pink gerbil babies in the cage. Ha! Turns out Fred and Dave were actually Fred and Davina. Mum wasn't going to be happy, so I didn't tell her. I told kids at school instead. Everybody wanted one. I charged £1 per gerbil and made £17! Result!

Then Fred and Davina had another brood, but this time I only made £4. Seems other parents have heard that gerbils breed like rabbits, too.

So I took them to the pet shop. The owner knows me – I'm always in there, looking at the tarantulas. They're waaay too expensive – I wouldn't even ask Mum; she could never afford it. But it's nice to dream.

This time I went up to the counter. The man raised his eyebrows.

"How many gerbils for a tarantula?" I asked.

He laughed.

"A lot," he said. Then, "Your mum know about this?"

I raised my eyebrows. He shrugged.

We struck a deal. Five gerbils for £1. Not quite my usual rates, but that's business.

Fred and Davina kept churning out the goods, I saved every penny and, last Monday, I got a real live tarantula! I called him Terry and hid him in a special box under my bed.

Then this morning, I heard the scream. When I reached my room, Mum had the box on her lap.

She looked up, her eyes were … shining?

"It's so COOL!" she gasped.

THAT was the surprise!

If you enjoyed this story, why not try some of Stella's books:
Mr Bickle and the Ghost and *My Dad, the Hero*

THE GIRL IN THE WATER | JOHN McLAY

The brave knights, under siege for what felt like an age, held strong in their castle fortress. One day a kitchen girl, sick of the hard work she was destined to do every day, decided to take flight.

As the defenders kept their eyes peeled for the stealthy approach of attackers from the forests below them, Mary the kitchen maid approached the entrance to the underground cavern. The cavern was precious: it was filled with the spring water that kept the besieged people inside the city walls from dying of thirst. Thin after months of little food and constant hard work, in the darkness she slipped easily between the sturdy wooden gate and the tunnel entrance.

Inside, she felt her way down an uneven stone staircase until the floor levelled out. She followed the sound of water for what seemed like hours until she felt herself climbing. As the water and her fumbled path converged, the walls closed in around her.

If the kitchen gossip was true, there was a way out here into the lowland forests. Ignoring the cuts and bruises, Mary pushed on until she spotted a chink of moonlight reflecting through a pool of water. Here, her path and the tunnel seemed to end. There she sat and waited until dawn. She was cold and exhausted, but determined to leave. Servant girls had it tough, and being a slave after the castle fell didn't appeal either.

As the cavern brightened, she took the deepest of breaths and plunged into the cold, clear water. She kicked towards the brightness, and when she could hold her breath no longer, burst out into a small lake, surrounded by trees. As she gasped for air and the sun shone down on her, she couldn't help but let out a small cry of joy. Free at last!

But the life she had imagined was wrenched from her dreams when she noticed soldiers on the banks of the lake. They stared at her with eyes agog. Her body stiffened up. Had she betrayed the castle? Shown them the way in?

Mary looked at the water. She could return and warn her people, or she could run, and save herself…

John recommends:
Mortal Engines by Philip Reeve and *Artemis Fowl* by Eoin Colfer

ALMA PATERSON WINS ANOTHER ROUND
PEDRO DE ALCANTARA

I woke up and stretched, curving my back and holding my arms above my head. It felt so good I started wagging my tail. And when the tail gets going it's kind of hard to stop it.

"Get up already," I heard Mum shout from the kitchen. "I do not want you to be late."

But what about what I wanted? Between the stretch and the tail wagging I was having a lovely time, and I stayed in bed a while longer.

"ALMA PATERSON!" she screamed. "COME DOWN!" Humans don't understand about dogs' ears. We're very sensitive, and certain vibrations are particularly painful for us: cats, Hoovers, mothers. I finally got out of bed and crawled on all fours to the kitchen downstairs.

"What on earth are you doing?" Mum asked. She was so predictable. She said the same things over and over again. "Get off the filthy floor."

I decided to tell Mum it wasn't my fault the floor was dirty. "Bow wow wow" is how it came out. "Arf."

"Stop your silliness," she said. "Eat your breakfast and get ready for school."

She placed a plate of bacon and eggs on the table. I stood on my hind legs, put my front paws next to the plate, and started gobbling it all down. Mum couldn't expect a dog to use a spoon, could she?

"Alma, you know how I get when you provoke me," she said. "Show some manners, or else."

"Bow wow," I said. "Arf."

Mum didn't understand me. Like a million times before. "Stop. It. Right. Now."

I growled at her. I didn't mean to, but what else could I do? A dog's a dog. Mum's face turned deep purple. I wondered if she knew how she looked when the veins popped on her forehead. Then the bacon and eggs hit my digestive tract, and, like a good girl, I did my duty: I pooped.

Mum let out a screech like no other. My ears rebelled and caused a frenzy of barking. It was so unfair. After all, I was eating my breakfast and getting ready for school, just like she had told me to do. Sometimes humans can be really crazy.

If you enjoyed this story, why not try some of Pedro's books: *Befiddled* and *Backtracked*

WHEN THE MARTIANS LANDED | ANDY MILLER

When the Martians landed, they didn't look much like Martians. Do you remember? We watched it together – everyone did. We thought there'd be antennae, the whole Bug-Eyed Monster bit. My little brother wanted tentacles. We weren't expecting them to look like the prime minister. Nobody was.

The ramp extended from the silver spaceship and the band struck up the national anthem. The prime minister – the original one – straightened his tie and got ready to address the first Martian. It was a historic moment. He had prepared himself for anything, even tentacles. But when he looked up and saw himself walking down the ramp, right hand extended, famous smile in place, you could see the prime minister – our prime minister – was completely flabbergasted. Whereas the new PM – the Martian one, the alien – looked supremely confident. He looked like the one in charge.

There was an explanation. The Martians can change their appearance. If we humans saw them as they really were, they said, we would be overwhelmed by their ugliness and sliminess. It was important to build a relationship of trust early on. And so the two prime ministers waved to the cameras and walked off arm-in-arm to continue their discussions in private.

In the months that followed, more silver spaceships landed. The Martians offered to help us eradicate disease and abolish hunger. "Our new best friends," the prime minister called them. They bombarded us with wonderful Martian food – irresistible cakes and chocolate bars and crisps which tasted out of this world. All gifts, they said. "Eat up!" said the prime minister. "Eat up, you lovely people!" Everyone's been getting fatter. Even my little brother, though he's not so little these days. They've started talking about an "obesity opportunity" instead of a crisis.

Yesterday, the government announced a new exchange scheme for Earth children – a trip to Mars for anyone who tips the scales at fifty kilos, with a lookalike Martian to take your place while you're away. On TV, the prime minister smiled his famous smile and then – just for a second – I thought I saw him lick his lips. "You lovely people!" he said. I don't know about you, but suddenly I'm not feeling hungry.

Andy recommends:
The Eighteenth Emergency by Betsy Byars and *Moominpappa at Sea* by Tove Jansson

LEAPS AND BOUNDS | STRAWBERRIE DONNELLY

Once upon a children's book, high on a dusty shelf
A perky princess in a story sat, all by herself.
"Someday soon my prince will come," she sighed. "But crumbs
    – he's late!
Idyllic though my fable is, just *how* long can I wait?"
The sweet princess grew restless for her True Love to appear.
"Perhaps he's lost," she mused aloud, "and needs a hand. Poor
    dear."
So, being quite a modern miss (and feisty for her age)
She made a vow to find him NOW, and strode … right off her
    page.
She marched across a nursery rhyme. "Shhhh!!" baa'ed all the
    sheep.
"There's no prince here! Unless, my dear, he's hiding from Bo Peep.
Try the cottage in the woods; you might just find him there."
She thanked them warmly, flipped the page and skipped into a …
A bear. "Grrrrrr," he growled, "NO GIRLS ALLOWED! Our sign's
    extremely clear.
Leave us be, to have our tea in peace – your man's not here."
The princess tiptoed from the tale to find another clue.
This quest for love, she thought, *is quite a hard one to pursue*.
Overleaf, in deep dark woods, she chanced upon a door.
Which opened – just a touch – to show a large and hairy paw.
A wild and wolfish grandmother bestowed a toothy grin.
"Looking for a dinner date?" he drawled. "Mmm … come on in."

"You're not the one for me!" cried she, and off the page she ran.

And stumbled on three little pigs, armed with some building plans.

"Forget old Princey – live with us!" they squealed. "We wouldn't
 mind!"

Tempting though the offer was, she wearily declined.

She sat beside a wise old spider, sharing curds and whey.

"I've been watching you," he winked. "You've had a busy day!"

The princess sighed and said, "Some prince! I *still* don't have a
 clue.

And now there's just one page to look – what *is* a girl to do?"

"You're a worthy heroine," he smiled. "So please don't cry.

Any prince would love a girl who's cool enough to try.

And as for 'happy endings'… Well! Let's turn the page and see."

The princess thought a while … then smiled – "Nah, let *him* look
 for ME."

If you enjoyed this story, why not try some of Strawberrie's books:
Hushabye, Bearcub and the illustrations in the *Magic Pony
Carousel* series

THE NAUGHTIEST ALIEN | TIMOTHY KNAPMAN

Eight squillion three hundred and two.

It isn't fair! thought Zark as his little rocket ship clanked sadly across the barren blankness of space.

Eight squillion three hundred and three.

I am not *the naughtiest alien in class!*

That's what his teacher, Mrs Neeeeeeeeeeeeep, had called him.

Zark was trying not to cry, which is hard enough if you've only got two eyes and they're both in your face. Zark had seventeen and they were all over his body, and soon his armpits, fins and webbed feet were wet with tears.

The naughtiest alien in class. Just because he said "bum"!

Eight squillion three hundred and four.

But he *didn't* say "bum"!

Eight squillion three hundred and five.

Not really.

And even if he did, so what? He didn't deserve to be sent out of the room and told not to come back until he'd counted every single star in the universe! Not for just saying "bum"!

How many stars were there, anyway?

Eight squillion three hundred and six.

No, and seven.

Eight.

Nine.

Oh, this was going to take *for ever*!

And anyway, some of the other aliens did things that were *far* worse than saying "bum"!

What about Frellch? He covered everything he touched with poisonous slime and only got away with it because he had a note from his mum saying it was an allergic reaction!

Eight squillion three hundred and ten.

Or Xflmptnqsh! He regularly ate people ahead of him in the lunch queue, then sicked up the bones all over the dinner ladies! And the only reason Mrs Neeeeeeeeeeeeeeep didn't tell *him* off was that she didn't know how to pronounce his name!

And while Zark was on the subject of who was the naughtiest alien in class, what about the Tyrannical Honk of Plonx? He ran his own fantastically evil interstellar empire in the holidays and spent his playtimes blowing other planets to tiny atoms! If anyone deserved to be out here, counting every single star in the universe, it was *him*, not Zark!

Anyway, thought Zark, *where was I? Eight squillion three hundred and...*

Eight, was it?

Or was it nine?

"Oh bum!" said Zark.

He sighed.

"One. Two..."

If you enjoyed this story, why not try some of Timothy's books: *Mungo and the Picture Book Pirates* and *Guess What I Found In Dragon Wood*

THE GRUM DECIDES TO CHANGE | GUY BASS

It was a simple, blue sort of day, the day that The Grum decided to change. *I would rather be anything than The Grum*, he thought. He packed a bag of useless things and ate his way out of his house. Soon he was full, but hungrier than ever for a change.

As he set off to town, The Grum spotted a Rogg rolling down a hill. *Shall I be a Rogg?* thought The Grum. *I would look down on the whole world. I would have legs enough to last a lifetime and the voice of an angel! But I'd never get used to that smell, and I'm sure I'd keep bumping my head.*

Further down the road, a cloud reminded The Grum of a Great Crested Yollop. *Shall I change into that?* thought The Grum. *I would never be cold again. I could swim like a fish and learn to ride a bike. But I'd miss brushing my hair, and my feet would hurt.*

The Grum sat down on a toadstool and had a proper scratch. A Red Pweet landed by his toes. *Shall I be a Pweet?* thought The Grum. *I would be able to go where I liked. I wouldn't have to work and I'd have the sort of teeth they write stories about. But I'd be forever having to wash, and I'd leave a trail of destruction wherever I went.*

By the time he reached the town, The Grum didn't know what he wanted. He stopped for a drink and a dance; then he ate so much that he had to lie down. The Grum slept, and as he slept he dreamt that he was as tall and round and strong as he had ever needed to be. He dreamt that he could eat whatever he wanted, and that he never forgot his friends, and that he loved all of the useless things that he carried with him in his bag, and that he lived a life full of small surprises. When he awoke he thought, *What a wonderful dream! I shall change into that.*

So he changed into The Grum, and for a while, he didn't want to change a thing.

Guy recommends:
The Lost Thing by Shaun Tan and *The Rabbits* by John Marsden

SIXTY SECONDS | SIAN PATTENDEN

At thirteen I became the youngest-ever leader of the British nation. I had already given the children free sweets on Thursdays, no school on Mondays and inexpensive dental care. I was popular, but there was just one thing…

My next decision was to add a minute on to every Saturday, at noon.

"One minute?" asked the secretary of state, himself just thirteen years old. "Why? No one needs it."

"Think of the possibilities!" I cried. "Time to contemplate the beautiful things in life."

The minister looked puzzled.

"Or to complete a fine poem."

The boy thought, then looked animated. "Or to clinch that deal and make a million!"

"…Or to do absolutely nothing at all." The health minister walked in, fourteen next birthday and always cynical.

"Where exactly will you be finding this extra minute from?" she sneered. "The sun is not going to shine for longer just because you ask it to."

I showed them the calculations. The finest brains in the country had worked it out. The rest of my young cabinet pored over the data, chattering about the proposal while the health minister furrowed her brow.

"What will you be doing with *your* extra minute?" she asked me.

I said that some matters were confidential; as PM, I had that advantage.

Saturday arrived and at twelve noon, everyone in the land would get their additional minute. News crews stood in suburban streets, waiting.

"Are sixty seconds enough, Prime Minister?" one asked.

"Of course," I informed him.

"What's in that plastic bag, sir?" shouted another.

"Why, that would be telling."

I approached the health minister's door and knocked. As the clock struck, she appeared.

"We haven't been getting along," I explained. "So I decided to use my minute to make peace."

I offered her the bag. She looked inside it and pulled out a self-inflating armchair, which steadily started to expand.

"During your minute you wished to do nothing at all ... so my scientists worked on this."

She smiled a beautiful smile.

I showed her the poem I had written, about the armchair. We talked and laughed – as happy Britain got its extra time.

Afterwards, the health minister suggested adding another minute on Thursdays.

If you enjoyed this story, why not try some of Sian's books:
The Awful Tale of Agatha Bilke and *Operation Ward Ten: Agatha Strikes. Again*

POCKET WITCH | CLAIRE RONAN

The birthday present Grandma handed Jackie was titchy. Inside the wrapping paper was a witch made out of felt with bead eyes.

"She's a pocket witch," explained Grandma.

"What will I do with it?" said Jackie. "Shall I hang it off a Christmas tree?"

"You won't pin ME on a Christmas tree!" said a squeaky voice.

This witch could speak!

"Her name is Ruby," said Grandma.

Jackie took Ruby to school. "I don't like school," she muttered. "There's this gang ... Isobel, Jade and Maisie."

Jackie's teacher was Mr Henderson. "Write a report," he said, "about what you did over the weekend."

Ruby perched on the end of Jackie's pen as she scribbled. When she'd finished, Mr Henderson said, "Would you like to read your report out for class, Jackie?"

"At the weekend my gran gave me a present," said Jackie. "A pocket witch. She can speak!"

"Rubbish!" said Isobel.

Ruby flew off the end of Jackie's pen. "I CAN speak!" She dive-bombed Isobel, Jackie and Maisie on her matchstick broomstick.

"NO! STOP!" yelled Mr Henderson.

"Haven't you noticed these girls have been picking on Jackie?" shouted Ruby. "You should have done something ages ago!"

"Why didn't you say something, Jackie?" said Mr Henderson.

Ruby turned Isobel into a frog, Jade into a chicken, Maisie into a Shetland pony. The frog hopped, the chicken scuttled, the pony's hooves tip-tapped across the floor. Everyone ran for cover when Ruby turned Mr Henderson into an elephant.

Jackie grabbed Isobel as she hopped past and dropped her out of the window into a puddle. She tucked Jade, the chicken, under her arm, and locked her inside the girls' toilets. She led Maisie out into the playing fields.

"STOP, Ruby!" begged Jackie when she arrived back inside the classroom.

Mr Henderson trumpeted as Jackie herded the class to the safety of the school playground. He smashed up the classroom and ground the desks and tables into matchwood with his elephant feet.

"ENOUGH!" cried Jackie.

Ruby waved her wand. Mr Henderson, Isobel, Jade and Maisie became their old selves.

But were they? Mr Henderson's feet had grown three sizes bigger. As for Isobel, Jade and Maisie? They never picked on Jackie again…

If you enjoyed this story, why not try some of Claire's books: *School for Trolls* and *Spooky Movie*

MISS FOX, OUR TEACHER | GWEN GRANT

Miss Fox, our teacher, has red hair.

So red, you can see it from one end of the school to the other.

Miss Fox also has a very loud voice.

One morning, she barked, "We are going to make a dark room, children."

Her voice was so loud that when she spoke, she made us all jump.

"We'll make the dark room out of cardboard boxes," Miss Fox went on, "and we'll paint it black."

So that's what we did.

We stuck the boxes together and made the walls.

Next we made a cardboard ceiling.

Miss Fox helped us to paint the ceiling and the walls black.

But afterwards, she snapped, "Stars, children! We need stars."

So we made stars.

Big silver stars and little silver stars and we stuck the stars on the cardboard ceiling.

"Hmmmm!" growled Miss Fox. "Planets! We need planets."

We made three planets.

A red, a green and a blue, and we hung them up on strings.

There was Planet Mars.

Planet Saturn.

And Planet Pluto.

Miss Fox said, "Who will make a big white moon?"

"I will," I said.

I cut the moon out of a sheet of snow-white paper.

Then we stuck the moon on the ceiling together with all the stars and the planets.

When Miss Fox shone her torch on the moon, it glowed white.

"Wild animals," Miss Fox yelped, "would love this room. They would feel safe in this room because there's no light, only the moon and the stars."

And it was very quiet.

That night, when we had all gone home and the school was empty, I lay in bed and hoped a real fox would jump in through a window, pad into our dark room and fall asleep, curling his tail around his nose and dreaming that he was safe.

So the first thing I did the next morning was to check and see if the fox was there.

But he was long gone.

Except I found a hair, as red as any of the hairs curling around Miss Fox's head. And I wondered if Miss Fox had such a loud voice because every night she went out and barked at the moon.

If you enjoyed this story, why not try some of Gwen's books:
Little Blue Car and *The Last Coal Barge*

THE PRINCE AND THE PILLOW
by TOM FLETCHER of McFLY

Once upon a time, there was a greedy prince. He had everything a man could ever want, but the prince wanted more. He lived in a giant castle, but he wanted bigger. He had a chest full of gold, but he wanted to be richer, and he wanted a beautiful princess to be his wife.

The greedy prince had a poor servant who lived in a hut in the shadow of the castle. He did not have much, but he was happy.

On the greedy prince's birthday, he ordered all the villagers to give him presents. Some people gave him clothes, others gave him food, but the wise wizard gave a different present. The wise wizard knelt before the greedy prince and handed him a white, feathered pillow.

"This is an enchanted pillow," said the wise wizard. "It will make all of your dreams come true."

The greedy prince snatched the pillow and ran straight to bed. That night he dreamt that he had everything. He dreamt he was the richest man the kingdom, with the biggest castle in the land and the most beautiful princess as his wife. When he woke the next morning, he saw that his dream had come true, just as the wise wizard said.

The greedy prince now had everything he ever wanted. He couldn't get any richer, his castle couldn't get any bigger and his princess couldn't be more beautiful. But since the greedy prince had everything, he had nothing nice to dream about. So that night when he fell asleep, he had a bad dream.

He dreamt that his poor servant lived in the biggest castle in the land with the princess and the pillow, and in the bad dream the greedy prince lived in the hut in the shadow of the castle. When he woke up, he saw that his dream had come true, just as the wise wizard said.

The poor servant now lived in the castle with the beautiful princess and the enchanted pillow and they were very happy. Every night the servant dreamt that everything would stay that way, and when he woke up his dreams had come true, just as the wise wizard said.

Tom recommends:
The Lion, the Witch and the Wardrobe by C.S. Lewis

SEVEN DAYS AT SEA | KATE O'HEARN

Sarah sat alone on the shore angrily watching the waves.

Before long, a light voice called "hello".

Gazing all around, she finally looked at the water and was shocked to find a dolphin staring at her.

"Did you just talk to me?" she asked.

The dolphin nodded. "What's wrong? You look so angry."

"I am," Sarah replied. "I hate spending holidays with my family in Cornwall. My gran's house smells weird and there's nothing to do."

"Where would you prefer to go?" the dolphin asked curiously.

"With my friends," Sarah said. "They're more fun than my boring family."

The dolphin sighed sadly. "I don't have any family. But I do have several good friends."

"You're lucky. I have two sisters. We share everything. I never get anything for my very own."

"I have an idea!" the dolphin excitedly called. "Why don't we trade? You could live in the sea with my friends and I could spend time with your family. Then we both get what we want!"

Sarah considered for a moment and then nodded. "But only for a week, right?"

"Absolutely," the dolphin agreed. "All you have to do is touch me and we can switch bodies."

Standing up, Sarah walked into the sea and touched the dolphin's head. Suddenly she was in his body and staring out through dolphin eyes as she watched her own body running to shore.

"This is wonderful!" cried the dolphin excitedly. "I have legs! Now I can run and jump and play. And I have a family!"

"And I can play in the sea!" Sarah cheered. Turning in the water, she gave a mighty flick of her tail and headed out to sea.

Such wonders Sarah saw as she explored the waters around Cornwall. But for each new discovery, she realized something was missing. There was no one to share her joy with.

By the end of the seventh day, Sarah was grateful to be switching bodies with the dolphin again.

"I loved your family," he said as he floated in the water. "But I missed the sea."

"You can keep the sea," Sarah cried as she started to run to her gran's. "I just want my family back!"

If you enjoyed this story, why not try another of Kate's books: *Shadow of the Dragon, Part Two: Elspeth*

SAVE OUR SCHOOL | CHRIS BUCKTON

You may not believe this, but that's up to you. I say it happened and I was there.

Our school is really old and really small. Almost everyone in the village has been to it, but that doesn't add up to many children now. Last summer there were only ninety on the roll.

Ninety children weren't enough. It cost too much to educate us, the government said. The school would have to close.

There's always been a school here. The village hasn't got a shop or a pub, so it's where everybody meets. People borrow the photocopier for their knitting patterns and the computer for working out their taxes and the playground for after-school matches and even the toilet when they get caught short.

Great-Grandma wrote a letter to the government in her best handwriting, telling them they couldn't do it.

But it was no good. The head teacher got a letter saying inspectors would visit in two weeks' time and then that would be that.

Great-Grandma just gave up on life. The last thing she said was that there must be something we could do.

A week before the inspection, three new pupils arrived. They said they'd just moved into the village.

The day after that, there were four more.

And by Friday we had a hundred and one children on roll.

"It's like a miracle," we said.

The new kids were a bit weird, but we didn't care about that.

The following week was the inspection. We passed. They said our handwriting was outstanding. Mind you, that was thanks to the new kids. They all had much neater writing than the rest of us.

When Mum was clearing out Great-Grandma's stuff, she found an old school photo.

"There she is." She pointed to a bright-eyed girl in a pinafore with button boots.

"Those boots look like Clemmy's." Clemmy was one of the new kids.

"Clemmy?" echoed my mum. "That was your great-grandma's name, short for Clementine."

The funny thing was, the children didn't stay. But luckily we didn't have another inspection for four years, and by then, new families had moved into the village, attracted by the inspection report, which praised our "old-fashioned values".

If you enjoyed this story, why not try some of Chris's books: *Shop Till You Drop* and *Survival*

ROGER IS BORING | GERALDINE McCAUGHREAN

Clarisse can turn seven cartwheels straight off. During the holidays, Hiram got stuck in a lift. And VJ was actually born on a train!

But Roger is boring.

Will is tyrranophobionic, which means if he eats peas he turns blue. (I think.)

Sheeharryzard can spell her own name – which is more than I can. Otto can spell his backwards – without looking, even!

But Roger's boring.

Karanjit says she's going to star in a movie and we can all go to the premiere (if it opens in Beccles). One of the teachers was arrested last year for being somebody else. And Mickey's dad knows how to win the lottery for sure, just by buying seventy million tickets.

But Roger? Roger is boring.

Megan can do long division (so long as it's quite short). She can crack her knuckles too, but Roger says, "Please don't."

Me, I'm building a boat from empty Ribena cartons taped together. I'm going to flatten all the straws and weave them into a matching life raft.

Meanwhile, Roger is boring.

It takes him all his time.

He's boring a tunnel under his desk, using a sharpened pencil, twirling it between the swish of his two palms. Roger's going to bore right through the world, stopping only to fight the mega-dragons clinging to the roofs of underground caverns there, by suckers on their ears. He'll wear armour made from turkey foil (wrong side out, of course, or he'd cook), and bore through the mantle (but not the molten middle, which makes your eyeballs melt). He'll surface in Papua New Guinea where they have guinea pigs big enough to ride.

It may take a while – his pencil keeps breaking – but nothing stops Roger once he's decided. (That's why I'm marrying him.)

Last year he bored into Lake Taal, a huge underground sea, and discovered three undiscovered fish. Unfortunately it took so long to climb back out that he had to eat them or starve.

I'm going this time. Hence the boat. Want to come?

Funny. To look at him, you wouldn't think he was anyone much. He never talks about himself. But when you know him like I do, Roger is utterly amazing.

If you enjoyed this story, why not try another of Geraldine's books:
Britannia: 100 Great Stories From British History

HOW TO POSSESS A CLASS | ALI SPARKES

"The pen is mightier than the sword," said Miss Hutchinson. Everyone slumped on to their desks. Oh no. The new teacher was *that* kind of teacher.

"Although personally, in a combat situation, I would recommend a thoroughly sharpened pencil," she added. Everyone sat up again. "Better still – carry one of these." She held a ruler on to the desk edge and thwacked one end of it so that it went *PWAPRRRRRRRRRRRRR*.

6C laughed uneasily. The ruler changed from grey to luminous blue. Miss Hutchinson swept it up into the air. It looked and sounded remarkably like a light sabre.

"Like from *Star Wars*!" gasped Darren.

"Better," said Miss Hutchinson. "*This* one isn't a special effect." And she cut through the leg of the desk, sending the battered oak post spinning across the classroom floor. "Hmmm." With a click, she returned the weapon to normal ruler. "A bit low on fission fuel."

"Miss…" breathed Samantha Pillis. "Is that allowed … in class?"

"Allowed? It's mandatory," replied their new teacher. "As of today. You've been targeted, you see. While you sit here wondering if I'm Princess Leia (and sorry – I can't do the Chelsea bun hairdo), a large intergalactic fleet of power-hungry aliens is hurtling through the upper atmosphere, planning to take over the planet. As your school is sited on the biggest radon deposit in Cornwall, and radon is their power source, they're hoping to start here."

"You're 'avin us on, miss!" chortled Darren.

"This breed of alien prefers to possess children and make them dig, rather than bomb them into oblivion, so as of today, we're on guard."

Everyone stared fearfully out of the window.

"You won't see them," sighed Miss Hutchinson. "They move so fast, they're invisible. They target idlers. Children who can remain totally focused on the lesson will remain unpossessed."

Darren sat up and stared at Miss Hutchinson with such intense scrutiny she could have been his Nintendo DS. So did Samantha. And Gaz, the loafer at the back. All twenty-eight pairs of eyes were fixed upon her.

I love first-day pupils! she mused, closing the drawer with the hacksaw in it. *They remind me it was worth giving up the old magic act.*

If you enjoyed this story, why not try some of Ali's books:
The *Shapeshifter* series

Roald Dahl was one of our best-loved children's authors. Here are 366 of his words. . .

"'Happy birthday!' cried the four old grandparents, as Charlie came into their room early the next morning.

Charlie smiled nervously and sat down on the edge of the bed. He was holding his present, his only present, very carefully in his two hands. WONKA'S WHIPPLE-SCRUMPTIOUS FUDGEMALLOW DELIGHT, it said on the wrapper... The room became silent...

Then Mrs Bucket said gently, 'You mustn't be too disappointed, my darling, if you don't find what you're looking for underneath that wrapper.'"

*

I still have vivid recollections of my first-ever birthday party. It was for my fourth birthday, held on 13 September 1920. "We'll put 'fancy dress' on the invitations," my mother said. "They'll all love it." It was decided that I was to be Little Boy Blue because it was my favourite nursery rhyme, and the local seamstress ran up a wonderful one-piece suit with long trousers made from soft powder-blue velvet. It had silver-coloured buttons down the front and a high collar and oh, it was grand! A long hunting horn was also dug up from somewhere for me to carry so that everyone would know who I was meant to be.

When the great day arrived I, together with two of my sisters (Little Bo Peep and Cinderella), stood waiting for the guests to arrive. I was in a paroxysm of excitement, and as about twenty Little Miss Muffets and Goldilocks and Dick Whittingtons began pouring into the drawing room, my excitement and nervousness caused such a ferment in my bladder that the floodgates opened and out shot a stream of pee pee, like the jet from a pressure hose. In no time at all the entire front of my beautiful powder-blue velvet trousers was covered with an enormous black wet stain that reached right down to my knees. I began to howl and I was quickly whisked out of the room by my mother, who changed me into ordinary grey flannel shorts and a white shirt. "Never mind," she said. "And if they ask you who you are meant to be, just tell them you are dressed up as yourself, because that's what you're going to have to be for the rest of your life."

If you enjoyed these extracts, why not try some of Roald's books: *More About Boy* and *Matilda*

MY PROBLEM IS I DON'T KNOW WHEN TO STOP | MORRIS GLEITZMAN

"Oh, Graham, pet," said Mrs Glossop, looking upset, "this sentence is so long," and it's true, I've only got myself to blame, I did completely ignore an instruction from a teacher, because as Mrs Glossop says herself, "full stops are our friends and we must learn to use them," but I ignored her on account of when I pick up a pen in an English lesson and use my imagination I don't want it to stop, so Mrs Glossop sentenced me to a week of lunch-time detention which wasn't that long really, not given I'd be completely finished now if I hadn't asked for another twenty-seven offences to be taken into consideration including skipping the full stops when I read a book and scratching my initials on to Anthony Webster's lunch box without any full stops and scribbling out all the full stops in all the books in the public library which was clearly an exaggeration (so was the lunch box) but on my last day of lunch-time detention two men in suits arrived at school and took me off in a car with tinted windows and asked me lots of questions in a very hot room about vandalism in libraries and completely ignored me when I reminded them that I'm a very keen reader and I've had my own library card since I was three, not to mention my own lunch box since I was four, facts they ignored because they were too busy yelling at me about criminal behaviour and then getting me convicted and sentenced to ninety-nine years in jail which made Mrs Glossop burst into tears when she came to visit me here in my cell and carry on about how my sentence is so terribly long except I have to say there was something completely fake about her tears and she had a look in her eyes which has left me very suspicious that the reason I'm locked up in this high-security prison isn't because of any scribbled library books or scratched lunch boxes, it's because – are you thinking the same thing, dear reader – it's because I gave Mrs Glossop a very long sentence and now she's given me one back?

If you enjoyed this story, why not try some of Morris's books: *Boy Overboard* and *Once*

WILLY, THE BOY WHO LOVED WORDS
LAURENCE ANHOLT

Willy loved words.

He kept them in a shoebox under his bed.

He liked odd words like **pumpernickel** and rhyming words like **poodles**, **noodles** and **oodles**.

He liked the sound of his sister's name, which was **Baby Eleanora**.

When someone told him a new word, Willy wrote it on a piece of paper. Then he put it safely in his box.

Everyone in the family collected words for Willy, except Eleanora, who was too young to talk.

On his birthday, Willy's dad gave him a dictionary. On one page they found **blink**, **bogey** and **boomerang**.

"Cool!" said Willy. "Now I have 366 words!"

"Enough for a story," said Willy's dad.

Once upon a time a little girl called Baby Eleanora found a box of words. They looked very tasty.

"Those are my words," shouted her brother. But Baby Eleanora did not reply – her mouth was full of words.

"Help!" cried Willy. "Eleanora has eaten my words!"

"**Supercalifragilisticexpialidocious**!" said Baby Eleanora.

"Quick! Call a doctor," said Willy's mum.

"**Doctor**, **proctor**, **helicopter**," laughed Eleanora.

Baby Eleanora ran out of the room with a mouthful of words. She shouted, "**ELEVEN ELECTRIC ELEPHANTS EATING ANTS**."

Then she ran round the garden, giggling, "**monkey**, **melon**, and **mongoose**!"

"My word!" gasped Willy's dad.

"No," groaned Willy, "mine!"

"Stand back," said Willy's dad. "I'll have a word with her."

"Not more words," sighed Willy.

They caught Eleanora by the ankles and tipped her upside down. Out came **snooty**, **snout** and **skunk**.

"Do something, Willy – they are your words," said Willy's mum.

But Eleanora was beginning to slow down. "**Yoghurt** … **yeti** … **yacht** and … **yawn**," she said.

"Listen!" said Willy. "She's running out of words."

Eleanora lay down and rubbed her eyes. "**Zigzag** … **zip** … **zing** … and … **zzz**." Then she fell fast asleep – without another word.

"Jumping jellybeans!" said Willy's dad.

"You took the words right out of my mouth," said Willy.

"Right," said Willy's mum, "we'll have no more words in this house, and that is my final word."

Willy's dad lay back on the sofa. "I'm completely lost for words," he sighed.

Then Willy picked up all 366 words and put them back in his shoebox.

And the last two words were … **THE END**.

If you enjoyed this story, why not try some of Laurence's books: *Matisse: The King of Colour* and *Happy Birthday Chimp and Zee*

www.scholastic.co.uk/zone

Find out about all your favourite authors, from Philip Pullman to Terry Deary, and be the first to see all our top new books, which will be coming to your local bookshop very soon.

The Zone is the best place for readers of all ages. And, if you're feeling lucky, check out the Competition Zone – there are new prizes up for grabs every single month!

Shiver

For years, Grace has watched the wolves in
the woods behind her house. One yellow-eyed
wolf – her wolf – is a chilling presence she
can't seem to live without…

THE HUNGER GAMES

Mystery and myth sweep in with the storm

Season of Secrets

SALLY NICHOLLS

The tale of a heartbroken child and an
age-old legend … a haunting story of love,
healing and strange magic.

Index of authors